The Past and Other Lies

The Past and Other Lies

Maggie Joel

FELONY & MAYHEM PRESS • NEW YORK

THE PAST AND OTHER LIES

A Felony & Mayhem mystery

PRINTING HISTORY
First edition (Murdoch Books, Australia): 2009
Felony & Mayhem edition: 2013

ISBN: 978-1-937384-75-3

Manufactured in the United States of America

Printed on 100% recycled paper

Library of Congress Cataloging-in-Publication Data

Joel, Maggie.
  The past and other lies / Maggie Joel.
     pages cm
  "A Felony & Mayhem mystery."
  ISBN 978-1-937384-75-3
  1. Sisters--England--Fiction. 2. Family secrets--Fiction. 3. London
  (England)--Fiction. 4. Mystery fiction. I. Title.
  PR9619.4.J63P37 2013
  823'.92--dc23
                        2012051200

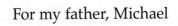

For my father, Michael

ACKNOWLEDGEMENTS

Thanks to Colette Vella, Kay Scarlett, Ali Lavau, Rhiannon Kellie, Tricia Dearborn, Louise Godley, Sheila Joel, Anne Benson, Liz Brigden and Sharon Mathews for your assistance, support, expertise and encouragement during the publication of this book.

The icon above says you're holding a copy of a book in the Felony & Mayhem "Wild Card" category. We can't promise these will press particular buttons, but we do guarantee they will be unusual, well written, and worth a reader's time. If you enjoy this book, you may well like other "Wild Card" titles from Felony & Mayhem Press.

———◆•◆•———

For more about these books, and other Felony & Mayhem titles, or to place an order, please visit our website at:

www.FelonyAndMayhem.com

Other "Wild Card" titles from

FELONY&MAYHEM

SARAH RAYNE
A Dark Dividing
Ghost Song
What Lies Beneath

MICHAEL MCDOWELL
Jack & Susan in 1913
Jack & Susan in 1933
Jack & Susan in 1953

BONNIE JONES REYNOLDS
The Truth About Unicorns

The Past and Other Lies

Jennifer and Charlotte

CHAPTER ONE

AUGUST 1981

O̲N THAT FINAL DAY of summer a drowsy wasp beat itself noisily against the French window. Through the open doorway the lawn had begun to turn yellow following five days without rain. The next-door neighbour's cat had trapped a vole and deposited it on Mrs Denzel's kitchen lino. And someone had taken a chair from the dining room and placed it in an upstairs bedroom.

At first no one noticed.

In the street beyond, a desperate last-day-of-the-school-holidays game of rounders was in progress. A bald tennis ball bouncing off a rounders bat and rebounding off a stationary Datsun sent up a cheer and a scurry of feet. A neighbour two doors up dragged his dustbin out to the kerb. A solitary, faded, red plastic triangle of bunting, left over from the royal wedding, fluttered limply from a lamppost. Gradually the game of rounders petered out.

In an upstairs bedroom that overlooked the now silent street, sixteen-year-old Charlotte Denzel climbed onto a dining-room chair that she had carried up to her bedroom for just that purpose. By balancing awkwardly on tiptoe she could just reach the light fitting around which she tied one end of a grey-and-red-striped school tie. She placed the knotted loop at the other end around her neck.

On the dressing-table stood the pot of shocking-pink nail polish with which she had intended to paint her nails. She had painted only one toenail, the big toe on her right foot, to see what it felt like, to experience the sure, broad stroke of the brush and the smooth, glossy sweep of the varnish the way her elder sister, Jennifer, did it. But her hand had shaken, the brush had jerked and the stroke had swerved, clotting in a lump that ran over onto her cuticle. A drop had splashed onto the carpet.

The pointlessness of painting her toenails, of painting anything, left her stunned.

And now the bedroom was heady with the sickly sweet odour of varnish and, looking down at the small pink jar on the dressing-table, she saw she had forgotten to replace the lid. She gazed down at her tartan-slippered feet, at the padded green velour of the dining-room chair on which she stood, and to the faded paisley carpet below. Their room—hers and Jennifer's—looked different from up here, smaller, more condensed, as though seen through a fish-eye lens. She wondered what people thought when they were about to do this. She wondered what people thought once they had done it.

She couldn't think at all. There were no thoughts left.

She braced her knees and prepared to kick the chair away.

Downstairs in the dining room the family ate shepherd's pie and peas from a packet. *Crossroads* had just come on the television and Mr Denzel was home early from the office. A chair was missing from around the dining table and Mrs Denzel seemed to ponder this as she lifted her fork to her mouth, holding it there, poised, with three squashed peas speared to the prongs. *The chair's missing—that's odd,*

you could see her thinking, then she popped the fork into her mouth and realised the gravy was still simmering in a pan in the kitchen.

'Oh, the gravy!' she said, pushing back her chair and going into the kitchen.

'Today's the final day of the school summer holidays in England and Wales,' announced her youngest, Graham, who had read this fact in Dad's copy of *The Times* earlier in the evening. Graham liked people to know he read *The Times*. Most people in their street read the *Mirror*.

'Well, the nights are drawing in now,' warned Grandma Lake with a satisfaction that seemed to suggest the family only had themselves to blame. Grandma Lake was Mrs Denzel's mother and a recent—though not entirely welcome—addition to the household. She sat now with her hands on the table before her in a rather helpless gesture that seemed to imply she was at the mercy of her family.

No one responded to her observation.

'Here we are!' announced Mrs Denzel triumphantly returning with a small white gravy boat cradled in a plaid oven glove. 'Will someone give Charlotte a call?'

Graham reached wordlessly for the gravy, barely lifting his eyes from his plate, and poured a steady stream over his peas and over the mashed potato that he had carefully scraped free of the mince. He lifted the lip of the gravy boat precisely so that none of the gravy went on the mince. This operation successfully completed, he would have placed the gravy boat straight onto the second-best nylon tablecloth had Mrs Denzel not whipped a table mat beneath it in the nick of time. A single drop of gravy hovered on the lip of the gravy boat, bulged for a moment or two, then slid silently down the curved side of the boat to plop onto the watercoloured print of Derwentwater (a gift from Aunt Caroline, Mrs Denzel's elder sister). Graham surveyed his be-gravyed plate thoughtfully before starting in on the peas, one at a time. He did not look like someone who was about to get up, go into the hallway and call up the stairs to his sister.

'So anyway, I told Peter to put it all in a memo and file it somewhere... I mean, what else could I do?'

This was Mr Denzel, seated at his usual position at the head of the table, his back to the open sliding doors that led to the lounge.

There had been a moment's pause as Mr Denzel opened his mouth to speak, but when it became clear he was going to talk about The Office everyone went back to their dinner.

'Did you, dear? Well, I expect that was the right thing to do,' replied Mrs Denzel absent-mindedly as she peered over his head at *Crossroads*.

The adverts had just come on and there was a preview for *Capital Tonight*, the program that followed *Crossroads*, and Mrs Denzel seemed to remember where she was. She frowned at the empty place beside Grandma Lake.

'Charlotte's dinner's getting cold. Jennifer, you go, dear,' she said to her eldest daughter, who sat opposite Graham. 'I don't know where that other chair's gone,' she added, looking around as though the missing chair was deliberately hiding itself from her.

So it was Jennifer who put down her unused napkin, pushed back her chair, left her half-eaten dinner and went out into the hallway to call her sister.

It was the final day of the summer holidays. The sun edged in through the French window and across the dining-room floor in a last show of force before succumbing to autumn. Two late starlings that had nested on the fencepost in the back garden flew in and out of their little wooden nesting box and a wary grey squirrel darted across the lawn, paused beneath the clothesline to inspect the remains of the dead vole that Mrs Denzel had tossed into the garden, then skittered off in search of the first fallen acorns. And tomorrow was the first day of the new school year.

'*Charlottedinner'sgettingcold!*'

Jennifer stood at the bottom of the staircase, one hand on the banister, her eye straying to the coat-cupboard door which was half open, a muddle of winter coats and boots and umbrellas spilling out as though someone had recently rummaged there. The open coat cupboard and the lack of response from upstairs suddenly caused her to wonder if, in fact, Charlotte was in the house at all.

She hesitated. A memory that she wished not to remember nudged her.

She took the stairs in bounds, two at a time, not out of any particular urgency, just because that was how she usually climbed the stairs.

Upstairs, the evening sunlight bathed the landing in an orange glow. Her parents' bedroom door was ajar, the bedspread neatly turned up, slippers and dressing-gowns stowed and hung, her dad's travel alarm clock ticking loudly like a time-bomb. Graham's bedroom door was closed but you knew that behind the door all was military-style precision. The study, which was now Grandma Lake's room, faced east onto the street and was now in shadow. The scent of lavender seeped from her room onto the landing.

Jennifer turned to the right, to the room she shared with Charlotte, and as she did she heard a loud thump as though something large had fallen over. The door was closed so she grabbed the door handle and went in, announcing as she went, 'S'dinner time!'

CHAPTER TWO

'AND WHAT HAPPENED next, Jennifer?'

Dr Kim Zaresky leaned forward just a little from her seat on the cream leather sofa, hands folded on her exquisitely bland, charcoal-grey suit, knees close together over soft Italian black leather shoes. She smiled in a way that was at once encouraging and supportive. No one sitting opposite such a smile could fail to be touched by it.

Jennifer Denzel was sitting opposite that smile and she swallowed nervously. She too was neatly dressed, though rather than a suit she wore French Connection jeans and calf-length boots, a sober black jacket over a plain white T-shirt—the sort of look you might see featured in a back issue of *Vogue* at the hairdresser's and decide, yes, I can do that, and it won't cost too much. She sat on the edge of an identical leather sofa, her knees similarly pressed together, though her hands twisted over each other, the fingers of one hand squeezing the knuckles of the other.

She was anxious, yes, but she felt strangely encouraged and supported. She took a deep breath.

'Well. That's when I found her. Charlotte. Hanging there from the light fitting.'

She paused but Dr Zaresky merely smiled encouragingly.

'And I—I didn't know what to do. Well, you don't, do you?... I think I grabbed her. Grabbed her legs. And I suppose I must have got her down though I don't really remember how... There was a chair, one of the dining-room chairs—it was green, velour—and the room stank of nail polish... And I thought, well she's dead. At first. But then she started thrashing about and—'

'I see,' said Dr Zaresky.

Between them was a smoked-glass and chrome coffee table, low-slung, on which stood a jug of water, two glasses and a tall crystal vase filled with white lilies. Jennifer squinted in the glare from the powerful lamp that bore down on her from overhead. A bead of moisture pricked her upper lip. Opposite, the dusky pink gloss of Dr Zaresky's lips shimmered like liquid in a Saharan mirage.

There was something about Zaresky's face—its length and narrowness, the slightly prominent nose, the hollowness of the cheeks—that was not quite English. If you saw that face sitting opposite you on the tube, you would know instantly that this was not an English face, though you wouldn't be able to put your finger on why.

Dr Zaresky sat back on the sofa, glanced at her notes and crossed her legs in one fluid movement, and Jennifer realised that her time was almost up. She sat back too, and smiled to indicate that she was perfectly in control, that this had not been an ordeal at all.

Dr Zaresky put her head on one side.

'Did it come as a great shock, Jennifer? I mean, you obviously had no idea that your sister—' she paused just long enough to let the impact of her question sink in, 'might try to kill herself?'

Jennifer sat very still as the words ricocheted inside her head. None of her muscles seemed able to move, except for her jaw, which opened slowly of its own volition though no words came out. There was something bubbling up inside her that seemed certain to erupt at any moment. She realised it was panic.

A second passed. Then another.

Dr Zaresky reached over the table, exposing a cuff of ivory silk shirt, and touched Jennifer's knee.

'But you really saved her life, didn't you, Jennifer?'

Jennifer swallowed the panic. 'Well, I—'

'And it's amazing how much detail you recall from that fateful day…how long ago?'

'1981. August. The thirty-first. A Monday.'

'Was it really? Yes, it is truly amazing.'

'It's sort of etched, you see. Although, well—I mean, some of it I'm not absolutely certain about… The shepherd's pie and peas, for instance. I can't actually remember if that's what we were eating but it's the kind of thing we would have eaten—'

'I'm sure. Well, thank you, Jennifer,' and Dr Zaresky again laid a hand on Jennifer's knee, then she removed it and turned away. 'We'll be back after this short break for more of "I Saved My Sister's Life!".'

Dr Zaresky's encouraging and supportive smile faded to be replaced by an advertisement for a ladies' shaver and the sound went mute.

❁ ❁ ❁

'But that's not true!'

Charlotte Denzel stood in the centre of her tiny, cluttered office on the eighth floor of the F.R. Moffatt Building and brandished the remote control at the television screen.

'IT. ISN'T. TRUE,' she repeated, clutching the remote so tightly the black plastic battery cover spun off the back and two Duracell batteries spilled onto the floor with a clatter. She turned to face the only other person in the small office—willing him to believe her.

Dave Glengorran, who was that other person, stared dumbly at the television, clearly unconcerned by such things as truth and lies.

'That your sister?' he said, even though Jennifer had been replaced on the screen by a suntanned young woman who was perched on the edge of a bath, a huge white towel wrapped around her, slowly and luxuriously drawing a razor blade through the soap suds on her shin. Dave moved closer to the television as though he might discover Jennifer hiding behind the shaving woman.

The television, a sixteen-inch portable, was perched precariously on top of a 1960s filing cabinet in their shared office—'office' being the somewhat optimistic description for what was essentially a cubicle wedged awkwardly between the dead-photocopier repository and the women's toilets, a space that seeped an acidic blend of stale urine, bleach and the decaying innards of superseded photo-copying equipment. It was located on the upper levels of the building which housed the whole of the Faculty of Humanities and itself occupied a prominent position on the main campus of Edinburgh's Waverley University.

On the TV screen the woman in the bathrobe had been replaced by a smiling teenage girl brandishing a gaily coloured pack of tampons.

'Is it? Your sister?' repeated Dave. 'She married? Seeing anyone?'

Dave, who was in his early forties, wore a tan-coloured leather jacket, smoked Marlboros and had an easy 'always a spare bed at my place if you want it, *nudge-nudge-wink-wink*' kind of attitude that was undermined by trousers that were a little too high at the waist and ankle to be entirely credible. He had the aura of one who, at heart, was still an undergraduate.

Charlotte saw him through a steadily growing haze of dismay and shock. Her throat seemed to be tightening, constricting. She thought of words like 'anaphylactic shock'. But that was caused by allergic reactions to certain foods and bee-stings—not by daytime television. Dave's words seemed to add to the haze.

'No, Dave. She's not married. She's divorced. And that's her sister-in-law. Her *ex* sister-in-law.'

'Who?' Dave looked baffled.

'*Kim.* Dr Zaresky. That's the only reason my sister's on the program, because she was married to Kim's brother.'

'Oh, right... Really?'

Dave turned back to the television where the teenage girl smiled implacably in a way that seemed to imply that, for her, a gaily coloured tampon pack was everything.

Charlotte found that her fingers were still clenched tightly around the black box of the remote control and aimed at the small television screen. She let her arm drop to her side, feeling a throbbing at her temples.

'She's fuckin' gorgeous,' said Dave, his Scottish *r* rolling even more than usual. 'Do you know her, then?'

The throbbing intensified.

'Of course I *know* her! She's my *sister.*'

'No, the other one, the doctor.'

Charlotte sat down on her desk, pushing aside her untouched lunch and a mountain of unmarked first-year semiotics essays. Dave reached out and deftly caught the pile of essays as it began to topple over.

'Your lot still doing *Buffy?*' he observed, momentarily distracted as he glanced at the title page of the top essay: 'The Place of "Good" and "Evil" in a Post-Dichotomous World in *Buffy the Vampire Slayer*'.

Charlotte took the essay from him and wordlessly replaced it on the top of the pile. Dave had once taught an entire semester on Britney Spears—Britney as post-feminist icon, the death of individualism in a post-Britney world, Britney as post-icon icon—so he was hardly in a position to criticise. Besides, the undergraduates always wanted to write about *Buffy* and *Angel*, it was a fact of cultural studies life. The days of *Bladerunner* were long gone.

She took a deep breath. There was not enough room in this office. It was increasingly difficult to find space to breathe.

'So all that stuff your sister talked about,' said Dave, nodding at the television. 'You're saying it didn't really happen?'

Charlotte *had* said that. At the time it had seemed like a reasonable thing to say. A face-saving thing to say. Now she was stuck with it.

'It was pretty believable, though, wasn't it?' Dave continued. 'All that detail. I mean, she was pretty convincing.'

Which was tantamount to him calling Charlotte a liar.

'Of course it was *convincing*. Of course it was *detailed*. Of course it was *believable*. That's because it's a true story— but it was *her*, not me!'

Charlotte turned away and began to sort the chaotic pile of essays on her desk. If she was going to tell a lie she might as well make it a big one.

'Aye, well. Folks always believe what they see on the telly.'

'No, Dave, they don't.' She could feel a lecture coming on and she did nothing to stop it. 'In our technology-saturated society, the average viewer is bombarded with such a volume of conflicting televisual and media images that they've learned to question the validity of those images. Cultural Studies 101, Dave. *Your* course.'

'Aye, well,' was all Dave would admit. He turned back to the television, putting his hands in his pockets and awaiting the reappearance of Dr Zaresky.

The thing about Dave was, if you unpacked all of his post-feminist, intertextual, queer theory ideas, you were left with just one concept: *Does she have big tits?* After three years of negotiating cramped office space, enduring departmental briefings and buying rounds of cheap bitter at the Union bar, it had become all too clear to Charlotte that this was the foundation upon which all Dave's philosophies rested. Charlotte would have preferred to share her office with a woman. Any woman. Except perhaps Dr Lempriere.

She turned back to the essays. The top one had a slightly sticky rust-coloured stain on the front page, the origin of which she didn't wish to speculate on. She stared at the words on the title page but they no longer seemed to make any sense. She put the essays down again.

Jennifer had actually said that. On national television.

But there was every chance no one had seen it. Certainly Charlotte had made a point of telling no one about the program—and that was when she was still under the mistaken impression her sister was going on television to talk about violence in children's computer games. (And what the hell was that? A smokescreen? How did 'Violence in Computer Games' become 'I Saved My Sister's Life!'?) But Dave had walked in, right in the middle of it, when surely—she glanced up at the clock that balanced on top of a bookshelf—yes, surely Dave should be running a first-year Subjectivity tute right now?

Her mobile phone went off with a series of alarming beeps and Charlotte jumped.

'I wish you'd change that,' remarked Dave, whose own mobile phone played the theme from *The A-Team*.

'Hello?'

'Charlotte? Why didn't you tell me Jennifer was going to say all those things on the television? Why would she make up something like that? Wasn't she going to be talking about violence and computer games?'

It was her mother.

Mrs Denzel worked Tuesdays at a respectable charity shop in the high street of a quiet commuter suburb in north-west London. She hadn't missed a day at the shop in eight years—not counting holidays and the Tuesday four years earlier when she'd accompanied Dad to the hospital for his hernia operation—which meant she definitely shouldn't be at home watching daytime television. Not on a Tuesday. And she never rang during office hours unless...

Charlotte couldn't recall a single occasion when her mother had rung her at work before.

'Charlotte?'

Various possible responses now presented themselves: excuses, evasions, platitudes, denials. She plumped for denial.

'Oh, hi, Mum. You mean Jen *wasn't* talking about computer games? I just turned on and caught the end—'

'She was talking about *you*! About *us*!' Mrs Denzel paused to let this sink in. 'Did you know she was going to do that? You should have stopped her.'

On the television screen Dr Zaresky had returned, her lip gloss touched up, her smile fully armed and aimed straight at the studio audience, whom she charmed mutely before turning to her left. The camera zoomed in on a middle-aged black woman in a red dress and large diamond earrings, an awed expression on her face. Dave turned up the volume then reached up to fiddle with the aerial and the image shuddered.

'I know nothing about it, Mum. I only caught the end. I can't really say. It's probably just some story she made up,' said Charlotte dismissively.

She closed her eyes and into her head popped a vision of Jennifer's face, Jennifer smiling and chatting, then not smiling or chatting because someone's fist, Charlotte's fist as it turned out, had smashed right into her mouth and shut her up.

Charlotte opened her eyes and little red spots flickered in the periphery of her vision.

'But I don't see why—'

'Really, Mum, I'm sure none of whatever she said is true—except perhaps the shepherd's pie and packet peas.' Charlotte laughed weakly. Denial hadn't worked, so maybe humour.

There was silence at the other end of the line. Then, 'I always tried to give you children fresh vegetables,' said Mrs Denzel, 'until that new Safeway opened up in the high street, then it was just easier to buy frozen.'

Charlotte waited. She knew her mother hadn't rung up to defend her cooking skills.

'But don't you think it's a bit...*odd*? That she'd go on the telly and make up such things? I know she's sometimes a bit...dramatic. Highly strung, they called it in my day. She got that from her grandmother, of course.'

She paused and Charlotte considered her grandmother. The idea that anyone might have considered Grandma Lake dramatic was baffling.

'But to make things up...?' said Mrs Denzel, then she fell silent as though a thought had just struck her. 'Do you think maybe she believes it herself? Thinks it really happened? They do say—'

'No, I don't,' interrupted Charlotte. 'I just think she enjoys the attention, particularly if it's at my expense. And she's been desperate to get on Kim's program for a year.'

That wasn't quite true—Kim's program had only been running since the autumn and the way the ratings were going it would be lucky to last till the spring. As for Jennifer being desperate to get on it, well, they'd never actually discussed it, but some things you just knew.

Violence in children's computer games! What a load of rubbish.

'Well, I think you should ask her about it... Or should we just pretend we didn't watch it?' said Mrs Denzel doubtfully.

Charlotte said nothing. She didn't need to ask Jennifer about it. She didn't need to ask Jennifer about anything.

There was a gasp at the other end of the phone.

'Who else do you think might have seen it?'

And that, of course, was the key question. Charlotte could almost hear her mother mentally flicking through an address book containing the names of every relative and acquaintance of the last thirty years and calculating their likely proximity to a television set at two o'clock on a Tuesday afternoon in late January.

Not many, surely?

Did they know anyone who watched daytime television? Who was unemployed? A housewife? Working from home? A student? Sick? Suddenly the possibilities seemed endless. And nowadays people had televisions in their workplaces—she was staring at one herself.

On the screen Dr Zaresky was now explaining the terrible toll that kleptomania took on families and Dave stood there transfixed.

'Mum, it's Tuesday afternoon, everyone's at work. And it's daytime TV—no one's watching it.'

And that was perfectly true. No one that she knew, no one who knew her, would have watched it. It didn't matter what complete strangers thought of her.

'And I can assure you I didn't tell anyone to watch it,' she added.

'I brought the small portable into the shop and set it up in the back room and we all watched it,' said Mrs Denzel. 'June Craven from head office came in halfway through and Irene Field's daughter-in-law from the cafe popped in too.'

Ouch.

Jennifer had wanted them to watch. They'd both received a brief email the day before informing them she was going to be appearing on Kim's show. It was supposed to be an alarmist and morally indignant segment on the trend towards violence in children's toys. Jennifer, who managed the toy department of a large London department store, would provide the retailer's viewpoint.

There was a silence on the line, then, 'I mean, we would have known, your dad and me, if anything like that had happened. You would have told us.'

It wasn't a question.

'Of course we would have told you, Mum.'

Afterwards, when Dave had remembered he had a tutorial and raced out of the office, Charlotte perched on the edge of her desk, contemplating the animated dramas of daytime television and praying for low ratings.

An ad came on for *Focus on Scotland* that evening—*'...turning the salmon farm into a theme park,'* announced the female presenter playfully with her perfect Home Counties enunciation (which was odd for a program called *Focus on Scotland*)—and Charlotte hit the off button.

She logged onto her hotmail account for the first time that day and saw Jennifer's email from yesterday morning plus an unread email also from Jennifer, sent late last night. Charlotte opened the new email, which explained that the segment on computer games had been cancelled at the last minute so there was now no point in Charlotte watching the show the next day, and could she please pass this on to Mum in case she didn't check her email?

Another new email popped into her inbox. It was from Graham. The heading read: *Hey Sis. What's Jen on and where can I get some???*

She logged out. The office phone rang and as she reached over, hand poised above the receiver to pick it up, she thought, just for a moment, that it might be Jennifer ringing to explain.

It wasn't.

It was Dr Lempriere, calling from Professor Pitney's office to report that she, and indeed the entire department, had watched the program and had Charlotte ever thought about counselling?

❖ ❖ ❖

Located on the westernmost borders of the city, Waverley University—formerly the Waverley Institute of Technology—was housed within the bleak walls of the old Northgate Hospital, a vast red-brick Victorian building which had, at various times during its lifetime, housed quarantine patients, destitute mothers, war-wounded and, most recently, psychiatric patients. Now, refurbished, refashioned, re-roofed and renamed, it formed the nucleus of the university's campus and contained the university's administrative services, the students' union, the international students' centre, the computer labs, various shops and cafes, and Northgate Bar, in which 99p pints of Auld Augie could still be purchased.

The old hospital had rested congenially amid ten acres of graceful woodland. Much of this woodland had now made way for a small cityscape of concrete and steel blocks, a crowd of prefabricated cabins, various sports fields, a gym and six car parks. It was into a secluded spot in the most remote and least-used car park that Charlotte, the following morning, slid her ten-year-old Fiesta. She had deliberately chosen this car park, the one behind the library, rather than her usual spot behind the Moffat Building. It was only the second week of term after the Christmas break and with summer exams so far off it seemed reasonable to assume that the library would be relatively deserted, particularly at eight thirty on a frozen Wednesday morning towards the end of January.

She had fled the office, the department, and indeed the entire university, soon after the phone call from Dr Lempriere, and had taken refuge in the remains of a bottle of Tesco's home-brand shiraz and a decision not to answer the phone to anyone.

The phone had not rung.

But today was a new working day and there were tutorials to get through, students to face and colleagues to avoid. Now all she had to do was get out of her car, cross the car park and enter the Moffat Building via the modern languages lab in the basement. She wasn't hiding; she was keeping a low profile.

She didn't move, her fingers still locked around the now motionless steering wheel. Before her eyes popped the image of Jennifer perched on the edge of that cream leather sofa telling Kim (*Dr* Kim, who was a doctor of philosophy, mind you, and knew as much about medicine as your average Cultural Studies undergrad), telling Kim, telling the studio audience, telling the whole daytime television world, *their* private business.

If Jennifer had suddenly decided to relate her little story at some family get-together that would have been awful enough. (What family get-together Charlotte couldn't imagine—the Denzels hadn't managed a Christmas in the same city for ten years.) But to do it *on television* on a Tuesday lunchtime, between an advert for incontinence pads and a segment on kleptomania in former child-star actors, was unforgivable. And now it seemed the entire Cultural Studies department had guffawed through it during their sausage rolls and pot noodles.

Footsteps crunched in the snow behind the Fiesta and Charlotte pulled her head lower into the collar of her coat. The footsteps passed by, and despite it being early on a frozen Wednesday morning in the unfashionable end of an out-of-the-way car park, she recognised the balding head, battered briefcase and duffle coat of Professor Tom Pitney, head of the department.

She sank down a little lower in her seat.

What was Tom doing at the library? And at eight thirty in the morning? No one went to the library—at least, none of the faculty did, unless it was to read the free newspapers. It was Tom Pitney who would be renewing or terminating her contract in September. He would have seen yesterday's program of course, and now he had come in early in order to work out who to reassign her classes to.

She laid her head on the steering wheel and closed her eyes.

'Hey!' The tap on the driver's-side window almost sent her head through the car roof.

'Jesus Christ!'

She wiped a gloved hand across the steamed-up window and made out Dr Lempriere standing beside the car with a bright smile as though the below-freezing car park on a Wednesday morning was a perfectly normal place to be—and perhaps it was if you were Canadian.

Dr Lempriere was Dr Ashley Lempriere of UCO, Toronto, and she had joined the Cultural Studies department on a twelve-month lecturing exchange to teach the honours class.

The same class Tom Pitney had promised Charlotte.

She had swept into the faculty in the middle of a Monday morning departmental meeting, filling Tom's stale office with a brisk New World breeze, a squeak of new leather, and the sort of teeth of which the average British person could only dream. The staff had exchanged curious sideways glances, Dave had sat up straighter and smoothed back his hair and Charlotte had looked over at Tom. Tom had started guiltily in his chair and dived into a large pile of papers on his desk and Charlotte had experienced a moment of doomed despair.

'Not the same Ashley Lempriere who wrote *The Author and the Death of Death*?' Bert Humphries, senior lecturer in Cultural Studies, had inquired, leaning forward, his bushy eyebrows twitching.

And Tom had smiled and shrugged sheepishly to indicate that, sadly, things were out of his hands—and even though you knew that was bullshit, what could you do?

Charlotte had begun scanning job ads.

And now Dr Lempriere—Ashley—was rapping on her window with her reindeer-skin mittens and some kind of interaction appeared unavoidable.

Charlotte fumbled for the button that made the window go down and not up. She found it at last and a shot of freezing air leapt into the warm car with her.

'Dr Denzel,' Ashley said. 'What a surprise! Who you hiding from?'

Charlotte smiled tightly back. 'I'm returning a book,' she said. They were outside the library, weren't they?

'That so?' Ashley raised one eyebrow significantly higher than the other as though returning books to the library was the last thing she would have expected of a colleague. She gave a long and meaningful look at the pile of books that was stacked on the Fiesta's passenger seat. 'Any of those mine?'

Dr Ashley Lempriere had written five academic texts, all of which were on various university course reading lists.

'I hardly need to visit the library for that, do I? You gave us all signed copies when you arrived,' Charlotte reminded her.

'I did too. Well, come on then. Can't spend all day skulking about round here, can we?'

Charlotte reluctantly unclicked her seatbelt and gathered her stuff together.

'So why're you parked way out here? Trying to avoid everyone, huh?' Ashley inquired, displaying the sort of bluntness British people did not need or appreciate, then she put an arm through Charlotte's, breaking another taboo, and steered her towards the library where Charlotte really didn't want to go. 'Y'know, everybody's talking 'bout nothing else but your sister's TV show,' she added.

'Are they? Well that's just great,' replied Charlotte coldly. 'And what do you suggest I do? Call a press conference?'

That sounded bitter. She didn't want to sound bitter, didn't want to sound like it was a big deal. On the other hand it *was* a big deal and she didn't want to appear too flippant either.

Ashley appeared to give the press conference suggestion serious consideration.

'I wouldn't advise it. Colleague of mine at UCO made a media statement after a rape accusation. No one even knew about it till that media statement came out. 'Course, he was finished after that. I took over most of his classes.'

I'll bet you did, thought Charlotte, mentally running through her own meagre class workload and wondering whether Ashley had designs on any of it.

'Still, I guess it might not be a bad idea,' mused Ashley. 'I'll even write you a media statement if you like: *Dr Denzel wishes to make it known that the allegations levelled against her yesterday by her sister are totally unfounded and absolutely without substance. Or so she claims...'*

She turned a frankly inquisitive look in Charlotte's direction but Charlotte refused to be drawn.

An earnest woolly-hatted early-morning group of undergraduates milled around the library foyer handing out pamphlets and copies of the *Socialist Worker.* Charlotte had handed out pamphlets too, once—anti-apartheid stuff probably—but that seemed a long time ago. She felt suddenly old and depressed. Either Lempriere did have designs on her own ever-decreasing class list and was even now plotting her downfall, or she was just a nosy gossip.

Charlotte declined an anti-whaling leaflet and reached into her pocket for a tissue. The icy air was making her nose run.

'So you say your sister's lying...?' Ashley continued. Charlotte didn't respond. 'Okay, I guess she has her reasons, right? Though I can't imagine what they'd be. And it ain't none of my business anyways. What is she, in therapy or something?'

'Not that I'm aware of,' Charlotte replied stiffly.

She wasn't at all sure how she felt about this question with its implication that her sister was a crazy person. On the other hand after yesterday's little drama perhaps she was. *Was* Jennifer in therapy? Charlotte felt, a little uncomfortably, that that was the kind of question a sister ought to be able to answer.

'Please, take this!' pleaded a girl in a grubby army-surplus overcoat, thrusting a photocopied sheet into Charlotte's hand.

'Excuse me,' Charlotte said, disengaging her arm from Ashley's and diving into the safety of the library even though she had no books to return and none that she particularly wished to borrow.

The leaflet, written in urgent forty-point Arial Bold, screamed: TEENAGE SUICIDE IS EVERYONE'S PROBLEM!

CHAPTER THREE

AUGUST 1981

THE MISSING DINING-ROOM chair was there in the bedroom and Jennifer, standing in the doorway, saw at once what had made the loud thump. It was tipped over on its side in the middle of the room where a dining-room chair had no business to be.

There was a strong smell of nail varnish.

She experienced a sudden rush of fury because she knew what she could smell was Shocking-Pink-for-Pink-that-Shocks nail polish, recently acquired from the make-up counter at Top Shop and new this season.

And Charlotte had stolen it.

She had stolen it and put it on her own nails *and*, as if that were not, in itself, a heinous enough crime, she had forgotten to put the lid back on the bottle afterwards. Everyone knew nail polish dried up if you didn't put the lid back on.

Jennifer kicked the bedroom door wide open in an explosion of anger that evaporated into something else entirely when she saw, before her, legs kicking a foot above the fallen chair.

Charlotte was wearing her tartan slippers, the ones Aunt Caroline had given her last Christmas. Jennifer had been given a similar pair, also tartan, and of the sort of suffocating blue and green that only a department store could produce and an aunt could purchase. Those slippers now dangled in the air beneath a pair of stone-washed jeans. Pepe jeans, so tight at the ankle you had to lie on your back to pull them on. The tartan-slippered feet seemed to burst out of the narrow legs like duck's feet: a cartoon Scottish duck's feet. At Charlotte's waist, wrapped almost twice around, was the yellow canvas belt, purchased at Wembley market only the month before, and above that was last year's Madness T-shirt, already shapeless and faded from too many washes, and from which two skinny white arms reached up, clutching wildly.

Which was when Jennifer saw the tie.

It was the school tie, Henry Morton Secondary, with its distinctive diagonal grey and red stripes. School uniform colours. Their school. And one end was tied to the light fitting, the other was tied into a loop and the loop, a tiny loop, barely wide enough for a person's head, was around her neck.

It was around her neck.

Above the loop was Charlotte. Charlotte's head. Twisted to one side, her hands scrambling for a hold, her face the colour of a washed-out February sky, of sticky window putty, of dough made from wholemeal flour. It was not the colour of skin. Her mouth was taut, the lips peeled back and an oddly bluish colour.

And the worst thing was—

The worst thing of all.

Jennifer knew why she was up there.

Someone screamed. Or perhaps it was more a groan. Either way it was cut short when Jennifer surged forward, snatching instinctively at the thrashing legs, her face buried in the denim of the dangling trouser legs in a desperate attempt to take their weight on her shoulders, in her arms.

And the legs were a dead weight. Jennifer kept trying to grab more and more of them, to take more and more of their weight and all the while she was thinking, *How long? How long has she been like this? All the time we were pouring gravy over our shepherd's pie? Taking our seats at the dining-room table? Since before* Crossroads *came on? Before Dad came in from work? How long?* And at the same time her mind raced forward to a time that hadn't happened yet but was about to: herself calling out, *Help! Someone help me!* and Mum and Dad running up the stairs, coming in, finding them, cries, screams, dismay. An ambulance being called, a lifeless body on a stretcher with the blanket (a red one) pulled up over Charlotte's face, the neighbours standing in clusters in their doorways, of hours spent sitting in white hospital corridors trying to get the attention of elusive doctors, of a policeman taking a statement and a WPC comforting Mum, someone asking, *Why? Why would she do such a thing?* Endless cups of tasteless vending-machine tea in white plastic cups. And life, her own life, stretching bleakly ahead from this point onwards into...nothing.

Jennifer groaned, sobbed and clutched even tighter and the legs kicked, they actually kicked, and she had the greatest difficulty keeping hold of those legs as her eyes sprayed tears and her mouth gasped, and she knew she must do something more.

The something more was the pair of tiny, slightly rusted nail scissors lying on the dressing-table beside the open bottle of shocking-pink nail polish.

Jennifer shifted the now wriggling legs to her right arm, reached over and snatched up the scissors, reached above both their heads and tried to cut the hated school tie. Which is when she realised it was impossible to cut using your left hand, so she sobbed and gasped some more and switched the legs to her left arm, the scissors to her right hand and began to cut and cut and cut like a manic dress-maker an hour before an important fashion show.

The tie proved to be made of good-quality material, and the cutting was more hacking than precision snipping, but eventually a tear was made in the awful stuff and the weight of Charlotte's body and of Jennifer hacking and snipping for all she was worth helped the strands to rip until at last it gave and the two bodies dropped to the floor with a bone-jarring thud.

Jennifer's forehead connected with her kneecap, the back of her head crashed onto the floor and there was a tangle of arms and legs. She found herself on her back staring up at the remaining length of tie, her thumb and forefinger still looped through the handles of the nail scissors, a red depression in her skin so deep it bruised the bone. As she stared up at that piece of tie it occurred to her that it was actually two pieces of tie—that is, two ties knotted together—which was how Charlotte had made it long enough to fasten to both the light fitting and around her own neck. And as Charlotte only had one school tie it was reasonable to assume that the other tie was Jennifer's. This time Jennifer did not experience a rush of fury that Charlotte had stolen something of hers.

On the floor beside her, Charlotte made a gurgling, choking, groaning sound. Jennifer lifted her head off the carpet and stared at her sister and opened her mouth to say something (what, she had no idea) when they both heard Mum's voice in the hallway downstairs.

'Charlotte! Jennifer! For heaven's sake, your dinners are getting cold and I'm not putting them in the oven. And you're missing *Crossroads*.'

As Mum spoke these words, they stared at each other and because Charlotte was alive and staring at her and because Jennifer knew why this had happened, she knew—they both knew—that neither of them was going to say anything.

'Al*right*. I'm coming!' Jennifer called back, her voice unnaturally high, quavering. She did not take her eyes off Charlotte. Downstairs the theme from *Crossroads* reached a climax then abruptly fell silent.

Jennifer eased herself up onto her elbows then, painfully, to her knees. Charlotte hadn't moved. She lay on her back, her—or possibly Jennifer's—grey-and-red striped tie, torn and askew around her neck, so that she looked like a punk rocker. She was no longer looking at Jennifer but was staring up at the ceiling and Jennifer wanted to demand to know what she was thinking. Then she remembered all over again why this had happened and she said nothing.

Instead she reached down and began, this time with careful snips, to cut the tie from around Charlotte's neck. The loss of two school ties was going to take some explaining, she realised grimly.

When she had finished Jennifer got to her feet. Then she dropped straight onto her bed as it became clear her legs were not going to hold her weight. So she sat on the edge of the bed and clasped her knees and discovered she was going to be sick.

At the same time, she saw that the two butchered school ties were the least of their worries, for around Charlotte's throat was a vivid red mark that looked exactly as though she had just tried to hang herself.

Jennifer wondered if she was going to make it to the bathroom before she was sick.

CHAPTER FOUR

O<small>N</small> THAT SAME Wednesday morning, as Charlotte was sliding her Fiesta into the library car park on Waverley University's main campus, Jennifer Denzel stood in the middle of the toy department on the fifth floor of Gossup and Batch's department store in London's West End pondering the problem of Barbie versus Action Man.

She had the same problem at this time every year: Christmas was over, the Grotto that had consumed almost a quarter of the toy department's precious floor space had finally been dismantled, the Santa Claus costumes had been dry-cleaned and stored away, and all of Santa's helpers had rejoined the dole queue or moved back to Vancouver or Dublin or Perth or wherever it was they had come from. The January sales had come and gone, and now she was stuck with the usual decision about which was to fill the gap: Barbie or Action Man?

Located in a six-storey early-Victorian mansion just off Regent Street, Gossup and Batch was one of London's oldest still-operational department stores, and even in the new millennium it still clung valiantly to an aura of late-Victorian gentility. The words *Emporium of Elegance* still adorned the main entrance in ornate italics and were picked out in silver letters on the store's famous burgundy shopping bags, and doormen in gold-braided livery still tipped their top hats as you entered and departed.

Unfortunately, it appeared the modern shopper no longer cared to traipse through dozens of departments and past hundreds of elegantly presented products in order to find a single item. They preferred to nip into a boutique in their lunch hour. They liked to park on a rooftop and take a lift down to a covered shopping mall. They chose discounts and wholesale prices over quality and excellent service.

An unspectacular stock market float in the late nineties had done little to halt the store's decline, and with shares dipping to just eight-seven pence the latest general manager had just been quietly and expensively dispatched.

As well as plummeting standards and a teetering share price, employee turnover was high and the title of the unofficial staff newsletter, *Gossip and Bitch*, gave some indication why. Jennifer was one of the very few exceptions in this perilous climate, having survived nine years at Gossup and Batch, and was now, thanks largely to an ability to keep her head down, manager of the toy department.

Peacekeeper™, she observed, wasn't selling well.

She frowned at the multitude of figures on the latest print-out from marketing and was only vaguely surprised to note that an interactive board game where players moved from one global trouble spot to another, settling disputes between warring nations through a combination of economic and diplomatic manoeuvres, and that had been extensively advertised on television in the run-up to Christmas, had failed to sell.

What kid wanted to *prevent* wars?

It was a relief she and Nick had never had children.

The more traditional board games were past their use-by date in a modern toy department. Who wanted to play Ludo or Snakes and Ladders when you could play Surveillance: Spy on your neighbours!™ with a micro digital video camera and a listen-through-walls bugging device?

'There's a phone call for you. Mr Gaspari.'

It was Gloria Clements, her PA, making a rare visit onto the sales floor.

Gloria was younger than Jennifer but had somehow notched up fifteen years' service at Gossup's. Her mother, Alfreda, a huge woman with an alarming bust, was one of an army of West Indian, Fijian and Turkish cleaning women who descended on the store at closing time, and on the rare occasions when her mother made it up to the toy department before Gloria had left for the evening, Gloria would scoop up her bag and sweep tight-lipped out of the office.

Gloria didn't have children either. In fact, oddly, no one in the toy department had children.

Or maybe it wasn't odd. Maybe it made perfect sense.

Jennifer looked up from the sales print-out and regarded Gloria thoughtfully. A telephone call from Mr Gaspari? Mr Gaspari was on the board of directors and as far as she could recall he had never, in nine years, rung her. It seemed surprising he even knew who she was. Could it be the Ring Me!™ thing? Surely that hadn't made it all the way up to the boardroom, had it?

Gloria returned her gaze expressionlessly.

'And did you ask what it was concerning?' Jennifer prompted.

'No. I didn't ask.'

Gloria, Jennifer felt reasonably certain, disliked her. It was possible to attribute this dislike to what is conveniently excused as a clash of personalities, but it would be more accurate to put it down to the incident with Gloria's fiancé, Adam Finch, four years ago.

'Well,' Jennifer said slowly and calmly, 'why don't you go and ask him, and if it's important I'll call him straight back and if it's not, take a message.'

She turned away and studied the first aisle of girls' toys. The single biggest seller in the pre-school section was My First Phone™, a plush mobile phone with nursery-rhyme ring-tones that middle-management parents picked out for the offspring they had just deposited at long daycare. For the pre-teens there was a Britney Spears version called Ring Me!™ in Barbie-pink fun-fur that imparted such profound messages as *'I rilly wanna see you tonight!'* and *'Can I go out with you?'* and *'I miss you so much!'* in a pre-recorded preppy American voice. After less than a month on the shelves, the toy department sales team had been so driven to the point of insanity by the continual playing of Ring Me!™ by excited eight-year-olds that they had removed the batteries and put the product on the top shelf out of reach. Naturally, sales had been affected and comments had been made at the monthly executive meeting upstairs. The phones had been returned to the lower shelves and the sales team had been given booklets on stress management.

Gloria hadn't moved.

'I need Saturday off,' she stated flatly and Jennifer perused her sales print-out in a leisurely fashion and waited for more.

'It's a fitting for the dress,' said Gloria finally. 'She can only do me Saturday morning. I have to go down to Camberwell.'

So that was it. The wedding. Jennifer squinted more closely at the figures. She chewed her lip to indicate that she might be listening and she might be about to approve this somewhat tardy request. On the other hand she might not.

The wedding was Gloria's wedding to Adam Finch. Adam was a fellow employee at Gossup's to whom Gloria had been engaged for more than a year. He was also the Adam of The Incident, which was why Jennifer was not going to the wedding and why Gloria was reluctant to provide it as a reason for wanting Saturday off. Jennifer tapped her pencil contemplatively on her print-out and thought she heard Gloria's jaw muscles clenching behind her.

'I was planning a stocktake this Saturday,' said Jennifer, still studying her print-out. Somewhere nearby a phone rang.

'I rilly wanna see you tonight!'

Gloria and Jennifer spun around to see a guilty-looking nine-year-old with a top-knot grinning at them nervously, a Ring Me!™ phone clasped in her hand and her finger on the talk button. They glared at her and the girl dropped the phone and fled.

'I miss you so much,' said the phone as it bounced onto the floor.

'I don't participate in stocktakes,' said Gloria calmly.

It was true that, as a rule, Gloria, as a PA, did not participate in stocktakes; it was a definite perk of not being sales staff. Still, procedures and processes were under continual scrutiny these days and perhaps, Jennifer mused, from now on non-sales staff *would* be expected to participate in stocktakes? She would give the matter some serious thought. In the meantime, this little power play had been pushed as far as it would go. She looked up and gave Gloria a bright smile.

'Of course. Naturally you must have Saturday off for your dress fitting.' She beamed benevolently and prepared to enjoy the gratitude that Gloria was now forced to bestow upon her.

Gloria's gratitude came in the form of a tight-lipped smile.

And perhaps at a sign from Gloria, or maybe just by coincidence, Adam Finch himself appeared at the end of the model airplanes and remote-controlled vehicles aisle and waved cheerily.

Jennifer raised a hand to wave back then she realised Adam was probably waving at Gloria and not at herself, and that in fact he was marrying Gloria and not herself, and her own raised hand went instead to straighten a stack of Tanya Starr, Supermodel™ dolls.

Adam Finch, who had a degree in Phys. Ed. from Loughborough and had been a Southern Counties 1500-

metre junior champion, was manager of the computer and software department on the third floor. He strolled up to them now in a shiny nylon tracksuit, in defiance of company policy, carrying a clipboard that ought to contain sales data on product availability and item price changes but which, Jennifer could see, actually contained running times (Adam frequently did laps of Regent's Park during his lunch hour). His face was shiny and there was moisture on his top lip.

'Sorry I'm late, my sweet,' Adam was saying, and he kissed Gloria's unproffered cheek dutifully. 'I stepped in something unpleasant in the park and didn't realise till I was in the lift coming up here. Stamped it into the carpet all the way from the front door to the fifth floor.'

He smiled ruefully in the manner of someone aware they've probably caused an inconvenience but who knows that someone else will always clear it up. Perhaps, Jennifer mused, it would be Gloria's mum who would have the task of scrubbing the something-unpleasant from the lobby carpet this evening. And possibly Gloria was thinking the same thing, as she responded to his apology with a cold look and Jennifer wondered, not for the first time, about this wedding they were supposed to be having.

'Gloria, is Mr Gaspari still on hold for me?' she asked abruptly, because she'd just remembered him and because she really wanted to break up this little fiancé-to-fiancée moment.

'Yes, he is,' replied Gloria, smiling sweetly. 'I told him you were just coming.' She turned towards Adam in the manner of someone about to go off for her tea break.

Jennifer returned the smile and marched off towards the Staff Only door and her office.

It did take some getting used to, this idea of Gloria and Adam getting back together and now hurtling, unstoppably, towards marriage. It changed the way you looked at things. For instance, it made you think that if that incident hadn't happened four years ago, perhaps Adam and Gloria wouldn't have broken up after all. Perhaps they would have stayed together and got married years ago. Perhaps (and contrary to what you had assumed at the time) they had been happy together then and were happy together now, and the awkward breakup and the three years apart had not been a blessing after all.

It made you wonder if, in fact, you hadn't got the whole thing totally wrong.

But that made it sound as if she had orchestrated the incident with Adam just for their sake, to help them out of a dead-end relationship, when in fact she hadn't thought about them at all. Not at the time. Only afterwards, when it had been necessary to explain her actions to herself. No, at the time she had been thinking entirely about Nick. Well, Nick and herself and their own forthcoming wedding. Actually, she had been thinking mainly about herself.

And she hadn't orchestrated anything. Not really. At least not until she had sat on Santa's lap at the staff Christmas party four years ago. She hadn't even wanted to go to the staff Christmas party but Nick had invited her to his own office's Christmas drinks at some Mexican-themed wine bar in Islington and she had definitely wanted to avoid that.

She'd found herself avoiding Nick quite a bit in the weeks leading up to that Christmas. Pretty much dating back, in fact, to that drunken night at Rafael's in early December when they had split a bottle of Frangelico and had ended up engaged.

It had seemed a hilariously amusing thing at 3 am in the back of a black cab somewhere near Victoria. An engagement had seemed less amusing the following morning, especially when Nick had excitedly begun drawing up guest lists and ringing caterers. By the time of the Gossup's Christmas party a date had been set for early spring and she was feeling distinctly odd about the whole thing.

Odd, bordering on panic-stricken.

Not about Nick exactly, just the wedding. It ought to have been the easiest thing in the world to say, Hold on, I'm not ready, let's not do this, but somehow it wasn't easy, and as the weeks had passed it had got less and less easy until she had woken up on Christmas Eve with a wedding date set, a celebrant organised, a reception booked and a roomful of guests already shopping for presents.

So she had gone along to Gossup and Batch's Christmas party staged, as per custom, in the executive meeting room on the sixth floor and, after some misgivings and three vodka and oranges, had sat on Santa's lap. Which was when she had realised that Santa wasn't Gary Harding from Sportswear this year, but Adam Finch, the new assistant manager in Computers who was going out with Gloria Clements and who, last time she had seen them together, had been arguing and looking pretty miserable.

After that moment of recognition, what had followed soon after had become as inevitable as the conga along the executive corridor. Two more vodka and oranges, and a half-hour of dancing to 'I Wish It Could Be Christmas Every Day', and she had found herself on the rooftop terrace leaning dizzyingly against the wall and peering across the clear icy night sky towards the Christmas lights along Regent Street.

She hadn't had to wait long to hear the footsteps behind her, feel warm breath on her neck and two hands placed on the wall on either side of her, enclosing her. She didn't need to look around to see who it was.

'All alone?' he had asked, and she had hoped he was in his own clothes again—she wasn't so drunk that kissing a man in a Santa suit seemed appealing.

'Not often, no,' she had replied, turning to kiss him. He *was* in his own clothes. But that hadn't stopped Clarice Fennel from Homeware identifying him, identifying them both, and before the night was much older, Gloria had left in a cab and Adam had thrown up in the women's toilets on the fifth floor.

And really that had been the extent of it. Except, of course, that Adam and Gloria had split up early in the new year, and Gloria had asked for a transfer which she hadn't got and had been frosty towards Jennifer ever since.

The other thing, apart from a nagging sense of unease at her own rather trashy behaviour, was a realisation that if Nick found out about the incident he'd be...well, not happy about it. Might even call off the wedding.

And actually that would be much simpler than calling the whole thing off herself.

So, with Adam a free man now, they had seen a fair bit of each other that January—just coffees and films and lunches and the pub after work—but it had made Nick stop and think. And that was all. Nick, it had transpired, was not the suspicious type—what woman would look twice at someone else when they had him?

But then she had had a stroke of luck. Adam had rung up and left a cryptic message on her answering machine on the one rare occasion that Charlotte had been at her flat.

Charlotte. If ever someone was going to take sanctimonious delight in spilling the dirt on her own sister, it was Charlotte.

'Oh, Adam!' Jennifer had said, rolling her eyes at Charlotte's arch questioning. 'Adam works with me, that's all. We go out. We have fun. It's not serious.' And Charlotte had pursed her lips and said nothing but you knew, you just *knew*, what she was thinking, that she couldn't wait to find some opportunity to tell Nick all about it. There would be a row, a falling out. The wedding would be cancelled. No need to break up, just a bit more breathing space. Perfect.

But it hadn't been perfect.

Charlotte had said nothing. Not a damn thing. And it wasn't as though there hadn't been ample opportunity in those final weeks before the wedding. Consequently, Nick had suspected nothing. The wedding had loomed closer and closer until only the last-minute discovery of herself and Adam sharing an illicit moment in Nick's own bed could have halted the steam train that was marriage.

But she couldn't do that to Nick, not that, not in his own bed. So she had stopped the lunches and the films with Adam and gone through with it. Oh well, a marriage isn't forever, she had told herself and so it had proved, for just two years later they were divorced and now Nick was living with Milli, and Jennifer saw almost as much of him as she had when they'd been married, only now he asked for her advice on things and told her what he was thinking. It was quite sweet really.

'Ah, hello. Excuse me.' She had almost made it to the Staff Only door and now some Hugh Grant type had accosted her. 'I'm looking for something for my little boy. He's eight—well, nine really. It's his birthday. Last week, actually.'

Jennifer stopped and turned round.

She took great pains not to wear a black suit or to look in any way like a sales assistant in order to prevent just this sort of thing happening but the clipboard she was clutching and her hand on the Staff Only door had given her away. Now this idiot was going to try and get her to choose a present for his brat of a son whose birthday he had obviously forgotten and who probably lived with his ex-wife and her boyfriend in Essex or somewhere and whose very existence he had probably forgotten about entirely until this morning when the boy's mother had rung him up at work to abuse him, and now here he was.

Jennifer turned on a smile. He did look astonishingly like Hugh Grant. Perhaps it *was* Hugh Grant, although she was fairly certain Hugh Grant didn't have a nine-year-old son.

'Of course, sir, I'll get someone to help you.' She raised her head to catch the attention of one of the sales assistants, but every cash register in sight appeared to be unattended, which meant a couple of staff were going to get it in no uncertain terms at the next staff meeting.

'Peacekeeper™,' she said, grabbing a long, flat cellophane-wrapped box from the top of an untouched pile nearby. 'It was our biggest seller this Christmas— you'll have seen it advertised on TV?' The Hugh Grant look-alike nodded vigorously. 'It's a thrilling adventure game but you learn about life at the same time,' she said.

'Oh. Right,' he said hopefully, and Jennifer thought, you haven't got a clue.

'Every boy in his class either has one or wants one.' That clinched it. She handed him the box and pushed him firmly in the direction of the cash register.

Mr Gaspari was still on hold.

She pushed open the Staff Only door and made her way along the drab uncarpeted corridor that ran the length of the fifth floor and at the far end of which was the office she shared with Gary Harding, the Sportswear Manager. Outside the office was Gloria's desk, neat and empty but for her PC (logged off) and her telephone, on which a red light was flashing urgently. It was late January but Corporate Services still hadn't removed the Christmas on-hold CD, which was Bing Crosby's *Christmas Classics*— though for some reason whenever you got put on hold he was only ever singing 'The Little Drummer Boy'.

She pushed her office door shut with her foot and was disappointed to see Gary Harding was still at lunch—a phone call from the board of directors was something she'd quite like him to overhear.

'Hello, Mr Gasp—'

'Arumpa-pum-pum!' sang Bing, and Jennifer stabbed at another button.

'Mr Gaspari?'

'Oh, Jennifer, there you are. It's Aunt Caroline.'

Aunt Caroline?

'Your secretary put me on hold. I've been listening to 'The Little Drummer Boy'. I think I prefer the Boney M version—'

'Aunt Caroline, I have to put you back on hold—'

'Oh, I only wanted to be very quick. It's about that television program yesterday—'

'Ah, you saw that? How—did Mum—?'

Jennifer had been about to say *Did Mum tell you about it?* but as the idea of her mother ringing Aunt Caroline for a cosy chat seemed unlikely she stopped herself.

'This might come as a shock to you, dear, but I do occasionally watch daytime television.'

It did come as a shock.

'Now I did want to talk to you and I thought you should come up. Shall we say tomorrow? Afternoon tea?'

Jennifer experienced a moment of panic. If Aunt Caroline had watched Kim's program, who else had? She had deliberately told no one about it—except Nick, of course. And Mum and Charlotte...though hopefully they hadn't, in the end, watched it. *Had* they? Neither of them had emailed her. Perhaps they had rung? She hadn't been home to check her messages.

'I can't possibly come up tomorrow, I'll be working. Sorry but—'

'Don't you get days off? Aren't you the manager?'

'Yes and that's why—look, I'll call you straight back,' and she stabbed the other line.

'Mr Gaspari?'

'At last! My dear girl, do you have any idea how long I have been kept waiting on this telephone?'

Mr Gaspari, whom Jennifer had never actually met, sounded exactly like a petulant great-uncle she dimly remembered from childhood. She had an idea most of the board of directors were well over seventy and she adjusted her manner accordingly.

'Yes, I am sorry, Mr Gaspari, I was just caught with a customer.' That was good, the older directors liked management to stay in touch with the consumer.

'Don't you have sales staff to do that?' he snapped back.

'Well, yes...'

'Never mind. It is about this television program. Yesterday afternoon—'

Surely the board of directors didn't watch daytime television? Had word somehow got out that she was going to be talking about kids' computer games? But the producer had cancelled that show and instead she'd done 'I Saved My Sister's Life!' because Kim was desperate. The board could hardly complain about that, could they? Anyway the show had been recorded on Monday night in her own time and you couldn't get in trouble for talking about your personal life in your own time.

'Board isn't happy. Company policy to clear all media interaction through Marketing and P.R. You know that. It's in your contract.'

Jennifer tried to recall that particular clause of her contract. Then she tried to recall if she had, in fact, ever read her contract.

'This is a clear breach. Board wants a letter of explanation before the next meeting. On my desk 9 am Monday. Understand?'

'Yes but—'

'Good.' The line fell silent and so did Jennifer.

CHAPTER FIVE

AUGUST 1981

IT SEEMED TO CHARLOTTE that everything changed after Grandma Lake came to live with them.

On a Monday evening nearly a year after Grandma Lake had moved in, Charlotte sat silently in the doorway of her and Jennifer's bedroom and looked across the landing to the study that was now Grandma Lake's room. Downstairs *Crossroads* had just ended and, in the bathroom, Jennifer vomited noisily into the toilet bowl. But here in the doorway it was still. Calm. The door to Grandma Lake's room was shut.

Even before Grandma Lake had arrived a year ago, silent and bewildered in the back of the Austin Maxi, the signs had been ominous. How, for example, could there possibly be room in the house for an extra person? It was a three-bedroom semi, five people already lived there. And for how long was she expected to live with them? No one had said, and to ask would have been tantamount to saying, how long will Grandma Lake live?

Dad had been furious.

They had all sat around the kitchen table at the tail end of last summer—Mum, Dad and Aunt Caroline—and, when the suggestion was made, Dad had looked up from the sports section of *The Times* long enough to halt the conversation around the table. Then he had shaken out the paper as though someone had been reading it on the beach and there was sand between the pages, folded it, stood up and left the room. He hadn't needed to say anything to make his position quite clear.

Who had first made the suggestion that Grandma Lake should come to live with them? It certainly wasn't Grandma Lake herself. She was living quite contentedly (you presumed, if you ever thought about it) in the poky Victorian terrace in Oakton Way, Acton, where she'd always lived. That was where she'd always been and that was where, in your mind, you always put her.

You didn't put her here in your own home.

Acton was less than twenty miles away, though Grandma Lake rarely came to visit. It had been left to Mum and Dad to drive over there to collect her at Christmas or on Easter Sunday or August Bank Holiday and bring her over for the day. This had meant a fraught ninety-minute drive into west London that encompassed twenty-two sets of traffic lights and eight roundabouts and probable road-works at Hangar Lane, as Dad never tired of observing. If Grandma Lake could just find it in herself to take the bus to North Acton and get the Ruislip train, he could pick her up there and save himself an hour-and-a-half round trip twice in one day.

But Grandma Lake didn't like to take the bus, much less the tube.

And once a year, on Grandma Lake's birthday, everyone piled into the Austin and spent a grim day in Acton, an ordeal that far outweighed the inconvenience of Grandma Lake coming to visit you because it was a whole day of your weekend gone and, worse, you were stuck there until Dad successfully caught Mum's eye and Mum announced it was time to leave.

On the face of it, then, you would think Dad had more reason than anyone to wish his mother-in-law closer to home. And perhaps he *had* wished it. Perhaps he had envisaged her selling up and purchasing a nice little bungalow or a ground-floor flat or a room in an old people's home somewhere close by like Uxbridge or Hillingdon or Ickenham. Close enough that Mum could tootle over there in the Austin every week to take her to the shops or for a pot of Earl Grey at the tea shop in the high street.

He probably hadn't envisaged her selling up and moving into the study.

So it must have been either Mum or Aunt Caroline who had made the fateful suggestion that morning. They were the only ones likely to notice a change in Grandma Lake's circumstances. And there must have been a change—no one would suggest their elderly mum move in with them unless there was a pretty compelling reason. Whatever the reason, one Sunday in late summer as the roast was spitting and hissing in the oven and Graham was watching *Happy Days* on the telly, Mum and Aunt Caroline and Dad had had a discussion around the kitchen table and by the end of the discussion Grandma Lake's house had been valued, her possessions assessed, her longevity and health analysed, the problem of the stairs up to the study sorted and Dad had shaken out the sports section of *The Times* and left in disgust.

There had been no question that Grandma Lake move in with Aunt Caroline.

Aunt Caroline, who was in her mid-fifties, had quite suddenly become betrothed to a Yorkshireman, Ted Kettley, whom she'd met a few months earlier at an auction in Skipton. He was a valuer or something, employed by the local council. This meant that, after a lifetime of having a maiden aunt whom you could reasonably expect to remain a maiden, Charlotte and Jennifer and Graham had found themselves in the unexpected position of preparing to attend Aunt Caroline's wedding in North Yorkshire to a red-faced, large-eared, pipe-smoking Yorkshireman who was, suddenly, their Uncle Ted. It had seemed to Charlotte at the time an example of the unforeseen and world-reeling changes that were suddenly dumped on you and that, as an adolescent, you had no control over. You were simply meant to deal with them. Grandma Lake's arrival was another example of this unsettling phenomenon.

Aunt Caroline had sold her high-ceiled Art Deco flat in Perivale and moved into Ted's modern and centrally heated bungalow in North Yorkshire. It had been disturbing, though not nearly as disturbing as the reali-sation that North Yorkshire was too far away to relocate Grandma Lake and that an ageing mother-in-law was hardly a wedding present Uncle Ted could be expected to take on.

'Grandma Lake will be coming to live with us,' Mum had announced one Sunday over lunch as she'd spooned roast potatoes onto each of their plates.

'Why?' asked Graham.

'Where will she sleep?' asked Jennifer.

How long for? thought Charlotte.

'In the spare room,' Mum had replied, craftily changing the name of 'The Study' to 'The Spare Room' as though by changing its name this room became a place they didn't really need and that could easily be handed over to someone else with very little inconvenience to anyone. She'd ignored Graham's question.

After that nothing was the same again.

The change came not suddenly, but bit by bit. An encroaching sort of change that you ought to have seen coming but somehow, because you were fourteen, fifteen, sixteen, you didn't. As the days and nights passed and record players had to be turned right down so as not to disturb Grandma Lake, and *The Professionals* had to make way for *3-2-1* with Ted Rogers and *The Big Match* was aban-doned in favour of *Songs of Praise*, as chicken curry and spaghetti bolognese made way for lamb chops and casse-role, as Dad's armchair became Grandma Lake's armchair, it began to dawn on everyone that this house that had for so long been a children's house and then, briefly, a teenag-er's house, was now, very definitely, an old person's house.

Everyone had dealt with the change in their own way. Graham, in a show of masculine territorialness, had decided to decorate his bedroom and spent long hours testing various colours, painting and repainting until the dimensions of his room must have shrunk by some inches and the fumes sent Grandma Lake to bed with a migraine. Jennifer had selected a boy at school—Darren McKenzie—to go out with and spent all her free time at his house.

Charlotte stayed late after school and no one ever asked why. She read books in the library that weren't on the curriculum (*War and Peace, Animal Farm, Madame Bovary*), she wandered aimlessly around the shopping precinct near school, avoiding the gangs of fifth-formers who gathered near the fountain and threw each other's school bags in the water. And she spent at least three evenings a week and most of the weekend over at Zoe Findlay's house.

Nearly a year after Grandma Lake had moved in, Aunt Caroline still hadn't been down to visit.

Mum alone had carried on as though nothing had happened, vacuuming around Grandma Lake as though she were a fixture that came with the house, reducing her array of culinary dishes down to about five that all included potato, carrots and peas as though potato, carrots and peas were what she had secretly yearned to cook all her life.

Dad said very little on the subject of Grandma Lake but he didn't have to. On a chilly March morning, some five months after Grandma Lake's arrival, he had turfed the Austin out of the garage and onto the driveway and in a day-long flurry of shifting and rearranging and throwing out and rewiring and hammering had turned the garage into a den. Here he had moved the second-best armchair, the desk that had once been in the study, a bookcase, a transistor radio, his case of dusty old 45s (the Everly Brothers, Billy J. Kramer and the Dakotas, Del Shannon, Dion and the Belmonts, Adam Faith), the old black-and-white portable television set that still occasionally worked and, finally, himself.

A sort of calm had descended.

Charlotte sat up, listening. The door to Grandma Lake's room was closed. Downstairs the theme tune to *Crossroads* had just ended and in the bathroom Jennifer coughed and sobbed noisily into the toilet bowl. And tomorrow was the first day of the new school year. Not just any school year: her first day in the lower sixth form, Jennifer's first in the upper sixth.

Tomorrow.

It was curious, mind-numbing even, to think of a tomorrow. To think of the rest of this evening. The next five minutes.

She wouldn't go in to school. She would spend the day curled up in bed even if it meant Mum telephoning the doctor's surgery. Perhaps she would never go in. Perhaps she would never get up.

Jennifer had stopped vomiting and was breathing loudly with jerky sobbing breaths as though she couldn't get enough air into her lungs.

'...*an unlikely place to find a soup tureen.*'

Crossroads had ended and in its place the carefully modulated voice of Derek Longstaff, the new *Capital Tonight* presenter, floated up the stairs from the lounge. Derek Longstaff had started the week before, replacing the previous presenter, much to Grandma Lake's disgust.

Each time he came on she scowled and said, 'He's not a patch on that Naomi girl.'

Charlotte closed her eyes.

From the bathroom the sound of the toilet flushing momentarily muffled the sobbing.

She opened her eyes. Soon Jennifer would emerge from the bathroom—and then what? Did she want to be found crouching here in the doorway? What was the alternative? She couldn't go downstairs and sit with everyone watching television. She didn't want to listen to Grandma Lake complaining about Derek Longstaff.

Funny that Grandma Lake was always Grandma Lake and never Grandma. It wasn't as though Grandma Lake had to compete for a place with a plethora of other grandmas—she was it: the sole grandparent. Her real name was Bertha, which made you think of ocean liners and little cabins with narrow bunks—but no one ever called her that either.

Grandma Lake's bedroom door was closed. You could almost imagine that behind the door it was still a study, with Dad's old desk in there and, on it, the old gramophone and the small black typewriter from the fifties on which Mum had taught herself to touch-type.

Now, what had once been the study was cluttered with the dusty, faded and moth-eaten collection of items that was all Grandma Lake had to show for eighty-odd years of living (or was all that Dad had allowed her to salvage from the house in Oakton Way). On the day of her arrival last October they had all been press-ganged into helping to carry her belongings up the stairs: dented Art Deco lampshades, musty wooden bookshelves and boxes of spineless Catherine Cooksons and Dorothy L. Sayers and a Mrs Beeton, an oppressive Victorian wardrobe and a rotting tea chest bursting with heavy silks and tweeds and a number of tatty furry items that looked suspiciously as though they had once been attached to living creatures.

And Grandma Lake had stood in the middle of the room pointing and saying, 'There, put it there! Oh, that old thing, I couldn't bear to leave it. You be careful with that! Oh dear! Oh dear oh dear...' Then she had sat down on the bed and said nothing.

On the mantelpiece and window sill Mum had placed a confusion of music boxes, ugly china and glass ornaments, empty brass candlesticks and yellowing photographs in ornate frames showing babies in long white christening gowns. Charlotte had recognised herself and Jennifer and Graham as babies. There was nothing more recent of any of them. Or perhaps Grandma Lake had a thing for baby photos, for there were photographs of Mum and Aunt Caroline too.

From the bathroom, the toilet flushed a second time.

Jennifer never ever threw up unless she was in the car. She'd been sick in the car on the journey home from Aunt Caroline's wedding last summer—all over the Ordnance Survey map of Norfolk.

On Grandma Lake's window sill there were also two much older photographs of people sporting between-the-wars fashions. One group was unmistakably a wedding party, presumably Grandma and Grandad Lake's. The second photograph, in a tarnished silver frame, showed a pretty young woman of perhaps twenty-one done up in a stiff black skirt and lace-up boots, wearing an armband and a jaunty black cap. Over her left shoulder hung a bulky box-like bag that looked like a gas-mask box but must surely pre-date gas masks by a good ten or fifteen years. The young woman waved a hand rather coquettishly at the camera, the sun in her eyes so that it was hard to tell if she was smiling or frowning. She was standing in what appeared to be a bus depot.

On the day that Grandma Lake moved in Charlotte had made the mistake of picking up the photograph, vaguely wondering if this was Grandma Lake as a young woman. But Grandma Lake had heaved herself to her feet and informed her with some ceremony that she was holding the Only Surviving Photograph of Great-Aunt Jemima.

No one had ever heard of Great-Aunt Jemima.

Grandma Lake had tapped the photograph meaningfully. Great-Aunt Jemima, her only sister, had died tragically during the General Strike of 1926 while on duty as a volunteer bus conductor—hence the bus depot, which was, she had explained, Acton Bus Garage—and during that turbulent and divisive period of Britain's history this was where Great-Aunt Jemima had been briefly and dramatically stationed.

'Turbulent and divisive' was not how Grandma Lake had described the General Strike. 'That daft strike' had been her exact words, but if you were studying the Rebellions and Revolutions course in O-level history you had to grant such a pivotal event its full historical significance.

Jennifer had muttered some excuse and fled downstairs but Charlotte, whether due to guilt or embarrassment, had remained.

And so now they had a great-aunt who had died tragically during the General Strike. This was unusual and perhaps mildly interesting, though somehow it failed to have the same pathos as, say, a great-uncle lost at Passchendaele. And according to Grandma Lake, Jemima had only signed up as a bus conductor because she was sweet on one of the drivers. Not a very glorious reason to die—particularly, Grandma Lake had explained, as Jemima had had a husband and a three-month-old baby at the time.

Her death had come on the fourth day of the strike at seven twenty-five in the morning (Grandma Lake had been most particular about the time) somewhere near Chiswick when the driver of Jemima's bus, a volunteer like Jemima, had taken a wrong turn and attempted to drive under a railway bridge. The bridge had proved too low and most of the top deck of the bus had been sheared off. Fortunately only four people had been on the top deck at the time—an elderly gentleman who had sustained a broken finger; a nanny and a one-year-old child who had both been thrown clear and who had, remarkably, sustained only mild cuts and bruises; and the bus conductor, Jemima, who'd been killed outright.

'She were the only casualty in the whole strike,' had been Grandma Lake's summing up of the tragedy. 'Lots of accidents and the like. Well, it's to be expected, all those young men and girls driving about helter-skelter—wonder it wasn't wholesale carnage. But no, on the whole, it went off remarkably well. Apart from poor Jemmy, of course.'

Charlotte had listened dutifully but henceforth had ensured she was never again alone in the room with Grandma Lake.

Now, nearly a year later, at a little before seven o'clock on Monday evening, it was safe to assume Grandma Lake was downstairs, dozing in front of *Capital Tonight*, and Dad's old desk and the gramophone and Mum's small black typewriter had been consigned to the garage, perhaps forever.

Everything had gone silent in the bathroom. Charlotte held her breath and realised that an elderly woman coming to live with you wasn't the worst thing that could happen in the world.

CHAPTER SIX

As JENNIFER WAS HANGING up the phone in her office and bleakly contemplating her career in retail, the Waverley University Graduations and Ceremonies Committee was in session.

This morning the talk was of academic dress.

'I'm sorry, but I fail to see why Media Studies shouldn't have the claret hood lined with silk of a lighter shade of claret and edged with gold silk,' declared Professor Kendall, who was chairing the Academic Dress Sub-Committee meeting in the faculty meeting room. 'After all, it's in keeping with the rest of the faculty.'

'It's not the claret hood per se,' replied one of the Media Studies lecturers, a thin, wiry lad of about twelve with a tufty goatee and impossibly skinny jeans. A series of sighs circled the table like a deflated Mexican wave. 'It's the lighter claret lining and the gold tassel,' he explained. 'We were told we could have malachite green and that we didn't need a tassel.'

'You. Have. To. Have. A. Tassel,' replied Professor Kendall between gritted teeth, and somewhere near the window a pencil snapped.

Charlotte glanced at the clock above Professor Kendall's head. It was nine forty-five on Wednesday morning. The meeting would have to be over by ten because the heads of department had a Finance Committee meeting at that time. Fifteen minutes.

It was time she said something. Made her mark on the meeting.

She shifted uneasily in her chair, aware that most of the fifteen committee members seated around the oval table had spoken, aware that if she'd just said something right at the very beginning of the meeting, she could relax now and zone out till the meeting ended. As it was, she knew she was in for an uncomfortable time until she could think of something to say.

Tom Pitney, seated beside Professor Kendall, had already given his report on Smalt and Begonia as defined in the British Colour Council *Dictionary of Standard Colours*, 1951 edition. Having given his report, Tom had taken no further part in the meeting and instead was scribbling timetabling revisions idly on his university notepad. Beside Tom, Bert Humphries, the department's senior lecturer, sat with a weary air about him, emerging from his stupor just long enough to challenge the assertion made by the Professor of Politics that a second colour in a hood lining must go to five centimetres by citing a little-known Australian university that used two and a half centimetres as its hood-lining measurement. The comment had been met with derision and raised eyebrows of the 'What can you expect from an Australian university?' kind and Bert had relapsed into silence.

Dr Ashley Lempriere was there too, tapping a pencil with loud impatience. Charlotte watched her through narrowed eyes. What was she doing here? There was no way a Canadian exchange professor was the least bit interested in academic dress, except perhaps her own academic dress when collecting some honorary degree from somewhere. Charlotte's eyes scanned the room. There were a lot of professors and department heads around the table and Lempriere's contract ended in June. Was she preparing the way for an extension? Tenure? A takeover?

She tightened her grip on her pen and took a calming breath. There was less than fifteen minutes of the meeting left. She squeezed her eyes shut. Concentrate. She must concentrate.

TEENAGE SUICIDE IS EVERYONE'S PROBLEM!

The problem was she still felt guilty about Darren McKenzie.

She didn't like the fact that she still felt guilty more than twenty years later. That she felt guilty despite having done more than enough over the years (some of it pretty morally dubious—lying to save her sister's marriage being one glaring example) to make up for it. And she couldn't understand why the bad things she had done over the years (borrowing people's cars without asking them, moving out of houses when the rent was due, lying on her CV on two occasions, pretending to be ill to avoid family Christmases) caused her no pangs of remorse whatsoever, not a shred of regret, and yet she still felt guilty about Darren McKenzie.

Of course, none of those other things had ended up with someone trying to kill themselves.

Except that it hadn't ended. Nothing ever ended—something happened and then something else happened and so it went on. And the most recent thing that had happened was that Jennifer had gone on national television and said all that.

It couldn't possibly be because of Darren McKenzie, could it?

She tried to remember. Jennifer hadn't cried for long. A couple of nights. Maybe three. By the end of that summer she'd been seeing someone else. Hadn't she? Or was that the following summer? At any rate, she'd got over Darren.

The clock above Professor Kendall's head inched forward to nine forty-nine. If she could just think of something to say. Of course, the obvious thing to say, the one thing that every single person seated around the table was thinking but hadn't said, was: Isn't this the most absurd waste of all our time and who the hell really gives a flying fuck what colours the Media Studies people choose to graduate in and why can't we all just pack up and go home right now?

The clock moved on to nine fifty and Charlotte twisted her pen around and around in her hands.

As far as she could recall, the main thing about Darren McKenzie was that he came from the north and wore a red-and-white-striped football scarf, which was the colours of Stoke City Football Club, when every other boy at Henry Morton Secondary had worn blue and white QPR or Chelsea scarves or the navy and white of Spurs who, that year, had won the Cup. This, and the way he said 'bath' so that it rhymed with 'maths', made Darren distinctive. Other than these scintillating differences, Darren McKenzie had been average-looking with acne and sticking-out ears and the usual Saturday job at Your Price Records.

Were our lives so dull, Charlotte wondered, that the arrival of a boy from Stoke seemed exciting?

Jennifer had started going out with Darren McKenzie not long after Grandma Lake had come to live with them, which meant Jennifer was over at the McKenzies' most evenings and so had avoided the nightly trauma of Grandma Lake sucking vegetable soup through her dentures and dribbling it onto the nylon tablecloth. By the start of the summer holidays, Jennifer and Darren had been going out for perhaps ten months, which was some sort of milestone for Henry Morton Secondary and a world record for Jennifer.

Going out with Darren McKenzie meant being seen out with him by as many people as possible—the more people that saw them lighting up a Silk Cut at the school gate or sharing a vanilla milkshake at Wimpey or queuing up to see *Conan the Barbarian* or whatever was on at the Palace, the more significant the relationship was. 'People', of course, referred only to other kids in Jennifer's year at school.

Such ostentation had been, and still was, inexplicable. Charlotte had spent her entire school life staring at her shoes, sitting at the back and generally going out of her way to avoid being seen by anyone and could not have imagined herself telling even her closest friend anything more revealing than her opinion on who had shot J.R. Ewing.

Right up until that Thursday at the end of term. The Thursday of the maths O-level.

'Would you believe, some people actually try to get themselves onto these committees...' murmured Geethan Chandrasekaran, the Professor of Celtic Runes, who had squeezed in next to Charlotte at the beginning of the meeting and who had been trying to catch her eye for the last half-hour.

Charlotte smiled faintly in reply. Somewhere in another building a fire alarm began to ring.

❀ ❀ ❀

Another bell was ringing. It was the bell in the school gymnasium signalling the end of the first period of the afternoon, a Thursday afternoon during the last week of the summer term. A summer that had ended twenty-five years ago.

Outside was the clatter of feet, the screams and shouts of a schoolful of children emerging from classrooms and corridors, swarming towards other classrooms and other corridors. The screams and shouts reached a crescendo then faded. Inside the gymnasium an exam was in progress and there was still an hour left to go. Heads raised, listening to the din outside, then lowered again. No one moved.

No one moved, except for Charlotte, who pushed back her chair from her desk in the seventh row, who stood up right in the middle of a trigonometry question, who knocked her chair with a loud thud onto the parquetry floor and ran out.

She'd been staring at the trigonometry question for ten, fifteen minutes and she knew the answer, had already worked it out in her head (because really trigonometry was quite simple) but had been unable to write down a single number because her eyes were stinging, her teeth were clenched so tightly her jaw was aching and the hand holding her pencil was shaking so that the only marks she made on the answer booklet resembled small bird tracks.

Funny how important a maths exam had seemed at the start of the year—at the start of the day, even. And it was odd how much time you spent preparing and practising and worrying about it and how a good maths grade had seemed essential to one's entrance into the A-level course, into university, into a career, the rest of your life. And yet it all came down to this one stupid question about a man walking five miles on a bearing of 092 degrees that any idiot could answer but that she was suddenly, bewilderingly, unable to put down on the paper.

Two hours before she had stood outside the girls' toilet block. Two hours ago someone—Julie Fanshawe, a friend of Jennifer's—had called her over, had said, all snide-like with that fake schoolgirl concern, *Hey Charlotte, there's something written about you in the girls' toilets.* And Charlotte had marched over there not knowing what to expect but angry. And with a sudden knot twisting her stomach in half.

And now here she was doing a question on trigonometry. A man walking five miles on a bearing of 092 degrees.

At which point she'd realised if she stayed in the gym one more minute she was going to be sick. Or worse, cry.

She hadn't made a decision to leave, just found herself pushing back her chair so that it had fallen with a thud onto the floor and she had fled the hall, leaving her exam paper and her answer booklet and her pencil case with her calculator and ruler and protractor on the desk and vividly, *agonisingly*, aware that every head had turned to stare at her, that three invigilators had started up after her, which was exactly, it was *exactly* what she hadn't wanted. Everyone staring.

A girl running at five miles per hour on a bearing of 092 degrees.

She escaped across the quadrangle and through the teachers' car park to the side gate and away. There was a bus pulling up at the bus stop that would have deposited her right outside her house but instead she turned in the opposite direction, running, needing to put distance between herself and the school. When, much later, she arrived home, she fumbled with the front door key, ran straight upstairs and shut herself in the bedroom she still shared with Jennifer.

If Mum had been home she might have wondered why Charlotte was home at three forty-five when the maths O-level wasn't scheduled to finish till four o'clock. But Mum wasn't at home, she was sitting in the waiting room of Dr Caddington's surgery with Grandma Lake, who needed a new prescription for some unnamed complaint. So when Charlotte arrived home with her school jumper tied around her waist and her face pale and carrying only a pencil there was no one to notice.

When it became apparent the house was empty she came to a dead stop in the middle of the bedroom, there being nowhere else to run.

Her school bag was hanging on the back of the door where she'd left it that morning because you were only allowed to take pens and pencils and calculators and protractors and rulers into the exam. Next to the bag was the pink jumper she'd bought Jennifer for her seventeenth birthday last September. Her own seventeenth was less than a month away and she stared at the jumper and her own fast-approaching birthday with equal dismay.

She snatched up the jumper and clutched it tightly in both fists so that the wool stretched taut. Then she remembered that one of the faces that had stared at her as she'd fled the exam hall had been Zoe's, and she groaned and sat down on the floor because she would never again visit Zoe's house in Beechtree Crescent.

Hours passed. Mum came home. Grandma Lake settled in front of the telly. Tea was served and Jennifer still hadn't come home from school.

'She's out with her friends,' Mum said and no one asked why Charlotte wasn't out too, when it was the last day of exams. Dad said, How did you do in the exam, then? and Mum said, Aren't you going to eat that, dear? and then Charlotte went back upstairs.

Perhaps they assumed Jennifer was out with Darren. But Darren came round at seven looking for her. Charlotte had already finished her tea and was standing at the top of the stairs when the doorbell rang, so it was she who saw Darren's familiar green parka through the frosted glass of the front door and she who, on the second ring, went woodenly downstairs and opened the door.

Darren. She stared at him. Jennifer wasn't with him. She almost closed the door on him because the last thing she wanted, the very last thing, was her sister's boyfriend standing there in the doorway staring at her.

'Is Jen in?' Darren said with his northern accent and it was such a normal, Darren thing to say that at first she just stood there.

'No,' she replied at last. Where was Jen? Probably out with her friends drinking milkshakes at Wimpey in the high street or down by the canal talking to boys from the grammar school. Having a good time, at any rate, while her boyfriend was standing here looking for her. Lucky Jennifer. Lucky, popular, pretty Jennifer.

The door to the lounge was ajar and Dad was watching *Capital Tonight*.

'...*a sheep dip in Tower Hamlets,*' Naomi Findlay, long-time presenter of the program, announced obscurely in her perfectly enunciated Home Counties voice. The incongruity of such words taken out of context seemed to give them portent, like words spoken by a prophet. *A sheep dip in Tower Hamlets.*

Charlotte took a deep breath, a hard lump filling her stomach. It had been there most of the afternoon, but now it began to glow hot and red, and it travelled up her spine and flushed her cheeks so that they burned. The pounding that had been beating away behind her eyeballs all evening quickened then suddenly vanished.

'I'm sorry, Darren.' Her mouth assumed the shape of a sympathetic smile. 'Jen's out with Adrian Cresswell.'

The words slid from her mouth as smoothly as the truth might have done. Adrian Cresswell. He and Jennifer had briefly been an item in third year, everyone knew that. The lie was so believable it could almost have been the truth.

Darren's lips parted slightly, his eyes widened. He swallowed, the way you did when you were in pain.

'She's been out with him a lot this week,' Charlotte continued. 'I expect she told you she was out with Nikki and Julie?'

Darren swallowed but said nothing.

'I told her to tell you, I told her it wasn't fair on you, particularly now everyone at school knows about it...'

That was it, of course. That was the killer punch: *everyone at school knows about it.* Yes, she knew how that felt.

She thought about saying 'I'm so sorry' again, but that would have been overdoing it so she just smiled awkwardly, the way a sister might have smiled in such a situation.

Darren's eyes glassed over and it seemed as though he was going to demand to know more but instead he turned abruptly and walked, almost ran really, down the driveway and into the light cast by the streetlamp. Then he was gone and Charlotte closed the front door after him and went up the stairs to her room.

'Who was it?' Mum called from the lounge.

'No one. Double-glazing salesman,' she replied, then she closed the bedroom door and there on the floor was Jennifer's pink jumper with red lipstick all over its front just as though someone had deliberately drawn on it.

Jennifer had come home eventually, giggling and tripping over the loose carpet on the landing and making the bedroom stink of cheap cider—it was a Friday night near the end of term after all. But by the following night Darren had been seen down at the canal with Roberta Peabody and Jennifer had sobbed noisily long into the night while Charlotte had lain hard and cold in bed and stared at the shadows on the wall.

In the unheated meeting room that was currently home to the Waverley University Academic Dress Sub-Committee, the clock inched forward to nine fifty-one and Charlotte was preparing to speak: *We could always take a vote on it.* These were the words she would say. Not the most scintillating words ever spoken, it was true, and as suggestions went it was hardly pithy, but it was at least constructive. She would say it.

Nine fifty-three.

A second scene popped into her head. Herself and Nick, who was now Jennifer's ex, though at the time he was her fiancé, seated in a small cafe just off the Embankment. Another scene and another lie twenty years after the first scene, the first lie. But connected, she suddenly realised, because she'd still felt guilty about Darren McKenzie. Had continued to feel guilty right up until Jennifer's wedding.

Nine fifty-five.

At least as far as lies went this one had passed unnoticed and that was important, more important than the fact that her sister had been having an affair with a work colleague a month before her wedding. But the lie had been told and the wedding had gone ahead.

Still, Jennifer and Nick were divorced now, so what did it matter?

The cafe was a classic greasy spoon tucked beneath the shadow of Waterloo Bridge. The lie was this:

'Honestly, Nick, do you really believe Jen would be out getting measurements for her wedding dress if she was having an affair with someone else?'

That was it. Hardly a lie at all, really, if you thought about it. Just a question, in fact. A question asked over a lukewarm coffee in a cafe just off the Embankment on a cold February lunchtime four years ago, and after she'd asked it, Charlotte picked up her chipped mug and held it to her lips and swallowed down a lukewarm mouthful because she liked her future brother-in-law and she had just lied to his face because she owed it to Jennifer.

It was a Saturday lunchtime and the cafe was busy with tourists staring mutely at the stale croissants and limp salads on their plates and at the stained cutlery with which they were expected to eat it. Nick was wearing a sweater and a sports jacket and looked wealthier than he really was so that for a moment Charlotte had felt proud to be seen with him—it was a novelty, this going out to lunch with a good-looking man—but the feeling had frozen inside her when Nick had said the one thing that he wasn't meant to say.

I think Jen's seeing someone behind my back.

This wasn't a question, not technically, so she could simply have not answered, but there was Darren McKenzie, always Darren McKenzie.

So she had answered him at once, reassuringly, unequivocally.

Anyone who had genuinely known nothing of the affair might have paused to ask Nick why he thought such a thing and who the affair was supposed to be with anyway. But she hadn't asked these things. Instead, she had jumped in with her denial so rapidly there was no room left for discussion and no time to ponder the morality of it all.

She'd already done the pondering. Had been pondering for the month prior to this conversation. In fact, ever since she'd overheard a message she wasn't meant to overhear on Jennifer's answering machine. A message from someone called Adam who had been very keen for Jennifer to come over that night.

'Oh, Adam!' Jennifer had said, rolling her eyes at Charlotte's questions. 'Adam works with me, that's all. We go out. We have fun. It's not serious.'

But the wedding was serious, and by the time Charlotte and Nick were sitting in the cafe just off the Embankment, the wedding was in seven days and Jennifer was still having fun with Adam. Charlotte had almost not come to the cafe. A part of her had believed Nick couldn't possibly suspect and that, if he did, there was no way he would ask her about it. A part of her, a large part, had believed it was none of her business and it was best not to get involved. A tiny, minuscule, insignificant part of her had remembered Darren McKenzie and felt guilty.

It was the tiny, minuscule, insignificant part of her that had said, 'Honestly, Nick, do you really believe Jen would be out getting measurements for her wedding dress if she was having an affair with someone else?'

The rest of her had been appalled.

'Why don't you ask her?' she added, swallowing the wretched coffee and trying desperately to rescue the situation.

'What's the point?' Nick looked down at the red and white plastic tablecloth then looked up into her face. 'She'd only deny it.'

'Well, there you are!' There had been a moment's silence. 'I mean, if you can't trust each other, what good is that?' which meant that now it was Nick's fault as much as Jennifer's if the marriage didn't work because he hadn't trusted her. It certainly wasn't Charlotte's fault.

What would he do, she wondered, if I said, *Yes, you're right, Jen's having an affair*? Would he believe me and not her? How is it that their marriage depends on me?

Instead, she had stood up, knocking the table and causing the coffee to spill over the edge of Nick's cup and form a pool in the centre of the table. She was going to be Jennifer's bridesmaid and Nick would soon be her brother-in-law. She liked Nick, he was a nice guy.

'I have to go. Look, it'll be fine,' and that was another lie, though perhaps not as shameful as the first.

'I believe Environmental Studies went with empire blue in the end,' Dr McGill of Linguistics was saying. 'Something to do with a charter from the sixteenth century,' he added mysteriously.

Charlotte jerked back to the present and caught Dave Glengorran's eye across the table. Dave had arrived late and was now tearing strips from the agenda and screwing them up into balls, which he was flicking off the end of his pen in the general direction of the wastepaper bin. Dave had said nothing either.

'Well, there's always damask,' he said suddenly and a little impatiently, as though this was a suggestion that ought to have been made some time ago. 'After all, that's what the University of London wears.'

'*Damask!*' spluttered Professor Kendall. 'The *Chancellor* wears damask, a damask robe. You cannot graduate with a Bachelor of Arts in a damask robe.' He took a deep breath and noisily reshuffled his papers. 'We need to decide today! I must make the Sub-Committee's recommendation to the Vice Chancellor this week.'

'All we want is gold cord,' insisted the younger of the three Media Studies lecturers, a girl with large spectacles and blue hair.

'Or sulphur, at a pinch,' said her colleague, the thin wiry boy with the goatee and skinny jeans.

There was a tense silence.

'Could we maybe look at a compromise here?'

Everyone turned to look at Ashley. She had tossed aside her pencil and was sitting up with a sudden air of determination and Charlotte's heart sank. That was it then. Dave had spoken, Ashley had spoken, and she was now the only one left who had remained silent.

'You guys want cord and you people say they gotta have tassels. Okay then, have both. Have the gold cord. Have the goddamn gold tassels. And why don't we all wear damask robes?'

The room erupted.

'Everyone, *please*, I must insist on one person speaking at a time!' Professor Kendall paused to mop his brow with a handkerchief despite the near-zero room temperature. 'It's ten o'clock and many of us have a Finance Committee meeting to attend, so may I suggest that we adjourn and meet again next week and may I *beg* you all to come to some sort of agreement on this issue?' He looked around the room.

Charlotte sat on the edge of her seat, the words *Isn't this the most absurd waste of all our time…?* perched right on the tip of her tongue, flexing and about to dive into the verbal arena. Her mouth felt dry and her palms started to sweat.

'I believe this room is free for a meeting next Wednesday, Professor Kendall,' she announced instead, the words bursting from her chest like a cough she had tried to suppress. 'There was a memo—the Misconduct and Discipline Review Board meeting has been postponed…'

She sat back again, her heart pounding. Well, at least she had said something. And then her mobile beeped and she was surprised to see she'd missed two calls from Aunt Caroline.

CHAPTER SEVEN

AUGUST 1981

JENNIFER RETCHED VIOLENTLY, bringing up barely digested shepherd's pie and peas. Perhaps, she realised afterwards, vomiting in such dramatic fashion actually helped things along a bit. At any rate, Mum came running up the stairs, buckets were proffered, glasses of water, soothing words, searching questions.

And all the while she knew that Charlotte was sitting silent and unnoticed in the doorway to their bedroom as though she had no part in any of this. As if she were merely a bystander.

When eventually Mum thought to look in on her, Charlotte had climbed into bed and was lying under the covers in a way that wordlessly and innocently proclaimed her own sickness. And she looked sick too, so still and pale and silent that Mum was on the verge of telephoning Dr Caddington. She was dissuaded, fortunately, from this course of action, but what could be more believable? Two sisters struck down with the same affliction. Some bug picked up at school, no doubt. Children are always picking up bugs at school.

When the first bustle of post-vomit activity had died down and the house had resumed its more usual after-dinner air, Jennifer sat on her bed, her knees drawn up tight to her chest, her arms wrapped around her shins, her throat raw. She stared straight ahead at a pile of geography and history textbooks on the floor, at the open jar of nail polish on the dressing table, at a poster Charlotte had blu-tacked to the wall. There were no posters on her own side of the room because at seventeen you no longer stuck pictures of pop stars on your bedroom wall. She reached behind her pillow for Peter Rabbit who was old and soft and battered and whose presence she hadn't noticed in five years. She held him close. Something was wound up very tight in her chest, so tight that were she to loosen her hold on him she felt that she might unwind suddenly, horribly and irreversibly.

Out of the corner of her eye she could see Charlotte's still and silent form beneath the sheets. The lid of the nail polish lay on its side on the dressing-table and the cloying smell of varnish hung in the air and coated the back of her throat.

She found that if she stared hard enough at the opposite wall, at the pencil case and the school bag on the floor, at the flaking putty on the window sill, at Steve Strange's eyes watching from a poster above the bed, she didn't need to think about anything else. If she just kept her arms wrapped very tightly around herself and refused to let go, everything else could be pushed to the edges, so far to the edges that it almost vanished. If she could just concentrate hard enough.

The dining-room chair lay on its side in the middle of the bedroom floor and, oddly, Mum appeared not to have noticed it.

Jennifer let go of Peter Rabbit, jumped up off the bed and fled the room. She bolted down the stairs to the lounge and the television and the remains of dinner—shepherd's pie and peas—which was beyond cold by that stage.

Mum was still in the kitchen while Dad, who had finished the washing-up, was reading the business pages, which meant the newspaper was open on his lap as he sat in front of the telly. On the screen *Capital Tonight* was ending and the new presenter, Derek Longstaff, smiled affably. '...*looking like the end of the road for jellied eels,*' he declared, one eyebrow raised in conspiratorial irony. Dad got up and flicked the channel back to BBC One, where the opening credits of *Angels* had just ended.

Grandma Lake had positioned herself in Dad's armchair to watch and was already asleep. At the other end of the sofa, Graham was curled up sucking a pencil stub, precociously studying *The Times* crossword puzzle. This necessitated much thoughtful frowning, pencil tapping and triumphant scribbling. As Jennifer appeared in the doorway, he paused long enough to glance up and cast a speculative glance in her direction, surprised, no doubt, that the sudden bout of illness that had so dramatically felled both his sisters had struck in the evening and not in the morning when it was time to leave for school.

'*One who pretends ill-health to be part male but more than dally.* Ten letters, something *a* something *i n* something something *r e r,*' pondered Graham out loud.

On the television a young male nurse in a lemon-coloured uniform ran silently in white plimsolls along a busy hospital corridor.

Jennifer stood in the doorway and reached up to touch her throat which was smarting from being sick.

'*He's stopped breathing!*' gasped the nurse in the lemon-coloured uniform.

Standing in the lounge doorway, Jennifer found she was unable to go any further. Little tremors ran through her body as though she had just climbed out of an outdoor swimming pool on a particularly wintry day. This was the final day of August, it was still mild, the weatherman had said so. Graham was in a T-shirt, Dad had his shirt sleeves rolled up. Grandma Lake was in a heavy-duty tweed skirt circa 1935. The skirt looked as though it had seen duty on many a cross-country ramble which was odd as Grandma Lake herself considered a walk to the pillar box at the end of the street to be an unnecessary journey fraught with peril.

There was a place on the sofa between Grandma Lake and Graham, and Jennifer made for this spot with wooden but dogged steps, finally reaching it, turning around and sinking down onto the sofa. It seemed an immense effort.

No one noticed. No one said a word. She stared straight ahead at the TV screen.

Somebody on *Angels* was on a life-support machine. Somebody was always on a life-support machine—last week it had been a young bride on her wedding day after a car crash (died), the week before a little boy after being bullied at school (survived), now it was one of the nurses following a drink-driving crash that had dramatically closed the last episode. This nurse—a young woman whose fiancé, another nurse, had been discovered having an affair—lay on the bed with a white sheet across her and a bandage around her head, various tubes taped here and there, her eyes shut, breathing noisily as though she had a blocked nose.

That would be a cushy acting job, Jennifer thought. I could do that.

'*Malingerer!*' cried Graham triumphantly and Jennifer spun around.

Graham innocently scribbled the letters into the crossword.

'Reminds me of when I wanted to be a nurse,' said Grandma Lake unexpectedly, and they all looked at her because they'd assumed she was asleep. Dad raised a silent eyebrow. She wasn't his mother, after all. It wasn't his suggestion she come and live with them.

No one said, *Does it, Gran?* or *When was that?* or *Why didn't you become a nurse, then?*

'The Great War,' Grandma Lake continued, conversationally, as though they had asked all these questions and more. 'All sorts of young girls became nurses. Volunteers they were, and stretcher bearers and ambulance drivers and all sorts.'

Graham, who was good at maths and equally good at history, chewed his pencil for a moment then said, 'But you'd have been about sixteen when the First World War ended.'

'That's what I'm saying—I wanted to be a nurse but I was too young, the war ended.'

'That's a pity,' said Dad wryly. 'You must have been choked when they signed the Armistice.'

'I was. I'd have made a good ambulance driver. I could drive, you know, I had an uncle taught me when I were a nipper. You didn't need no licence then, just hop in and off you go. I drove tractors and all sorts. Yes, I'd have made a good ambulance driver.'

With this she resettled her hands on her lap and concentrated once more on the television.

The nurse on life-support lay very still and breathed noisily. Beside her, her mother held her hand and looked worried. An image of Grandma Lake in two cardigans and an antiquated tweed skirt, skilfully driving an ambulance across a muddy field in France, flashed unconvincingly before Jennifer's eyes.

She wished they would all be quiet.

'*Overdose,*' announced another young doctor in another part of the hospital. '*But why?*' cried the patient's distraught mother. '*Why would she do such a thing? Why would she try to take her own life? She seemed so happy.*'

There must have been some colour left in Jennifer's face because she could feel it now drain away like blood down a sink in some B-grade horror film and at the same time Graham and Dad and Grandma Lake and Mum, who was laying out breakfast things in the kitchen, and the hospital ward and all the frantic nurses and distraught patients seemed to peel away on every side so that she was left, clinging to a tall and very narrow pinnacle where no one could possibly reach her but where everyone could see her. She swayed dizzyingly for a moment or two, expecting to fall. Expecting someone, everyone, to stare at her, to demand of her *Why? Why did you let this happen? What could you have been thinking? How could you have been so—*

'We've moved her to Intensive Care,' said the young doctor. *'But she's stable.'*

'Oh God,' said the girl's mother.

Cruel. That was the word Jennifer might have used.

'Do you think she'll be alright, doctor?'

'We've pumped her stomach. But…'

The young doctor—a Brummie with a broad accent—spread his hands in a gesture that clearly said, the rest is up to you, Mrs Whatever. The camera zoomed in on Mrs Whatever's face as his words sank in.

And Jennifer realised, too, with a thud that felt like a netball hitting her in the face: Charlotte was up there alone and what was to stop her trying it again? What was to say she wasn't even now climbing back up onto the dining-room chair, retying the bits of dead tie together, slipping the loop over her head and kicking the chair away?

Jennifer leapt up from the sofa, dived through the door and hurled herself up the stairs with an acceleration that would have astonished Miss Penge, who coached the school netball team. Scrambling up the stairs, partly on hands and knees, she threw herself at the bedroom door, every fibre already recoiling at what she might find.

What she found was Charlotte lying exactly where she had left her, on her bed, the sheet across her chest and under her arms, breathing noisily, a scarf wrapped high around her neck and beneath her chin. Her head was turned towards the wall but, as Jennifer burst in and stood there, reeling, she turned slowly, awkwardly, and gazed up at her. The pieces of dead tie were gone. Charlotte's slippers, the hideous blue and green tartan ones, stood side by side, neatly and innocently, beneath the bed.

Only the dining-room chair, still on its side in the centre of the room, hinted at anything amiss.

Fear turned to fury and Jennifer grabbed the dining-room chair and noisily marched it and herself out to the landing and downstairs and into the dining room where she thumped it down in its usual place. Mum looked at her and said, 'Oh, thank you, dear...' and then, because the anger had dissipated as rapidly as it had come and she realised it was merely a reaction to being scared, Jennifer went slowly back upstairs.

Now that she knew Charlotte was not trying to kill herself, at least not right at this moment, she paused, long enough to notice that the landing was swaying dizzyingly. She held on to the wall and wondered finally if she ought to tell someone, Mum for instance, and dump the whole thing in her lap. But as the vertigo slowly eased and Charlotte lay, unmoving, in her bed, the moment for telling passed, the likelihood that she could form the words to describe what had happened evaporated. It would mean questions. Questions that didn't need to be asked let alone answered.

She returned to the bedroom. Charlotte still gazed at the doorway and this time Jennifer spoke because someone had to.

'Are you...okay?' she asked, which was pitiful, all things considered, but it was important someone said something.

Charlotte's answer was to turn back to face the wall, so Jennifer lay down on her own bed and stared up at the ceiling and understood that this was it, that from this point onwards this was how it was going to be: that she would never know if Charlotte was upstairs in their bedroom trying to kill herself. Or not.

CHAPTER EIGHT

A SKIN HAD FORMED on the surface of Jennifer's tea where the milk had cooled. She wrinkled her nose in distaste and vaguely recalled some conversation she had had with Charlotte a few months back about skin forming on milk. Charlotte had, inevitably, turned it into a cultural theory lecture. Come to think of it, that could have been the last time they had spoken.

'I never realised you disliked those tartan slippers, dear,' said Aunt Caroline a little indignantly. 'I remember choosing them very carefully from Dean's, the shoe shop in the high street. Old Mr Dean especially recommended them. He said they were Gordon tartan. Or perhaps it was McLaren? I really can't remember.'

They were sitting—Aunt Caroline in an upright winged armchair of the variety you saw in nursing homes, and Jennifer on the edge of the two-seater settee—in the front room of Aunt Caroline's bungalow in Skipton. A plate of Sainsbury's Eccles cakes lay untouched on the coffee table between them.

It was Thursday afternoon and it had been a long drive from Clapham to North Yorkshire. Jennifer had missed the A65 turnoff at Leeds and almost ended up in Bradford. Driving into Skipton she had intended to bypass the town centre and had instead found herself in a congested market-day street on the wrong side of the canal and the castle.

Negotiating snow drifts, partially gritted roads and a one-way system that seemed to serve no purpose, she had eventually arrived at Aunt Caroline's neat ivy-covered bungalow on the other side of the town just in time for a late lunch.

Now she reached uneasily for her jacket and wondered if it was too early to leave. She'd dressed in work clothes—a charcoal-grey suit and black leather boots—and was hoping to make it into the office by late afternoon. Gloria had been told she was visiting a supplier. What her real purpose was in being here, Jennifer still had no idea. Except that she had been summoned. And now she found herself defending what she'd said on TV. The slippers! Those awful tartan slippers that Charlotte had been wearing—why had she ever mentioned them?

'We aren't Gordons or McLarens,' she pointed out patiently. 'We're Denzels and there isn't a Denzel tartan as far as I'm aware. It's French,' she added.

Aunt Caroline sat back in her armchair, as far as it was possible to sit back in such a severely upright piece of furniture, a china teacup resting in its saucer on her lap, and considered this.

'Yes, dear, I know. And your mother and I were Lakes and they haven't got a tartan either.' She shook her head a little sadly at this obvious family deficiency. 'Of course your grandma and her sister were both Flaxheeds and that's a very old word dating back to the Anglo-Saxons, I believe. It means flaxen-headed. Blond.'

Jennifer stood up abruptly, almost spilling the contents of her teacup, but the membrane of milk prevented the tepid liquid from leaking over the side and onto Aunt Caroline's settee. It was a tartan settee, she noted even as she stalked across to the window and stood there looking out at the street. Outside the snow was coming down in ever-increasing flurries.

She hadn't meant to get into this discussion with Aunt Caroline. She hadn't meant to come north at all. It was totally unreasonable to just ring someone up and expect them to drop everything and come motoring all the way up to North Yorkshire at a moment's notice. Especially someone who had the Christmas sales figures to sift through and now the January sales to analyse, who had fifteen casual staff to monitor, not to mention the third-quarter figures to present. It simply wasn't going to happen. Aunt Caroline was living in a different era. An era where people still took afternoon tea.

And yet here she was. She had hurried through yesterday afternoon's staff meeting, got Gloria to rearrange two other meetings, lied to a director, her PA and two senior staff members and invented a supplier who didn't exist, and now here she was drinking Earl Grey tea in Aunt Caroline's front room in Skipton.

She ought to have ignored her aunt's summons. After the phone call from Gaspari the only thing that mattered was her immediate future as a Gossup and Batch employee, a future that now looked likely to include a series of alarming possibilities: an appearance before the board, a letter of reprimand, a letter of termination, an undignified clearing out of her desk, Gloria's barely restrained glee, explanations and lies to family and friends, the Jobs Vacant pages of the *Guardian*, unpaid rent, the benefits office, despair.

It was only once this appalling downward spiral had been envisaged, rationalised and tentatively dismissed, and a suitably cringing letter to the board composed in her head, that she had even remembered Aunt Caroline's phone call and guiltily rung her back.

A cold flicker of unease that had nothing to do with Mr Gaspari and the board and everything to do with the repercussions of her television appearance had fluttered in her stomach. It had been naïve to think they would all just let it pass unremarked.

Would it help to explain it had been an accident? That she had only been told at the last moment of the program change? That she was merely helping Kim, whose show was dying in the ratings? She hadn't even told Aunt Caroline she was going to be on TV in the first place.

Funny, you couldn't imagine Aunt Caroline watching daytime television. But watch it she had, and after they had discussed the icy roads and the roadworks around Newport Pagnell and the health of various family members over bowls of minestrone and crusty bread rolls and had sat down in the lounge with cups of tea, Aunt Caroline had said: 'So, dear, this thing you talked about on the television. Tell me again. And tell me what happened—afterwards.'

So Jennifer had repeated her story, and had told her aunt what had happened afterwards, though not what had happened beforehand because Aunt Caroline hadn't asked for it and because, even if she had asked, Jennifer wasn't sure she would have told her.

Aunt Caroline sat quite still, wrapped in a furry blue cardigan and a Marks and Spencer wool skirt, a rug over her knees and only a politely curious expression on her lined face.

She doesn't know whether to believe me or not, thought Jennifer. I should have lied. I should have told her I made the whole thing up.

But she hadn't said that. And she hadn't driven up here just because Aunt Caroline had requested it; she had done it because it was important to be believed, it was important they knew. That *someone* knew.

'I hope you didn't make too much of a mess on the carpet.'

Jennifer stared at her aunt blankly. 'I'm sorry?'

'When you were sick. You didn't say whether you made it to the toilet or whether there was a rubbish bin or perhaps a plastic bag you could use.'

Jennifer stared at her. Then she remembered.

'I did make it to the bathroom,' she replied thoughtfully, which was odd, because in her memory there was no gap between what had happened in the bedroom and then having her head down the toilet bowl, though she must have leapt up and scrambled out of the room, crossed the landing and got herself across the bathroom lino in time.

'That's a relief. I know Deirdre was always fussy about those carpets... I suppose she still is.' She looked up suddenly. 'Are they still beige?'

Jennifer frowned, remembering the beige carpet in the lounge and dining room at her parents' home that some-time during the eighties had been replaced by an awkward red, black and white geometric design. What were the carpets like now? She found she couldn't remember.

'No, I don't think they are,' she replied. Slippers? Vomiting? Carpets? What am I doing here? she wondered. She thought of the long drive home and closed her eyes.

It was warm by the window due to the radiator that ran the length of the sill and was turned to full blast, judging by the waves of heat that wafted above it. By contrast, the window was cold and Jennifer pressed both palms against the windowpane and felt the ice seep into her skin.

'I remember that summer,' said Aunt Caroline.

Outside a milk float rattled past and a robin landed on a branch of a yew tree and busily inspected its plumage.

'Ted and I had only been here a few months. We planted the roses in the front garden and we had two weeks in the Greek islands that year. Crete. Something big happened that summer...'

'The Royal Wedding,' Jennifer supplied with a sigh.

'No, the riots. I was thinking of the Brixton riots.'

And that was typical of Aunt Caroline. Just when you thought she'd become the sort of old lady who cooed over things like royal weddings, she brought up the Brixton riots. Jennifer looked across at the corner table beside Aunt Caroline's chair and saw that day's *Guardian* nestling beneath *Sporting Life*. I should visit more often, she realised. Well, here she was and it wasn't too late.

The robin shook its wings and darted off. An elderly neighbour, a man with thinning white hair and thick glasses, walked past in the street and waved through the window. Aunt Caroline watched him go into the house next door.

'Mum died a few months after that,' she continued. 'We drove down for the funeral. You were doing your mock A-levels. And Charlotte was at that college. She'd just resat one of her O-levels. She was a bit peaky. Deirdre said something about it at the time.'

A bit peaky.

Grandma Lake's funeral had been in December, four months later. Yes, Charlotte, she recalled, had indeed been peaky. They had both been. She couldn't remember Mum saying anything about it.

'I so wanted Charlotte to come down today,' said Aunt Caroline, shifting the teacup in her lap. 'But she was busy.'

She'd invited Charlotte? And Charlotte hadn't come?

I was busy too! Jennifer thought indignantly, and now she felt annoyed with her younger sister who had saved herself this journey in this weather. There was something wrong here, she realised curiously—it should have been she who was unable to come up because she was too busy, and Charlotte playing the good niece, sitting patiently on Aunt Caroline's settee, sipping Aunt Caroline's Earl Grey.

Why had she invited Charlotte?

Because of the television program.

'We had a good few years together, Ted and me,' said Aunt Caroline as though they had been discussing Uncle Ted. Jennifer moved away from the window and came and sat down again, wondering if this was leading anywhere. She couldn't imagine where.

'Fifteen lovely years. There was no fuss, no bother. Just a contented, shared life. We liked the same things, and that's important.'

Jennifer nodded, thinking of all the things she and Nick had both liked: Middle Eastern food, experimental home-made cocktails, guilty cigarettes after they'd both quit, sex in unlikely places (especially in other people's houses when the other people were downstairs), affairs with other people. That last one they hadn't realised they both liked until just before the marriage broke up. She didn't equate any of these things with Aunt Caroline's marriage to Uncle Ted.

'And I was quite happy to move to Skipton,' Aunt Caroline remarked, 'even at my time of life.'

Aunt Caroline had been in her mid-fifties when she'd married Ted Kettley. Mum, who had never even heard of Ted until a month before the wedding announcement, had been tight-lipped at the news. 'I'm not saying a word,' she had declared vehemently to anyone who would listen. 'I'm not saying anything about this man, whom none of us know. I'm not saying anyone's too old or too set in their ways for such a life-changing decision—a decision that, after all, affects us all. I'm not saying anything at all.'

But Mum had been wrong, and until Ted's death four years ago, he and Aunt Caroline had lived quite happily in Ted's bungalow and Aunt Caroline appeared to have made the transition from London spinster to Yorkshire wife with commendable ease. At least, Jennifer supposed so. She'd never really given it much thought. She glanced ever so discreetly at her watch.

Aunt Caroline pulled the rug a little closer about her knees and Jennifer stared at her aunt's hands, which were the hands of an elderly lady. She looked away. It had been over a year, nearer eighteen months, since her last visit.

'And even when you have a loving husband and wonderful friends,' Aunt Caroline was saying. Then she paused, as though she had suddenly realised Jennifer no longer had a loving husband, and who knew what sort of friends she might have? '...the one thing that's always there is your family.'

Jennifer stifled a groan.

'We don't choose them, and Lord knows, if we could, we probably wouldn't choose the ones we've got.'

Amen to that.

'Your mother and I didn't see eye-to-eye on a lot of things. Most things, really.'

And now Jennifer saw where this was going—it was a not-so-subtle reference to what Aunt Caroline no doubt saw as a rift that had developed between herself and Charlotte. That stupid TV program. She should have been prepared for this, she realised, as Aunt Caroline went on talking.

'You can grow up with someone, live in the same house, but your experiences, your outlooks, can be totally different.'

Jennifer had no idea at all what Aunt Caroline's outlook might be, or Mum's for that matter. They had always been fairly cordial with each other, hadn't they? Indeed, they hardly referred to each other at all, and that was about as much as she cared to know.

A memory came into her head of Aunt Caroline, years ago, standing on the doorstep outside the kitchen at Mum and Dad's house, smoking a cigarette and making no effort at all to keep the smoke out of the house. It must have been spring or summer because the kitchen door was open and it wasn't cold. And it must have been before Aunt Caroline had met Ted, while she was still living in Perivale. What Aunt Caroline had been doing outside their kitchen smoking a cigarette, Jennifer couldn't imagine. She'd been a rare enough visitor, even before Grandma Lake had moved in. It was the middle of the day and Mum was going on and on about what a business it was, running a house for five people. So many meals and so much washing and always cleaning and the shopping that never ended and Lord knows, she didn't expect Caroline to understand.

It was the first time Jennifer had heard her mother say anything like this, complaining about the house, about them. About her life. She must have been about twelve, she realised, eleven or twelve. Not yet angry with her parents, though this might have heralded the start. And Aunt Caroline, standing in the doorway, had taken a drag of her cigarette and said, not turning around, speaking to the garden it had seemed, 'You chose it, Deirdre. You chose your life.'

Jennifer remembered the shock these words had been to her. The harshness of it. Then she'd looked at her mother and thought, Yes, you did choose it. You chose your life.

'Of course, there was a good few years between Deirdre and me,' Aunt Caroline was saying now. 'In some ways it was as though we were different generations.'

Jennifer rubbed her temples. Aren't we talking about me and Charlotte? she thought impatiently. If this was meant to be a parallel it wasn't a very good one. She and Charlotte were not years apart, they were eleven months apart. Although, we could be from different generations, she mused, Charlotte seemingly having been born with a middle-aged sense of seriousness and disapproval.

'We tend to let things fester, don't we?' said Aunt Caroline.

Do we? Jennifer wondered, remembering Nick's affair with Milli and her own fury. Now Nick and Milli were living together in Nick's flat in Rotherhithe and Jennifer often went over there for cocktails or Sunday brunch. Who was festering?

'Spite. Petty jealousies. Envy. They're a normal part of growing up together. But sometimes they can get out of hand. People's lives can be affected. Changed.' Aunt Caroline tapped her silver teaspoon against the side of her teacup then looked up brightly. 'But still, you learn to get on. To get by. And as you get older those differences seem to count for less.'

She frowned suddenly, and pressed a hand to the side of her head. Jennifer waited. Was there more? But the tapping of the teaspoon seemed to have signalled the end. It was time to go. And if she wasn't careful she'd be snowed in and that would mean either spending a night on Aunt's Caroline's sofa bed or asking some taciturn Yorkshire farmer to dig her out. Neither prospect appealed. She pushed herself up off the settee with a 'Well!' that was intended to convey a sense of finality to the visit. She reached for her gloves and coat and bag.

'Are you leaving, dear?' said Aunt Caroline.

'I ought to, so I get back before dark.' Fat chance, it being past two o'clock already and with contraflows on the M1 either side of Newport Pagnell.

Aunt Caroline got up and as she did so she swayed and put out a hand to steady herself against the wall, a slight frown creasing her brow.

'Well, it was lovely of you to come and visit,' she said, her hand still pressed against the wall. 'I'm only sorry I haven't made any cake or nice little biscuits for you to take back with you. But I don't bake, you know. Well, why would you when there's a Sainsbury's in town?'

Why indeed? Jennifer kissed her aunt's cheek and tried not to notice that it had a greyish tinge and was the same consistency as crepe paper. The same consistency, too, as Grandma Lake's cheek all those years ago. She had a sudden vision of Grandma Lake seated at the dining-room table at Sunday lunch twenty-five years earlier, chasing a pea around her plate with a spoon, her mouth open and a shining bubble of spittle balancing on her lower lip. She shuddered. She hated all things old, people most of all, and those two years when Grandma Lake had lived with them was no doubt the root cause of this phobia. And now Aunt Caroline was old. But not as old as Grandma Lake had been at the end. Besides, she was Aunt Caroline who had married Uncle Ted, and who went to the races at Doncaster and had her own life up here in Skipton. There was no comparison.

As she turned to leave, Jennifer saw a row of postcards along the mantelpiece, one of which she recognised as a card she had sent from Mykonos last year showing a laden mule struggling up a winding cobbled street, and she remembered she hadn't seen any mules, laden or otherwise, during her week on the island. She'd seen the inside of a lot of clubs and tavernas, but no mules. Next to her own postcard was a card showing a vast and darkly oppressive building topped with bulging domed roofs and spikes with a distinctly Eastern European appearance. She remembered that Charlotte had gone to Moscow a while back. Moscow was a typical Charlotte tourist destination: cold, bleak and austere. No danger of having any fun there.

Beside the two postcards three photographs were lined up: one in a modern, transparent plastic frame of a smiling Uncle Ted in a tweed jacket and corduroy trousers standing in a muddy field, taken perhaps eight or nine years ago; one in a more conventional wooden frame of a serious-looking boy with Brylcreemed hair and an RAF uniform who definitely wasn't Uncle Ted; the third, in a plain silver frame, was a grainy black and white photograph of a young woman with a 1920s bob standing in what looked like a bus depot waving jauntily at the camera. Jennifer picked up the photo and studied the young woman for a moment, wondering if she ought to find something more to say, if she were being rude leaving this early. Then she put it down and, with a cheery wave, let herself out.

As soon as the front door closed behind Jennifer, Aunt Caroline eased herself away from the wall and walked stiffly over to the window, watching as her niece swept a dusting of snow from the bonnet and front and rear windows of her Peugeot, climbed into the driver's seat and started the engine, sweeping the windscreen wipers back and forth a couple of times. Then she revved the engine and held up a hand in farewell as the back wheels spun on a patch of ice and went nowhere.

In no time at all Mr Milthorpe from next door burst from his own bungalow, spade at the ready, and was soon busily shovelling away snow and putting down stones beneath the tyres and calling out things like: 'Easy! Easy now! Tek it steady, lass. Back her oop now. Aye, that's right.'

Eventually the car was freed and with a final wave and a loud rev of acceleration, the Peugeot leapt away from the kerb and roared off down the street.

Aunt Caroline stood at the window for a while longer, noting the grey clouds overhead and estimating that it would be dark by three thirty.

The sudden wave of dizziness had surprised her but it had gone as quickly as it had struck.

She drifted over to the mantelpiece where a moment before her niece had stood and she too picked up the silver photo frame. She didn't look at the photograph because she didn't need to. Instead, she tapped the frame with her forefinger and for a full minute she considered telephoning her sister, Deirdre, in London.

CHAPTER NINE

'W,' JENNIFER SIGHED IN a tone that was meant to convey her total indifference to the letter 'W' and her utter boredom with the game as a whole.

Hangman! And on a Saturday night.

Graham said nothing, just raised his eyebrows in that ironic, rather smug way he had and drew the long downward stick of the hanged man's left leg. Jennifer stared in silent contempt at the top of his neatly brushed, precisely parted, mousy-brown head. She had one remaining chance and seven letters on the piece of paper that didn't look as if they belonged together in the same word.

'*Ae_rotat*! Anyway, there's no such word. You just made it up.'

Sadly, denying the existence of Graham's word, though satisfying, was a futile gambit: Graham had no need to make up words. Despite being a whole two years younger than Jennifer, he appeared to have memorised Dad's *Complete Oxford Dictionary* and was a self-professed authority on words of which no one else had ever heard. That made it impossible to win against him at hangman or Scrabble or anything else.

It was Saturday night. The first week of a new school term was still fresh in everyone's minds—everyone who'd

bothered to actually go to school that was—and Jennifer
was sitting at home playing hangman with Graham.

Ae_rotat, for God's sake.

Mum and Dad had gone out for the evening and
Charlotte was alone upstairs. On the television, *Wonder
Woman* had been replaced by *The Generation Game*. Mother-
and-son team, Irene and Greg from Cirencester, were
attempting to ice a giant wedding cake.

Jennifer picked up the pencil and her fist clenched tightly
around it so that her nails cut into the palm of her hand.
Something, a throbbing rush of blood behind her eyes, a flash
of painful white light, blurred her vision, and she saw herself
reach out and draw a vicious line right across Graham's note-
paper, tearing the paper, her hand sweeping it from the coffee
table, flinging the pencil against the wall so that it made a mark
on the wallpaper then bounced harmlessly onto the carpet.

But she did none of those things. She sat calmly on
the sofa holding the pencil and staring at the word. That
damned word.

Ae_rotat.

On one side of the paper was the neat list of discarded
letters: *i, u, b, c, m, n, s, p, l, v, d* and now *w*. That left *f, g,
h, j, k, q, x, y, z*, none of which looked remotely possible.
Aezrotat? Aekrotat? Aefrotat? They sounded like a Central
American tribe, a Soviet news agency and an African hairstyle. The throbbing started again.

On the television, Greg from Cirencester dropped a
stack of plates and the audience shrieked with laughter.

'Anyway, who cares?' she declared, throwing down
the pencil and snatching up last week's *Smash Hits*. She
proceeded to flip irritably through its pages. Graham leapt
forward triumphantly and with a flourish drew the man's
second foot to complete the hangman.

'Hangman!' he exclaimed, just in case she wasn't
already aware. 'It's a *g*. *Aegrotat*,' he said writing in the
missing letter.

'Aegrotat! Crap,' Jennifer snorted, refusing to acknowledge the existence of such an absurd word.

'It means a certificate of illness to excuse a student from an exam,' explained Graham, as though someone had asked for a definition.

'Yeah? Well, it's not hangman because I never guessed the final letter so I never got it wrong,' Jennifer pointed out.

'Hangman! Hangman,' sang Graham just as Charlotte drifted into the lounge.

Jennifer looked up and felt the blood drain from her face. The room fell silent. So silent she could hear her heart beating, the blood rushing in her ears, pulses throbbing at her temples and at the back of her neck. She could hear the hum of background noise from the television set, the settling of floorboards on the stairs, the rustling of leaves on the sycamore tree in the garden, the buzz from the streetlight outside the house, the footsteps of a neighbour in next-door's driveway, the slam of a car door at the end of the street.

'Wanna play hangman?' said Graham.

And Jennifer thought, Why aren't we playing noughts-and-crosses? Monopoly? Snap?

Charlotte ignored the question. She slunk across the room and flopped herself down onto the sofa, staring blankly at the television, her arms folded across her chest as if no one else was in the room.

Smash Hits had a double-page feature on The Teardrop Explodes. The band members posed in black leather trousers and bulky leather flying jackets in a derelict inner-city landscape. Jennifer began to read the first paragraph of the accompanying interview, but she couldn't make out the words. They seemed to make no sense.

From the other side of the coffee table Graham scooped up the discarded pencils and pieces of paper and tidied them away, then he reached beneath the table and pulled out the battered Monopoly box.

'I'll be the racing car,' he said. 'What do you want to be? Char, you in?'

It was Saturday evening. The first week of the new school term. Mum and Dad were at the Bunch of Grapes in Northolt with Doug and Judy Farrelly, who had once been their next-door neighbours but now lived in Kilburn, which meant she, Charlotte and Graham had the house to themselves. At the moment Grandma Lake was taking a nap in her room, and with any luck she wouldn't bother to get up and come down before retiring to bed. The crunch would come at eight thirty when Grandma Lake liked to watch *The Les Dawson Show*.

Graham leaned forward, carefully placing the little red racing car on the board.

'Do you want to be the ship or the boot or the dog, Char?' he said.

Charlotte continued to stare at the television. Ted and Julie from Ipswich were attempting to spin a potter's wheel.

For the last year Charlotte had spent every Saturday night at Zoe's house and Jennifer had been out with Darren. But Charlotte hadn't gone over to Zoe's since the start of the summer holidays. And Darren was going out with Roberta Peabody even though he'd said, not three months ago, that Roberta had a nose the size of Concorde. And tonight Julie Fanshawe was having a pyjama party because her parents were in Marbella for an entire fortnight and here was Jennifer at home sitting in Dad's armchair playing stupid games with Graham.

Darren wouldn't speak to her. He wouldn't even say why.

Sod him.

She peered across at Charlotte. There had been graffiti in the girls' toilets in the last week of term. Jennifer had seen it. She didn't know who'd written it but she knew what it said and she knew why it was there.

Someone needed to say something. *She* needed to say something.

Graham began to count out a wad of brightly coloured Monopoly notes. She didn't know what she should say and Charlotte didn't look up, so the words—whatever they were—remained unspoken.

There was a thump from upstairs followed by the creak of a floorboard and they all looked up.

'Golf Romeo Alpha,' Graham announced ominously, which was police-radio code for the letters GRA: Geriatric Relative Alert. Grandma Lake, evidently, was awake and up and about. Perhaps she'd fallen or knocked something over? They waited silently but no further sound came and, anyway, she'd call out if she'd fallen over. Everyone lowered their eyes. Graham picked up a thick wad of red five-hundred-pound notes and patted them into a neat pile.

On the television the audience applauded and Ted and Julie from Ipswich waved goodbye. Squeezed tightly into the farthest corner of the sofa Charlotte studied the program's end credits as though they held the key to some great mystery.

Jennifer observed her with a sideways glance. Everything she did with Charlotte was sideways now. She didn't look at her anymore, she peered at her from underneath her fringe or around a corner or through a doorway or over the top of a magazine. Charlotte sat with her arms locked around her knees gazing with vacant eyes at the announcer who previewed a forthcoming program. *The Les Dawson Show* came on and Jennifer thought, Why has she come downstairs? Surely it can't be because she wants company—not our company, anyway?

The television audience broke into tired sit-com laughter. Graham had given up on the Monopoly board and the three of them stared gloomily at the screen and Jennifer thought, if Graham wasn't here this might be the moment I could say something. She could say, for instance, that Tina Davies in 5B had seen Adam Ant last week in Sainsbury's in Ruislip. That he was buying breakfast cereal. The whole school was talking about it.

The audience laughed again and Graham remained in the room and Jennifer said nothing. She realised that Charlotte didn't care about Adam Ant. That she didn't even listen to records anymore, that she no longer went over to Zoe's house.

What *had* she been doing over at Zoe's house all those Saturday nights?

No one really believed *that*, Jennifer reminded herself. Not that.

'Alright then, Battleships,' said Graham at last, as though this was positively his final offer on the games front and if they didn't accept this, well then frankly they were all in for a pretty dull evening.

'Oh, grow up,' said Jennifer.

Why didn't Charlotte go over to Zoe's house anymore? And why hadn't Zoe come round to their house all summer? Not once during the entire six weeks. Not one phone call. Perhaps her family were away on holiday?

On the television two fat elderly comedians sat wedged onto a sofa in drag, vast sagging fake breasts resting on their folded arms.

Could Zoe have been on holiday for six weeks? And after term had started? But Jennifer didn't know whether Zoe had been at school this week or not.

There was a creak on the stairs, then the door to the lounge was pushed open and Grandma Lake shuffled in wearing fluffy powder-blue slippers and a floral dressing-gown. Everyone looked up then looked away again.

She made her way across the room and lowered herself down onto the sofa, losing her balance at the crucial moment, so that she fell backwards with a whomp of fake leather that made Charlotte bounce upwards. Once this would have made Jennifer laugh but nowadays, after a year, it just made her despair. The television audience laughed again and a second or two later so did Grandma Lake, a curiously high-pitched, girlish giggle that was faintly disturbing. It reminded Jennifer that Grandma Lake had probably once been a girl herself.

'I couldn't sleep,' announced Grandma Lake, suddenly and to no one in particular. 'Not with all that racket.'

The idea that Grandma Lake's operatic night-time snorts and snores could be interrupted by any noise they themselves could make seemed unlikely but no one was inclined to remark on this. Except perhaps Graham.

'Sierra Oscar Bravo,' he announced cheerfully, which meant Silly Old Bat.

'Eh? What's that?' said Grandma Lake.

'Ow!' protested Graham, his face suddenly flushing red with shock and pain because the slap had been unexpected, because Jennifer had hit him harder than she had meant to. He kicked her shin in retaliation then sat there with arms folded angrily.

Charlotte said nothing.

There had been graffiti in the girls' toilets. It had turned up in the last week of term.

Jennifer shut her eyes.

It was Julie Fanshawe who'd seen the graffiti first and perhaps it was Julie who had written it. She'd come bustling into registration full of it, bursting with the importance of it, flushed with the excitement of someone else's downfall, of her own immunity. And what had she, had any of them, expected Jennifer to do about it—defend the family honour? You couldn't just march in there and wash it off, everyone would have thought you'd had something to do with it. That you were a part of it. That you had something to hide. That there was some truth in it.

Jennifer had had nothing to do with it. Nothing. And everyone knew that there was no truth in it. But she had run over there anyway because she had to know. And she'd seen Charlotte standing outside the toilet block. Just standing there and she'd known that whatever it was, whatever was written on the wall, Charlotte had seen it. That she had been too late.

Charlotte stood up and stabbed at the television set and *The Les Dawson Show* vanished, replaced by a film on ITV. *The Magnificent Seven*. A parched, desert landscape and a crumbling Mexican village.

''Ere! I'm quite partial to *Les Dawson*,' protested Grandma Lake, but no one moved to change the channel.

Jennifer had had nothing to do with what was written on the wall of the girls' toilets. All she had said was one little thing to one person. Just an observation really, a stupid throwaway line. And everyone knew Charlotte and Zoe were always together. There was already talk. There must have been. That's what schools were like. You said one little thing to one person and before you knew it...

'And I can't be expected to sleep when your mum and dad are out in that car,' said Grandma Lake. 'Not until I know they're back safely. Can't sleep a wink till then.'

This was patently untrue but no one said anything. Besides, most of what Grandma Lake said was aimed at the television and required no response.

Jennifer realised she needed to do something. That someone had to do something. They couldn't all go on sitting here, staring at the TV indefinitely.

On the television bandits rode into the village. Their leader entered the cantina and lit a cigar while the villagers looked silently on.

Charlotte hadn't moved. She had been wearing the same jeans and black sweatshirt for four days now. Why didn't anyone else see? The same clothes for four days? *Four days!*

A sudden burst of gunfire shattered the silence and a lone Mexican peasant fell dead in the dust, a red circle on his back.

What was worse—no one else seeing or this constant

state of dread in case someone *did* see? But so far no one had noticed. What were they all *doing*?

What they were doing was talking to the television or sipping beer at the Bunch of Grapes in Northolt or waiting impatiently to play Monopoly.

But what if Grandma Lake stopped talking to the television? What if Graham gave up the idea of Monopoly? What if they both noticed Charlotte sitting there, saying nothing, in the same clothes she'd had on for four days? What then?

'Fine. I'll be the boot,' Jennifer said picking up the Monopoly counter and placing it next to Graham's on the board.

Grandma Lake was asleep, her chin resting on her chest, arms folded across her vast bosom, an occasional snort erupting from between puckered lips and *The Magnificent Seven* was over halfway through by the time Jennifer bought her first hotel.

It was after eleven and Charlotte hadn't moved a muscle, not once, not even to see what was on BBC One. Every time car headlights lit up the hallway and a car engine neared the house Jennifer paused, waiting, but each time the headlights swept on up the street. It was too early, anyway, for Mum and Dad, only just last orders.

Was no one ever going to go to bed?

All she had said was *one little thing* to one person in the last week of term. *One little thing...*

What ought to have been another crap Friday night at the community centre's under-eighteens disco had, surprisingly, not been crap at all. It had been pretty good, in fact. Briefly.

'There's Adrian,' Julie had shouted above the synthesised beat of 'Planet Earth' and loud enough that anyone could have heard her. 'He's coming over!'

And Adrian Cresswell had come over, weaving between Sonya Marshall and Mark Bickley from 4C who were slow-dancing to Duran Duran, circumnavigating a cluster of white faux leather handbags, and Jennifer had known he was coming over to her. After all, he'd been watching her from the other side of the room for the last fifteen minutes. About bloody time too. She'd been working up to this point since *Christmas*. A smile here, a word there, a walk home from school, a look across the classroom when Darren wasn't there, and now it was June, the end of term, and finally Adrian was free of that Jackie Parfitter cow and very, very soon she was going to be free of Darren.

'Alright?' Adrian had said, throwing back his head and talking to her out of the side of his mouth. 'Planet Earth' had ended and Julie had melted discreetly into the background. Yes, Jennifer had replied, she was alright. And Adrian was alright too, in a black button-down Gary Numan shirt, narrow red tie, black straight-leg pegs and black winkle-picker boots with buckles on the ankles.

And he had said: 'Yeah, so. I was looking for your sister.'

That was what Adrian had said. That was what Adrian had weaved his way across the dance floor to say to her: *I was looking for your sister.*

'Charlotte,' he'd added, as though she might not know who he was referring to.

Charlotte!

'You what?' she'd replied, mystified, and already a sense of things not going as planned had begun to creep over her.

'Well, she never comes here, does she? I was wonderin' where she goes, tha's all.' A shrug. 'She's not going out with anyone, is she?'

'Why?' Jennifer had replied coldly, already aware that she didn't really want to know.

'I was just wonderin'.' Adrian had turned away and

sipped his Coke and surveyed the disco critically, his foot tapping to Spandau Ballet. Then he'd turned back. 'Think she'd go out with me?'

'Come on. Your go,' urged Graham, pointing impatiently at the Monopoly board.

Jennifer tossed the dice and got a five.

'Park Lane!' crowed Graham jubilantly. 'With two hotels, that's…five hundred pounds, please.'

Graham always said *please* when he was fleecing you at Monopoly.

'Park Lane. I went to Park Lane once.'

Grandma Lake was awake and addressing the television once more.

'We both went. Late summer it were. There were a lovely brass band in Hyde Park and so many handsome young men. A real treat, it was, to take a tram into town. Me and Jem sat on the top deck and shared a bag of sugared almonds.'

A shot pierced the air and on the television a bandit slumped dead over a low stone wall.

Think she'd go out with me?

Adrian Creswell had come over in a black Gary Numan button-down shirt, the one with the red buttons. He had come over to ask if she thought Charlotte would go out with him.

Julie Fanshawe, along with half the lower-sixth, had been standing just a short distance away, watching and listening. Waiting with barely concealed glee. Meanwhile

Charlotte had not ever been there because Charlotte didn't go to discos. Charlotte didn't go out. Charlotte spent all her time over at Zoe's house.

'No, Adrian, I don't think she'd go out with you, *actually*.'

There. It had ended right there. That was what Jennifer had said. Just that, nothing else. Then she had spun around and swept out, leaving Julie to retrieve her handbag from the pile on the floor and Adrian standing there in the middle of the disco with everyone staring at him.

Laughing at him.

Sitting cross-legged on the floor, Graham was busily helping himself to Jennifer's last fifty pounds and mort-gaging off her few remaining properties, joyfully scooping up her set of main-line stations, flipping them over and calculating their mortgage value.

A croupier, thought Jennifer. He'd make a great croupier.

On the sofa, Charlotte suddenly looked up and stared at Grandma Lake as though she'd only just noticed her grandmother was sitting beside her. There was such inten-sity in her look Jennifer held her breath.

Outside a car approached, its headlights lighting up the hallway. Everyone paused, silent. Waiting. Its engine geared down and the car turned into the driveway.

Mum and Dad were home.

Instantly the atmosphere changed. Charlotte turned away and squeezed herself into a tighter ball, her gaze resting somewhere to the left of the television screen. Grandma Lake got unsteadily to her feet and said, 'Well, that's them at last. I'm off to bed.' Graham began to pack up the Monopoly board. Jennifer presumed she had lost.

A front door key sounded in the lock.

'—always busy, no matter what time of the day or night,' said Mum from the hallway.

'They should never have put a roundabout there in the first place,' said Dad.

'Oh, you still up, Mum?' said Mum to Grandma Lake, who was in the hallway.

'I'm off to bed, it's past my bedtime. You need your sleep at my age,' said Grandma Lake accusingly as she commenced her ascent of the stairs.

'Goodnight then,' called Dad, a little ironically.

Mum and Dad came into the lounge and Jennifer jumped to her feet. Dad stopped in the doorway, unzipping his jacket. Mum stepped around him, placing her handbag on the sofa, pulling off her coat. The room suddenly smelled of damp autumn air and alcohol and cigarettes.

They both stared at her wordlessly.

This was the moment they were going to notice Charlotte's black sweatshirt and jeans.

'I won at Monopoly,' said Graham, pre-empting a question he clearly assumed Mum and Dad were poised to ask. 'I had everything but Whitechapel and Old Kent Road and Angel and the Waterworks.'

'Doug still owes us for that last round, you know,' said Dad, turning to Mum and pulling his wallet out of his coat pocket. 'And I bought him a double, too.'

'Not *The Magnificent Seven* again!' groaned Mum, and it became obvious no one was going to notice the black sweatshirt and jeans. No one was going to notice anything.

'No, Adrian,' she had said. 'I don't think Charlotte would go out with you, *actually*.' And then she had said: 'Because she's already going out with Zoe Findlay, *actually*!'

And everyone had stared. Not at Adrian. At her. She'd spun around and run out and no one had come after her and no one had retrieved her handbag from the pile on the floor so that she had had to come back later and get it herself. And the next week there had been graffiti on the wall of the girls' toilets.

CHAPTER TEN

THE TOP-FLOOR LANDING of number 86 Randolph Gardens, SW4, was lit by the feeble glow of a single twenty-five-watt light bulb and by the time Jennifer had run up four flights of stairs and negotiated the double-key dead-lock in the semi-darkness, dumped her briefcase, coat and keys and reached for the telephone, whoever was calling her had finished leaving their message and hung up and the answering machine was flashing self-importantly.

'Shit!' said Jennifer.

She closed the front door, cutting off the feeble light from the landing and plunging her hallway into darkness. Distant hip hop flooded up from the ground-floor.

Her flat was the converted upper floor of a mid-Victorian terrace in Clapham. An attic, perhaps a servant's quarters in some other era, it was now the abode of a never-ending stream of unmarried city workers. In that earlier era cattle had still grazed on the nearby common and marshes still bordered some parts of Clapham village. A century and a half later Randolph Gardens was situated in the centre of a triangle formed by Clapham Junction, Wandsworth Road and Queenstown Road station. In summer the rattle of two thousand trains travelling daily to and from Waterloo and Victoria carried over the air. But in January, four flights up, the sounds were muffled: traffic on the main road, a single police siren, a distant shop alarm, hip hop.

The light on the answering machine flashed once, twice, three times, reflecting off the window and bathing the room intermittently in a lurid red glow.

It was freezing.

Jennifer flicked the light switch and turned the central heating on full. It had a timer switch which meant you could set it to come on an hour before you got home, but she had never figured out how it worked. Besides, what kind of person always knew what time they'd get home?

She recovered her coat, keys and briefcase from the hallway and carried them to the sofa, then turned to study the three envelopes she'd retrieved from her letterbox. Internet bill. British Telecom bill. Mobile phone bill. She cleared a space on the kitchen table and filed them there. Most of the calls would be to Nick's mobile, and when most of your calls were to your ex, that was depressing. He, too, rang her much more often now that they were no longer married.

It was ten o'clock on Friday evening. She'd worked late to catch up after yesterday's jaunt up north then gone to Vino Tinto around the corner where she'd downed two overpriced caipiroskas, been propositioned by a Norwegian software manufacturer, seen Gloria sitting in a dark nook with Adam Finch, their heads bent close together, and come home. The Northern Line had been experiencing delays and she'd waited twenty minutes at Stockwell for a train and now it was too late to make arrangements with anyone and too early to go to bed. Ten o'clock at home on a Friday evening.

She pressed the PLAY button on the answering machine.

'Jen, sweetie, it's Kim. Just wanted to say thanks so much for helping out Monday evening—it went well, didn't it? And you were fabulous, of course. Sorry about the last-minute mix-up; Gerry is an idiot but you rose to the occasion sensation-

*ally. Anyway, I owe you. Come over for stuffed aubergines one
night. Ciao!'*

You sure do owe me, thought Jennifer sourly, particularly if anyone else in her family had decided to watch the
broadcast on Tuesday.

But it was Friday night and so far it seemed that,
aside from Aunt Caroline and the entire board of Gossup
and Batch, Kim's program had found itself a format and
timeslot spectacularly free of viewers. This might not bode
well for Kim's future television career, but it made Jennifer
very relieved.

There were two more messages on the machine.

*'Heya! I'm...traffic on Streatham...way to Gino's...haven't
heard how it went? Didn't catch the show, but Mill said it was
cool...very convincing. Haven't spoken to Kimmy. Anyway...
find out where you got that Albanian fetta...Mill's doing
a Greek...do you think it's tacky—Albanian fetta in Greek
salad?... Catch ya.'*

Nick. Great. So now she was his cookery consultant.
And it had been Algerian fetta, not Albanian. Jesus. As
for Milli making a salad, Greek or otherwise, who was
he kidding? Nick's girlfriend, who worked in marketing,
was good at persuading teenagers they needed sneakers
that cost half their parents' weekly income, but she was a
crap cook. And Nick ringing up to ask about fetta when
he'd spent the two years of their own marriage existing on
sardines on toast and Safeway's frozen ravioli?

One message remained. She pressed PLAY and heard
a burst of her mother's voice. She pressed STOP.

Okay. Well, it wasn't Charlotte, that was the main
thing. Good. Perhaps Scottish TV didn't show Kim's
program? She cautiously pressed PLAY again.

*'Oh, you're not there then? It's Mum. It's—let me see,
Friday evening, about ten o'clock. I know it's a bit late to call but
I was worried. We haven't heard from you for ages. Your father's
well. He's just watching the news at the moment. I was thinking,*

why don't you come over for Sunday lunch? This Sunday. Oh, I meant to say, we both watched your television program on Tuesday. I thought it was going to be something about computer games? I rang Charlotte straight after and she—'

At this point the answering machine took great delight in cutting Deirdre off and beeping smugly.

Shit, thought Jennifer. Hadn't she emailed them both not to watch it? Didn't people check their emails?

She erased all three messages. Then she had an uneasy thought. She flicked on her computer, opened her Hotmail account and saw, among all the Viagra and porn emails, a message from Graham headed *Hey sis, anything you want to tell me???*

So, in fact, everyone had watched it.

She logged off, turned off the computer, filled a glass with Australian cab sav and switched on the TV.

'...went off the rails and slid down an embankment onto a main road at Streatham causing a heavy tailback of traffic,' said the newsreader pleasantly on the late news. *'A Southern Railways spokesperson blamed frozen points for the derailment. Meanwhile, in North Yorkshire, heavy falls of snow...'*

Jennifer shivered. She had first-hand knowledge of the heavy falls of snow in North Yorkshire. She flicked the mute button and took a fortifying swig of wine.

Mum could be fobbed off. Mum would prefer to be fobbed off, it would be doing her and Dad a favour. A quick phone call should suffice: 'Oh, it was just TV, I was helping out Kim. I made it all up. You shouldn't believe everything you see on television...' Simple.

She wished she hadn't been quite so believable. Even as she had been relating to Kim details she herself barely remembered and some that had never actually existed, she'd thought, Damn! This is good, this is *really* good! I'm telling a *great* story! I should write a book.

Now, with four days' hindsight, she was realising her newfound storytelling skills were more to do with being in a television studio under swelteringly bright lights with a captive audience of bored housewives whipped into a frenzy by the warm-up man. And Kim, damn her, leaning forward and doing that faux-psychiatrist routine.

She had been sucked in. Well and truly.

On the news the political situation in Iraq had deteriorated, tensions had escalated in Kashmir and twenty asylum seekers had been discovered dead in the back of a meat lorry in Dover.

She went into the kitchen and crumbled off a hunk of Algerian fetta, some olives (Bulgarian), a pickled onion (Burnley via Sainsbury's) and a lump of crusty bread (the deli in Wandsworth Road). Thus armed, she stood over the phone, hit the speakerphone button and pressed 9 on the memory pad. The phone rang twice before it was picked up.

'Hello?' said a surprised voice.

Jennifer picked up the receiver. 'Hi, Dad, it's Jen.'

Odd. Usually Mum answered the phone.

'Hullo, love. Your Mum's talking to someone at the front door,' said Dad, recognising at once that his eldest child had not rung to speak to him.

She thought about saying, 'Oh, actually I phoned to talk to you, Dad,' but she couldn't summon up some fake reason why she needed to talk to him.

'Thanks, Dad, I'll wait,' she said. Then, 'Oh, aren't you and Mum off to Barcelona soon?'

'We've cancelled,' said Dad. 'Too expensive.'

'Oh. Well, didn't you know that when you booked it?'

'Your mother bought the new car. She should've sold the old one privately and bought a twelve-months-old one. We'd have saved five hundred in on-road costs.'

'Why didn't you do that then?'

'Oh, your mother takes care of all that.'

'Oh.'

'Here she is... It's Jennifer.'

There was a slight pause, then: 'Hello dear, I was just at the front door. It was one of those market research people. They came by earlier when we were eating dinner so I said to come back later. I didn't think they'd come at ten o'clock though. Wanted to know if we wanted to buy cable television.'

'That's not market research, Mum, that's a salesman.'

'It was a girl, she seemed very nice. She lives up on the estate. She gave me a brochure. Anyway did you get my message? I called at ten but you were out.'

'Yes. I worked late. You've no idea how busy—'

'Well, I told you from the start retail was a bad idea. Working all those Saturdays. And nowadays all the shops are open Sundays too. Betty Willoughby's youngest, Denise, just got a job at the meat counter at Tesco and she works all hours.'

'Dad says you're not going to Barcelona, now?'

'No, it didn't seem wise, not with the elections. The Basque is still a very volatile region.'

Good, this was safe territory.

'It's not in the Basque region, Deirdre,' called out Dad from somewhere in the distance. 'Barcelona is in Catalonia.'

'Oh, did I mention, your Dad and I watched your television program on Tuesday. I didn't realise it was going to be one of those American tell-the-whole-world-your-private-business things?'

This wasn't such safe territory. Jennifer took a deep breath.

'Well, Mum, those sorts of program rate highly.' (Except, perhaps, this one.) 'And anyway they can act like counselling for some people. I mean, you know, it encourages people to talk about issues, to access their emotions…'

'To air their dirty laundry in public. I think it's tasteless.'

Mum had a point.

'Don't you think that's a rather elitist viewpoint, Mum? Based entirely on—on the paradigm of so-called high culture versus low culture where popular culture is inevitably seen as low and is therefore—' She searched for the word 'devalued.'

God she sounded like Charlotte.

'You sound like Charlotte,' said Mum.

'Bilbao,' called out Dad. 'You're thinking of Bilbao. That's in the Basque.'

'It was just a telly program. I was helping out Kim—Nick's sister? Anyway, I made it all up. You know, you shouldn't believe everything you see on TV.'

'You *lied* on television?'

'It's not a court of law, is it? I wasn't under oath. Anyway, it's a low-rating program, they needed an additional guest at short notice, so I went on and—and made up the whole thing. That's it. End of story.'

She could tell that this was not the end of the story so she ploughed on. 'Kim said they'd give me a false name but then the producer forgot and put up my real name, although it was only my first name. Plenty of Jennifers in the world.'

'Not who have sisters called Charlotte.'

'Yes. That was…unfortunate. But what does it matter? No one believes it's true. God, no one even saw it.'

'Charlotte said her work colleagues all saw it.'

'So she just tells them it's not true! *God*, it's TV—no one believes what they see on TV.'

'I do. And so does your father.'

There was a silence as though something important had been said.

'I just wish you'd think a bit more carefully before you say things about people, that's all,' Mum continued. 'Because it's just not fair on Charlotte—or on your father and me.'

No, it wasn't fair. And perhaps now was the time to say: Actually, Mum, it wasn't a lie at all. It happened and perhaps, therefore, you ought to be asking Charlotte about this, not me.

But when you'd kept something hidden for twenty-five years you didn't just suddenly come out with it.

Except on national TV.

'Well, I'm sorry, I have to go. I've got someone here,' Jennifer lied.

'Oh. Well, are you coming over for Sunday lunch?'

'No, I'm doing a stocktake.' Jennifer rang off.

To Mr Alberto Gaspari and the Board of Directors, Gossup and Batch PLC

Dear Sirs,
In response to a concern that has been raised regarding my appearance on national television last Tuesday—

Jennifer's office phone rang.

Despite it being nine thirty on Saturday morning, someone was ringing her in her office. No one should even know she was here.

She glanced at the display. It was an external call but she didn't recognise the number. The ringing stopped then the office door opened and Gloria stuck her head around it.

What was Gloria doing here? Hadn't she asked for the day off to get her wedding dress fitted?

'It's your sister for you,' said Gloria, adding a raised eyebrow that was a clear reproach for not answering the call herself.

Jennifer ignored her and picked up the receiver.

'Yes?'

'Jen. It's Charlotte.' Silence.

'Oh. Hello.'

Jennifer tried not to think about what she had said on national television four days ago.

'Mum rang me. About an hour or so ago. I've been trying to find you—'

'I do have a mobile.'

'—because Aunt Caroline's had a stroke.'

A stroke? And Jennifer thought, Why would Mum ring Charlotte and not me?

Bertha and Jemima

CHAPTER ELEVEN

SEPTEMBER 1924

Now, THIS TIME, surely!

With a final well-placed jab the hatpin pierced the felt of the hat, her hair and her scalp, and Bertha yelped.

It was impossible! How were you meant to affix a hat to your head if you had short hair? It was like trying to hold a knob of butter between your fingers on a hot day. She threw hat and pin onto the bed in disgust.

How did Jem do it? She'd cut her lovely long hair into a slick bob more than twelve months ago and yet she never seemed to have any trouble at all keeping her hat on.

Jemima was downstairs in the lounge and the murmur of voices—Dad's, mostly, but Mum was probably there too—travelled up the stairs to the bedroom at the front of the house in Wells Lane. It was a Sunday-lunchtime kind of murmur, a murmur softened by a stomach full of roast mutton and boiled carrots and baked potato and steamed pudding and, judging by the quietness of the street outside her window, the rest of Wells Lane was recovering from Sunday lunch too.

But not Bertha. Bertha had an appointment.

She picked up the hat and pin and, despite the importance of the occasion, decided not to ask Jemima for help. There wasn't time, she told herself, when really there were a good many other reasons not to ask for Jemima's help.

It was getting on for two o'clock and she needed to be at the tram depot by ten past and then—

And then.

Her heart jumped the way a needle on a gramophone record jumped if you danced the foxtrot too close to it. And then she would take the number 36 tram to Hyde Park where Mr Booth would be waiting for her.

She drew a quick breath and crushed the rim of the felt hat between her fingers. It was too exciting, too nerve-wracking—but deliciously so.

What if he wasn't there?

What if she couldn't find him in all the crowd?

Naturally, Mr Booth—Ronnie!—was not going to Hyde Park simply to meet her; not as such, no. He was going to be there on important League business, but he had asked her to come along, to join him. Mr Booth's exact words had been: 'You ought to come, Miss Flaxheed—it is every woman's duty.' And that was true because politics was not merely a man's duty, not any longer, not since the War, and anyway, it was every woman's duty to get married, though she did not think that was quite what Mr Booth had meant. Yet.

Right, hat, this is it, she thought grimly, shoving onto her head the oddly shaped object that two years ago someone in Paris had decided was a stylish thing to place on one's head and that someone else in a factory in Dagenham had copied and sold at a tenth of the price in Baxter's Millinery in Acton High Street. With a prod and a final twist, the pin, hat and hair were fastened together and Bertha took a final look at herself in the narrow mirror.

She felt a little uncertain about the coat. It was a long black affair that reached to her ankles and was her best coat and had cost thirty shillings. But the fact remained it was still early September and autumn had barely set in. Indeed, as she glanced through the window, the lane outside was bathed in bright early afternoon sunlight and the sky was a clear, pale blue. The elms that lined both sides of the lane were still in full leaf and Mr Creely from number fifty-five was heading off to the George and Dragon in only his shirt sleeves, despite it being a Sunday.

No, the coat would be too hot, she would look absurd and feel uncomfortable. On the other hand, suppose it suddenly turned chilly, or suppose it was late and becoming dark by the time she got home? (She tried very hard not to imagine how it would be if Mr Booth escorted her home, all the way to her front door. Well, to the garden gate, at any rate.) Yes, she *would* wear the coat. Elsie Stephens at work had said it was 'very Gloria Swanson' and that was good enough for Bertha.

Well then. This was it! The brass clock that hung on the wall at the top of the staircase indicated she had twelve minutes to get to the tram depot.

'Bertha!'

It was Dad.

Bertha froze, fingers halfway to her hat, two startled eyes staring back at her from the mirror. It was fine. He probably just wanted her to say goodbye before she left.

'Bertha!'

That wasn't a 'Hope you have a pleasant afternoon out,' Bertha. That was a 'Get here now, I want to talk to you!' Bertha, and for a moment she dithered with both hat and coat—take them both off? Leave them both on? Take the hat off and leave the coat on?—then she scurried out of the room, picking up her skirt and dashing down the narrow flight of stairs. Once downstairs she paused outside the lounge (there was silence from within) then pushed the door open and stepped inside.

Her mother was sitting in her usual chair near the lamp in the corner, peering curiously over the top of a pair of spectacles at her knitting. The knitting, a green jumper for her sister's youngest, covered her lap and balls of similar coloured wool crowded at her feet. She didn't look up.

'Bertha.'

Her eyes snapped across to her father, who was standing at the empty fireplace, one foot on the fender, hands locked awkwardly behind his back, a stern expression on his face, in a pose he had probably once seen the King adopt in a photograph in *Picture Post*.

'Do you think you are off to meet this young man, then?'

Bertha flushed and then, because she had just given herself away, her flush deepened.

How could Dad *possibly* have found out?

The answer came at once courtesy of a slight movement of skirts and rearrangement of hands near the window, and Bertha's gaze fixed on her sister sitting in the other corner of the room.

Jemima. Sitting meekly, straight-backed in the hardest wooden chair the house had to offer—which was saying something, in a house crowded with uncomfortable chairs—her hands folded in her lap, looking every bit the demure and dutiful youngest daughter. Looking, in fact, like everything that she was not.

Jemima. Bertha felt her face burn. How could Jemima have found out? She'd been so careful! Only Elsie Stephens knew, and Mr Booth himself of course, but Mr Booth had never met Jemima. No, Elsie it must be—Elsie, with whom she and Jemima had gone to see Charlie Chaplin at the Globe on Friday night; Elsie, who had waited with Jemima when Bertha went to purchase the tickets; Elsie, who, regardless of being Bertha's work colleague, seemed to share more secrets with her sister than with her. Elsie, who only knew the secret in the first place because she had agreed to provide the excuse for this Sunday afternoon excursion.

'Well? Do you not have anything to say for yourself?'

Bertha's gaze swung back to her father, who at this moment resembled less a father and every inch the butler he had once been. Actually, Dad resembled a butler more than a father most of the time and Bertha felt like an errant scullery maid more often than someone who wasn't a scullery maid ought to feel.

How much did he know? How much did Jem know? A quick glance at her angelic sister showed a head modestly bowed and yet the faintest hint—not that faint, in fact—of a smile. A triumphant smile. Damn you, Elsie Stephens!

Well, she would not be beaten so easily!

'Oh, but Dad, I thought you'd be pleased! Elsie and I are going to Hyde Park to listen to the speakers. You know how inspiring you said they are, all standing on their wooden boxes...preaching the word of the Lord.'

That was pushing it, that last bit, but it was worth a try, and Jemima's head came up, no pretence now of not listening.

'Preachers! If you want preachers we've got preachers enough at our own church,' retorted Dad, meaning St Mary's, at which they had all taken communion that morning. 'And it's not men of God you'll be hearing if you go to that place now, it's unionists and socialists. And communists too, if I'm not much mistaken.'

'Oh Dad!' said Bertha with growing frustration as the clock sped beyond two o'clock. Of course there would be unionists and socialists! That was why she was going—Mr Booth was one of them. As for communists, well, she'd never even seen one, and as far as she knew Dad hadn't either, though the way he went on about them you'd think folk were tripping over them at Crown Street market.

'I understand they are all sorts, not just socialists and unionists. Men speaking about all manner of things, and I'm twenty-two. I shall be able to vote in eight years... If I become a householder...'

'Ha!' said Dad. 'How do you think you'll become a householder? You'll never vote and so you never ought to—a woman has no place in the parliamentary process, nor in the industrial or commercial processes neither. A woman's place is—'

'Yes, but in whose home?' she interrupted impatiently. 'How shall I meet a husband if I never go out?'

'So. There is a young man.'

Damn. She saw Jemima's smile reappear but Bertha stuck her chin out defiantly.

'I expect there will be a great many men, Dad, seeing as how only men are allowed to speak, but Elsie will accompany me—'

'I understood Elsie was unable to come.'

So that was it! Jemima had undone her alibi. Judas!

Bertha faced defeat, her shoulders drooping. What would she say to Mr Booth? How long would he wait? Would he notice she wasn't there? Would she ever see him again?

'Don't worry, Dad, I'll go with her,' said Jemima and Bertha heard these words but she didn't look around because that would be to admit defeat. Jemima coming with her? But this was exactly what she did not want and she felt giddy, faced with the sudden choice of taking Jemima or not going at all.

Fortunately, the choice did not appear to be hers to make.

'Well. Alright. So be it,' said Dad as though he were passing judgement on some great act of God rather than simply allowing his two daughters to take a tram into town. Then he reached for the *Gazette* and shook it out purposefully. 'And mind you be back before tea,' he added.

'I think they should go,' said Mum, looking up from her knitting now that the disagreement had been sorted. 'I'm sure they'll come to no harm.' But Dad was deep into the latest carryings-on of Mr MacDonald's government and Bertha and Jemima had left the room.

'Oh! We shan't make it!' wailed Bertha as they sailed around the corner of King Street and into High Street.

The coat had been a mistake. The afternoon sun was beating down and her full-length skirt with her best coat over the top of it was making her perspire in a fashion that was hardly becoming. As for running to catch a tram, that was out of the question in the long coat. She could do little more than shuffle rapidly. The alternative, picking up both skirt and coat, was not worth the frowns of the Sunday afternoon folk who seemed to be out and about in Acton with the sole purpose of getting in her way and staring at her.

But Bertha's shuffle was an Olympic sprint compared to Jemima's saunter, and with one eye on the brick walls of the tram depot ahead, one eye on her dawdling sister Bertha felt she would burst with the frustration of it all.

'Oh, *do* stop being so hysterical, Bert,' called Jemima from twenty, now twenty-five yards behind. 'The 36 is always late anyway. And there's another afterwards.'

The 36 was not late when it was leaving the depot, only when it was returning to it during the evening rush. And as for there being another, the next one was not due to depart for a whole hour, which would mean they would not arrive at Hyde Park till nearly four o'clock, by which time Mr Booth would have long given her up.

'Oh do come *on*, Jem!'

It occurred to her that Jemima was deliberately going slowly so that they would miss the tram. But that would mean they would have to go home and give up the whole idea and why would Jemima have volunteered to accompany her if she did not wish, for her own devious reasons, to come? No, it must just be her usual perverse need to make her older sister squirm. Bertha took a deep breath and resolved not to squirm, no matter what.

'And they're bound to be on strike,' continued Jemima as though the thought had just that moment occurred to her. 'The trams are always on strike.'

On strike! Bertha felt that she might collapse. As they neared the brown brick archways of the tram depot, a double-decker London United tram lumbered out of the entrance and onto Uxbridge Road with a terrific clanking and screech of metal, a large 36 stuck above the driver's cab, and Bertha gasped in dismay.

'Wait! Wait a minute!' she cried, raising her hand and running alongside the tram.

It had barely got up speed and the conductor, perhaps taking pity on the flushed young lady with the inappropriate winter coat, or perhaps seeing her prettier younger sister tripping merrily behind in a charming light summer dress and a sudden smile in her eyes, pulled his bell and let them on board.

'Two to Hyde Park,' gasped Bertha, as they settled themselves upstairs on the top deck and the conductor swung his ticket machine at them.

'Off for a Sunday stroll?' he asked conversationally, aiming this remark at Jemima.

'No. We are attending a political rally,' said Bertha haughtily, handing over her money.

'Pretty girls like you shouldn't be wastin' a lovely Sunday afternoon on no politics,' came the reply, still aimed firmly at Jemima.

Jemima smiled briefly and dismissively. 'We're not the ones wasting our Sunday afternoon. You're the one who's stuck on a tram all day.'

The tram conductor, who until that moment had appeared to be enjoying his job, shuffled off, scowling, and Bertha, a deep beetroot colour, stared fixedly out of the grimy window.

'Why do you have to be so rude to people?' she hissed, not turning around in case the conductor had returned.

Jemima pouted. 'Rude? *He* was the rude one! Didn't you see how he was ogling us? Disgusting. He was older than Dad.'

Bertha had not noticed that he had been ogling them, she'd thought he was just being friendly. Well, it was over now and she would not think of it again.

The tram gathered speed and was soon trundling at a heady twelve miles per hour eastwards along High Street. A breeze gusted in through the open windows and they clutched their hats. Bertha gazed out the window. They were already passing the new aircraft and motor vehicle factories where so many people seemed to work nowadays. She saw them every morning, slow lines of pasty-faced girls with stooped shoulders and filthy overalls, girls who before the War would have been in service. Think they're too good for it, Dad said, and what was so good about stuffing aircraft parts into other aircraft parts anyway, he wanted to know.

'Shove over,' complained Jemima, wriggling her hips on the narrow seat they shared.

Bertha, annoyed, wriggled back at her. 'Well, I don't know why you wanted to come in the first place,' she replied tartly, glaring at the sailors' cap worn by the little boy on the seat in front and refusing to look at her sister.

'I could hardly let you go on your own, could I?' said Jemima sweetly.

'I wasn't going to go on my *own*, was I? Elsie was going to accompany me.'

'Elsie was going to accompany me,' mimicked Jemima, putting on the posh voice Dad used when he was reminiscing about his butlering days. 'Elsie wasn't going to accompany you anywhere. You were going off on your own to meet some man.'

Damn and blast Elsie!

'I'm twenty-two, and I shall come and go on my own if I wish to. I go off to work on my own every day and no one gets excited about that.'

'That's because you're not meeting some man at work.'

'Ha! How do you know I'm not?' replied Bertha.

Jemima sniggered and Bertha, humiliated, resumed her observations through the bus window.

And Jemima was right, of course; she was not likely to meet a young man at work seeing as how there were forty women operators at the West Western Telephone Exchange, and one woman supervisor, Mrs Crisp. There was a manager, of course, Mr Littlejohn, who was married and whom she had seen only once in the two years she had worked there. She was more likely to meet a young man on the top deck of the number 36 tram than she was at work.

Bertha glanced swiftly around but the top deck was full of families and elderly ladies. Then she remembered Mr Booth—Ronnie!—and she smiled to herself.

'You should be grateful I offered to chaperone you,' said Jemima, nudging her for a reaction.

'*Offered!* You're a nosy parker, Jemima Flaxheed! You just want to stick your nose in where it's not wanted.'

'Oh, don't think I don't already know all about your Mr Booth,' said Jemima in a bored voice, and Bertha clenched her jaw and cursed that Judas Iscariot, that viper in her bosom, that Elsie Stephens.

'He is not *my* Mr Booth, he is an acquaintance,' she retorted. 'And he has a Social Conscience,' she added, as though that clinched it.

'A social conscience? I'll bet he wants more than a social conscience from you!'

'How dare you! Mr Booth is a gentleman.'

'Sounds very dull.' Jemima yawned. 'And I bet you want more than that from him. Poor man, I hope he's prepared to defend himself.' She tapped the place on her gloved finger where a ring would go.

'That says a lot about your gutter mind if that's what you believe.' Bertha lifted her nose in the air and sniffed. 'If I'm going to vote one day, I shall want to know some-thing about the world. I'm not content to live in ignorance. It's 1924! There's more to a woman's life than…than… than serving tea and madeira cake to wealthy American businessmen!'

'Ha!' Jemima responded, and a silence fell as both sisters stared out of opposite sides of the tram.

Jemima had worked for the last year in the tearoom at Gossup and Batsch, a large American-style department store just off Regent Street. The store—a six-storey early Victorian monstrosity—had suffered somewhat during the War. It was rumoured to be owned by Jews and since 'Batsch' was obviously a Hun name the building had come under sustained attack in those first few excitable weeks in August 1914. Indeed, the windows had been broken so many times they had had to be boarded up. But 'Batsch' had miraculously become 'Batch' and since the War ended the store had flourished. Lots of young people shopped there because it sold fifty-shilling suits and ready-made dresses of the type you saw in American films at the Globe. And now there was a tearoom on the lower ground floor, so after you had strolled around and wanted to rest your feet, you could have a nice cup of tea and a slice of cake.

A year ago, Bertha had seen a small advertisement in the *Herald* seeking 'Superior Serving Staff' and, though she had not considered herself a serving person as such (it was a little too close to domestic service), the idea of working in a smart new tearoom in a glamorous American-style department store just off Regent Street, even if it was owned by Jews, was exciting. More exciting than plugging telephone lines into an exchange and wearing an uncomfortable telephone receiver fastened to your head all day long, ruining your expensive Marcel-wave and giving you a sore ear to boot. She had shown the advertisement to Jemima.

'What do you think? Does it sound like a good position? Do you think I should apply for it?'

'Only if serving fat old cats "keps of tay and a slace of Madeira cake" all day long is your grand ambition,' Jemima had replied scathingly, and while Bertha had spent some days reconsidering and thinking about it a great deal, Jemima had applied, attended an interview and been awarded the position.

Bertha reached out and with her glove wiped a circle in the window so that she could see through the accumulated smoke and grime. The tram passed the cricket ground then creaked to a stop by the isolation hospital, and a stooped elderly man with a stick tried to get on. He could hardly manage the step and the conductor had to reach down and pull him up. As she looked down from the top deck Bertha saw that it wasn't an old man at all: it was a young man of perhaps twenty-five, his war medals pinned lopsidedly to his chest. She thought again of Mr Booth whom, she presumed, must have been in the last years of the War, though he had said nothing of this and she certainly had not inquired.

Really, she did not know very much at all about Mr Ronnie Booth, she realised, feeling a knot of nerves begin to form in her stomach. It had been all very fine, this planning and waiting and imagining what might be and counting down the days and getting ready and running for the tram. But now that she was here (with her sister!) hurtling along the London streets towards a young man she had met only once and about whom she knew almost nothing and whose intentions towards herself were utterly unknown, it suddenly seemed somewhat reckless.

Somehow the tram was already clanking past Shepherds Bush and fast approaching Kensington. Soon they would be on Bayswater Road and then—

She gulped. Thank God Jemima was here.

What if Mr Booth failed to turn up? She experienced a moment of panic. Well then, she would simply hop back on the first tram home and no one would be any the wiser—if she were here alone. But she wasn't alone, she was here with her sister.

Damn you, Elsie Stephens!

She watched the crowds of couples strolling along the pavement enjoying the unexpected September sunshine. So many bodies, so many faces. Suppose she failed to recognise Mr Booth? Their meeting—miraculous though it had seemed at the time—had been fleeting to say the least. And if she hadn't been late posting that letter, it would never have occurred at all...

There had been a commotion in the post office. Bertha, joining the queue late on Saturday morning with errands to run for her mother and a letter for her great-aunt's birthday which ought to have been posted three days before, had been in no mood for a commotion.

'Express letters and other postal packets are sixpence a mile over and above normal charges,' boomed a resolute male voice, carrying above the restless queue that stretched as far as the doorway.

'This is a public service and yet you make it accessible only to those that have wealth!' came the unlikely reply, also a man's voice, younger and higher pitched, more emotional.

Bertha, and indeed everyone in the queue, craned their necks, but she could see little more than the back and shoulders of a shop-bought grey suit and a shiny auburn head.

'Not me that makes it accessible or otherwise,' replied the postmaster in a bored fashion and Bertha recognised him as Mr Lake, who was actually the sub-postmaster and who had often served her in the past. 'Now, do you want to send this letter or don't you? I've got a lot of customers besides you.'

'Aye, there's other folks want to post their letters too!' grumbled an elderly woman just in front of Bertha amid a growing murmur of discontent.

The shiny auburn head swivelled around and seemed to sense the mounting air of menace behind him. Bertha saw a man in his mid-twenties with pale skin and a large bushy moustache, a narrow face with a strong nose and chin, and rather nice vivid green eyes. She liked that face. It immediately turned away from her and back to the counter.

'Brother, you are a cog in a capitalist conspiracy that is so vast you cannot even see it!' he declared angrily, then turned and marched out of the post office, braving the line of damning looks and disappearing around the corner.

Bertha watched him go and felt a little astonished. And a little disappointed.

After purchasing a stamp for the letter and dropping it into the postbox, she stood in the street looking to the left and right as though she were contemplating the next task on her list of errands. When she saw the young man, now with a small bowler hat on his head, sitting on the bench outside Mulligan's tea shop, it was almost as though she had willed him there. He was fishing in his pocket for something, a coin perhaps, but his fingers emerged instead with a large fob watch at which he frowned. Then he looked up.

Bertha quickly looked away. Around her, people bustled past with market-day urgency, banging against her with their Saturday shopping. A tram trundled to a stop at the kerbside, disgorging a family of small boys and their young nanny. The conductor leaned out calling, 'Room up top!' and pulled the bell. A motor car rumbled up behind the tram, its engine spluttering, and tooted its horn impatiently. But all these noises faded into a distant murmur as Bertha stared straight ahead, her heart fluttering very fast in her ribcage, aware that this was An Important Moment.

Something was going to happen that would change her life forever, or if it did not then an opportunity would be gone and it might never present itself again.

''Scuse me, miss, you forgot your change.'

Bertha spun around to see Mr Lake from the post office standing beside her, his green clerk's visor pushed to the back of his head, an apron tied around his middle and a small collection of coins in the palm of his ink-stained hand.

'One and ha'penny for a standard letter. You gave me threepence.' He tipped the change into her hand then jerked his head down in an oddly formal salute, glared at the young man who was still sitting on the bench, and disappeared back into the post office.

Bertha stared at the coins in her hand and, with a sinking sense of despair, realised that if the young man had noticed her at all, he would now think her a silly, flighty girl with not even a rudimentary grasp of arithmetic.

'Are you alright, miss?'

She froze and stared with even more intensity at the two coins in her hand. He had stood up! Had spoken to her! What ought she to do?

'Yes, thank you for asking, I'm perfectly alright.' She managed a glance at him. Had that been too formal? Too dismissive?

Smile. That was what people did; she must smile at him. She turned her head and smiled directly at him (he *did* have such nice vivid green eyes!) and he smiled back.

'I, er, I'm afraid I made a bit of a fool of myself in there,' he said then, nodding his head at the door to the post office, and his slight stammer, the tinge of colour to his cheeks, gave her courage—he was shy!—and even though she thought he had indeed made a fool of himself, she rushed to his defence.

'Oh no! I thought it was marvellous!' She swallowed. Had that been too much? 'I mean, I think it's wonderful when—when people say what they mean. When people believe, really believe strongly in something!'

He took a tentative step towards her, his eyes observing her eagerly. 'Do you? So few people do...'

'Oh *yes*!' said Bertha, unsure what it was that she was agreeing to and then realising she could think of nothing to follow up with. 'Oh yes,' she repeated, less certainly.

'It's so refreshing to hear you say so, miss. So many people, young people like us who have seen first-hand the horrors of the world our fathers have created, who ought to be concerned, who ought to be shaping the world we shall some day inherit, are just…apathetic. Too concerned with dances and American films and mass-produced garments from these foreign-owned stores that are squeezing out honest working people…' He stopped, his face quite red now. 'Sorry. No manners.' He snatched off his little bowler hat and ducked his head at her. 'Booth. Ronald Booth. Ronnie.'

Ronnie. Bertha sighed. She had always liked the name Ronnie. It was friendly, sort of. Familiar.

'Bertha, Bertha Flaxheed. Miss.' She flushed at this last word. Was she being too forward?

There was a slight pause, the initial rush of emotion and then the formalities of introductions leaving a gap that for a while appeared too vast to ever be bridged. Bertha skidded from one corner of her mind to another, seeking with increasing desperation a subject, a sentence, a word that would break the silence. There was nothing, her mind was empty.

'Are you—do you involve yourself in politics, Miss Flaxheed?'

She experienced a rush of relief.

'Well, Mr Booth, I was saying to my father just the other day how I am twenty-two years old now—' Dear Lord, she had told him her age! 'and how in eight years' time I may find myself in a position to exercise my democratic right and vote for a government and…and how I intend to…to understand, to read, to *know* as much as possible before that time so that when that time comes, I should be able to make the correct choice.'

She had said nothing of the kind to Dad, though now that she thought about it, it was something she felt she might tell him, one day.

'Bravo!' exclaimed Mr Booth enthusiastically. 'If only more of your sex felt the same way, Miss Flaxheed, then we would show them, eh?'

'Indeed!' said Bertha, wondering who 'they' were and what exactly she might show them.

'I am a teacher, a teacher of music, at the grammar school and it is fair to say that few, very few indeed of my female pupils take but the slightest interest in the current political climate, or indeed in any political climate.' He reflected sadly for a moment or two. 'In fact, they take only the slightest interest in music, it must be said.'

'Girls are so silly and self-absorbed,' said Bertha, who had once been one and felt this excused her betrayal of her sex. 'But I beg you not to lose hope, Mr Booth, for out of every class of silly and self-absorbed girls there will be one who will trouble herself to learn about the world.'

This sounded pompous but she hoped he would ignore this and instead look upon her as the one girl in the class.

'I'm certain you are right, Miss Flaxheed, and if every classroom in England can produce such a girl then there is hope for the New World.'

This seemed a little excessive, but Bertha smiled brightly.

Mr Booth seemed to hesitate before reaching a decision.

'You see, I am involved in a group that meets occa-sionally to discuss just such issues as these, Miss Flaxheed: the rights of the worker, the role of the trade unions, the place of socialism in our world, that sort of thing.' Bertha nodded wisely. 'Indeed, this letter I was intending to post was concerned with a rally we are holding this Sunday coming. It—I—the rally is open to all, and we welcome our sisters in the fight. Should you care to come, I would be honoured.' He swallowed. 'It will be at Hyde Park at three o'clock. You ought to come, Miss Flaxheed—it is every woman's duty.'

Bertha swayed and the pavement gradually melted away and so too did the tram and the market-day shoppers into the September sunshine far away so that all she could see was his vivid green eyes.

'Yes, Mr Booth, I should like to very much.'

The tram trundled along Bayswater Road and elegant young courting couples swam before Bertha's eyes. The north side of Hyde Park was on her right, surrounded by black-painted railings over which she could see the bandstand decked with red, white and blue pennants and a brass band in scarlet tunics tuning their instruments. The waters of the Serpentine glittered in the distance.

The tram swung around the corner into Park Lane. One side of the road was lined with the magnificent mansions of London's wealthy and a number of the newly built American hotels. On the other side of Park Lane, within the park itself, was a great crowd of people and their noise, and the shouts of the men on soapboxes, could be heard above the rattle of the tram. This was Speakers' Corner.

They must get off! This was their stop.

Bertha found she couldn't move.

'Have a peanut,' said Jemima and Bertha stared at her sister then down at the white paper bag in her sister's outstretched hand.

'A peanut?' she said incredulously. Was this a moment for peanuts?

'Left over from the Globe on Friday night. Thought we might need nourishment.'

'But we must get off—this is our stop!' gasped Bertha, lunging from her seat, which, as Jemima had yet to move from the aisle seat, proved ineffectual.

'Do be careful!' protested Jemima crossly, extricating herself from her sister's lunge. They untangled themselves, tumbled down the spiral staircase as the tram screeched to a halt, and skipped down onto the kerb, Jemima forgetting her crossness of a moment ago and laughing at their near miss.

Bertha stood on the kerb trying to regain her balance and feeling quite sick.

'We 'ave been *betrayed*!'

From inside the park a cheer went up, followed by a few jeers.

'Aye, brothers, *betrayed* I say—betrayed and *duped* by the very men we voted for! The *very men* we trusted to deliver us from this *yoke* of poverty and *degradation*!'

The words, a hoarse shout delivered in a thick northern voice, were drowned out by another cheer and a flurry of shouts and whistles. From across the road Bertha and Jemima strained to see through the railings. Two red double-decker Generals had swung into Park Lane and disgorged their passengers, so that for a moment it was impossible to move at all. When finally they were able to cross the road and to hurry arm in arm, and with growing excitement, into the park, they were confronted by a throng of people that stretched from Park Lane all the way to the Serpentine.

Groups of young men, some in cloth caps and shirt sleeves, others in brown Sunday-best suits and bowler hats, stood around heckling the speakers and bantering with each other. Courting couples strolled from one speaker to another, amused as much by each other as by the words they were hearing. Children dodged between legs, chasing each other and running from their parents.

Of the speakers themselves, there were preachers of a dozen different hues, from Baptist to Methodist to Jew to a single Hindu in a white turban skilfully dodging the rotten fruit that routinely came his way.

'Mr Ramsay MacDonald! Ha! I say you are no friend to the working man, Mr MacDonald! What have you done, in your eight months in your fancy new office at Downing Street? What have you done for the likes of us?'

The speaker was a lean and heavily moustachioed young man in a striped shirt and braces, with a cloth cap on his head, who stood on a wooden box punching the air with his fist.

'He's done more than the likes of you 'ave, anyhow!' shouted a bearded man in wire spectacles, and as Bertha and Jemima hurried off the shouts of a dozen speakers pursued them...

'I've seen first hand, brothers, the conditions of our brothers in the northern collieries and I can tell you it's a *scandal*! *Poverty*, brothers, poverty and *famine*! Wages have been cut by forty per cent! *Forty per cent!*'

'This government cares *nowt* for the working man. You were better off with a *Tory*—at least then you knew who your enemy was!'

'And I ask you *why*? Why is it, brothers, that this government, and all governments, hunt down the communists? Why it is that all across the country, laws are passed and free-speaking men—men like yourselves—are hunted down and imprisoned? I'll tell you why: it's because they are *afraid*!'

'Beware! Beware my friend, for they are everywhere! The communist is in your place of work, he is in your street, he is your neighbour, he may be in your family—he is everywhere! Pervading and spreading his revolutionary filth, for make no mistake, my friend, *he will stop at nothing.*'

It was quite dizzying, all these different voices, made more so by the crowds who seemed in no mood to listen to anybody for more than two minutes, and regularly called back responses to the questions posed, often in sarcastic or rude tones.

'Where is he, then, this young man of yours?' gasped Jemima, as they dodged to avoid a scuffle that threatened to erupt near by. 'He'd better not be one of these cloth-cap-and-braces sorts.'

Bertha looked all around, but the number of speakers was so great she felt quite confused. Mr Booth had said a rally and she had taken that to mean a great political assembly of people of a like mind, come together to share their thoughts and to rouse themselves to action, not this chaotic and inarticulate rabble.

(*Would* he be in a cloth cap and braces? Surely not.)

'This way!' she said, dragging Jemima past a particularly large white banner. The banner belonged to the League of Women for a Return to Domestic Duties and was held by two stuffily dressed middle-aged ladies. Above them, a third lady, in a wide-brimmed hat and clutching a parasol, stood atop a small stepladder.

'...*urge* you, my dear sisters, *not* to be tempted by the ways of the man's world, for it is not for us! It is God's bidding that we, the fairer sex, embrace the duties that He has deemed are ours. Do *not* be tempted by these changes in the laws that offer suffrage for all, for that way lies *disaster*! It will spell the end of home life, the end of marriage, the end of childbirth. It my dear sisters, the end of Femininity itself!'

'Piffle!' said Bertha, annoyed.

'Miss Flaxheed! Miss Flaxheed, over here!'

Bertha saw him immediately, only a few feet away, waving to her though prevented by a particularly thick crush of people from reaching her.

'Mr Booth! There he is!' she said triumphantly, and she waved at him to seal the matter.

'Ha!' said Jemima enigmatically.

Bertha elbowed and pushed her way through the crowd, pulling Jemima after her, until they had reached a little group of younger men and one or two young women who were gathered around an elaborate speaker's box. It was really more of a lectern, and over it was draped a large red and gold banner on which was embroidered a crest. Closer inspection revealed it to be two crossed arms in red and black with the words *Socialism Through Unity* woven around the top, and *People! Organisation! Rights!* along the bottom.

They weren't communists, were they?

'Stupor,' said Jemima.

'What?' Bertha turned to her distractedly.

'Socialism Through Unity. People! Organisation! Rights! STUPOR.'

'Miss Flaxheed!'

He was not, thank God, in a cloth cap, and he was wearing a Sunday jacket over his shirt so Bertha couldn't see if he was wearing braces or not. On his head was the smart little bowler and his auburn hair was smoothed back very neatly, the large moustache trimmed and very tidy, his eyes still that quite dazzling shade of green.

'Mr Booth!'

'Miss Flaxheed!' He came forward, fighting his way through the throng, and Bertha despaired of them ever getting beyond this heralding of each other.

'Oh, you must be Mr Booth. Charmed I'm sure,' and Jemima swept ahead and held out her gloved right hand.

Immediately Mr Booth, who had been about to offer his hand to Bertha, changed direction mid-stride and, registering her sister, withdrew his hand to tip his hat to her instead.

'Oh. My sister, Mr Booth, Miss Jemima Flaxheed,' explained Bertha, feeling uncomfortably that she had been outmanoeuvred.

'A pleasure, Miss Flaxheed, indeed a great pleasure.' His eyes shone as though he were thrilled that they were, both of them, there. Then he turned and hesitantly reached for Bertha's hand, and as Bertha had assumed she had been forgotten where hand-shaking was concerned, there was a moment of confusion as his hand hovered unanswered in the air and Bertha, realising her mistake, dived at it, missed and stumbled into him.

'Sorry, I'm so sorry,' said Mr Booth and Bertha smiled bravely and was mortified. 'You had a safe journey, I hope?' he asked, which, considering they had come on the tram from Acton and not on the *Mauretania* from New York seemed excessive.

'At least the tram was running,' complained Jemima. 'They seem to be on strike more or less all the time at present.'

'And that is the very reason we are here, Miss Flaxheed!' exclaimed Mr Booth, turning to her eagerly. 'We—' and he spread his arm in a sweeping motion to take in the crowd surrounding the lectern, 'are the embodiment of all that is wrong with England today!' He paused. 'By which I mean, we are here to try to put right all that is wrong with England today.'

'Rather a tall order, wouldn't you say?' remarked Jemima.

Bertha rounded on her impatiently. 'A tall order is only tall until you scale it!' she declared, trusting Mr Booth wouldn't recognise the quote, which she had stolen from the Girl Guides handbook.

'That's it! That's it exactly, Miss Flaxheed,' replied Mr Booth. 'You've hit the nail on the head. The Socialism Through Unity league endeavours to identify the many injustices in our society and bring them to the attention of those in the opposition parties, in the unions, in various political leagues and organisations...'

'In other words, to get them to do your dirty work for you,' finished Jemima, and Bertha felt her irritation reach such a level that she was quite breathless.

It was a very warm afternoon now, the trees around the edge of the park and down by the Serpentine offering little shade to the crowds at Speakers' Corner, and Bertha could feel her dress sticking to her underarms. A pinkish tinge had appeared on Mr Booth's forehead and cheeks as though his fair skin was already catching the sun. Jemima, in her slim cotton summer dress was the picture of cool disdain. She gazed past Mr Booth at the scowling, pale-faced man who had just stepped up to the lectern.

'Mr Jamie Cannon,' explained Mr Booth. 'Our West London delegate and one of our founding members.'

Mr Cannon, who was wearing a dark suit that was a size too small for him, paused, fingering his collar, which was buttoned tightly at his throat. He suddenly gripped both lapels and his eyes—black, unblinking eyes—swept the assembled crowd.

'Mr Cannon has just returned from a tour of the north,' whispered Mr Booth.

'Ah,' said Bertha nodding, and Jemima, with a snort of derision, wandered off.

'I find myself troubled,' announced Mr Cannon in an oddly soft, almost conversational tone, and Bertha strained to hear, curious to find out what it was that troubled him. 'Yes, troubled, my friends. And I shall tell you why. Our King has chosen to open an eighth wonder of the modern world: the *Empire* Exhibition, no less, at *Wembley*, not four months ago. Yes, my friends, a great *exhibition* to rival The *Great* Exhibition of eighteen hundred and fifty-one, an exhibition to show the world the *might* of England's empire. Oh yes, a wondrous thing indeed. And in Paris! Paris, *France*...' He paused to let this sink in. 'In Paris, France, if you please, we have the Olympic Games. The *Olympic* Games, mind, not the people's games. The Olympic Games.' A murmur of unrest rippled through the onlookers. 'Where, if you please, the winners of athletics races win medals, *gold* medals, for their efforts!'

The murmur rose to a growl and Mr Cannon's tone rose too.

'And my friends, that great seafaring vessel the *Mauretania* has this very week set a *new record* for the crossing of the Atlantic—a famous endeavour indeed!'

'Shame!' called someone from the crowd, and Bertha, who until that moment had thought the fastest crossing of the Atlantic a very fine thing, began to realise that it was not a fine thing at all.

'And why do these things trouble me? *I shall tell you.*' And suddenly Mr Cannon's voice was no longer soft; it boomed across the raised faces, and the crowds who were turned away from him now turned to listen. 'Because in our *cities*, in our *towns*, in our *villages*, in our *factories* and *collieries* there is *poverty*! Poverty and *desperation* and *unemployment* the like of which this nation has *never* before witnessed!'

He paused to let the swell of discontent that swept through his audience reach a crescendo.

'Yes, my friends, whilst our King entertains the King and Queen of Italy…'

'No!'

'Shame!'

'…of *Italy*, our friends in the north *starve* and have *no* work. And those few that *do* work are faced with *wage* cuts whilst the price of *food* goes up. And what does this government do? *What*, I ask you? It *debates* German reparations!'

'They're a disgrace!' called out Mr Booth, his face flushed and excited.

'In*deed*, Brother Booth! A *pitiful* disgrace. For the first time in our history we have a government run by *working* men—and what have they done? Brought in the troops to break up the dockers' strike, that's what! Allowed the Germans to pay their war debt in coal and meanwhile our *own* coal industry is collapsing. Friends, the very *enemy* you sacrificed your youth to fight in the trenches, this very enemy is favoured over *our own people*!'

Someone held up a bottle of beer to him and Mr Cannon reached down and took a mouthful, wiping his sleeve across his mouth in a rather coarse way. Mr Cannon took a second swig and nodded to his audience, accepting the shouts of approval and the smattering of applause that broke out. It seemed that he had finished and Bertha thought it had been a very fine speech, though she wondered why he did not now go on to say how these things could be changed.

Standing beside her, Mr Booth was clapping enthusiastically.

She ought to remark that she had found Mr Cannon's words very inspirational but if Mr Booth asked her what she was inspired to do, she would, she realised, be unable to say. So she clapped loudly, throwing in a 'Bravo!' for good measure.

'A most inspiring talk,' said a smartly dressed lady who had appeared next to Mr Booth. The lady, who was dressed in a long white coat with a fur stole and an elegant little hat, clapped silently with white-gloved hands. Bertha, whose gloves were black and a little frayed at the edges, felt a stab of unease.

'Inspiring? What does it inspire you do?' said Jemima, who had returned and was now standing on Mr Booth's other side. For the second time that afternoon Bertha was glad Jemima had accompanied her.

Mr Booth spun around.

'Oh. Mrs Grantham-Jones, may I present Miss Jemima Flaxheed and her sister, Miss Bertha Flaxheed.'

Oh, so now *Jem's* the Miss Flaxheed, and *I'm* the sister, thought Bertha, silently outraged.

'May I introduce Mrs Caroline Grantham-Jones. Mrs Grantham-Jones is a very good friend to the league, a sponsor and benefactor.'

'Charmed,' said Bertha, who wasn't.

'How wonderful,' said Mrs Grantham-Jones, 'to have more women supporters at the grassroots level.'

'What are you a sponsor *of*?' asked Jemima.

'Why, of social change,' said Mrs Grantham-Jones, raising her elegant eyebrows.

Jemima sniffed and looked vaguely off towards a family of mallard ducks frolicking on the surface of the Serpentine, and Bertha suddenly found that she liked Mrs Caroline Grantham-Jones a great deal.

'How wonderful!' she said, to make her own position quite clear. She was rewarded by a smile from Mrs Grantham-Jones and a beaming grin from Mr Booth.

'Are you for social change, Miss Flaxheed?' inquired Mrs Grantham-Jones with an encouraging smile, and Bertha decided that she was, very much so.

'And I believe that it is every woman's duty to get involved,' she said firmly.

'Well said! Our sex has fought a long, hard battle to reach these giddy heights of equality, Miss Flaxheed, and we must be on our guard not to retreat one inch!' declared Mrs Grantham-Jones with a chilling glance at the ladies from the League of Women for a Return to Domestic Duties who were, at that moment, launching into a full-blown denunciation of birth control and the evils of wearing trousers.

'Well, Ronnie lad, how did we do?'

Mr Cannon, his oration completed, came over and clapped Mr Booth vigorously on the shoulderblade.

'Splendid! First class!' said Mr Booth. He grabbed Mr Cannon's hand and pumped it up and down energetically.

'Oh yes, very inspirational,' agreed Bertha, not sure whom she was trying to impress, but suspecting it was everyone and anyone.

Mr Cannon turned to inspect the young woman who had said this.

'Well hullo, and who might you be?' he said. 'Introduce us, Brother Booth.'

'Oh, ah, Miss Bertha Flaxheed, Mr Jamie Cannon. Miss Flaxheed is, uh, is a fellow West Londoner.'

Bertha forced a self-conscious smile as Mr Cannon clasped her hand in a grip that seemed, for a moment, as though it would never end.

At the temples of Mr Cannon's strong face were two squiggly veins that reminded her of worm casts on a beach first thing in the morning.

'And what brings you to our humble gathering, Miss Flaxhead?' he said. 'Are you here to lend a hand in the struggle for social justice?'

He had mispronounced her name. Well, she could live with that but not the tone of mocking irony in his question.

'No, I'm here because Mr Booth invited me,' she replied tartly.

'Ah.' The worms wriggled. 'Ronnie's a good one for the recruiting, I'll say that for him. That's how we got Caroline there,' he added, with a nod and a wink towards Mrs Grantham-Jones, who had marched over to confront the League of Women for a Return to Domestic Duties.

Bertha smiled stiffly. She did not like the familiar way he called Mrs Grantham-Jones 'Caroline'. Mrs Grantham-Jones quite clearly was not that sort of person. But what had he meant by implying Mr Booth had recruited Mrs Grantham-Jones? Or, for that matter, herself? *Had* she been recruited? She looked across to where Mr Booth was explaining to Jemima the various elements of the crest embroidered on the Socialism Through Unity banner. Jemima was studying the seam on her left glove and Bertha knew her sister would not put up with this for very much longer.

Did Mr Booth call her Caroline?

'I believe we shall turn you into a very fine socialist, Miss Flaxhead,' murmured Mr Cannon in a low voice, weighing her up with his head on one side as though she were an unknown port whose vintage was questionable but most likely still drinkable. Then he reached around as though he would put his arm around her waist and Bertha prepared to be outraged, but instead he placed his hand on her bottom and held it there and she was so shocked she was unable to move.

'Really, it makes me quite incensed!' declared Mrs Grantham-Jones, reappearing before them with a dark scowl.

Bertha used the interruption to dodge out of the way of the offending hand, almost landing on her rescuer's toes.

'We women need to be striving onwards, not scurrying back into our domestic holes!' added Mrs Grantham-Jones, aiming this remark at Bertha and obviously anticipating Bertha's own thoughts on the subject. But Bertha was busy smoothing down her dress and willing her face to return to its normal colour, wondering why Mr Booth had introduced her to this loathsome man and then deserted her. Perhaps now that Mrs Grantham-Jones had joined them Mr Cannon would leave her alone.

'Quite right!' declared Mr Cannon, clapping his hands together and then rubbing them as though he were about to commence something enjoyable. 'And Miss Flaxhead here has agreed to join our little gathering. More hands to the wheel, eh, Miss Flaxhead?'

'Oh bravo, Miss Flaxhead!' said Mrs Grantham-Jones, and now she too was party to the mispronunciation of Bertha's surname and where on earth was Mr Booth?

'I'm sorry, I must go, I must... I just have to... Do excuse me.' She gave an apologetic smile and hurried after Mr Booth, whom she could now see a little way off in the crowd.

'Mr Booth!'

'Miss Flaxheed!'

He waved to her and, as she approached, smiled that wonderful green-eyed smile which quite took away her breath and, with it, all the discomfort of the last few minutes.

'Miss Flaxheed, do join us. I've been explaining to your sister a little about our organisation, our aims and methods.' His eyes sparkled. 'I must say, having you both here and being able to talk about—about—' he waved his arm expansively, 'all this, is quite—quite invigorating!'

Beside him Jemima stifled a yawn.

'It *is* invigorating!' Bertha agreed emphatically, to counteract Jemima's yawn and because, after all, Mr Booth had invited her to attend. And he had such lovely green eyes. 'I feel like I could stay here all afternoon!' she added, turning to take in the impassioned voices and the bustling crowds that surrounded them, and pushing the horrid Mr Cannon to the very back of her mind.

'And yet we must be home for tea,' said Jemima, 'and the next tram is in a quarter of an hour.' She nodded pointedly at the fob watch Mr Booth wore attached to his waistcoat.

'Oh, but you can't leave yet,' protested Mr Booth, looking from one to the other of them in disappointment.

For one heady, insane moment, Bertha imagined Jemima departing on the next tram and herself staying on alone with Mr Booth, with nothing but the evening and a lifetime together ahead of them.

'And yet we must,' sighed Jemima, gazing mysteriously off across the sea of heads towards Victoria and Belgravia as though some force greater than themselves was propelling them onwards. It was: the London United Tramways Sunday afternoon timetable.

'Then I shall escort you to your tram,' Mr Booth declared, proffering his arm with a little bow.

'You needn't bother, we can find our own way,' said Jemima and she strode into the crowd. Bertha lost sight of her almost immediately, and felt a little spurt of panic. She turned back to Mr Booth in anguished indecision.

'I am sorry, we must—we do have to—my dad—tea will be ready...'

It sounded a bit lame. Could she, dare she, stay here on her own, with Mr Booth? Allow Mr Booth to bring her home, later?

She swallowed. 'I mean, there *are* probably later trams—I could, if—well...'

Mr Booth looked horrified. 'And if you were to miss this one, you would be late? Of course, Miss Flaxheed, you must go, I understand perfectly,' he said obviously not understanding her meaning at all. 'But you will lose your sister,' he said, scanning the crowd in the direction Jemima had just taken.

'It's—no, I shall be fine. Thank you so much. Goodbye, Mr Booth. I... Perhaps we shall—? I shall—?' Bertha paused in an agony of fresh discomfort.

'But of course! We are here often, you must come again. And I shall look out for you at the post office!' and he grasped her hand in farewell. Bertha turned and skipped through the crowd weaving, no *floating*, in a way that transformed her heavy coat and the hot sun into things lighter than air.

'*Do* come on!' called Jemima crossly. She was already standing at the tram stop on Park Lane, hailing her from across the road. 'Lord, what a dreary bunch,' she added when Bertha had floated over and drifted to a halt. 'That odious Mr Cannon would have put his grubby paws all over me if I'd given him half a chance.'

(And Bertha stopped drifting and felt her face redden in humiliated recollection—had *she* given Mr Cannon half a chance?)

'And as for that simpering Mrs Whatsit-Thingummy, who did she think she was? Lady Muck?'

'I liked her,' Bertha declared. 'She was...graceful.'

'Graceful!'

'Caroline,' mused Bertha. 'If I have a baby girl, I shall call her Caroline.'

'Ha!' said Jemima.

'But what about Mr Booth?' Bertha asked, this being the only question that really mattered. Not that it mattered a fig what Jemima thought. Still, she was curious. She glanced sideways at her sister and held her breath.

'Oh, if you like dreary little music teachers, I suppose he'll do, but really!'

And even though she knew she should be glad that Jemima didn't care much for him, Bertha sat on the tram and stared out the window and refused to speak to her sister the whole way home.

CHAPTER TWELVE

MARCH 1925

THE ELM TREES THAT LINED the pavement either side of Wells Lane had burst into fresh green buds and the cherry tree in Mr Jack's tiny front garden at number seventy-five had thrown up an early confetti of pink blossoms. Carefully arranged vases of daffodils and early carnations and scarlet geraniums stood in the windows of neighbours' houses and Mr Creely at number fifty-five had polished and waxed his brand-new black Baby Austin.

There was to be a spring wedding in Wells Lane.

At number eighty-one the frenzy of activity resembled below-stairs in a great country house during a pheasant-shooting weekend. The sort of weekend, observed Dad, who had experienced such occasions, when most of the staff had gone down with the flu and a peer of the realm had turned up unexpectedly and without a valet.

On the morning of the wedding, Mr Cyrus Flaxheed, retired butler and father of the bride, was swaying dangerously on the top rung of a stepladder outside his front doorstep attaching two white streamers to the porch. The white streamers were homage to some vague rural custom that no one had ever heard of, but everyone was too afraid to question. His elder brother, Alan, retired dairy farmer and up from Shropshire especially for the wedding, stood at the bottom of the ladder, holding it steady and calling instructions.

'Left a bit, Cyrus—no, no, left. *Left*. Too far. Right. *Right*.'

'Make your mind up!' said Mr Flaxheed, leaning his forehead on the brickwork above the door, a white streamer in each hand high above his head. His face was red, the tendons in his neck taut like cords where they shot out of his very high, very starched collar. It was warm for late March and a bowler hat and frock coat were not the most practical attire for this sort of work. But Mr Flaxheed, who had moved to this area upon his retirement from the post of butler to Lord and Lady Parker-Soames of Leadheath Hall in Sussex some ten years earlier, was not the sort of man to be seen out of doors without a hat or coat on. His brother Alan, who had inherited the family farm, was bareheaded, in shirt sleeves and braces.

'Left one's too low,' he announced and Cyrus Flaxheed tutted crossly.

In the kitchen, Mrs Flaxheed—Alice—was overseeing the baking of the wedding breakfast. Her sister, Nora Lasenby, and Nora's youngest, Edie, were busy steaming puddings and baking custards and icing cakes and slicing fruit loaves and cutting out gingerbread shapes. Alice stood in the middle of the kitchen tapping a stub of pencil against a long list and pursing her lips.

'Cider,' she said. 'The men will want cider and that brother of Cyrus's hasn't been out and fetched it yet even though he said he would. And there's meant to be someone at the church hall with the curate opening up and if we don't get those extra trestle tables from the vestry the boy scouts will have them for their goings-on. Now, there's cream in the ice box for those fruit trifles but Edie, you'll need to go out to the shop and see if you can't get some extra currants and some of those glacé cherries. And...'

She paused long enough to glance up at the ceiling. 'What *is* going on? I shall have to go upstairs and see where they've got to with that dress.'

At the kitchen table Nora and Edie stirred and baked and cut and sliced with silent urgency.

Upstairs, that dress, a creamy-white muslin affair, cut down, restitched and reseamed, had last seen service at Alice Flaxheed's own wedding in the tiny chapel at Leadheath Hall, a modest ceremony attended by the housekeeper, two footmen and a scullery maid on a frozen January morning more than a quarter of a century earlier. It was now lying slung across the back of a chair in the girls' bedroom and was the centre of a spirited discussion.

'But it's so dreary!' complained Jemima, who was perched listlessly on the window sill watching her father as he attempted to string up two rather tatty streamers. Beside her stood a glass vase and ten white roses, delivered that morning from the groom. Ten! Whoever heard of the groom sending ten white roses! She supposed music teachers at grammar schools did not earn much of a wage.

'Oh, but I think it's got class!' exclaimed Elsie Stephens.

Jemima observed her sister's friend silently. Elsie thought a ride in a tram to Putney was 'class'.

'And it's so wonderfully old! Look at it, all kind of... yellowy.' Elsie fingered the intricate lace of the bodice reverently. She wore apple-green herself, an unwise choice that made her and anyone standing near her look ill.

'I'll bet it's an heirloom,' said Janie Lasenby, who was Aunt Nora's eldest. 'My mum says your mum wore it at her wedding.'

'A hand-me-down, then,' pronounced Muriel Barmby, who worked at Gossup's tearoom with Jemima.

'Hardly!' said Bertha from the doorway, scowling. 'It was owned by Lady Parker-Soames of Leadheath Hall in Sussex and she wore it to balls and dances and—and all sorts. It's hardly a hand-me-down.'

'What is it then? Stolen?' said Muriel, lighting a cigarette.

'It's the colour of rotting teeth, is what it is,' announced Jemima from the window sill. 'And it smells musty. And what's more, it's so hideously long anyone wearing it will trip up and fall flat on their face at the altar.'

'It's a wedding isn't it?' giggled Elsie Stephens looking up from her position on the floor. 'You're meant to fall over.'

'I think you're supposed to get drunk first,' observed Bertha.

There was a clatter followed by a loud thump in the street below and Jemima leaned out of the window to see her father lying on his back, a streamer in each hand. She turned back to survey the bedroom. Elsie looked downright ridiculous. Who'd invited her, anyway? That dreadful green dress with the scarlet trim that she'd worn to the Palais last autumn, and that hat which looked like a flowerpot. Dreadful. Well, it wasn't Elsie's wedding, so who cared?

Muriel, in stark contrast, was all in black, which suited her deathly white complexion and would send Mum and all the family into a frenzy. Black! At a wedding!

As for Cousin Janie, well the Lasenbys were not noted for their sense of style and no one, least of all the Lasenbys themselves, was pretending otherwise. Still, at nearly eighteen Janie ought to be wearing something a little less nursery and a little more cocktail. Polka dots indeed!

She heard footsteps on the stairs, followed by her father's booming voice.

'Right, then, are the young ladies decent? We have precisely one and one half hours to get to the church. I expect you all to be dressed. The bride in particular.'

That was his butlering voice, a voice not to be argued with, and all the young women looked at the bride expectantly.

Jemima pushed herself up off the window sill. 'Nearly ready, Dad!' she called in her singsong voice, and they waited in silence until they heard his footsteps retreat.

'For goodness' sake, Jem, I don't know why you must leave everything to the last minute,' complained Bertha from the doorway and she turned and flounced off down the stairs after her father, leaving Jemima to get herself into the dreary bridal dress.

The dress *was* dreary. No one seeing it for the first time as the bride emerged from the family home on the arm of her proud, Sunday-best father could fail to be disappointed by such a dreary dress, thought Jemima peevishly.

Behind her, at a dignified distance, came Bertha and Janie—Janie fidgeting with the back of her dress and Bertha walking stiffly as though she were a pallbearer not a bridesmaid. They were followed by Muriel, who tossed her head at the watching crowd, and Elsie who flushed shyly. Then came Uncle Alan, hitching up his trousers and offering his arm to little Edie. Aunt Nora and Mum stood at the kitchen window waving white handkerchiefs and dabbing their eyes.

Outside a good-sized crowd of neighbours had gathered in their front gardens and in the lane and a small cheer went up and a smattering of applause and someone said, 'Oooh, look at that hat!' and someone else agreed, 'That's class, that is, a hat like that,' and Jemima closed her eyes for a moment.

Thank God for Muriel.

Muriel's elder sister, Evadne, worked at the motion picture studios at Ealing and had borrowed for the bride an elegant black hat with a veil and a rather striking little embroidered jacket of grey silk which was fitted across the shoulders and bust in such a way as to enhance one's already perfect figure.

She raised her chin a little higher and bestowed a smile on Mr Creely's head.

Mr Creely—neighbour, retired police constable and Wells Lane's sole possessor of a brand-new motor car— had gallantly offered his Baby Austin and chauffeuring skills for the wedding. So here they were climbing into the back of the gleaming black car, Mr Creely holding the door open and looking like he wanted to salute them, his hair oiled so that it gleamed as much as the duco. He tried to catch the bride's eyes as she swept into the back seat but as he had once attempted to kiss her in a dark alley when she was eleven years old, the bride did not catch his eye and, had he not been the sole owner in Wells Lane of a brand new Baby Austin and the only alternative to an undignified hike on foot to the church, the bride would not have deemed to travel in Mr Creely's motor car at all.

'All aboard then,' said Mr Creely, tipping his hat and confusing chauffeuring with bus-conducting. He closed the gleaming door of the Austin after Dad got in and marched around to the front of the car with much ceremony. Finally, and at a pace that would have slowed a funeral procession, they eased away from the kerb and set off up the lane. The family, neighbours and other guests now had about five minutes to dash up the alleyway between numbers thirty-four and thirty-six, turn into Gunnersbury Lane, and get to the church and into their seats before the car got there. The groom, one assumed, was already there.

The groom.

Jemima sat back in the plush leather seat and regarded the rounded bowl of Mr Creely's hat. They turned into Acton Lane and passed sedately beneath the red-painted wrought-iron archway of the railway bridge. As they turned left, not right, into High Street, she realised that Mr Creely was going to take them the long way round, possibly to allow the guests time to take their seats, but most likely to prolong his self-appointed role as driver of the bride. Beside her on the seat Dad patted her hand reassuringly but stared straight ahead at the Saturday afternoon shoppers and street vendors.

The groom.

If it hadn't been for that tedious Sunday afternoon at Hyde Park last September she would, she supposed, not now be sitting here in the back of this gleaming black Baby Austin heading towards her own wedding.

They passed the fire station, the town hall and the Globe Cinema, the library and the tram depot and Crown Street market, then they turned right into King Street and ground to a halt outside the King's Head, where a dray cart blocked the road and barrels were being rolled off. Mr Creely appeared to be giving them a tour of Acton's Places of Interest. Beside her, Dad pulled out his fob watch and frowned. Mr Creely swung out beside the dray so that two wheels mounted the kerb, scattering a group of elderly ladies and a shop boy on a large bicycle.

Perhaps, she mused, it might even have been Bertha sitting beside Dad in the back of a motor car in this dreadful dress (Bertha would suit it much better than she herself did) and she, Jemima, might be the one hurrying along to the church on foot. But there you were, life was funny like that.

Having exhausted Acton's sites, Mr Creely finally pulled up outside the church. And there he was, the groom, standing on the steps in a dark grey suit, waving. Was it a new suit, or had he just borrowed it? He was standing beside a man with one leg.

Jemima thought about waving back but in the end she just smiled.

'There he is! That's 'im, over there. Behind the palm tree. Second from the left.'

Muriel Barmby, four months earlier, buttoned, laced and pinned into the stuffy black waitress dress, heavy black shoes, spotless white linen apron and starched white linen headpiece that made up the regulation dress code of Gossup and Batch's tearoom, ducked behind a pillar and nudged Jemima sharply with her elbow.

Jemima looked up distractedly. She was trying for the third time to add up the bill of the elderly couple on table five, who had ordered a plate of cakes and a pot of tea and who might have had cream and jam too, though someone had forgotten to put it on the bill.

She followed Muriel's gaze, but all she saw was the usual Monday morning tearoom crowd: elderly ladies from Maida Vale and Hampstead and Belgravia in fox furs and boas and elaborate and unbecoming hats who always smelled faintly musty and told you to mind the teapot was warmed before the water was poured. Otherwise, there was a young couple, wealthy by the look of them, her dripping jewels and furs; an elderly gent of the retired-colonel type; a younger, tweed-suited man with his back to her sitting with a slightly older woman in an expensive coat and a very stylish hat and—ah! Now she saw him.

Mr Oklahoma in camel-hair coat, wide-brimmed hat, rings on the fingers of both hands and a fat cigar between his lips and (they had it on good authority) an even fatter wallet in his pocket. As usual he was studying an American newspaper which was spread out on his lap and whose pages he flung over and reshuffled noisily in the manner of someone accustomed to being the centre of attention.

'Told you,' hissed Muriel. 'Monday mornin', regular as clockwork. Mr Oklahoma.'

Of course his name wasn't really Mr Oklahoma. It was Mr van den Gelfenhoogen. Or something. He had told Muriel he was in newspapers and that he hailed from Oklahoma City, so he was known as Mr Oklahoma for simplicity's sake. He had been coming to the tearoom every Monday morning for the last four or five weeks, where he sat and noisily read his newspaper and sipped his black coffee. Occasionally he ate a pastry or a scone (though he called it a biscuit. He called biscuits 'cookies'). Sometimes he met other gentlemen, suited, often with attaché cases, some American like himself, some English. One a German. They talked 'business', reported Muriel, who always returned from Mr Oklahoma's table (table seven) rather breathless and bursting with news. This particular morning, a Monday in late November, Mr Oklahoma was seated alone, which was a good sign because it generally meant he would exchange a few words with whoever was serving him (Muriel, if she got in quick enough) and invariably left a large tip (half a crown last week).

'How do I look?' asked Muriel, turning to Jemima and smoothing down her hair, which was a soft chestnut brown—though you wouldn't know it, thanks to the regulation hairnet. Muriel checked her nails for dirt (but as Mr Gilfroy, the tearoom manager, checked the nails of every girl before she began her shift, it was safe to conclude they were scrubbed clean). Then she checked the line of her stockings and hitched her unbecomingly long black dress up a little to expose a vital extra inch of calf.

Muriel had designs on Mr Oklahoma. Or, rather, Muriel had designs on moving to America. Since her older sister, Evadne, had landed the job at the motion picture studio, her interest in all things American had intensified. Mr Oklahoma, who was unquestionably American and undoubtedly wealthy, had walked into the tearoom at exactly the right moment, and Muriel, who was young enough and pretty enough to keep her East End antecedents temporarily hidden, felt that she was In With a Chance.

Jemima felt that Muriel had about as much chance of marrying the Prince of Wales. In fact, she fancied herself as having more of a chance than Muriel and, though she was too preoccupied with her own affairs to bother too much with a loud, cigar-smelling American, she still made it her business to pass his table surprisingly often and to bring him his change when Muriel was in the kitchen. And she flattered herself that the smiles he bestowed on her were friendlier, more suggestive, than any he bestowed on Muriel.

'You. Gel. Gel. Yes you.'

One of the old cats was waggling a crooked finger at her and Jemima fixed a surly look on her face and slouched over in the accepted Gossup's way. She swayed between the crowded cane furniture and pot plants and her somewhat circuitous route took her very close to Mr Oklahoma's table. He didn't look up.

Well, perhaps she could catch his eye on her way back. She flounced past, brushing against the table of the young man in the tweed suit and the slightly older lady in the expensive coat as she went by.

'I've told Mr Cannon we ought to concentrate our efforts on the Opposition to lobby on our behalf. We really have very little of what one might call "clout" on our own.'

'Yes, yes, indeed. You're right there. Yes, quite right.'

Jemima looked back and was mildly surprised to see the posh lady and Bertha's funny little man from that dreadful political thing two months back. What were they doing here? Having an assignation? But no, she saw that they were having a dull political discussion and that an assignation was the furthest thing from either of their minds.

'Gel. Over here. I have been waiting a quarter of an hour for my pot of tea and cake.'

'It's just coming,' Jemima said with her sweetest smile (they usually tipped a penny each).

'Say, miss! Miss!'

She saw Mr Oklahoma calling her from over his newspaper. He smiled broadly as Jemima sidled over. A half a crown was good, but what if—what if…

'What is it, sir? Can I get you something special today? Chef says the pastries are fresh out the oven.'

Chef hadn't said anything of the sort but it was the kind of thing you were encouraged to say. Particularly to wealthy American customers.

'Well, now,' he said, lowering his newspaper to the table and settling back in his chair and taking a long, smiling look at her. 'That's a mighty fine offer and I believe I'll have to give it some serious consideration. But in the meantime what I require, young lady, is a telephone. I have a real important overseas call to make.'

A telephone? What did he think this was—the Ritz hotel?

'I'm terribly sorry, sir, we've got Madeira cake and Danish pastries and cupcakes and scones and Chef's special almond slices but telephones are off today.'

He let out a shout of laughter, throwing his head back and rewarding her with an even bigger smile, and Jemima glowed and prayed Muriel would stay in the kitchen or wherever she was.

'Okay, honey, why don't you run along and make up my check' (he always called it a check when he meant a bill) 'and I'll see if there's some place in this tiny store where a fella can make a call,' and he winked at her in a way that seemed to suggest vast prairies and gleaming skyscrapers and endless roads. And money. Jemima winked back and sashayed her way to the counter to make up his bill and work out how to slip him her name.

'Miss Flaxheed!'

Well, now he would know her name. Everyone would.

Mr Gilfroy had emerged from the small manager's office that was wedged between the counter, the cloakroom and the kitchen and was now summoning her frostily like the Grim Reaper on Judgement Day.

Oh go away, thought Jemima irritably.

'I'll just finish making up this—'

'*Now*, Miss Flaxheed. Get Miss Barmby to finish that.'

Miss Barmby had just emerged from the cloak-room (strictly forbidden during work hours) where she had applied a smear of powder and lipstick (an offence that would normally warrant a stern reprimand) but Mr Gilfroy had gone straight back into his office without even a second glance at Muriel. Jemima glowered at his retreating back, passed the bill to Muriel and followed him into the office.

'Close the door.'

Jemima closed the door and stood before his oversized Victorian desk. Apart from an inkwell and blotter the desk was empty and, other than serving as an object behind which one could sit, its purpose seemed to be purely decorative. Aside from the desk, the office contained only a bookcase stuffed with thick black ledgers and a rather sick-looking potted palm.

Mr Gilfroy, his brilliantined hair parted like the Red Sea, his moustache so waxed that it looked like a single strand of hair, sat behind the desk, arms straight at his side, regarding Jemima with a stern frown. His thin, wiry frame was encased in a pinstripe suit that he must have been born wearing, so impossible was it to imagine the man without the suit. He ruled the tearoom the way you imagined an NCO ruled a barracks. There were rules, there were regulations, there were transgressions and there was discipline.

There was a high turnover of staff.

It was rumoured he had a wife and two children in Hertfordshire, though no one had ever seen either.

'Miss Flaxheed,' he said, thrusting out his chin and fixing her with a severe look. Then, with a glance at the closed office door, he stood up, came over and kissed her passionately on the mouth.

'Jemima!' he moaned, his words somewhat smothered by Jemima's hair and the starched linen headpiece that kept it in place. 'I've missed you! Your smell, your softness, your divine taste. Oh God!'

Aside from this morning's regulation clocking on and checking of nails, it had in fact been less then twenty-four hours since Mr Gilfroy had last set eyes on her. Jemima stifled a sigh. His response to this enforced separation was gratifying though a little pitiful.

She noted that beneath his pinstripe suit he wore, as usual, a freshly laundered shirt, that he was scrupulously shaved and smelled of the hair oil that made his hair shine in the dimly lit office. Jemima approved of these touches; they were the details that made certain exchanges possible.

Mr Gilfroy's hand slid down over her buttocks and he pulled her towards him so that her breasts were pushed up against his starched white chest. Jemima turned her head slightly to one side so that his kisses landed on the side of her mouth rather than on her lips.

When she had first started working in the tearoom a year ago, she had sniggered along with the other girls at Gilfroy's primness. What sort of wife, she had wondered, could endure such a starched, pinstriped and priggish man? A starched, dull, priggish wife presumably, probably tucked away in a semi in Ilford or Epping. (She had since found out it was Rickmansworth and that the wife's name was Irene, but otherwise her assumptions about Mrs Gilfroy remained unconfirmed.)

But last December, a sudden snowstorm, a store-wide electricity blackout and a twenty-year-old bottle of vintage port that Mr Gilfroy had been saving for his eldest child's wedding had changed everything. Now Jemima was supremely, triumphantly aware that every starched collar, every lick of hair oil, every stroke of the razor was for her and her alone. When she lined up with the other girls before the start of each shift for the ritual nail check, Gilfroy's white fingers caressed her palms and stroked the back of her hand in a way that recalled what had happened in his office the evening before, when everyone else had gone home. She was careful to keep her gaze on the floor. Even so, Muriel had proven to have hawk-like eyes.

'Filthy old goat,' she'd muttered in an aside after one such caress. ''Im with a wife and kids at 'ome too. And he's old enough to be your father. Disgustin'.'

Jemima had smiled, recognising a note in Muriel's tone that suggested that had Mr Gilfroy come to her first, it might very well be Muriel herself spending her evenings in this cramped office, Muriel wearing a small silver ring around her neck on a piece of string, Muriel estimating how much Gilfroy took home in his monthly wage packet and how much of it he gave to his wife.

Godfrey Gilfroy. It was rumoured he would be moved Upstairs in a year or two. Senior management, perhaps a directorship in time. And if you wanted to get on, you didn't need a dull little wife called Irene in Rickmansworth. You needed a lively and stylish young thing, someone who knew how to dress, who said the right things. Someone like Jemima.

'Silly!' she admonished him now, playfully. 'S'only been a day. Honestly, you'll be wanting to stay here all weekend next and never going off home at all.' And though this was intended as a hint, a vision of things to come, his reaction was not what she expected.

'Stop! Please do not go on!' He let her go abruptly, as though she were on fire, his face taut and pale, and for a moment Jemima felt a flicker of concern. 'Miss Flaxheed, I'd rather… You must listen. This is precisely the reason that I have asked you here, and during work hours, which would never—I—'

Gilfroy paused and Jemima stared at him, fascinated. She had never seen him so ill at ease.

He took a deep breath and continued. 'You see something terrible, something quite, quite dreadful has occurred.'

This was it. His wife had found out. She had left him. *He* had left *her*. At last!

'My wife—'

'Yes?'

'My wife has found out about—about this.' He paused, looked down at his hands that now lay flat on the desk and swallowed loudly in the sudden, crushing silence.

Jemima felt her fingers curl themselves into tight fists. She straightened them out at once so that he wouldn't see.

'So stupid,' he continued with a tight smile. 'She—my wife. Well, I shan't go into the sordid details. Suffice to say there was an indiscretion on my part, some laundry, some discolouration...' He coloured and Jemima stood quite still, breathless. 'At any rate, there was a confrontation, an accusation you might say, that I was honour-bound—'

'To leave her!' blurted out Jemima.

'To *atone*!' Mr Gilfroy countered in shocked tones. 'To *atone*, Miss Flaxheed. I am not one to shirk my responsibilities. So. There it is and I am afraid...' He took another deep breath. 'Yes, so very, so *dreadfully* afraid that we must desist at once. There must be no more. It is quite, *quite* out of the question. You understand, of course?'

Jemima did understand, perfectly. He was ending it in favour of his wife, who was small and dull and whose name was Irene. He was choosing *her* and his two daughters and his semi-detached brick house in Rickmansworth over Jemima.

It was inconceivable. Had the wife threatened blackmail?

And was she to go meekly back to being Miss Flaxheed, waitress, whose nails must be checked, whose cash-till calculations must be supervised, whose clocking on must be overseen? Whose future, suddenly, looked uncertain?

Well, she still had her dignity.

'Will that be all, then, Mr Gilfroy?' She stared at the calendar on the back wall of the office. It had been sent by a tea supplier and showed a view of an Indian tea plantation.

There was a pause. Gilfroy seemed to hesitate. 'Yes, yes. That's all,' he said and turned away awkwardly, seating himself at his desk, fumbling in a drawer, dismissing her.

Jemima turned and left the tiny office. She stood very still on the other side of the door, breathing quickly, willing herself not to think, but a quick, hot, solitary tear welled up in one eye. She blinked it away furiously as Muriel advanced.

'Tight bleeder,' announced Muriel with a scowl, nodding towards the now-vacant table seven. 'Shot off when me back was turned and only left a shilling.'

So while Jemima had been trapped in that odious little office being pawed and then unceremoniously dumped back in with the dregs, Mr Oklahoma had escaped, and the fact that neither she nor Muriel had really stood any chance whatsoever of catching someone like that only made her all the more humiliated.

'Will you get this one, Jem? Me stockin's laddered,' said Muriel, nodding towards a customer standing expectantly by the cash register.

Jemima didn't want to get this one, or indeed any one. She didn't want to be here in this cramped, pot-planted, cane-chaired dungeon surrounded by acid-tongued, dried-up old ladies and wealthy, cigar-smoking foreigners who looked right through her. She didn't want to be here in this tearoom with a manager who couldn't take his hands off her one minute then couldn't look her in the eye the next. A manager who would probably make her pay for his lapse for as long as she continued to work for him.

'Er, miss. 'Scuse me—can I pay?'

No you can't. Push off! she thought irritably, but at that moment the office door opened and Mr Gilfroy emerged, chin up, nose very high, hands locked behind his back, a fierce look in his eyes, a look that for the last three months she had been protected from, but that now, suddenly, she knew would seek her out. She scuttled over to the cash register.

'Pot of tea and a slice of walnut cake, it was,' said the young man helpfully and Jemima saw that it was him, the man from the park—Mr Booth.

Mr Booth. Mr Ronnie Booth. Music teacher and political agitator. Mr Booth who had been so pleasant, so attentive to her that afternoon. Mr Booth who had seemed to be Bertha's young man but who, once one had actually met him and talked with him and observed him, had turned out not to be anything of the sort. Mr Booth who, now that you looked at him closely, was a pleasant enough young man, with nice hair and lovely green eyes. Yes, really quite nice eyes and well-dressed—in a schoolteacher sort of way. And now here he was at her cash register, wanting to pay for a pot of tea and a slice of walnut cake. Well.

Jemima smiled. 'Why, Mr Booth, what a lovely surprise. It's Miss Flaxheed. Miss Jemima Flaxheed.'

❀ ❀ ❀

'Friends, most of you know me. I am Cyrus Flaxheed, proud father of the bride, and I consider myself well versed in speech-making, having for some fifteen years held the position of butler at Leadheath Hall in Sussex, home of Lord and Lady Parker-Soames. So you'll forgive me, I hope, if I stand up here and say my piece.'

A chorus of murmurs rippled down the trestle table that ran the length of the church hall. Whether the murmur was of agreement or encouragement or an acknowledgment of Mr Flaxheed's illustrious career depended on who you were.

The bride and groom were at the centre of the table. Dad stood beside Jemima, Mum on his other side, and as

Dad launched into his speech the only murmur Jemima heard was a groan. The last time Dad made a speech had been at Aunt Mary's funeral in the parlour of Uncle Alan's farmhouse in Shropshire three years earlier. Some terrible and unmentionable illness had struck Aunt Mary down and whittled her away to nothing and, following her eventual demise, Uncle Alan had been unable or unwilling to say anything at all about his recently deceased wife. So Dad had stepped in and, even though he had seen Aunt Mary perhaps twice in the last quarter-century, he had still managed to talk about her for a full thirty minutes.

And this was a wedding—he had a captive audience and a role to play. Lord knew how long he might go on for.

'This is an auspicious occasion in the life of any father. Marriage, the holy union of two of God's children...'

Jemima closed her eyes. The honeymoon was to be in Torquay. She and Ronnie were catching the six o'clock train from Paddington and she began to wonder if they would make it.

'...happens only once in a person's lifetime, a state not rashly or injudiciously entered into, but one that, nevertheless, forms the basis for...'

Jemima opened her eyes. She had lost the thread of what Dad was saying. Judging by the glazed expressions around the table they all had.

She caught Muriel's eye across the room, where her friend sat at the second table, between two of Mum's distant cousins. Muriel gave her the cross-eyed look she usually reserved for when Gilfroy was being particularly officious.

Mr Gilfroy had been officious a lot lately, not to say downright mean in his insistence on timeliness, cleanliness and courtesy far beyond what duty demanded. His pursuit of these aims had been directed mainly at Jemima, so much so that in the end it had been a relief yesterday evening to triumphantly announce her engagement and to hand in her notice, to tell him exactly what she thought of his ideas of hygiene and to sweep out of there with her head held high before going for a celebratory port and lemon at the Cat and Fiddle over the road.

'...a foundation, indeed, on which the very pillars of our civilised world stand firm!'

In fact it had become a celebratory four or five port and lemons, not only at the Cat and Fiddle, but at the Pig's Head too, and the Station Arms, and finally some dingy little basement club called Jellicoe's, where two middle-aged city gents insisted on buying her and Muriel outlandishly coloured cocktails and had then offered to escort them home. Actually, not home exactly, but to the Tunbridge Hotel over the road. She and Muriel had excused themselves to powder their noses and run giggling up the stairs and onto a passing tram.

Jemima glanced again at Muriel, who made no attempt to stifle a huge yawn, and after all those port and lemons it was a miracle they were here at all. And as for Mr Godfrey Gilfroy and his 'clean nails are a sign of a clean mind, Miss Flaxheed', well, he could think himself lucky she hadn't decided to provide Mrs Gilfroy with some of the details of where exactly those oh-so-clean nails had been and how often.

But the moment had passed. Now she was a free woman. A wife.

'...that fateful day, more than twenty-five years ago, when my dear wife, Alice, gave me the honour of her hand in matrimony...'

Oh, please!

Monday morning. She pictured Muriel hurrying along the lower-ground floor corridor at Gossup's, late as usual, smoothing down her uniform, patting her hair into place, furiously scrubbing her nails clean at the tiny enamel sink in the staff lavatory, putting the urn on, rushing out to set up the tables before Mr Gilfroy came out of his office—and all with no one to help her. Jemima's uniform, her apron and headpiece, would remain hanging on the peg in the changing room. That horrible white lace thing they had to wear on their heads that made them look like ladies' maids in some big old house! And that awful starchy apron that was like having a piece of cardboard tied round their legs! She wouldn't miss that or the spilled tea on the white linen tablecloths or the cake crumbs floating in tea dregs or the dried-up old spinsters from Maida Vale who left no tips and quibbled over their bills. No, she wouldn't miss any of it.

'...when I held her in my hand—a tiny, red-faced, screaming little thing she was; loud and angry even then—and I said to Alice, "Alice," I said...'

Good Lord.

Muriel caught her eye again and winked conspiratorially. Her family all lived in Wapping, which was right the other side of London. Jemima returned her smile vaguely and looked away. People's lives, she realised, went in different directions, and the friends you had today were not the friends you would have tomorrow.

'...and now, here she is, a grown woman, on her wedding day, and I'll tell you now, my friends, it makes me a proud father, and I hope—yes, friends, it's my sincere hope—this lad sitting here beside my little girl appreciates what it is he's won.'

For heaven's sake!

Everyone was watching her now, Mum smiling indulgently as though she were reliving her own wedding. Would you smile if all you had to remember was a plain little wedding ceremony a quarter of a century ago in the bleak anteroom of someone else's house? But time could make you nostalgic about anything. Twenty-five years ago Mum had been a second scullery maid and Dad had been a butler, a man so much older, so much above her in every way, that it must have been like marrying a prince. Here was a man who had taken her out of that life of servitude and drudgery to this: a different life of servitude and drudgery.

Sitting opposite Mum was Uncle Alan, his hair shining wetly and parted precisely down the centre so that you could see his scalp. He was silent, his smile creased with a slight frown. Was he, too, remembering his own wedding to Aunt Mary, who had withered away and was now dead, and whose only son, George, had survived more than four years in the trenches only to be taken by the flu epidemic of 1919? Uncle Alan's frown deepened in concentration and she saw that his gaze was directed down the far end of the room, where Muriel was touching up her face powder in a little mirror.

Aunt Nora, sitting next to Uncle Alan, had the kind of fixed smile on her face that people had when they weren't really listening. It was unlikely she was fondly remembering her own wedding, Uncle Harry having run off in 1915 with a VAD from the local hospital. Beside Aunt Nora sat Janie and Edie, both perched on the edge of their chairs. They worked, the two of them now, at the Hoover factory at Perivale. As Jemima watched them Edie slid a furtive hand up to her face to rub a large red pimple in the crease of her nose. Beside her, Janie hissed something and slapped Edie's hand away.

At the other end of the room was Ronnie's sister, Rose, and her husband Clive Trent. Rose and Clive were publicans, Ronnie had explained during the introductions after the service.

'S'right—the Boar's Head in Camberwell,' Clive had announced proudly, as though she ought to have heard of this place and would be suitably impressed. Jemima hadn't and wasn't.

'Oh yes, next time you're down Camberwell way you shall have to pop in,' gushed Rose, who was older than Ronnie but dressed like a little girl. She talked like one too.

Jemima had smiled demurely. 'I can't imagine a single reason why I should be down Camberwell way', she had replied. As for 'popping' into the Boar's Head, she'd as soon present herself at the doors of Holloway Prison.

There had been a short silence then Ronnie had coughed. 'Well, my love, now we shall have a reason, shan't we?' he said, and Rose had smiled with relief, and Clive had positively beamed and looked as though he might actually slap his thigh. Jemima had waved at someone across the room and walked away. And now here they were, Rose and Clive of the Boar's Head, Camberwell, grinning down the length of the table at her and actually holding hands as though this was the second-best day of their woeful little lives. As though she were now family. Well, she supposed she was. Dear God.

Bertha sat on the far side of Mum, but as she was leaning back in her chair all Jemima could see of her was her nose. Bertha was not smiling and no doubt this was because she was too busy daydreaming about herself and her own wedding to think about her only sister's big day. Who Bertha was daydreaming about marrying, one could hardly imagine. Someone dull, that was certain.

Then there was Ronnie.

Ronnie sat beside her, staring straight ahead, the tips of his ears pink, his nose shiny with moisture, chin thrust out. His groom's attire consisted of a hired slate-grey morning suit that was shiny around the elbows and knees where it had been steam-pressed too often, a cream carnation buttonhole that clashed with the buttercup yellow of the bridesmaids' dresses, and his everyday, schoolmaster's shoes that he had polished so highly it merely drew your attention to the fact that they were shop-bought and some years old. His neck squeezed out of the tiny opening afforded him by his too-tight collar so that he resembled a soldier on a parade ground awaiting the sergeant-major's drill commands. The hand that reached beneath the linen tablecloth and grabbed her fingers was as stiff as a salute.

But instead of turning his gaze on her, he turned and grinned sheepishly at his best man. The best man was a rather sorry-looking chap named Collie Westing whom Jemima had only met for the first time at the church. He was the man with one leg who had been standing beside Ronnie on the church steps. She hadn't asked—well there hadn't really been a moment—who this Collie Westing was. She had been under the impression that Mr Cannon from the league was going to be the best man but now it appeared that Mr Cannon wasn't here, nor indeed was the rather pompous Mrs Grantham-Jones, and the task had fallen to the one-legged Mr Westing. You presumed Mr Westing had been in the War with Ronnie, which was even more reason not to ask too many questions.

'...sallying forth into the Kingdom of Heaven!' announced Mr Flaxheed with some relish.

Sallying forth?

Ronnie's fingers flexed then tightened around hers uncomfortably. Why did he stare straight ahead like that? What was he looking at? Why wasn't he looking at her?

She looked across the table. Mr Westing had a wooden crutch that he had laid against the front pew at the church, and he had stood on one leg throughout the entire service so that she had kept glancing at him, fascinated, wondering if he would wobble and perhaps fall over, but he hadn't.

Ronnie swallowed noisily. He would be making his speech next. She felt for the strangeness of the ring on her finger, twisting it round.

'...and so I give you Mr and Mrs Ronald Booth— health and long life!'

'*Health and long life!*' came back the shout as two dozen glasses were raised with dry-throated relief.

Jemima forced a smile. Ronnie turned pink and glared at the tablecloth.

'Up you get, lad,' ordered Dad, nodding at his new son-in-law in the way that he would once have commanded the hall boy at Leadheath to empty the master's chamber-pot.

Ronnie took a hasty swig of his beer, wiped his sleeve across his mouth, then scraped his chair back across the polished floor of the church hall leaving two grooves on its parqueted surface. A silence fell. Ronnie swallowed and said, 'Ah…' and his eyes flickered around the room as though he expected someone to hand him a speech. Jemima reached for her glass and raised it to her lips, staring into its gently fizzing amber depths and imagining herself elsewhere.

'Um. Thank you. Yes, thank you, one and all for your kind toast…er… And to my, er…to Mr Flaxheed, of course—' he tipped his head in his father-in-law's direction without actually looking at him, 'for his kind and, um, generous speech.'

Silence.

'We—that is, myself and Miss—I mean, Mrs Booth, my new wife. Um. We'd like to thank you all for coming to this, our wedding. So, thank you.'

The bubbles in Jemima's cider had dissolved and it tasted like ordinary apple juice. She wondered if she ought to have had beer instead but that looked just as flat. What she really wanted was a cocktail, but she might as well have wished for a honeymoon in Paris.

Ronnie, who had confided to her on their first night out that his ambition was to be a public speaker like Mr Cannon, had ground to a halt, but just as it appeared that he had run out of people to thank and might, therefore, have to sit down, he reached into his jacket pocket and fished out a folded scrap of paper, which he hurriedly unfolded and smoothed out.

Jemima twisted her glass between her fingers and wondered why, if you had gone to the trouble of writing out a speech, would you then forget to actually use it?

'Ah, I just wanted to add, just finally, that it's a great honour to be here and, more than that, that it's—that I'm—

that we're all very fortunate to be here. Many of us aren't here...'

Jemima looked up and glanced along the length of the two tables to see which of them wasn't here, but apart from the odious Mr Jamie Cannon and Mrs Grantham-Jones, she couldn't see anyone.

'...many hundreds, well, thousands of us aren't here.'

Ronnie squinted at the scrap of paper and Jemima's heart sank. Socialism, he was going to talk about socialism and the working classes. Dad was going to be furious.

'...I'm talking about the thousands of unemployed miners and shipbuilders and textile workers and their families in the north, men who fought for the future of this country and who now find themselves facing years, *years* of unemployment. In parts of Tyneside and Durham and South Wales the unemployment rate is as high as fifty per cent. *Fifty!*'

Ronnie paused and looked up into the roomful of frozen, waiting faces, wiped a sleeve over his top lip and plunged on.

'The War cost this country nine million pounds—nine *million*—and who is it that pays this debt? It's the poor, the impoverished, the sick, the elderly, the unemployed, through increased taxation and higher prices and lower wages and lost jobs! And we—we who are here—we...'

We *what*? thought Jemima, exasperated. For God's sake, sit down.

'We are here...at this wedding.' And Ronnie did sit down, very quickly and grabbed his beer glass and drained it.

A silence settled over the room, eyes twitched from side to side. Mum raised her head and smiled hopefully at no one in particular. Bertha, leaning forward, her head bent, appeared to be studying the hymn sheet from the service, and on the other side of Ronnie, Jemima could see Dad glowering down at his hands where they rested on the table. And then she realised, with a suddenly freeing sensation, that it really didn't matter what Dad thought or how furious he might be, as she was now a married woman.

She was Mrs Ronnie Booth.

They would be in Torquay by ten o'clock. It seemed incredible that they could be seated around this table in this church hall in Acton drinking flat cider and then in six hours they would be checking into a hotel on the seafront at Torquay. Seven nights at the Majestic Hotel.

What would they do?

She had never been to Torquay and neither had Ronnie, though his own parents had apparently honeymooned there. They were both long dead now, his father employed on the railways and dying of some work-related accident, his mother of scarlet fever when he was ten. He and his sister had been brought up by an aunt in Stockwell.

She knew more about his parents, Jemima mused, than she did about Ronnie himself, who complained a lot about the conditions at his school and of the conditions of the mines in County Durham, but who said almost nothing about his childhood, his War service or how he came to be attached to a socialist league and living in a boarding house in Acton. Maybe he was waiting till she asked him about himself? She hadn't asked him. Well, there was plenty of time. Perhaps in Torquay.

What would they do in Torquay for a week? What did anyone do?

She had seen married couples at Eastbourne, sitting silently opposite each other over their dull little boarding-house meals, holding doors open for each other and politely saying 'Thank you, dear' to each other and walking arm in arm along the seafront on moonlit evenings with an awkwardness that told you they would never walk arm in arm if they weren't on holiday. She hoped there would be a cinema in Torquay where she could sit in the dark and watch the screen and no one would have to say anything to anyone.

But the speeches were concluded, general conversation began again around the table, and Mr Westing sat back in his seat and beamed at the happy couple.

'Didn't know you was into that all that communist stuff, Ronnie,' he commented loudly.

Ronnie turned purple. 'Not communist,' he hissed, leaning right over the table. 'Socialist. We're a socialist league.'

'Socialists never helped me,' said Uncle Alan in his slow West Country drawl, picking up his spoon and pointing it at Ronnie. 'No socialist turned up in my cowshed to milk my cows morning I were laid up bad with me back. That Mr MacDonald and his Labour cabinet didn't come rushing round to rub ointment on my cows when their teats got bad with the udderwort.'

He placed his spoon neatly beside his plate and Aunt Nora, who was seated on his left, slid a few inches to her left.

'As if the Prime Minister's going to give two hoots about your cows' udders, Alan,' boomed Dad. 'And in my opinion you're better off without that sort so much as setting foot on your land, Al—mark my words, they mean to take it from you and turn it into a collective.'

'It happened in Russia,' added Aunt Nora, who read the newspapers and recalled something like this happening in 1917.

'Do the Russians get udderwort?' whispered Janie to her mother and beside her Edie piped up: 'What *is* udderwort, Mum? Have we had it?'

'No, dear, that was the whooping cough and you were very lucky to survive it, praise be to God.'

'They'll have a fight on their hands if they try and take my land, I can tell you. They'll have to take me out feet first or not at all!'

'Whooping cough! Really, Nora, Doctor Durnley said it was a nasty chest infection and a tickly cough,' said Mum.

'Anyway, communist, socialist, what's the difference?' yawned Jemima. She couldn't see what were they all getting so excited about. What was one word versus another?

'It was indeed the whooping cough, Alice. Mrs Vance at number ninety said it was and her three got taken by it last winter.'

'What's the *difference*?!' gasped Ronnie, turning to her.

'Telegram!' exclaimed Mum suddenly, and even though the War had been over for seven years you could still feel a ripple of tension sweep through the room. Conversation ended abruptly and all eyes fixed on the telegram boy, who was standing in the doorway holding a plain brown envelope in his hand. It was only after Bertha calmly got up and went over to him that the guests seemed to recall that this was a wedding and that telegrams were often received on such occasions.

Jemima sat up. She had never received a telegram before. The telegram boy—who, come to think of it, wasn't a boy at all but was, in fact, Mr Lake from the post office—looked very self-important with his peaked cap and his Royal Mail armband and his sign here, please.

Bertha, who probably knew Mr Lake better than anyone as she'd taken to loafing about the post office a great deal towards the end of last year, had taken possession of the telegram, just as if the telegram were for her. After smiling and exchanging words with Mr Lake as if there was no urgency whatsoever and a whole hall full of guests were not waiting to see who it was from, Bertha excused herself and brought the telegram over. Jemima reached over and took the telegram before Ronnie could get hold of it because she knew very well he would make an absolute hash of reading it out.

'Telegram!' she exclaimed, waving the brown envelope in the air, because she knew how to create a dramatic moment. She tore open the envelope and pulled out the single sheet of typed paper.

'MR RONNIE BOOTH STOP DOUBLE CHANCE WINS NATIONAL STOP BAD LUCK STOP JC STOP'

A cheer went up, mingled with rather a lot of laughter, and Jemima sat down furiously. A horse race! The Grand National, for heaven's sake! Who would send a telegram about the Grand National on the day of her wedding? It was humiliating.

'Damn,' muttered Ronnie crossly. Then he saw her face. 'I had a little flutter,' he explained, adjusting his cravat. 'Jamie had a tip. I thought it might pay for the honeymoon.'

Jemima laughed sweetly and patted her husband's hand. 'Never mind, dearest, it won't spoil our honeymoon,' she reassured him because everyone was still watching them.

The honeymoon wasn't *paid* for? They needed to rely on bad tips from Ronnie's unsavoury friends to *pay* for it? *Her wedding* was a place where *racing results* were read out and discussed?

On the far side of the hall Muriel was laughing heartily and Jemima felt the blood rush to her face. Common little East End tart. And to cap it all off, there was Bertha actually asking the telegram man to sit down at *their* wedding table and have a slice of the wedding cake!

'Aren't you going to give him a farthing?' she said crossly to Ronnie, nudging him and nodding in the direction of the presumptuous Mr Lake.

Ronnie looked round guiltily. 'Oh, well, I suppose…' And he got up awkwardly and sidled over to where Mr Lake was tucking into a large slice of currant and orange fruitcake with pink and white icing on top. Jemima watched with grim satisfaction as Ronnie made a show of handing him a farthing which Mr Lake stiffly refused. Instead he pushed back his chair, replaced his peaked cap on his head and backed out of the hall with a muttered apology. Bertha flushed darkly and looked along the table at her sister.

But Jemima was up and on her feet because someone had finally cranked up the gramophone and the dancing was to begin and in less than an hour she and Ronnie would be on the train to Torquay.

CHAPTER THIRTEEN

AUGUST 1925

'I SAID MAYFAIR NINE-six-eight-oh-*eight*!' repeated the testy male voice down the telephone line and Bertha winced, feeling her ears burn red, and prayed that Miss Crisp was not standing behind her.

'Thank you, caller, hold the line, please,' she said in the singsong voice you were supposed to adopt. Her eyes skimmed across the bank of indicators in front of her and her fingers hung frozen in midair. *Nine-six-eight-oh-eight, nine-six-eight-oh-eight.* Finally her brain, eyes and fingers began working as a team. 'Connecting you now,' she gasped as she stabbed the jack into the switchboard. The male voice disappeared and Bertha drew a deep breath.

'Rude so-and-so,' she muttered half to herself, half to Elsie, who was perched on a stool beside her, but Elsie was in the middle of a complicated trunk call connection to the Glasgow exchange and didn't hear her.

The West Western Telephone Exchange was housed in a square, solid red-brick structure built in a style of architecture reminiscent of a Victorian workhouse that thumbed its nose at the new trends of concrete, chrome and decorative facades. The switchroom was situated at the heart of the exchange. A vast, chilly, hollowed out, cathedral-like hall, it was forty feet from floor to ceiling at its centre, its roof held aloft by a series of cold steel arches, its floor covered with dark polished parquet. In the centre of the switchroom was Miss Crisp, seated before a forbidding Victorian desk, surrounded by thick black ledgers and with command over the single gas heater. Except that Miss Crisp was not at her desk.

'*Miss* Flaxheed. I should like a word, please.'

Bertha froze. And for a split second, every operator in the switchroom froze too, forty pairs of hands hung motionless in the air, forty heads jerked perceptibly in one direction and forty unseen callers continued speaking into their receivers even though no one was listening. It only lasted a moment before the constant murmur of female voices resumed its normal level, and a sea of pale, unadorned hands once more flickered over the switchboards connecting and disconnecting as seamlessly as machines.

Bertha brought her own pale, unadorned hands down into her lap and swivelled around on her stool to face Miss Crisp.

'Yes, Miss Crisp?'

Miss Crisp was West Western Exchange's switchroom supervisor and had been so since before the switchroom went automatic in the nineties. She wore her hair up in a severe bun when everyone else in the switchroom—even Nancy Probart who was over thirty and had a nine-year-old daughter—had their hair cut short in a bob or else shingled. Miss Crisp was also the only woman in the switchroom who wore, each day without fail, the sort of starched, white, high-necked blouse and heavy, black ankle-length crinoline skirt that your mother might have thought quite smart in 1901. Her face was very pale, her lips were the colour of lips—quite remarkable in a workplace where every other pair of lips was brilliant scarlet. In fact, Bertha now saw, when you looked closely, Miss Crisp had no lips at all, which was no doubt down to the fact that for thirty years she had pursed them so tightly they had simply vanished.

Miss Crisp pursed very tightly the area around her mouth where her lips ought to have been. 'Is there...a *prob*lem, Miss Flaxheed?'

She pronounced the word 'problem' in the same way a Victorian lady might have pronounced the word 'illegiti-mate', as though she had heard of such a thing but until this moment had never believed she would encounter it. She raised herself to her full five feet and one quarter inches and quivered. Bertha almost expected to hear the creak of whalebone.

Bertha opened her mouth but instead of saying some-thing turned beetroot red. A long second passed.

'No, of course not, Miss Crisp. No problem at all,' she replied at last.

'And yet you appear to be making more mistakes than usual, Miss Flaxheed. More. Mistakes. *Than. Usual.*'

Bertha concentrated on Miss Crisp's highly polished Balmoral boots. Boots that ought to have clicked smartly across the parquetry floor of the switchroom but which, due to some cunning piece of cobbling, made no sound at all, allowing the wearer to slide stealthily and silently about her domain. Out of the corner of her eye she became aware that Elsie had cocked her head to listen, leaving her Glasgow caller dangling on the line. On Bertha's other side, Fliss Cutler tutted beneath her breath with mock disapproval. And on the far side of Fliss, Nellie Trenoweth had gleefully terminated a call and whirled herself around on her stool to watch.

There was a perceptible drop in volume in the switch-room, so much so that it was quite likely the callers on the end of the telephone lines would be able to hear Bertha's reply to Miss Crisp's observation—if she ever made one.

'Very well then,' declared Miss Crisp, having received no satisfactory reply—indeed no reply whatsoever. Her bosom rose in majestic indignation. 'Be warned, Miss Flaxheed, that your conduct is under observation and that any further transgressions on your part shall, indeed *will*, warrant a full disclosure to Mr Littlejohn!'

And with this, Miss Crisp swept away with all the grandeur of the Orient Express pulling out of Victoria station.

Mr Littlejohn.

A shiver ran the length of the switchroom to the furthest end of the hall, where the single shuttered window high in the ceiling looked out over the rooftops of northern Acton. The shiver rippled back up the opposite side of the room and stopped dead at the solid, firmly closed door that led, by means of a corridor, a second door and an outer office, to Mr Littlejohn's office.

Someone sniggered. It sounded like Nellie. 'Spiteful old cow,' murmured someone else, and with such perfect diction that it must have been Fliss Cutler.

'She wouldn't dare, Bert,' hissed Elsie, leaning over and patting Bertha's hand.

No doubt this was intended as a sign of her solidarity. But Bertha had not forgotten that it was Elsie who had let the cat out of the bag to Jemima a year ago about her meeting with Ronnie.

'You have a temporary connection now, caller,' sang Elsie into the transmitter at her mouth.

Mr Littlejohn was controller of West Western Telephone Exchange. Few in the switchroom had ever actually seen him until the occasion—now part of West Western folklore—when a raven had flown in through the solitary window and had, for an hour, flapped and squawked and swooped amid the steel rafters of the switchroom, causing mayhem and terror and the whole of the West Western Exchange had come to a complete halt, leaving all of west London from Shepherds Bush to Ealing incommunicado. Eventually Mr Littlejohn himself—six foot tall with steel-grey hair and brandishing a pistol—

had emerged through the solid and usually closed door. A number of shots had been rattled off and the raven disposed of. The solitary window had been shuttered immediately and had remained shuttered ever since.

Bertha had been off sick that day, the result of a nasty head cold contracted after a disappointing picnic at Kew the previous Sunday, and so had missed the one and only exciting event to happen in the switchroom's history.

Remembering that particular picnic at Kew five months ago—just two weeks, in fact, after Jemima's wedding to Ronnie—Bertha forgot entirely about the threat of the mythical Mr Littlejohn and the reality of the vitriolic Miss Crisp. Instead, she allowed herself to dwell on the reason for her 'more than usual mistakes' that morning.

That reason was Mr Lake, of the post office.

Mr Lake, whose Christian name was Matthew, had appeared unexpectedly at the wedding reception that ghastly Saturday afternoon in March bearing a telegram that had irked Jemima and caused her to summarily dispatch him very shortly afterwards.

Far from being discouraged, Mr Lake had taken up a position outside the church hall from where he could observe the departure of the newlyweds at his leisure. He could also accost the bride's older and as yet unmarried sister, Bertha.

Leaving the reception hard on the heels of the newly married Mr and Mrs Ronnie Booth as they had boarded a taxicab bound for Paddington Station and thence to Torquay, Bertha had walked straight into him.

'Oh, beg your pardon,' mumbled Bertha. Looking up she was surprised to see Mr Lake who, not half an hour earlier, had delivered the telegram.

'Miss Flaxheed. It *is* Miss Flaxheed, I believe?' replied Mr Lake, in a way that dared her to contradict him.

Mr Lake's somewhat conceited and over-familiar manner made Bertha very much want to contradict him. She also had a suspicion that he had lurked about on this street corner so that he could get a last and lingering look at the young bride as she was whisked away on her honeymoon. Bertha bridled.

'Yes it is. Now please excuse me, I am in a great hurry.'

Bertha was not in a hurry, great or otherwise, but it seemed prudent to give that impression. To substantiate her claim she thrust out an arm and made as if to stride purposefully onwards. But Mr Lake, who was a solid-looking man and tall besides, seemed in no particular hurry to stand aside and her departure was thus thwarted.

'Perhaps you would care to accompany me on a picnic to Kew one Sunday afternoon, Miss Flaxheed?' suggested Mr Lake.

This was such an astonishing thing for Mr Lake of the post office who must be well into his thirties, if not older, to say, that for a moment Bertha was dumbfounded.

'The crocuses are quite delightful, you know, at this time of year and the greenhouses have all manner of orchids in bloom at the moment, from South America and the Asias and other such places, I believe,' said Mr Lake. 'Young ladies are partial to flowers in bloom,' he added, as though he had read this fact somewhere and was determined to make the most of it.

Bertha was unmoved by this appeal to her femininity. She was, however, in a state of acute anxiety over the suggestion from an almost unknown man that she accompany him—alone?—on a picnic. To Kew.

A response was undoubtedly required and, to give herself time, she stepped back a little, the better to view Mr Lake.

He was certainly in his thirties, though perhaps not as close to forty as she had at first assumed. His face was clean-shaven and large, his nose proportionally vast and his neck not much narrower than his face. He wore the uniform of the post office counterman, which was a dark grey serge jacket and trousers, with a wing-collared shirt beneath, and a dark grey felt hat that he was now holding before him in two vast hands. He was easily six foot tall and Bertha experienced just a flicker of nervousness.

But his face was friendly enough, she decided. His eyes, though you couldn't tell the colour at this time of the evening, nevertheless appeared friendly too. The post office, one supposed, would not employ someone who was not of good character. Besides, when he worked behind the counter he wore a sort of green visor on his head and a bottle-green apron tied around his waist and he used a pair of tweezers to tear off quantities of stamps. She didn't equate that sort of thing with opium dens and white slave traders.

But why Mr Lake was now standing outside the church hall, accosting her with invitations to picnics at Kew on Sunday remained a mystery.

'I believe I have an engagement this Sunday,' she said at length. From this he was to infer that she was a young lady with options, that she was not at all impressed by his unwarranted proposition, and that he should most certainly consider this a refusal.

'Well then, the following Sunday?'

Bertha turned to look rapidly from left to right to see who was within hailing distance should she need to call for assistance, and—of more immediate concern—who might be observing this exchange between herself, older and unmarried sister of the bride, and an employee of the post office.

But the wedding party had moved on so she turned back to Mr Lake. There were ink stains on the pads of his fingers and around the nails of his right hand, the stains a very faint blue as though he had made every attempt to scrub them clean. The stains and the scrubbing had an oddly comforting effect.

It occurred to Bertha that in two Sundays' time her younger sister and her younger sister's new husband would have returned from their honeymoon in Torquay and be living as man and wife in Ronnie's home. Much to her own surprise Bertha found herself saying, 'Yes, I believe I have no engagements the following Sunday.'

Accordingly, two Sundays hence, a mild and partly overcast day in early April, she had announced after lunch to her astonished father and her silently knitting mother that she was going to meet Mr Lake from the post office at the District Railway station and that she was going with him by means of a railway train to Kew Gardens, whereupon they would take a stroll in the Palm House and perhaps also the Orangery, and then partake of a light picnic tea prepared for that purpose by Mr Lake, and that she would return in time for supper.

And that is what she did. More or less.

The mild and partly overcast Sunday lunchtime promised to become an unseasonably warm and brilliantly blue-skied afternoon, and as she made her way a little breathlessly, in daringly high court shoes, to the railway station, Bertha was glad she had discarded her Gloria Swanson coat at the last minute. She wore instead her best dress—beige with an irregular hemline that rose almost to the knee on one side—and carried a natty Dorothy bag with tassels in grape that almost matched the aubergine of the second-best cloche hat that Baxter's Millinery in the high street had to offer.

She would not think about that other time she had rushed to meet a young man on a Sunday afternoon.

It was better not to imagine how things might have been.

This morning Jemima had swept triumphantly into the house, Ronnie following sheepishly in her wake, to announce that they were returned from their honeymoon. Had, in fact, returned some days before but had been so preoccupied with home-making and other sundry marital duties that they had been unable to visit before now. When they had gone (less than an hour after they had arrived), Bertha had made her announcement about meeting Mr Lake.

She turned the corner and there, immediately outside the station booking office, was Mr Lake.

For a moment her courage almost failed her.

He stood, legs slightly apart, hands behind his back in the manner of a soldier standing at ease. He was dressed in a neat dark suit and collar and tie. The only concessions he had made to the Sunday afternoon were the brown shoes in place of his boots and the soft collar in place of the starchy wing collar. On his head was a soft grey hat and she silently thanked God that he had not worn a bowler. He was, when all was said and done, Mr Lake from the post office.

He hailed her with a wave of his hand and a 'Hullo, Miss Flaxheed!' and Bertha, alarmed that someone she knew would see her, hurried over to silence him. 'A beautiful day for a picnic,' he added loudly, reaching down and picking up a very small wicker picnic hamper.

Ought she to have brought something too? Bertha wondered in sudden horror. Was the arrangement that they would both provide their own picnics and here she was empty-handed so that she would either have to starve or ask to share Mr Lake's? She decided to say nothing and see what transpired.

'There's an east-bound train in three and a half minutes,' announced Mr Lake, taking a large gold fob watch from his waistcoat pocket and studying it with a satisfied frown.

I'm out with my father, thought Bertha, dismayed.

'I have taken the liberty of purchasing our tickets,' said Mr Lake, holding up the two tickets as proof of this liberty.

Bertha followed him onto the east-bound platform where they stood, side by side, close to the platform's edge, and cast desperately about for something to say. The picnic? No, that was dangerous territory. The weather? Always safe but he had already beaten her to it. The price of the tickets? He might think her grasping and miserly. Or careless and irresponsible. The train was late. There was still time to back out.

But she knew she would not back out; that was the one certainty. The embarrassment of turning and fleeing now, at this stage in the proceedings, would surely outweigh any embarrassment the rest of the afternoon could mete out.

She was here for the duration.

Mr Lake—surely he would ask her to use his Christian name?—pulled out his watch again and gave it a disapproving glance.

'I understand this station used to be called Mill Hill Park,' Bertha remarked. 'I mean, before it was renamed Acton Town,' she added, lest he should be in any doubt. And surely this was the most idiotic thing she—or indeed anyone—could have said. But really, what did it matter? Here she was, Bertha Flaxheed of Wells Lane, twenty-three years old, operator at the West Western Telephone Exchange, worrying about what Mr Lake of the post office thought of her conversation.

'Oh? You're a bit of a train buff, are you?' replied Mr Lake, turning to her in some surprise and perhaps even approval. 'I'm a big one for all forms of transportation myself, and communication—it's the way forward, you know. What attracted me to the postal service in the first place. That and my old father,' he added as the train arrived. And with this newly established interest in common, they sat in perfect silence the two stops to Turnham Green, changed platforms and caught the Richmond train to Kew Gardens.

As they left the station, crossed Kew Road and entered the gardens through Victoria Gate, the first black clouds began to gather and the sun dipped behind them. Bertha looked up at the sky and decided she could risk a comment about the weather.

'I hope it doesn't cloud over?' she said, making it a question because she felt sure Mr Lake would hold some firm opinion on the matter.

'I believe it already has,' replied Mr Lake, keeping his eyes firmly on the path ahead, and Bertha felt foolish because obviously it had already clouded over, anyone could see that, and now he must think her a perfect idiot. She must be more definite in future. More alert.

Future? They were only going to be here for a couple of hours. Less if it rained.

'I've never been to Kew before,' she said, because she hadn't and this was something he could not call into question.

'Then you are in for a treat. Spring is always the best time to view the flowerbeds—the daffodils, the wisteria. Maybe early azalea and rhododendrons. Follow me!' And he set off down another path with such long strides that Bertha had quite a job keeping up. I thought he said we would stroll, she thought to herself as they sped around the pond, whirled through the Rose Garden, dashed past the Azalea Garden and shot out into the Bamboo Garden, where Bertha had to pause to draw breath.

'I need to sit down,' she said, putting words to action and dropping herself and the Dorothy bag down onto the nearest wooden bench and resisting the temptation to pull off her shoes and rub her fast-blistering heels. She had an idea no man liked to see a lady pulling off her shoes and rubbing her blisters in public. She was beginning to realise she might possibly have worn the wrong shoes. However, it was too late to worry about such things and, as Mr Lake made to sit down beside her, she took the opportunity to enjoy the view.

They were sitting on Riverside Walk, their bench overlooking a tributary of the river. A signpost pointed towards the Herbarium, the Orangery and Kew Palace and Bridge, and in the other direction to Old Deer Park and Richmond. A large number of young, springtime couples strolled arm in arm along the river. The couples, she noticed, or at least the young men who formed one half of these couples, were dressed in light slacks and brightly coloured jerseys, or wide-legged Oxford bags. Some even wore plus-fours and tartan knee-length socks. Those who wore jackets wore them unbuttoned and showed a large quantity of jauntily coloured knitwear beneath. Aside from Mr Lake, there was not a single dark suit, fob watch, collar and tie or waistcoat to be seen.

Bertha sank lower on the bench lest someone should see them and take them for father and daughter. Why wasn't he wearing a small, neat wristwatch? Why didn't he at least undo his waistcoat?

It seemed inevitable that every passing couple must surely turn and stare and perhaps snigger but no, all the young people strolling past were far too engrossed in each other to notice the stuffy couple sitting silently on the bench staring at the river.

Mr Lake hitched up his trousers an inch, crossed his legs and moved the picnic basket, which was lying on the bench between them as a sort of barrier, one inch to the left and then one inch to the right.

'And is that why you became an employee of the telephone exchange, Miss Flaxheed?' he said, and for a moment Bertha was so baffled by this question that she offered no reply. Then she remembered the conversation about trains and communication.

'Oh, no, I got a job there because my friend, Elsie Stephens, told me they were advertising. Elsie worked at Western Exchange at Kensington, and she transferred to West Western when it opened two years ago,' Bertha explained. 'I was working at the bakery in the high street before that. And before that at Hanson's Shoes for Ladies in Ealing,' she added, as though becoming a telephone operator was a natural progression.

Mr Lake nodded wisely and fell silent.

And was this to be the sum total of their conversation? Bertha wondered, panic-stricken. She ought to ask him why he was working at the post office yet this seemed impossible, like asking a vicar why he had become a vicar—you just didn't. But she must say something.

'And have you worked long at the post office, Mr Lake?' she inquired, and on balance it seemed like a safe enough question: polite, not too intrusive, yet displaying a respectful interest in his affairs. She relaxed for a moment, not the least bit concerned with what answer he gave but relieved at having done her bit for the conversation.

'Long enough,' replied Mr Lake.

Surely he was going to say more than just that?

Then, 'Shall we have tea?' and Bertha nodded.

The small wicker basket was turned around, the buckles undone, the lid lifted and the first drops of rain began to fall. Mr Lake surveyed the contents of the picnic with a critical eye so that it occurred to Bertha someone had made it on his behalf.

The drops of rain quickened and became a fine spray that covered Mr Lake's hat and collar and the sleeves of his coat in a shower of tiny glistening diamonds.

'Sardine? Or ham and shrimp paste?'

'Um...' Bertha tried to think. 'Sardine.'

She was carefully handed a square of soft white bread, the crusts cut off, containing between the slices a thick layer of mashed sardine.

'Thank you,' she said, waiting until Mr Lake had selected a sandwich for himself (ham and shrimp paste) and taken a bite. She took what she hoped was a dainty nibble and then, because this might look as though she disliked the look of the sandwich, and was being very rude, she took a second somewhat larger bite, and suddenly found her mouth quite full.

'Well. This is very pleasant,' declared Mr Lake, leaning back and dusting the raindrops from his left trouser leg.

'Mmm.' Bertha tried to swallow and nod at the same time.

They munched silently for a while, then Mr Lake delved into the basket and came out with two bottles and a little packet wrapped in brown paper.

'Now, lemonade. And I have flapjacks, Bakewell tart or mother's home-made gingerbread.'

Mother's home-made? Did that mean his own mother had made it at home, or was it just a figure of speech? She couldn't risk it.

'The gingerbread, please.'

He smiled approvingly and handed her the packet from which she carefully selected a slice of moist, dark-gold gingerbread.

'Mm, lovely,' she said through a mouthful.

'Yes. Although it's really my Aunt Daisy's recipe, and rumour has it she got it from a housekeeper who once worked in the kitchens at Windsor Castle.'

'Really?'

'Yes.'

The rain had eased off and just as Bertha was thinking of looking skywards and commenting on the fact, it came down again in a sudden flurry that blew straight in under her hat and wet her face.

'The rain. Perhaps we'd better...?' she suggested.

'We'll head for the Palm House,' agreed Mr Lake, getting up, repacking the basket and offering her his arm in such haste that Bertha had to jump up and grab her bag. She was still clutching the partially eaten gingerbread and she had to transfer it swiftly to her other hand in order to take his arm.

They scurried along the path in the direction indicated by the signpost as the rain became heavier and began to drip down the back of Bertha's neck. Really, it's rather romantic, she thought, stepping into a puddle, and losing half her slice of gingerbread. Mr Lake strode rapidly, his breath growing louder and heavier, the wicker basket banging against his legs. The sleeve of his jacket was cold and damp beneath her hand.

Ahead loomed the vast iron and curved glass structure of the Palm House. It was certainly magnificent, particularly as the rain was now driving down on them and the Palm House seemed to offer the only shelter. Making for the entrance, they eventually drew to a halt, Mr Lake grabbing the door handle and gallantly standing aside to usher her in.

Bertha stood, catching her breath, aware of a rush of moist hot air that clogged her lungs as Mr Lake came in after her, closing the misted glass door and shaking the raindrops from his collar.

The glass of the Palm House was completely fogged up so that she could see nothing of the outside. A narrow gravel aisle led down the centre and fenced off on either side were vast green leaves and stalks and tendrils that thrust upwards in a way that was almost claustrophobic. Half a dozen other couples, in various states of dampness, also stood around shaking off the rain and steaming gently.

'This is exactly why I am not a postman,' announced Mr Lake in a loud voice. Bertha smiled painfully at one or two of the young people who had turned to regard them.

'Well, no harm done,' she said, which was an appalling platitude; if Mr Lake was a younger version of Dad, then she was turning into her own mother. 'Shall we walk?'

she suggested to smother this discomfiting thought and, boldly taking his arm, she set off down the aisle away from the crowd in the entrance.

They stepped in unison and the gravel crunched noisily beneath their feet so that they sounded like a whole platoon of guardsmen drilling. Above them the rain pattered down on the glass roof and on either side the foliage rose above them, each giant frond dripping with fat beads of moisture. The air was so thick that Bertha felt the need to draw more and more of it into her lungs to catch what little oxygen there was.

'A bench!' exclaimed Bertha, seeing a little seat up ahead and making a desperate bid for it, whereupon she sank down and fanned her face with her glove.

'That's better,' said Mr Lake, settling himself down beside her. 'Very pleasant,' and he nodded approvingly at the array of orange and pink and white flowering orchids that surrounded them on three sides.

Bertha had never seen an orchid before. The heads of the flowers appeared to rear thirstily out of the foliage, their long tongues snaking towards her, sucking up what little air there was. They were monstrous. She hated them.

'Did you ever consider the postal service, Miss Flaxheed?'

The question echoed noisily inside Bertha's head. *Had* she ever considered the postal service? Well, yes, many times when she had had occasion to post a letter, but she felt sure this was not what Mr Lake meant.

'There are a great many opportunities in the post office for young ladies, more so than teaching and nursing, I expect,' continued Mr Lake, 'and more so than the telephone exchange, I wouldn't wonder. Not just counter service either—there's telegraphy, sorting clerks, the savings bank.'

Bertha stared at him in some consternation. Had he brought her all the way here to offer her a position at the post office?

'My dear old father was in the postal service, you see,' he went on. Bertha nodded faintly. 'Joined as a boy messenger in the sixties and in those days, well...' And here Mr Lake paused to raise his eyebrows, shake his head and utter a loud 'Hmmm!' so that Bertha understood that being a boy messenger in the sixties was a decidedly dicey business. She bit her tongue rather than ask why. 'No job for a respectable lad in those days, Miss Flaxheed, but I shan't embarrass you by going into that.'

'Oh no, I shouldn't be embarrassed,' Bertha assured him.

But Mr Lake would not be drawn on the matter. 'He enlisted soon after. Royal Engineers. Fought in the Zulu War in '79, then when he left the army he became a postman. Auxiliary, though. Not what we class as an established position, you see. Very hard it was, for a man like my father.'

'Yes, indeed it would be,' agreed Bertha, though she had never met Mr Lake Senior, and therefore had no idea what this meant.

'Fifteen years he did it, and they never did make him established. He reckoned it was on account of his being an ex-soldier. Employers didn't like them, you see—thought they were trouble.'

He fell silent. Bertha waited in case there was a further revelation to come but a careful sideways glance at her escort showed that he had resumed his contemplation of the orchids.

Well! thought Bertha, not a peep out of him all afternoon and then a potted family history tumbles out of him all in a rush. She ventured a reply.

'You forget, Mr Lake, that I *am* employed by the post office,' she retorted boldly, because was she not a fully trained and experienced telephone operator at the West Western Telephone Exchange, and had not all the telephone companies come under the auspices of the General

Post Office more than ten years ago? Mr Lake was not, she smiled to herself, quite so knowledgeable as he presumed to be.

He turned and looked at her in surprise and she saw that a bead of moisture had settled on the bridge of his nose.

'Ah, you are referring to telephone communications which, I do concede, is now a part of the GPO. But it is, I am sure you will agree, merely a means of frivolous gossip for the wealthy minority.'

Bertha did not agree.

'What about Dr Crippen?' she retorted hotly.

Dr Crippen had been the first man to be arrested as a result of a wireless message from ship to shore, a fugitive from justice in transit in the Atlantic, no less! And what of the *Titanic*? Hundreds of passengers' lives saved because of a wireless distress call!

But Mr Lake appeared unmoved by Dr Crippen and the *Titanic*.

'Consider,' he said, 'there are some quarter of a million telephone subscribers, Miss Flaxheed—well, I need hardly tell *you*—compared to a population of some forty-two million. It will hardly replace the postal service as a means of doing business, I would venture. No, the future lies, Miss Flaxheed, with the postal service.'

Bertha pursed her lips and smothered a frown. The bead of moisture had travelled down to Mr Lake's left nostril and he reached into a pocket, pulled out a large white handkerchief and wiped his nose.

'I believe the rain has eased off. Shall we go?' said Bertha, standing up abruptly and not waiting for a reply.

As she turned towards the exit she saw a rather nice-looking young man standing by himself a little way off near the door by which they had entered. She hadn't noticed him before and wondered how long he had been standing there watching them, for watching them he most certainly was, and as Bertha caught his eye he gave her a smile. Quite a cheeky smile too, one that might just have been accompanied by a wink.

Bertha glanced behind her to see if the smile and possible wink had been intended for someone else but the only person nearby was Mr Lake, who was getting to his feet and placing his hat back on his head.

Well, fancy! thought Bertha, putting on her jacket rather self-consciously. She made a great show of repositioning her hat, tucking her handbag under her arm, ensuring her arms were kept firmly by her sides and generally keeping her eyes averted. Her face, she felt certain, had turned a deep scarlet, though this was surely due to the oppressive climate.

'I don't know that the rain has eased off entirely, Miss Flaxheed, however it is rather warm in here, so shall we venture out?' suggested Mr Lake as they set off down the aisle. As she neared the doorway the young man, and he was very young she now saw, perhaps even a little younger than herself, continued to smile, turning his head boldly to watch her pass and reaching out only at the very last minute to take hold of the door handle and open the door for her.

As she swept past, Bertha decided he must be a manual worker of some kind, as he wore a jacket with no waistcoat and his hat was an old cloth cap pushed to the back of his head. This was all she saw as she re-entered the gardens and a blast of wet, chilly, early April air hit her. The raindrops, still softly falling, doused her cheeks, cooling them, and she stood for a moment breathing in the fresh, light air.

'Ah, that's better,' remarked Mr Lake, coming up behind her and raising both eyebrows expressively as though he had made an observation of some consequence. Bertha replied with a tight smile and set off down the path in what she decided must be the direction of the railway station. She wondered if the young man in the Palm House had overheard this and whether he now assumed Mr Lake to be her father. Perhaps it would be better if he did.

'I think it must be getting late,' said Bertha, not really having much sense of what time it was but aware that she had spent enough time in Mr Lake's company and that she was a young lady with a life to live. She was sure she had heard the door of the hothouse open and close again, and footsteps on the path behind them.

'It is in fact five minutes to four,' announced Mr Lake, having whipped out his fob watch and taken a long look at it. 'Meaning we shall catch the ten past four train, if we are quick about it.'

Bertha walked in silence, not sure what irritated her more: his ridiculous old fob watch, his precise pronouncement of the time, his memorising of the entire District Railway Sunday timetable or his insistence that they go everywhere in a terrific hurry. She deliberately slowed her pace; the footsteps behind them slowed too.

'It was in memory of my old dad that I joined the postal service myself,' continued Mr Lake and Bertha closed her eyes for a brief second. Did he really think she cared two bits about how or why he had joined the blasted postal service?

'Yes, when Father died, Mother and I had to move in with Mother's sister, Daisy—she of the gingerbread—in Acton. Oakton Way. We had lived in Shepherds Bush prior to this, you see.'

Bertha did see. She saw that this was the dullest man she had ever met, that she would as soon have spent her valuable Sunday afternoon in the lounge with Dad reading the newspaper, Mum knitting and Jemima and Ronnie coming round for tea and chattering endlessly about home-making and wifely duties.

'When I was seventeen I tried out for an established position, only I couldn't get one, on account of the Boer

War had just ended and suddenly they were reserving all the jobs for ex-servicemen. But I persevered, took the sorters and telegraphists exam and worked for a time in the telegraph office, then became a sorter and now I am, as you know, a counterman.'

He paused but Bertha was too busy calculating his age to make comment. The Boer War had just ended? That was, well, twenty-three years ago which made Mr Lake... made Mr Lake forty if he was a day! Dear Lord!

'It's a good, steady profession. A man can support a family in such a profession. I have been able to assist my mother and aunt so that we now own our house in Oakton Way outright.'

Forty!

'Eventually, I hope to advance further to the position of postmaster.'

They had reached the edge of the gardens and were about to pass through the gate and onto the street when suddenly Mr Lake paused and spun around, frowned and slapped his hand irritably against his thigh.

'The picnic basket. I've left it on the bench in the Palm House. Do excuse me, Miss Flaxheed, I'll get it directly,' and he hurried back along the path, excusing himself as he almost collided with the young man who was standing just behind them.

It was the young man who had smiled at her in the hothouse. He was smiling now as he sauntered right up to her. Most certainly a manual worker, she decided, his clothing being quite patched and his boots being very well worn. Maybe he worked here at the gardens. She turned away and stood her ground, taking in the air and definitely unaware of anyone who might be approaching her.

'Arf'noon,' he said, and Bertha continued to take in the air but she inclined her head an inch in his direction.

'Lovely day for it,' he ventured.

'Is it?' replied Bertha.

'Thought you was never gonna be rid of yer old man,' he said with a wink and Bertha felt herself blushing hotly. 'Bit of a tyrant, ain't he?'

'I don't think that's very polite...'

'Anyway, the old bloke's gone now.' A second wink. 'Where is he? Gone to meet someone and left you on all yer own, I bet.'

'Mr Lake has gone to retrieve his picnic basket,' Bertha replied coolly, and she could see Mr Lake already at the door of the Palm House, disappearing inside. This information seemed to encourage the young man, who took a step closer.

'Anyways, reason I come after you, I thought you must 'ave lost yer purse, miss,' he said. Bertha frowned and turned to look at him. 'Yer purse,' he said loudly as though she were deaf. 'Thought you must 'ave lost it in the gardens because I found one.' He held out to her a small and rather tatty black leather purse.

'Oh no, I have my purse, thank you.' Bertha held up her bag to reassure him that her own purse was quite safe inside. In one sudden movement he snatched her bag and was off, running through the gate and across the street, then round a corner and was gone.

'Stop! Thief, stop there!' Mr Lake, having just emerged from the Palm House, dropped the picnic basket and took off after him.

Bertha stood helplessly in the gateway, staring after them both and thinking very seriously about bursting into tears. After some minutes Mr Lake reappeared, shaking his head and breathing rather heavily.

'No luck, I'm afraid—fellow was long gone.' He came to a stop and bent over to catch his breath for a moment. 'Are you...alright? Did he...hurt you or anything?'

'No, nothing like that, just—just sort of grabbed it and ran. It happened so fast.'

'These fellows are professionals, they don't work for a living, most of them are…socialists and union men.' He took another deep breath. 'Did you have much in it?'

Bertha tried to think. 'No. Well, just some bus money. But it was a lovely bag, my favourite bag…' She stopped because she really didn't want to cry.

'Well, I'm sure we can find another exactly like it. Now, I think we had better find a police station.'

'Oh no, I'd really rather not,' said Bertha quickly.

'Can't let them get away with it.'

'I'd rather just forget about it and go home.' She felt very cold all of a sudden and she rather hoped it might start to rain again so that if she did burst into tears it might not be so obvious.

Mr Lake took her arm, tucked it into his and patted it comfortingly. 'Very well, then. Come on.' They retrieved the abandoned picnic basket and he led her across the road. 'Must say, you were very brave, Miss Flaxheed. Incident like that, a lot of ladies would have panicked, but you were very stalwart. Very stalwart indeed.'

Bertha ventured a timid smile.

'Thank you, Mr Lake.'

'Please, do call me Matthew,' he said.

CHAPTER FOURTEEN

AUGUST 1925

THE FOLLOWING DAY SHE had carried an old navy handbag to work but no one had noticed.

Even apart from the handbag, she had felt rotten all day, stuffy-headed and lethargic, and she had sneezed so many times during lunch that no one had been in the least surprised when she had sent word the next day that she was ill with a violent head cold and could not come in to work.

That had been the day of the raven in the rafters and Mr Littlejohn with the pistol, an incident about which the whole switchroom still talked, five months later.

And now, finally, today was the day.

Bertha knew it with a certainty she couldn't voice, and even had she been able to voice it she wouldn't have, not to her family and certainly not to her co-workers. Bitter experience had taught her that if you talked about something it did not happen. And this was going happen.

Matthew had called it A Special Reason. He had arranged to meet her this evening after her shift. He had never met her straight from her shift before. It was unprecedented.

This was it.

'Oi, Flaxy, you been at the gin or something?'

Bertha jerked her head up and met the inquiring eyes of Nellie Trenoweth, who was perched two seats away and was scrutinising her with a piercing gaze, a lipstick poised over her mouth ready to reapply. 'You been a million miles away all day,' she observed. 'Wouldn't be keeping something from us, would you?'

Nellie had a way of reading people that was quite unnerving. The slightest retort, denial or explanation could prove fatal, but Bertha found that her headset required immediate readjustment at precisely that moment.

'Am I missing something interesting?' said Fliss Cutler, looking up from her call with a sparkle of curiosity in her eye. 'So sorry, caller. *Do* be a sweetie and hold the line, would you? Thanks so much.'

Thank *you* very much, Nellie, thought Bertha, jabbing a jack into a new call. 'Operator. May I help you?'

'S'obvious,' Nellie was saying. 'Read her like a book, that one. Something's up, sure enough... Battersea nine-two-double-six, that line is engaged. Would you like to try again later, caller?'

'Perhaps she's anticipating a special delivery courtesy of the Royal Mail,' replied Fliss with a wink. 'Do please stay on the line, caller. Shan't be too much longer... There we are, you have a connection.'

A special delivery from the Royal Mail, yes, most amusing. Well, she'd made no secret of her weekly excursions with Matthew, not since Elsie had seen them at the Lyons in High Street a few months back and made it her mission to broadcast the news as far and wide as possible. Anyway, there was no shame in it—Matthew was a very respectable man, no one could argue with that. And in these times, well, a girl had to look out for herself and take what she could. Elsie had recently been courting the awful Bernie Sampson from the Switch Adjustment team who wore a too-small bowler hat on the weekends and had a thin moustache and lived in a sordid little flat above a greengrocer's in Ealing with his sister, according to Elsie.

The bell went for the early shift's lunch break.

'Time for tiffin!' announced Fliss, ripping off her headset and slipping off her stool. 'Come on, Nance,' she said, grabbing the hand of Nancy Probart, who was seated on Fliss's other side, and leading the charge for the lunch room.

Finishing her own call—a belligerent old woman from Belgravia who kept getting a crossed line with a young man in Islington—Bertha removed her own headset, climbed down from her stool and followed Elsie and Nellie and the rest of the early shift as they trooped out for their thirty-minute lunch.

By the time she reached the lunch room most of the bench space was taken. Bertha found a spot and squeezed in beside Nellie and Elsie and opposite Nancy and Fliss and contemplated her lunch. It was potted shrimp paste sandwiches again. She bit into her sandwich and listened to the lunchtime chatter.

'Well, far as I'm concerned we'll all be out of a job,' said Elsie, launching resignedly into her usual ham and tomato sandwich.

'They're always gonna need operators, though, ain't they?' said Nellie, shaking her head at Elsie's defeatist approach. 'Stands to reason. Some muggins has gotta push the button and pull the lever. Always 'ave, always will.'

They were discussing the new Telephone One-Fifty, a subject they'd all been discussing with boring repetitiveness on and off for most of the year. The Telephone One-Fifty had been introduced the previous year and was a new type of handset which had an automatic finger-dialling facility, meaning callers would now be able to dial their own numbers and no longer need to go through the operator. It was not yet widespread, and if you wanted to make a trunk call you still had to go through the operator, but the long-term implications for exchange staff were ominous.

Bertha took a bite of her sandwich and smiled to herself. She too had been worried about the Telephone One-Fifty only a few short months ago, but soon it would no longer be her concern. None of it would. Not Miss Crisp, not the mythical Mr Littlejohn, not Elsie's trials and tribulations with the awful Bernie Sampson or Nellie's gossiping or anything really. In a few short hours it would all be over. That is, in a few short hours she might—probably would, in fact—become Mr Matthew Lake's intended. And knowing Matthew as she felt she now did, he would be unlikely to ask her to marry him if he were not entirely ready and in a position to carry it through pretty much at once. She could be married and out of here in a few weeks. Perhaps less.

She listened as the conversation followed its usual pattern and she pitied them. She pitied poor Elsie who had only managed to land herself the horrid Bernie Sampson and whose future married life looked dismal. And Nancy, her husband killed in the Battle of Jutland, with a little girl to care for. What were Nancy's prospects? And Nellie, who tried so hard to give the impression that she knew all there was to know about men when the reality was she had never managed to keep one for longer than three weeks. There was no denying Nellie had fun—or she gave the impression of having fun—but what was it all for, in the long run, if not to find a husband? And at the far end of the lunch table sat Miss Crisp, opening her little wooden lunch box, pulling out her two fish paste sandwiches, her stick of celery and her orange, as she did every day, in silence and on her own, a wide space either side of her and not a soul in the place speaking a word to her.

Bertha averted her gaze. She was, she realised, in a privileged position. But she would not brag.

'You're looking jolly pleased with yourself, Bert. What's up?' said Fliss, leaning over the bench to peer at her. 'Talk about the cat that's got the cream,' she added in an aside to Nancy.

They were all looking at her. Well so be it! Was she not about to become engaged to be married? To announce her wedding, her imminent departure? But it hadn't happened yet. Nothing had been said, nothing spoken out loud. There was nothing to be gained by setting herself up for a great fall.

She pulled down the corners of her mouth lest she give herself away. 'I've no idea what you're talking about.'

'It's the postman, isn't it, Bertha?' said Nancy, leaning forward with a conspiratorial wink at Fliss.

'He's a counterman,' retorted Bertha tartly, feeling her colour rise. And then she felt awful because Nancy's husband was dead at the bottom of the North Sea. Or was it the Baltic Sea? At any rate it was a heart-breaking story, though you heard such stories all the time. Actually, he might not be at the bottom of the sea at all. She had an idea Nancy had once said he was buried at Portsmouth, but she might be mixing him up with a nephew of Matthew's. So many dead boys, it was hard to keep track.

'A counterman,' Bertha repeated more calmly, amid a few guffaws. 'And if you must know, I shall be seeing him this evening after work and having afternoon tea with his mother and his Aunt Daisy this Sunday.'

This resulted in a second, louder round of guffaws, and Bertha wished she had said nothing.

'Well, but that's very nice, Bert,' said Elsie loyally. 'Good for you,' she added, and well she might because Elsie, as Bertha knew very well, had not been allowed to invite Bernie Sampson to afternoon tea at her parents' house in Shepherds Bush. Some match that was.

The bell went, heralding the end of lunch, and as they traipsed back into the switchroom Elsie remarked that her new shoes were pinching her toes and Fliss said that that was the last of the sardines and tomorrow it was back to fish paste. It was all so normal, so exactly like any other

Friday afternoon in the switchroom, that Bertha wondered if she really was meeting Matthew this evening after work with the understanding that they would become betrothed...or if she had, in fact, imagined the whole thing.

The afternoon dragged on and, apart from a breakdown in the Exeter exchange which meant all calls to the south-west had to be diverted via Bristol and Cardiff exchanges, was uneventful. Bertha passed the time pondering all the different ways a man could ask you to marry him.

At long last the bell rang to signal the end of the shift. Transmitters were ripped off, coats grabbed and hats thrust onto heads, and everyone surged out into the warm air and sunlight of the August evening.

And there was Matthew! Standing on the steps waiting for her, just as he had told her he would be, just where everyone finishing the shift could see him. Bertha felt a surge of pleasure and quickly made her way over.

'Evening, my dearest,' he said, leaning over and offering her a kiss on the cheek, which she accepted gracefully as she did each time they met.

'Hello dearest,' she replied a little breathlessly, offering him her arm. She allowed herself to be led down the exchange steps, unable to resist a glance over her shoulder to see who might have observed her.

But no one had. Nellie and Elsie were still standing in the doorway, cigarettes already lit, madly applying lipstick. Fliss and Nancy, first out of the door, were already halfway towards the railway station, hurrying arm in arm and laughing at some joke.

'Dearest, shall we go?' said Matthew, and Bertha reminded herself what day it was and how she had been waiting for this day all week. And perhaps a lot longer.

'I thought we could go for a fish and chip supper,' Matthew suggested and Bertha stared at him, her mouth falling open.

A fish and chip supper?

This had become something of a Friday night tradition over the past five months and meant Pontison's Fish Café in Gunnersbury Lane—haddock and chips for Matthew, plaice and chips for Bertha, hers with vinegar, his without, served with a plate of bread and butter and followed by a pot of tea for two, after which they either strolled through the park or, if it was a chilly evening, had a bottle of stout at the Red Lion. Either way, the evening ended up at the path leading to the Flaxheeds' house in Wells Lane with a peck on the cheek and an arrangement for Sunday afternoon.

That was not what this evening was supposed to be.

Already they were walking along the street towards Horn Lane, Matthew discussing with obvious relish that afternoon's sorting at the post office. Sorting was an event in which he, as a senior counterman, no longer had to participate but, as an ex-sorter himself, took some pleasure in observing. The current team of sorters were all ex-servicemen—a group, according to Matthew, so intensely dull and stupid they could only have survived the trenches by sheer dumb luck. It was, he concluded, a daily miracle that the post got sorted, placed into the appropriate mail bags and loaded into the delivery vans at all. One could only imagine where some of the more obscurely addressed parcels ended up. Last week, for example, a registered letter bound for Salisbury had, he revealed with grim relish, turned up in Salford, Manchester a week later.

Bertha experienced a tightness in her chest, a light-headedness and flickering of lights before her eyes like when you'd run for the last tram and not quite made it to the stop in time. This was not how she had imagined her evening. It was not why she had waited so impatiently for the week to come to an end, had counted the minutes each morning, lying in bed, waiting to get up and wash and dress so that it had seemed her heart would burst out of her chest and her brain would erupt from her skull with the effort of lying still, the agony of waiting. And for what? So that they could go for a fish supper at Pontison's!

She couldn't speak. Her throat was parched and her tongue was numb and lifeless in her mouth. She walked in silence and her hand, where it rested on his arm, was dead and cold.

'Careful, m'dear,' said Matthew suddenly. She looked down and narrowly missed stepping in a steaming pile of horse dung on the road. A little way ahead, a horse and dray from the brewery were stationed outside the Red Lion, where barrels were being unloaded and rolled down a wooden ramp into the cellar.

The Red Lion. She looked up and realised they were walking east along High Street and not south down Gunnersbury Lane as usual. They passed Acton Lane and she could hear a train rattling over the bridge. They were not, in fact, very far from Matthew's aunt's house in Oakton Way. She paused, confused, and looked at Matthew, who had fallen silent. He had a sort of dogged secretiveness about him. Bertha felt quite sick.

'And did all go well at the counter today?' she blurted out, because now she needed the familiar and ordinary when just a moment before she had despised it.

'A little fraught, m'dear, in actual fact,' Matthew replied with a slight frown.

'Oh?'

'The unions, stirring up a hornet's nest as usual. I won't bore you with the details. Suffice to say the new lot are every bit as bad as the old lot. We shall all be Bolsheviks by Christmas, at this rate.'

'Oh dear.'

The new lot, she knew from previous discussions, was the National Federation of something or other who were an offshoot or a rival branch of the Union of something else and were always on the brink of calling out the postal staff on a strike.

Bertha made no further comment. Somehow the familiar and the ordinary had not proved as comforting as she had imagined. And now they were turning, very definitely, into Oakton Way. Things had gone far enough.

'My dear, aren't we going to Pontison's?' she inquired lightly.

She felt a slight pressure on her hand as Matthew reached across and squeezed her fingers. That was all, just a slight pressure, but it was enough, and in a rush the giddiness returned and she felt little pinpricks of perspiration on her skin.

They continued to walk almost to the end of Oakton Way and at last came to a stop outside number fifteen.

The houses in Oakton Way dated from the 1880s and had been built as cottages for the workers at the nearby railways yards. They were similar to the houses in Wells Lane, though the front gardens were smaller, and while Wells Lane had elm trees dotted along its length, Oakton Way was treeless and bordered at one end by the blackened walls of the new gas works that cast a shadow over one half of the road. Number fifteen had a dark-green front door and in the lounge window hung a pair of ancient white net curtains. The little garden was bordered on one side by rosebushes and the flowers, now past their bloom, had shed pink and white petals onto the little pathway that led up to the front door.

It was a little after six o'clock and the sun had yet to set, though in this part of Oakton Way the street was already deep in the shadow cast by the gasworks. Bertha pulled her jacket a little closer about her shoulders.

They paused now at the garden gate, but rather than opening the gate Matthew stood and gazed up at the house with obvious satisfaction and then, with another squeeze of her hand, he looked down at her. Bertha, frozen into inaction, couldn't decide whether to gaze up at the house, turn towards Matthew or return the squeeze. So instead she contemplated the last full bloom of the nearest rosebush.

'We own this house now, of course,' he said, which meant that she ought to be gazing up at the house. 'Bought it whole from the landlord and now we own it—I own it. Not a brick belongs to the bank either.'

Bertha gazed more intently, her eyes settling on the geranium in a vase that stood on the sill of an upstairs room. She had not visited the upstairs rooms during her previous visit, the closet and wash room being situated downstairs behind the kitchen and down a cold passage.

'My salary at the post office is not excessive,' Matthew continued. 'However, as a senior counterman I do earn a little over five hundred pounds.' He paused, scrutinising the upstairs window.

Five hundred pounds! That seemed rather a lot, certainly more than double her own salary at the West Western. But the exact size of his salary was unimportant compared to the fact that he had told it to her. When a man told you how much his salary was, it meant only one thing.

'Indeed?' she replied.

'However, it is steady work and the prospects for a hard-working, dedicated employee are more than satisfactory. I intend to become sub-postmaster in time and then, well—' he sniffed and appeared almost abashed, 'it is not inconceivable that I should make postmaster before retirement.'

She tried to decide whether a response was required at this point and, if so, what that response might be. She nodded, her head a little to one side, implying an intelligent understanding of the situation.

'I therefore consider myself to be...to be in a position, a good position you might almost say, to make an offer of matrimony to a young lady and to hope that that young lady might accept it.'

What young lady? Me? thought Bertha, confused then flustered and finally a little annoyed—after all, what sort of a proposal was that? It hadn't even been a question. She took a deep breath.

'Well, I think that that young lady is in a position to accept a proposal of matrimony—should one come her way,' she replied tartly, fixing her gaze as haughtily as she could on the one remaining bloom in the rosebush.

There was a short silence and she was pleased to see she had nonplussed him.

'Miss Flaxheed—Bertha—would you consent to be my wife?'

'Yes, I would,' she replied unequivocally, and now there was no reason at all not to turn and face him and allow him to take both her gloved hands and to risk, yes, to give him a smile. After all, it was the happiest day of her life.

'Well! This is marvellous, quite marvellous!' exclaimed Matthew and then, remembering himself, he put a hand inside his jacket and pulled out a ring. 'May I?'

She nodded and let him unbutton her left glove and roll it slowly down her hand and her fingers, then slip the ring over her engagement finger. It stuck at her knuckle and had to be worked around and around a number of times before it would go any further, but when it had and she was able to look at it, it was very fine. A simple narrow gold band with two tiny rubies on either side of a slightly larger pearl. Victorian in style, it was true, but with a certain understated elegance. She was very pleased.

'Shall we go inside? I know Mother and Aunt Daisy will be keen to offer their congratulations.' He opened the wooden gate to let her pass.

As the gate banged back against the fence post the one remaining rose shed its petals in a pink arc on the path and Matthew stepped on them as he went to open the front door.

'Do have another muffin, Miss Flaxheed.'

Bertha contemplated the almost-transparent china plate that was being offered to her and on which were another eight buttered muffins. On the small mahogany tea trolley beside Aunt Daisy were three more such plates, one laden with slices of gingerbread, one with Madeira cake and one with teacakes. The piece of uneaten Madeira and the large chunks of Aunt Daisy's homemade ginger-bread on her own plate were, she hoped, hidden by the remains of her last muffin.

'Oh I don't think I can,' she said, looking to Matthew for assistance but he, she was fairly certain, had only had one muffin and less than half a slice of gingerbread. The two old ladies had themselves barely nibbled a teacake each. There was a lot of food left over. 'Well, perhaps just a small one?' she suggested helplessly, took the smallest muffin and placed it on her plate.

That Mrs Lake and Aunt Daisy had been expecting her—and possibly her entire family—was evident from the quantity of tea they had laid out. Mrs Lake had triumphantly wheeled the trolley in from the kitchen only seconds after she and Matthew had stepped into the lounge to share the happy news.

'How marvellous! Daisy, isn't it marvellous?' Mrs Lake had exclaimed, turning to her elder sister.

'Marvellous!' agreed Aunt Daisy beaming at them. 'You will join us for tea?'

Bertha took a small nibble of her second muffin and looked up into the radiant faces of Mrs Lake and Aunt Daisy who were perched side by side on the settee. Matthew, on a chair, was smiling brightly at her. She swallowed her mouthful with difficulty and smiled brightly back.

In the hallway, a huge grandfather clock ticked noisily. And then it ticked again. And again. The silence grew until very soon it had filled the whole of the tiny lounge so that there was hardly space enough to take a breath. Bertha focused on the plate balanced on her lap and prepared to take another mouthful of muffin, even though the crumbs of her last mouthful were clogging her throat.

Would she be living here, in this house? The dimly lit room they sat in was so crammed to bursting with heavy Victorian furniture that there was barely room for the four of them to sit.

'You will be glad to leave the telephone room, I expect, Miss Flaxheed?' said Mrs Lake suddenly, and Bertha looked up.

'Oh, the exchange! Yes, I—' she began automatically, and then she paused.

That was a rather big assumption, wasn't it? That she disliked the world of business and was just waiting for the excuse to leave paid employment forever? Then she thought of the endless hours she had spent perched on a high stool speaking into a transmitter that flattened her hairstyle and gave her a sore ear, and of the endless callers who either treated her like she was a machine or were rude to her. And she thought of Miss Crisp, creeping around the switchroom like a belligerent spirit, and Elsie, who was stuck with Bernie; of Nellie who was fortunate to be working at the West Western at all, and of poor Nancy, widowed with a little girl. What future did any of them have?

Her reply was emphatic. 'Yes, indeed, I shall be very glad to leave. And very glad to take up my new duties and responsibilities,' she added as an afterthought, and saw Matthew nod approvingly.

'Telephones are such fearsome beasts, of course,' announced Aunt Daisy, with a glance at Mrs Lake for confirmation. 'We do not have one here as we have no need for one, and I feel sure they are not quite respectable nor healthy either.'

Bertha smiled tightly because she knew all this, Aunt Daisy having said the very same thing on her previous visit.

Mrs Lake and her elder sister were as alike as two sisters divided by seven years in age and a lifetime of marriage and motherhood for one, and spinsterhood and paid employment for the other, could be. They were perhaps in their late sixties and early seventies, both tiny of frame with child-sized hands, thin-faced with long narrow noses, their wispy grey hair tied up in a neat high bun. They both dressed in heavy black crinoline skirts that rustled at every movement and high-collared white blouses. By comparison, Miss Crisp seemed the height of fashion.

The two sisters operated as a team, so that it was a constant challenge to remember which was which. One would open a door, the other would pull the trolley through, one would hold up the plate, the other would cut the cake and place the slice on the plate. It all happened wordlessly and seamlessly. They both perched on the edge of an overstuffed maroon leather settee and stared at her in unblinking silence.

'These muffins are delicious,' Bertha said, and Mrs Lake and Aunt Daisy looked collectively pleased.

'We made them specially,' confided Mrs Lake and Bertha thought, Supposing I had turned Matthew down?

'I do like a good muffin,' she replied.

'You'll soon be making your own,' observed Matthew proudly as though he had offered to show her how to drive or had made her captain of a cricket team.

The clock chimed the hour loudly and for seven counts no one had to say anything at all. Seven o'clock. They had been here one hour.

'And what about your own people, my dear?' said Mrs Lake abruptly, her tea cup poised in mid-air halfway between saucer and mouth.

'Yes indeed, you'll be wanting to tell your own people the wonderful news,' agreed Aunt Daisy, and the way they said Your Own People made Bertha feel as though she were of some other race entirely rather than just Bertha Flaxheed of Wells Lane on the other side of High Street.

'Well, yes, I expect I shall tell them,' she replied. 'You must come over to tea on Sunday, Matthew, and we shall tell them then.'

And this was such an odd, such a significant thing to do—arranging for your new fiancé to come to tea so that you could tell your parents you were engaged to be married—that for a moment the room, the plate, the muffin in her hand, the two little old ladies leaning eagerly towards, seemed quite unreal.

Then she saw that her fiancé was Mr Matthew Lake of the post office whom Mum and Dad had already met and whom they had thought rather old and had said very little to, and suddenly it all seemed very real indeed.

'Yes, that would be very nice,' said Matthew, and he didn't appear nervous at the prospect.

Now that tea had been settled, they plunged into another silence until Matthew finally said, 'Well, perhaps we had better be getting along.'

'Yes, yes indeed, we must,' Bertha agreed, putting down her plate.

'Oh, but Miss Flaxheed hasn't finished her muffin, Matthew.'

'That's alright, really.' Bertha was already on her feet.

'Don't want to spoil our fish supper,' agreed Matthew.

Oh, they were going to Pontison's after all.

Aunt Daisy went out to the hallway and retrieved their jackets. 'Don't tire Miss Flaxheed out, Matthew,' she said in a chiding manner.

'Yes, you mind Miss Flaxheed gets home at a respect-able hour, Matthew dear,' agreed Mrs Lake, holding out Bertha's jacket.

'Now then, Mother, we're only going for a fish supper at Pontison's then I shall escort her straight home. Ready, my dear?'

Bertha nodded and made for the front door. How, she wondered, did you say goodbye to your future mother-in-law and her elder sister? Her mind baulked at the idea of kissing them. She turned as she reached the door, smiled as brightly as she could, and waved a cheery farewell. 'Thanks ever so much. Goodbye,' she said, and Mrs Lake and Aunt Daisy smiled brightly back and waved goodbye. Bertha stumbled out into the cool night air and made her way quickly along the path to the gate.

'Well. This is lovely, isn't it?' said Matthew as they walked arm in arm back along Oakton Way.

'Yes, lovely,' said Bertha.

Sunday came around, as Sundays do, very quickly indeed—quicker, in fact, than most, because this was a Sunday filled with nervous trepidation.

Bertha had remained steadfastly silent on the subject of engagements for forty-eight hours. Not that either of her parents appeared to have noticed the fact, Dad's attention being entirely taken up with the curious machinations of the local council with whom he had become increasingly obsessed to the point of considering standing for election himself, and Mum's time being taken up with The Saving of Janie, her sister's eldest, who had got herself in the family way by some young man at the factory who looked in no hurry to marry her. Amid such uproar, a secret betrothal and the appearance of an engagement ring on the finger of their own eldest daughter went entirely unnoticed.

And so be it, thought Bertha. She certainly did not need their approval any more than Jemima had sought their approval to marry Ronnie. Jem had simply come home late one evening and mentioned it casually over breakfast the following morning, right between the first pot of tea and the arrival of the Sunday paper. Then she had flounced out and acted like Lady Muck all the rest of the day and Dad had been absolutely furious. But there was little he could have done about it because it had already happened. It was soon after that he had begun to get interested in the local council.

No, announcing your engagement so casually over Sunday breakfast, without your intended even being there, was not quite right, Bertha decided. She and Matthew would do it properly and respectably and everyone would be glad and congratulations would be offered and toasts made and perhaps Dad would pour them all a glass of sherry. And the best part was that Jemima and Ronnie would be there too, because they usually came to Sunday tea if they weren't doing something more important. And of course she would make it absolutely clear that Matthew had Prospects, that he Owned his Own House and was Comfortable. Ronnie and Jemima lived in a dreary little flat above the butcher's in High Street. She had only visited the place once. It had smelled of sawdust and fresh meat.

Matthew arrived as the clock on the mantelpiece struck four and Bertha, who had been brazenly studying the wedding announcements in the *Gazette*, looked up and met Dad's eye.

Dad's expression said, *Punctual—I like a fella to be punctual*, which was the sort of thing Dad did say, but he could just as easily have said, *Ay ay, this chap's a stickler, better watch out for him.* Either way, both Bertha and Mum, who was knitting for cousin Janie's baby ('poor little mite') remained in their seats while Dad got slowly to his feet, smoothed down his trousers, buttoned up his waistcoat, flattened his head where his hair had once been, and generally acted as though this was Leadheath Hall and he was still Mr Flaxheed, the butler.

He's going to call the lounge the 'parlour', thought Bertha.

'That'll be your Mr Lake,' observed Mum, as though there were any number of gentleman callers at this time on a Sunday afternoon and she had, by means of clever deduction, surmised which one it was.

'Of course it's Mr Lake,' Bertha replied, and she recalled with sudden clarity the tea with Matthew's mother and aunt on Friday evening. Did Matthew think of her parents in the same way she thought of his? The idea was unsettling but, once entertained, would not be dislodged.

'You'll find us in the parlour,' Dad was saying in the hallway.

'Goodness! I'd better see about tea,' exclaimed Mum, as though she hadn't been preparing the tea all morning. She jumped up so that wool and needles cascaded in all directions, and Matthew and Dad, entering the room at that exact moment, were met by a particularly rebellious ball of sky-blue wool ('Bound to be a boy, they always are').

Matthew stooped to retrieve the recalcitrant ball and held it out to Mum, who looked momentarily disconcerted, as though unsure whether to greet Mr Lake or to thank him for returning the wool. She settled on the latter.

'Oh you're too kind, Mr Lake. Isn't he too kind, my dear?' she said.

Bertha agreed that Mr Lake was too kind and silently wished her mother would go and see about the tea.

'Bertha,' said Matthew, coming to her and touching her hand. Behind him Dad's nostrils flared, which meant he was shocked to his core that this man had addressed his daughter by her Christian name in his parlour.

'Hullo,' she replied, not quite able to return the greeting in full. But still, in a few short minutes the news would be out and they could all relax.

Matthew was shown to the second-best armchair and Dad settled himself in his own armchair. Bertha sat down too. She exchanged a glance with Matthew: they must wait until Mum had returned. And Jemima and Ronnie weren't here either, though they often arrived late—sometimes by a quarter of an hour.

There was a silence. A bewildering list of conversation topics flashed through her mind—the post office union issues, tea with Aunt Daisy and Mrs Lake, the worsening conditions of the miners—but they were all unsuitable. Something, she felt fairly certain, had just happened with a well-known cricketer, but what, and which cricketer, she didn't know.

Finally Dad said, 'You'll have seen what those daft idiots at the council have gone and done, Mr Lake?'

Bertha sank down a little into her chair. What had the council done?

'The bus route between Rosemont and Creffield roads?' said Matthew, obviously hazarding a guess.

'Allotments!' said Dad, dismissing the bus routes with an angry shake of the head. 'Daft idiots are threatening to do away with residents' allotments *permanently* in order to sell the land to developers.'

Ah yes, the tricky allotment question. Dad had been banging on about it for the best part of a fortnight. Not that he had an allotment or knew anyone who did, but it was the principle of the thing, whatever that principle might be.

'No, I haven't seen anything about it,' said Matthew. 'I've been glued to the cricket news this last week.' He sat up, suddenly enthusiastic. 'You saw that Mr Jack Hobbs has beaten Grace's record of one hundred and twenty-six centuries—and fourteen in a single season!'

Yes, that was it, thought Bertha; Mr Hobbs getting some big score or other. Then she looked carefully at Matthew, not having realised before that he was a cricket follower. Dad, of course, detested cricket. It was a game for Eton schoolboys, or something like that.

Silence fell once more and Bertha's heart raced anxiously. Where on earth were Jemima and Ronnie?

'Here we are, a nice bit of tea,' said Mum, carrying the tray into the lounge, and Bertha leapt up to help her. The next few minutes were filled with the normal questions and thankyous of polite company at Sunday afternoon tea, but all too soon the four of them were seated with cups of tea at their elbows and plates of sardine sandwiches on their laps and only the weather left to debate. It was quarter past four—surely Jemima was on her way?

'You are knitting baby clothes, Mrs Flaxheed. Is there a happy event on the horizon?'

Horror of horrors! Bertha froze, the sardine sandwich dissolving to dust on her tongue, and her eyes flew to her mother, who had flushed red and seemed frozen in horrified inaction. Dad was expressionless but for a twitching of a muscle in his jaw.

'Dad, Matthew and I have some news,' said Bertha, smiling grimly and turning to include Matthew in her announcement. Matthew hastily put down his plate and scrambled to his feet. 'Yes, yes, so we have. Indeed, we do. We...' He turned to her, then back to Dad. Mum appeared to be redundant in this conversation. 'I have asked Miss Flaxheed, Bertha, to be my wife and she has done me the honour of consenting.'

There, it was out. There was no going back, there need be no more silences, no more raised eyebrows or flaring nostrils, it was done and she was officially engaged. All they needed was to await the congratulations.

But the front door was at that moment flung open and there were hurried footsteps in the hallway.

'Alright, we're here at last. Don't fuss, Mum. Ronnie had some piano recital thing on and I don't know what else. Anyway, it doesn't matter because we're here now and we've got news, so you'd better stop what you're doing and listen!'

And here was Jemima marching into the lounge, plonking herself down on the settee with Ronnie bringing up the rear, suddenly remembering to remove his hat.

'Give me a kiss, Mum, as we shall be having a baby! What do you think of that? Well, aren't you going to congratulate me?'

CHAPTER FIFTEEN

MAY 1926

THE BABY WAS THREE months old and so far all it had done was cry, soil its nappy, dribble and vomit, and sometimes it did all those things at once.

Jemima kicked the kitchen door shut and clamped her hands over her ears. But the miserable flat that she and Ronnie lived in was so poky and cramped it was impossible to block any sound out at all no matter where you were or how many doors you slammed.

The baby paused, hiccoughed and let out a louder yell.

What was wrong with it? She had fed it, changed it, turned it over. She had even held the rotten little thing in her arms and paced up and down the hallway to calm it down but even that had only stopped it for five minutes.

'*Stop* it! Stop *crying*!' she ordered, but that only caused it to cry more.

It had cried all last night from the moment she had put it down to the moment when Ronnie had noisily let himself in, sometime after midnight, and then it had cried until he had left again for work this morning.

It was the Union. The Union and their stupid threats of a big important strike. A pathetic, pointless waste-of-every-body's-time strike, a strike that wasn't ever going to happen. And Ronnie was coming home after midnight because of it and leaving her alone with this...this...this *crying* thing. Coming home at all hours, full to bursting with this resolution and that demand and the stupid government saying this and the even more stupid Union saying something else and what did it matter anyway when everyone knew, they all *knew*—except Ronnie and his stupid little league— that there wasn't going to *be* a strike tomorrow or the next day or next week or next year, and in the meantime here she was all alone with the baby crying day after day after day and driving her to distraction.

'STOP! *Stop crying!'* she shouted, hands over her ears, but the crying continued and she flung open the door and marched into the hallway and into the baby's tiny boxroom. When she saw it lying there, so small and helpless and red-faced and wretched, she wanted to pick it up and shake it and shake it until it stopped.

It had looked so sweet, so small and vulnerable, she remembered, the first few days after it was born; sort of tawny and downy, like a little chick. Her heart had melted. Its face and hands and feet so tiny you wondered how they could possibly work. But work they did, and soon the face was screwed up in rage and the hands and feet plucking at the blanket and grabbing at everything and the downiness and the tawniness, which was just a touch of jaundice, had faded to a bald pink. Not a chick, a monster.

She turned and fled back to the hallway and into the mean little lounge, but the sight of the mean little dining table with the three mean-looking, mismatched chairs and the patched and overstuffed settee left over from the previous tenant and the single bookshelf donated by Dad and the horrible, ugly dresser (a present from Clive and Rose in Camberwell) that looked as though it belonged in some other century made her want to shout again, louder, and she returned to the kitchen.

It was the second day of May, a promisingly warm spring Sunday that had turned into a damp spring evening, and now the kitchen was as chilly as an icebox in January.

It was 1926—*1926!*—and most houses, certainly most houses in Acton, had gas cookers, but not Mr and Mrs Ronnie Booth, oh no! They had a range, a solid fuel range that you had to kick into action first thing in the morning when it was still dark outside, then feed constantly with coal or wood to prevent it dying. Other people—people who lived in Maida Vale and Kensington and whose husbands wore suits and bowlers and worked in the City—had machines that did their washing for them. Or, rather, their maids had machines to do the washing for them. Their wives no longer had to sit in front of the tub and scrub for a whole morning then drag everything downstairs to the yard to put it through the wringer and hang it, still sodden, on the line just in time for a downpour. But it was laughable to think of Ronnie ever buying such a machine for her. And laughable that she, Jemima Flaxheed, late of the tearoom of Gossup and Batch of Regent Street, should actually desire one!

She let out an abrupt laugh and for a moment, in the other room, the baby paused in surprise, then, with a deep breath, it started up again.

So this is it, thought Jemima, her hands still pressed to her ears, this was her lot: to feed the baby one minute and the range the next; to scrub Ronnie's dirty clothes with her bare hands and hump great loads of washing up and down the stairs; to spend all afternoon making tea then all evening cleaning it up again in that dirty, cracked enamel sink; to heave Mum's old black perambulator up and down the stairs each time she took Baby outside and, when she had the bright idea of leaving the wretched perambulator in the downstairs porch in the yard, to have Mr Parson the butcher tell her to move it and get angry when she refused.

And that was another thing, they were living above a shop! A *butcher's* shop! Parson's in High Street, a place you never went to unless you were living on charity because the cuts were small and sometimes the meat wasn't fresh and here they were *living over it*! As if the baby's crying wasn't enough to send you to a madhouse, at five o'clock every morning except Sundays they were woken by the delivery van and the sawing of bones. Every morning, *saw saw saw*, enough to set your teeth on edge—and after having to go through all that you'd think old Parson, the stingy old miser, would at least have the decency to give you a bit of shoulder or a spare chop or something but no, all you got from him were demands to move your perambulator. Well, she was *damned* if she was going to move her perambulator for anyone, let alone him. The old sod could just step around it and no matter if he did bang into it all the time.

The back window was open and even though it was Sunday and Parson's was shut on Sundays, a sudden waft of sawdust and raw meat seeped into the flat.

What kind of a man brought his wife to live *here*?

The kind of man who thought more of his comrades in the league than he did of his own wife, who cared more for some unknown miner's family in Worksop than he did for his own family right here in Acton. Lord knew, she didn't need a big house; a poky terrace would do; a two-up, two-down with a parcel of yard out the front and a WC out the back would do. It wasn't much to ask, was it? And they could rent at first, couldn't they? But oh, no! While other wives lived in comfort with gas cookers and washing machines, she was meant to be content with this mean little one-and-a-half-bedroom flat above Parson's.

Bertha, meanwhile, was queening it in a three-bedroom house with a garden and rosebushes in Oakton Way.

In the other room the baby gulped, choked, and fell silent.

Jemima held her breath and stood motionless, her heart thudding noisily.

With a little cough the baby began to grizzle once more.

The creamy-coloured peeling wallpaper that covered the walls began to turn a violent red colour and a pulse started throbbing in her forehead. She couldn't remember getting up but now, somehow, she was standing in the hallway, the blood hurtling through her body so that her arms ached and her fingers clenched the air. But her body had nothing to do and nowhere to go except out into the yard to rescue the washing off the line.

She would go outside. She would rescue the washing off the line.

But it had been spitting all evening and the washing, she knew, would already be wet through. And anyway there was another pile of nappies to wash and Ronnie's work clothes still not dry for tomorrow though she had washed them on Thursday. Perhaps it would be a good thing if there was a strike because then she wouldn't have to wash his work clothes, but then she remembered the schools weren't going on strike no matter what happened with the government so really there was no escape.

No escape at all.

She flung open the door to the flat and stepped, stumbled, down the cold concrete steps to the downstairs door, which was permanently ajar because the hinges were rusted. She tugged open the door and pushed the huge old black perambulator out of the way and stood in the yard, breathing deeply.

Breathing deeply.

The rain sprayed a fine mist onto her face and it felt cool and calming and she liked the way her hair grew damp and heavy and had that wet hair smell about it, and how her dress clung to her legs and the drops dribbled down her arms and along her fingers and hung in droplets at her fingertips before sliding off and splashing on the muddy yard beneath her feet.

She smiled. She thought about laughing out loud but there was no one to hear, Parson's being closed on a

Sunday and the shop empty and silent for once. The smell of sawdust and raw meat still lingered. It had begun to seem like there would never be a time when she couldn't smell sawdust and raw meat.

She would go out for a walk. No matter about Baby, Baby never noticed if you were there or not, except when it was hungry or needed changing, and even then you never knew if it realised it had been fed or changed or not. What did it matter if you went out on your own and left Baby asleep while you did the shopping or went to the park or looked at the fashions in the shop windows? Baby had never come to any harm and it was ridiculous to be tied to the house like a slave when your husband was at work every day, or out at yet another pointless rally, and only took Baby out in the perambulator on a Sunday afternoon for all the world to see what a wonderful dad he was. Oh yes, a wonderful dad—didn't they all say so? And she, stuck indoors like a slave.

Like a prisoner.

The rain eased a little and she looked up at the grey dusk and wondered when Ronnie would deign to come home. He had come home late nearly every night of the last week filled with all the news as though what Mr Baldwin said and what the government did or what the union demanded could have anything to do with them. With her. And now someone was on strike—the coalminers, no doubt; it was always the coalminers—and you'd think that would be an end to it, but no! Now they were saying it's a general strike or revolution! And what did they think that would accomplish? she had asked. Did he think the Russians were better off now than before?

So they had fought and Ronnie had gone out. Although there had been more to it than just the Russians.

Baby had stopped. Jemima cocked an ear in the rain and listened. There was traffic in High Street, she could hear the splash of tyres as a bus passed by and in the distance the bells of All Saints calling people to Evensong.

They would get a good turnout tonight, despite the rain, because people were eager to hear the latest about whether there really was to be a strike or not in the morning.

The strike. It was all people talked about. It was all they had talked about at tea that afternoon at Mum and Dad's.

Dad had been reading from the *Gazette* when they'd arrived—late, thanks to Baby regurgitating its milk all over Ronnie's shirt front and he not having another shirt to change into (and now everyone thinking it was Ronnie who fed Baby because it was his shirt ruined and no one thinking that most of her own dresses had been ruined weeks ago and no one noticing because where did she ever go that she got a chance to wear a nice dress?).

So Bertha and Matthew had already been there and settled on the settee this last half-hour or more with their cups of tea and their bread and butter and jam and all nice and cosy and she and Ronnie arriving late and getting a look from Dad that said, *You might at least make an effort to arrive on time for tea that your mother's made and your own sister and her new husband already here and settled,* but he'd said nothing, only shook Ronnie's hand and said 'Evening, love' to her and tickled Baby under the chin and Baby had chuckled and gurgled as though butter wouldn't melt.

'They say it'll be anarchy and revolution,' announced Dad, sitting down, and Jemima had groaned because it was obvious they weren't discussing the Cup Final or the Residents' Allotments Association.

'I'll have a cuppa, Mum,' she said, sitting on her old chair by the window and passing Baby to Ronnie. Bertha wanted to hold Baby, you could tell even without looking, but Bertha would wait to be asked. She was sitting, all prim and wifely, beside her new husband.

Her new husband: Mr Matthew Lake who worked behind the counter at the post office and who was forty if he was a day! His and Bertha's wedding at the registry office in the town hall had been a small affair compared to her own. Perhaps the bride was ashamed of marrying a man so much older than herself? At any rate, the ceremony had been very brief with no organ music or hymns, and if Jemima hadn't got the confetti herself it would have been as flat as cake you'd made yourself. They'd had a wedding breakfast at the Duke of York Tavern and Aunt Nora and the girls—Janie so big you wondered how she dared show her face—and Mr Lake's mother and aunt, who looked old enough to be at their own funerals. A very sober affair it had been, with speeches so stiff and formal you'd have thought someone had died, and perhaps someone had because what kind of a young girl, even someone like Bertha, would get herself saddled to a man who was forty and worked at the post office?

Afterwards the newlyweds had gone to Scarborough for the week and good luck to them in late November with the sky as grey as the sea and who knew what sort of lodgings. She shuddered, remembering the Sea View Bed and Breakfast in Torquay where she and Ronnie had stayed for six grim nights last March.

And here they were, Mr and Mrs Matthew Lake, married these five months gone and playing the Happily Married Couple, if you please!

'Another slice of bread, Matthew dear?' asked Bertha, offering the plate.

'Thank you, my dear,' said Matthew, carefully selecting a slice and placing it on his plate.

'Jam?'

'Thank you kindly.'

Sickening. Who were they trying to fool? What kind of a marriage could it be, him so old, her grateful to finally be someone's wife? And as for the bedroom! Well, the mind reeled to imagine it:

Another go, my dear?
Thank you, my dear.
Pyjamas?
Thank you kindly.

Ugh! It was disgusting. It was unimaginable. Did he think about it, she wondered, during the day when he was stamping the mail and tearing off a sheet of stamps for you behind the counter? Did he think about tearing off a sheet of stamps when he was in bed with Bertha?

'Jem, a slice of walnut cake?'

Jemima quashed the image and stared at the plate her mother was holding out. She took a piece of cake absent-mindedly. Did people think about *that* with her and Ronnie? Did they wonder what went on in the bedroom? Funny, she hadn't thought about it before the marriage, so satisfied had she been to be Mrs Ronnie Booth, and then suddenly she was heavy with the baby and she had walked about the park and up and down the lane proudly with her still-unmarried elder sister on her arm and never a thought for what folk might think. Except, of course, what a pretty mother she would make. Now she wondered. Now she took a sideways look at Ronnie and wondered. He was thin, he always had been, and his clothes had a tendency to be too large, and his bones, if he showed them to her when the light was still on, were sharp and tending to jut out of his skin. He wasn't a tall man, and not manly perhaps, like Jamie Cannon was manly, but you never felt out of your depth with him like you might with Jamie. You always knew what he was thinking and how you could get him to think what you were thinking, and it was like that in bed when the lights were out and it was so cold you had to keep your nightdress on and hope the old bed didn't creak too much in case old stingy Parson was still in the shop downstairs.

Ronnie had been so funny on their wedding night, treating her as though she might break—as though it were her first time! She hadn't said anything—some things you didn't tell your husband—and after that every night, regular as clockwork, not as frantic perhaps as old Gilfroy, but regular and no more fiddling about in stock cupboards and fumbling to do yourself up quick-sharp in case anyone came by. But since Baby, nothing, almost as though he was too scared of hurting her, and here she was with her figure back and men looking at her and not thinking for a moment that the baby could be hers. And Ronnie off at his stupid meetings every night and not back till late and thinking her already asleep.

'Folk have got to eat,' proclaimed Dad solemnly, wrenching her thoughts back to the present.

'We *are* eating, Dad,' she pointed out through a mouthful of walnut cake.

'And we're the lucky ones!' declared Ronnie, and the way he pounced on her, it was as though he'd been waiting for her to say just those very words all afternoon. All week.

Jemima pinched the piece of walnut cake between her thumb and first finger until it crumbled and collapsed onto her plate in little bits.

'Do you think,' she said, 'we could go for five minutes without discussing the dreary old, boring old miners? It's so *dull!*'

Beside her she felt Ronnie stiffen, but he said nothing. Sitting opposite, Bertha picked up her teacup and took a quick sip, her eyes fixed on a point on the carpet between them.

In his armchair, Dad frowned. 'It's what I just said, folk have got to eat, whether they be rich folk or poor folk, and folk that don't have food in their bellies will be restless until they do. Stands to reason. Don't take no fancy parliament fella in Westminster, nor no red-faced union leader on a soapbox, to tell us that. We can see it with our own eyes. Question is, what's to be done about it and how are they going to go about doing it? That's the only thing far as I can make out.' And he cast a challenging glance at his audience, or more precisely at his two sons-in-law, as they, at least, could be trusted to have some grasp of the nation's current precarious political situation.

Jemima snorted.

Next to Bertha, Matthew licked his lips and faced his father-in-law thoughtfully as though he doubted the validity of what Dad had said and his authority to say it. Just as though he was aware that he was almost of Dad's generation and was waiting, none too patiently, in the wings to assume the role of Head of the Family.

'That's true, of course,' he conceded carefully, and you knew from the way he said it that he was merely being polite and that Dad's opinions really counted for very little, 'but there will always be rich and poor folk. That's human nature. You see it in every society from Calcutta to the New Guinea tribesman...'

Oh Lord, what did he know of New Guinea tribesmen? thought Jemima, silently rolling her eyes. He weighed parcels in a post office, for heaven's sake!

'...but the fact remains we live in a civilised society where a chap and his family can get on in life if they so desire, and we have a very good system of parliament that is the envy of every other civilised nation and which allows us to resolve disputes and find solutions without recourse to violence.'

Ronnie fairly jumped up from the settee in his agitation and Jemima braced herself.

'*Violence?*' he replied furiously. 'If you were...were... were *starving* and your family was starving because your wages had steadily been decreasing for the last *ten years* and your hours have been cut and you see your boss living in a big house with servants and driving a big car and when you complain you're thrown out of your job and left to live on the...the *charity* of others not much better off than yourself, what would you do then? I bet you would have recourse to violence then. I know I would!'

Ronnie's voice had risen during this little speech and he had got to his feet in his excitement. As he finished on this defiant note that seemed to be aimed straight at Matthew there was a silence. Ronnie sat back down and upset his plate, which was resting on the arm of the settee, so that the walnut cake fell onto the carpet butter-side down and crumbs scattered over his lap and over the chintz fabric of the settee.

'Oh dear,' said Mum amiably, and it was hard to know if she was lamenting Ronnie's overheated little speech or the demise of the walnut cake and her carpet. She got up and went over to pick up the debris at Ronnie's feet. 'You'd think,' she added, slowly straightening up and surveying them all pointedly, 'that with two sides on which to fall, a slice of cake would occasionally fall on the unbuttered side, but no, never happens. Every time it's butter-side down,' and, having imparted this nugget of wisdom, she placed the errant slice on the trolley and gave the plate back to Ronnie. 'Flapjack?'

'Thank you,' mumbled Ronnie shamefacedly.

'Anyway, I really don't see how a stupid strike in a coalmine should have the slightest effect on us,' Jemima pointed out, because someone had to say it.

Opposite her, Bertha gave one of those pursed-lips tutting noises that, as elder sister married to a postal worker, seemed to be her duty now. 'That,' she declared, 'is because you don't keep abreast of the State of the Nation.'

'The State of the Nation!' Jemima scoffed. 'What do you know about the State of the Nation? What do any of us know except what we hear in the queue at the greengrocer's?'

'We read the newspapers, we see the newsreels...'

'You young ladies don't know anything about it,' Dad interrupted, 'and can't be expected to neither. It's not a lady's duty to know these things.' He turned to Ronnie, who swallowed and suddenly looked quite young. 'As for starving miners turning to violence, I won't hear of such things in my house, if you please. This is a law-abiding Christian household and we don't hold with that kind of communistic talk.'

Ronnie opened his mouth to protest but Dad held up a hand and continued. 'I'm sure we all agree those poor men and their families are doing it tough and that Mr Baldwin and his government have not done all that they might to assist them, but that's no excuse for the kind of behaviour they go in for in Foreign Parts.'

Ronnie, duly reprimanded, studied the floral pattern on the edge of his plate and turned pink from his chin to the tips of his ears. Jemima felt a rush of fury—fancy being so outspoken and then so cowardly as to allow Dad to tell him off in front of everyone! Why didn't he say something in his own defence? At least look Dad square in the eyes? But no, he sulked like a schoolboy and she, his wife, was humiliated.

'Yes, Mum, thank you, I will,' said Matthew to his mother-in-law as she offered him a flapjack. He sat back with a relaxed attitude and Jemima thought, You wouldn't put up with Dad telling you off, would you? You'd stand up for yourself. She observed her brother-in-law carefully and she observed Bertha reaching up and brushing a crumb from her husband's shirt front then sitting up so primly and proudly and surveying the room as if to say, Look at my husband, Mr Matthew Lake of the GPO, who thinks before he speaks and knows how to defend himself and who won't be told off by anyone.

'Aren't you giving Baby any tea?' asked Bertha sweetly.

Jemima smiled back at her even more sweetly. 'If you knew anything at all about babies, you would know that when Baby is asleep the one thing you don't do is wake Baby up.'

Bertha flushed.

'Any rate, I doubt it'll come to a general strike,' declared Dad with a finality that was intended to prevent further discussion. Unfortunately Ronnie, who had remained infuriatingly silent when he ought to have spoken up, was at once on the edge of his seat again.

'I believe there will be, sir. And if not tomorrow then in the next few days—it has to happen. The government's pushed the unions into a corner so they've nowhere else to go and the unions are solid enough that—'

'The unions are infiltrated with red sympathisers intent only on anarchy and revolution!' interrupted Matthew, and beside him Bertha squirmed, perhaps unused to hearing her husband raise his voice. 'It may be all very well on the Continent,' he went on, 'but it's not the British way of going about things. Your union pals will find out soon enough that the British people have no stomach for that kind of thing.'

Jemima waited, her eyes on Matthew. He spoke with a clear, strong voice that rang out with the authority of conviction and made you believe what he said. Well, it made you listen. Unlike Ronnie who ought, you would expect, to be used to expressing his viewpoints in public by now. Perhaps it was just that Matthew was so much older than Ronnie. A man, in fact, compared to Ronnie, who at this moment looked like a silly schoolboy hauled up before the headmaster.

Ronnie's eyes were almost popping out of his head.

'Why can't any of you see?' he demanded. 'Things can't go on as they are! This—this *Empire* is built on the... the backs of workers who are now starving in the streets! *It just isn't fair!*'

Jemima stared down at her hands in her lap and in that moment she despised him. Despised him as she had never despised Dad or Mum or Bertha or Matthew or the fat, smug customers in the tearoom or even spineless

Godfrey Gilfroy and his little wife at home in leafy, dull Rickmansworth. No, this was a burning fire that raced through the limbs and made her fingers rigid in her lap and her face burn with white heat.

'It just isn't fair!' she mimicked. 'Most people stopped saying that when they left the nursery. Wouldn't you say, Matthew?'

There was a silence and she smiled at Matthew, who returned her look with a rather surprised and somewhat embarrassed expression. Bertha had flushed even redder and wasn't looking at anyone. Jemima couldn't see what Ronnie was doing and frankly she didn't care.

'That's enough, girl,' said Dad in a stern voice, but Jemima ignored him because it was fine for the men to speak their minds so why shouldn't she?

'Anyway, I've got some leftover ham from dinner in the icebox if anyone'd like a slice?' inquired Mum, as though finishing a conversation from earlier. No one replied.

Jemima nibbled a crumb of walnut cake which, perhaps in deference to the atmosphere in the living room, had gone distinctly stale at the edges.

Suddenly Ronnie stood up. Jemima remained perfectly still, though her heart beat loudly.

'There's a rally tonight,' he announced. 'Steyne Hall. We're to wait for word from Westminster to see if the strike's on.'

He paused, no one said anything and Jemima thought, Is he waiting for us to offer our congratulations? Or is he expecting us to accompany him? In the end it appeared that all Ronnie was waiting for were the right words to excuse himself. 'So if you'll pardon me leaving early, sir...' He swallowed as he dipped his head at Dad. ('Sir'! Why couldn't he say 'Dad' like Matthew did?) Then he nodded at Mum and turned to Jemima, but there was no question of her going with him, surely he could see that there was

Baby to think of, anyway. So Ronnie ducked out and a moment later the front door opened and closed.

'I'll have some of that leftover ham, Mum,' she had said, and she had eaten two slices before Matthew had offered to escort her and Baby home.

And now it was late, the rain had stopped and the traffic was silent on High Street and still Ronnie hadn't returned.

Jemima brushed the raindrops from her shoulders irritably. How childish. How like Ronnie to stay out late to punish her. Did he really think she cared? Did he really think she noticed his presence or not? It was like having another child underfoot. She turned and climbed the stairs to the flat to be met by silence.

Thank God.

But...

She crossed the tiny hallway in two strides, threw open the door to the little boxroom, and stood there in the moonlight staring at the cradle. Baby was quite still. And silent, utterly silent.

For a moment she was paralysed, every limb weighted down, and it seemed as though she might never be able to move again. Then Baby snuffled and sighed and all the feeling in her limbs flooded back so that she lurched forward and snatched the little thing up and clasped it tightly to her. She closed her eyes and fought down something hard that was stuck at the back of her throat, choking her.

Loud footsteps sounded outside and a moment later the front door opened then banged shut.

'Jem!'

A beam of light hit her but she didn't turn around. Baby stirred restlessly and let out a murmur of protest.

She held her hand over its eyes to shield it from the sudden light.

'Jem!'

He was behind her now in the bedroom doorway but before she could turn around he had come in and taken her roughly by the shoulders so that suddenly she was afraid. But only for a moment.

'It's happened!' he gasped, shaking her. 'It's really happened, from midnight it began! The strike has begun!'

She spun around, stunned. Ronnie's face was shiny with perspiration, the hair sticking up in a peak at his forehead. His eyes were wide, wild, excited.

Was this her husband? Was this the man she had married? She thrust Baby into his empty hands.

'Do you really think I *care* about your stupid strike? How can you be so *stupid*?' and she marched into the bedroom and slammed the door behind her.

CHAPTER SIXTEEN

MAY 1926

THE FOLLOWING MORNING IT was not, for once, Baby who woke her but a shout from outside in the street, followed immediately by an answering roar from what sounded like a large crowd of people. The roar was abruptly muffled by the growl of a bus engine, gears cranking and a conductor's bell, all of which made Jemima sit up with a start.

The strike. Had it started? If so, why could she hear a bus?

She was up and out of bed, grabbing her shawl and pulling it around her shoulders. She pulled aside the faded blue curtains, rubbed the mist from the window and peered out to the street below.

The first thing she saw was people, droves of them, in their working clothes and all on foot, moving in excited clusters east towards the city. On the road was every sort of motor vehicle you could imagine. From the earliest horseless carriages to the latest Morris, from charabancs to delivery vehicles, milk carts and even a hearse, all laden with passengers and all making their way slowly east. One vehicle, a fruit delivery van, carried a dozen bowler-hatted city gentlemen, crammed in like apples in a barrel. Behind it a brewer's dray pulled by a sluggish cart horse contained a gaggle of shop girls who waved at the crowds and blew them kisses until, accompanied by loud shrieks, the cart slid into a rut, tipping them all forward so that they tumbled over each other.

The bus that Jemima had heard was a few yards further up High Street. It was a big red double-decker General and it was surrounded by a vocal crowd of furious young men intent on stalling its progress, their faces contorted with rage.

Such hatred and the day had only just begun. She felt a shiver run across her shoulders and she pulled the shawl closer about her.

Forcing the reluctant window to open, she leaned her head out to hear their shouts. The slow-moving bus lurched to a halt in the congested traffic and the small crowd surged forward as though they would storm it by force.

At that moment a large open-topped touring car packed with police constables veered through the traffic, mounting the kerb and sending pedestrians scattering in all directions. It bore down on the stranded bus and disgorged its troops. They at once flung themselves at the crowd of boisterous strikers who had surrounded the bus, and for a few moments a confused scuffle ensued, during which punches were thrown, helmets were knocked to the ground and the traffic came to a complete halt before the strikers made a run for it, the constables in hot pursuit.

Yes, the strike had begun. And was this Ronnie's glorious revolution? Men brawling in the street?

In the next room Baby suddenly awoke and began to wail. And yes, there could be a General Strike, there could be a biblical flood or the Second Coming, but there was always Baby to feed and change, wasn't there? And where was Ronnie?

Baby's wails increased and as Jemima pushed herself up off the window sill to shut it up, the bedroom door opened and Ronnie stood in the doorway, already dressed.

'I'll be off then,' he announced, not meeting her eyes, instead reaching for his hat on the peg behind the door.

'Where are you going at this time? School won't even be open for another hour.'

She knew the answer before she'd finished asking the question.

'The strike.'

And for a moment she was dumbfounded, stunned. How could someone be so single-minded? So certain about something? So *excited*? It defied belief. Defied logic. He was a little boy counting off the days to the start of the school holidays. The agony of waiting had nearly killed him and now it was here.

'There's work to be done,' Ronnie went on, and Jemima felt her nerves stretched taut. God, why were men so self-important?

'Oh? And what exactly are you going to do?'

Annoyance flashed across his face and she felt a moment of triumph.

'How can you not *understand*?' he demanded, advancing into the bedroom. 'This is *it*! This is the moment we've waited our whole *lives* for—longer!'

'How can we have waited *longer* than our whole lives?'

The irritation grew. 'Not you and me: the unemployed, the miners, the dockers, starving families...'

'And meanwhile I live in a cupboard over a butcher's shop!'

In the boxroom Baby's crying had reached a critical point and Mrs Avery in the flat next door began banging on the dividing wall.

'I've got to go,' he declared. 'The league needs me. The people need us.'

She shrugged. All her energy of a moment earlier had dissipated.

'Go then. I'm sure the strike will collapse if you're not there.' She pulled the curtains shut and prepared to get back into bed.

Ronnie stood in the doorway for a moment as though he would argue with her but then he turned and left. The front door opened and slammed behind him and in the street outside a horse whinnied and someone swore angrily.

Then quiet.

For a while Jemima lay in bed refusing to move. She had little enough time for herself what with Baby and her husband and the flat all demanding more hours from her than she had to give. She was damned if any stupid strike was going to make her get up. So she lay there, rigid, with the counterpane pulled up to her chin against the early morning chill. But it soon became obvious she wasn't going to get back to sleep, she couldn't even doze. Baby's cries continued, Mrs Avery's banging became more insistent, and the shouts and laughs and curses from outside weren't just disturbing, they were making her want to get up and see what exactly was going on.

'Load of socialist rubbish!' she muttered to herself as she jumped up and hurriedly got dressed.

She grabbed Baby and, leaving the horrid little flat, together they went down to the street.

Rather disappointingly, the disturbances of earlier had died down. Yet a slow-moving stream of workers on foot seemed to be growing by the minute. So too the line of overcrowded lorries and delivery vans that made their way cautiously and, in some instances, recklessly, through the congestion.

And what difference, wondered Jemima, is this daft strike going to make? Folk were still going to work, weren't they? And pushing Baby before her in the perambulator she headed along High Street towards her parents' house.

At Wells Lane there was no indication a strike had even been called. No one was about, and the street was silent. Jemima wondered for a moment where Ronnie had gone. Was he even intending to go to work today? The schools weren't officially part of the strike. If he failed to turn up he would be sacked.

Sacked. Husband and father, a rented flat above a shop, and he was risking it all for *what*? Some coalmining family in Stockton-on-Tees that he'd never even met. And who probably weren't even grateful.

As she wheeled Baby in between the elm trees lining the lane she felt a rising hysteria that was partly fear about what on earth would happen to them if Ronnie got sacked, and partly a secret delight at the thought of seeing him finally realise what a fool he had been. Well, she wouldn't hang around too long to see that; she'd move back in with Mum and Dad before it came to that.

'Hullo, Jem—what do you think? Isn't it exciting!'

And here was Bertha coming along the lane from the direction of Oakton Way, her face flushed and perspiring in the May warmth. 'How's Baby? Can I have a push?'

'No, you can't. We've just come from the flat and we're tired. And no, Bertha, it isn't exciting,' she added, forcing her way past and negotiating the front gate. 'Actually, it's daft and pointless. I'm surprised you can't see it,' and she thrust open the front door with a loud, 'Hello-oh!'

'In the kitchen,' called out Mum.

'Here,' said Jemima, leaving Baby and the perambulator in Bertha's care, and she walked down the hallway into the kitchen.

'Hullo, dear,' said Mum. 'We're just having tea.'

'We' was Aunt Nora, Cousin Janie and little Herbert, Janie's baby. Herbert, who was now nearly five months old, was a miserable red-faced little thing that you knew, with depressing certainty, would never amount to anything much.

'Hullo, girls,' said Aunt Nora. 'Isn't it exciting?'

'Your dad's gone off to be a special constable,' announced Janie, jiggling the wretched Herbert on her knee.

'Really?' replied Jemima in a bored voice, fetching herself a teacup off the dresser. Who did Janie think she was, telling her things about her own dad? Of course, Janie didn't have a dad of her own. And she didn't have a husband either, come to think of it. Rather a careless girl, Janie.

'Dad a special constable?' exclaimed Bertha. 'Fancy!'

'Yes, he went off first thing,' said Mum proudly. 'Over at Steyne Hall, that's where they're enrolling 'em. A Special Constable of the Metropolitan Police! What do you think of that?'

'I think Dad's been waiting his whole life for it,' said Jemima, pouring tea into her cup.

'Fancy!' said Bertha again. And then, 'Do you think he'll get a uniform?'

'Probably,' said Janie. 'Else how would folk know he was a special constable else?' Herbert made a gurgling noise and began to regurgitate something.

''Course he won't get a uniform,' said Jemima, exasperated. 'He'll probably get some wretched little armband. Like the VADs in the War.'

This remark was met with a disappointed silence.

'Well, never mind,' said Mum cheerfully. 'I expect he'll get to guard something important and keep folk under control.'

'Folk are walking to work—what's he going to do? Help them cross the road?'

'Really, Jemima, I don't think you appreciate how dangerous it might be,' said Mum indignantly. 'Nora said she saw some young men attacking a bus in High Street earlier.'

'I did!' confirmed Aunt Nora, leaning forward eagerly. 'And some of the young men looked quite *rough*. Dockers, I shouldn't be surprised. There was some shocking language, I can tell you.'

'It *is* a general strike, Aunt Nora,' admonished Bertha, putting on her serious face. 'It's not tea at the palace. Men are fighting for their rights. You have to expect that kind of thing.'

'What's Matthew doing?' inquired Jemima.

Bertha shuffled about in her seat. 'He's at the post office, naturally. The GPO isn't on strike, you know. Folk still need to send letters and telegrams.'

'And people have got to get to work but that doesn't stop the buses and trams and trains being on strike.'

'That's different.'

But how it was different, Bertha did not elaborate on.

'Your Matthew's a very principled young man, Bertha,' declared Aunt Nora, who obviously was a good judge of husbands.

'He's going to volunteer, too,' said Bertha with a sideways glance at Jemima. 'On the buses. As a driver. He drove ambulances, you know. In the War.'

Jemima hadn't known and frankly she found it difficult to imagine her dull, ponderous brother-in-law dodging machine guns and mortars at the wheel of a rickety old ambulance on the Western Front.

'At Portsmouth,' Bertha continued (and Jemima thought, Ha! I knew it). 'He's going to go down to the bus garage after work to volunteer to drive on the early shifts. They're enrolling people today.'

'A bus driver!' gasped Janie in hushed tones, as though Bertha had announced Matthew had signed up for the Secret Service and was being posted to Bolshevik Russia. But then, Janie had no husband of her own with whom to be impressed.

'What's young Ronnie up to, love?' said Mum suddenly, as though she'd just remembered she had two sons-in-law.

'I bet he's excited,' said Bertha rather too casually. 'The big day, finally come...' And as Jemima turned to her Bertha looked away and flushed.

'The big day? An excuse for grown men to skip work and play about in the streets like schoolboys? Oh, he's excited alright. I hope he doesn't see your Matthew driving a bus, that's all.'

'Perhaps your dad will arrest him?' suggested Janie in wide-eyed delight, and Jemima gave her a withering look.

'How long do you think it will last, Alice?' asked Aunt Nora of Mum. Why Aunt Nora thought Mum would know anything at all about it was a mystery to Jemima.

'Matthew says they will be lucky if it lasts the week,' said Bertha. 'He said folk'll just get fed up with the strikers and the strikers will just give up. That or there'll be anarchy and the army will be called out. But either way it'll be over by the weekend.'

'*Anarchy!*' said Jemima. 'What does Matthew know of anarchy? He works in a post office!'

Bertha's face darkened.

'The post office is at the heart of a society's communication network!' she retorted, so pat that Matthew himself might have said it.

'If it goes on too long there'll be food shortages,' warned Aunt Nora. 'There were queues outside the butcher's this morning. We've already begun rationing, haven't we, Janie dear?'

'Well, I don't know about all this strike business,' announced Mum, heaving herself to her feet, 'but I've got the washing to start and your dad'll still be home for his dinner at twelve.'

'Shall we go and watch the strike?' said Janie, holding Herbert out for Aunt Nora to take.

'Watch it? What's to see?' said Jemima. 'People hanging about waiting for the end of the world? I'd rather be stuck at home with Baby.'

And that was exactly where she was for the rest of the day, though it was true that she spent a large portion of it watching the street from her bedroom window. Not that there was much to see. By afternoon High Street was deserted and Jemima began to wish she'd made some arrangement to see Bertha. Even tea at Oakton Way with the odious Mrs Lake and the shrivelled-up Aunt Daisy was preferable to being cooped up all day in the flat.

By four o'clock things suddenly became more lively as the first workers began to drift back home again. By five, the street was teeming with a steadily increasing stream of pedestrians and a growing procession of vehicles. The noise and congestion grew alarmingly and onlookers stopped to watch, cheering loudly whenever a particularly colourful or overladen vehicle came into view.

At that point Jemima, unable to remain alone in the flat a moment longer, went next door and persuaded Mrs Avery to take Baby for five minutes then hurried down the stairs to join the throng. She almost ran straight into Bertha and Janie, who popped out of the side passage and were about to knock on the downstairs door.

'Jem! Come on! Come and watch the procession!' said Janie. 'Everyone's out watching!'

'I know, I know. I can see it from my window,' Jemima replied, but she allowed herself to be led out to the street and they took up a position in front of the butcher's.

For an hour the noisy, colourful procession continued. At one point a scuffle broke out in front of the old fire station when a delivery van that had driven all the way up from the country tried to unload its goods and was met by a group of angry strikers. A carload of special constables came roaring up Gunnersbury Lane and screeched to a halt outside the shop, the constables diving into the scuffle to break it up. Dad wasn't among them.

'See? Armbands,' said Jemima, pointing.

'What a shame!' said Janie, standing on tiptoe to see over the heads of two very large women with big hats. 'I like a man in a uniform.'

You'd like just about any man at this moment, thought Jemima.

'Look! A bus!' cried Bertha, and Jemima rolled her eyes because it had come to this, the three of them standing in High Street, excited because a bus was coming along. And yet here she was craning her neck as much as anyone to see another double-decker General come careering round the corner, a Union Jack fluttering on its bonnet, swerving erratically and nearly running into the back of the fruit delivery van. It braked, almost stalled, then set off again, and through the cab window Jemima could see a very young-looking chap pulling desperately at the gearstick. Beside him, the window was smashed and paint was daubed on the side of the bus obscuring the *Gen* of *General*. One or two game passengers sat outside braving catcalls from the onlookers, and on the back platform balanced a youthful conductor in a gaily striped blazer, holding grimly onto the rear handrail and clutching his ticket machine.

Behind the bus ran a group of strikers in shirt sleeves and braces, keeping up a stream of abuse. They attempted to jump up onto the platform but with a neat swerve, whether deliberate or accidental Jemima couldn't tell, the bus evaded them and plunged down Gunnersbury Lane. Which route the bus was following was a mystery and perhaps that wasn't the point.

'*Demo tonight! Demo this evening at Horn Lane Cinema!*' cried a man in an armband who was working his way through the crowd handing out badly printed fliers, one of which he gave to Jemima. 'Demonstration in support of

the strike, tonight at six thirty sharp! Horn Lane Cinema!'
he said, moving off.

'How daft! Do they think we have nothing better to
do?' said Jemima, dropping the flier on the ground.

'Oh, do let's go!' pleaded Bertha.

'I wish we had armbands,' sighed Janie.

But her disappointment was quickly forgotten as the
distant strains of a brass band could be heard further
down the street. Around them the crowd strained to see.
The sounds of the band grew louder and someone called
out, 'It's the Band of the Royal Marines!' and someone
else shouted 'It's the Metropolitan Police Band!' but as the
band finally came into view a large banner identified the
Acton Labour Party, led by the band of the National Union
of Railwaymen, which wasn't quite as good but everyone
cheered anyway. The marchers strode proudly past, many
of the men wearing their War medals, and there were
women, too, among their ranks and Bertha waved excitedly as though she knew them all personally.

'Careful, don't want Mr Lake to see you cheering the
enemy,' remarked Jemima above the noise. Bertha pulled
her hand down and bit her lip.

Afterwards everyone made their way to All Saints
parish hall where an impromptu concert had been organised. The headline artists—a Miss Valda Langhorne,
pianist, and a Mr Tommy Scarlet, comic and entertainer—
failed to turn up because of the strike, so the vicar and
Miss Morgan from the Women's Institute had to impro-
vise. Lots of people got up to do turns and sing songs and
it was all very hilarious and at last Jemima could stand it
no more and got up to leave.

Outside it was dusk and a small crowd had gathered
in front of the parish noticeboard to read badly printed
and hastily pasted-up copies of something called *The
British Citizen* and something else equally makeshift called
The British Worker and it didn't take much brain power to

decide which side had produced which newspaper. She couldn't imagine why anyone was bothering to read either of them, when all that one paper was going to report was the glory of the noble workers and all the other paper was going to say was beware the Red Scourge.

'Mrs Booth—Jemima!'

It was Matthew coming out of the darkness, wearing an armband.

Jemima stopped politely, raised her head and greeted him cordially.

'Good evening, Matthew. Bertha said you were driving the buses,' she said airily, making it clear such things did not impress her.

'Indeed I have been—I enrolled after the evening sorting and have been out on the number 17C to Putney and back!' He made it sound as if Putney were somewhere off in the African Veldt.

'Does the 17C go to Putney?' inquired Jemima suspiciously.

Matthew looked a little abashed. 'No, I don't believe so—not normally—but these are testing times. And my conductor was supposed to be navigating but he was a young chap from Taunton. Up here studying engineering. We ran the gauntlet, you know,' he added, and Jemima was surprised to note a glimmer of excitement in his normally dull postal clerk's eyes. 'Quite a set-to we had at Hammersmith. Hooligans chucking bricks and so forth.'

'You went to Putney...via Hammersmith?'

In the light from the streetlamp she saw him flush. 'Testing times, Mrs Booth—Jemima.'

She wished he'd stop calling her 'Mrs Booth—Jemima'. It was quite irritating.

'Well, clearly it's all very exciting,' she observed, stifling a yawn. 'However, I've got Baby to feed and Ronnie will no doubt be home and wanting his tea.'

Would Ronnie be home for his tea? She wasn't entirely sure.

'Oh,' said Matthew, 'I oughtn't let you go home alone, not with gangs roaming the streets,' and he hesitated as though seeking someone from whom he could ask permission to accompany her.

'Don't bother, I hardly think a gang is going to roam into me. Anyway, Bertha's in there...' She indicated with her thumb the church behind her just as a raucous burst of laughter erupted from the direction of the hall.

'Ah yes, I gathered this was where everyone was headed.'

Matthew hesitated, seemingly torn between an archaic sense of gentlemanly duty and a fear of what his wife might think of him going off without her. Jemima stood coolly by and watched his discomfort with interest.

'It is rather dark,' she said, looking around and giving a little shiver.

And that seemed to clinch it.

'I'll go and find Bertha and let her know I shall return once I've seen you safely home,' and he scuttled off towards the hall.

Enjoying the idea that Ronnie might have come home and found her not there, and even more the idea that she might return home late with her brother-in-law in tow, Jemima waited impatiently for Matthew's return. He did so after some minutes, apologising and, she could see, a little awkward.

'They're having an interval,' he said breathlessly. 'Looks set to go on for a while yet so I said I would escort you home then get back for the second half.'

'If you like,' she replied, making it clear these domestic arrangements were all very dull. She held out her arm and he took it quickly, as though embarrassed not to have offered her his arm first, and they set off towards High Street.

Despite the threat of roaming gangs, the streets were

all but deserted now and their footsteps echoed in unison as they walked along the pavement. Her brother-in-law was, Jemima noted, much taller and broader than Ronnie, his voice deeper, his face clean-shaven and not in need of the drooping moustache that Ronnie sported.

'You are very brave, volunteering on the buses, Matthew,' she observed suddenly, surprising them both. She felt him stand up taller, his head go back.

'Oh well. I should hope we all know our duty in difficult times.'

'Bertha supports the strikers, you know.' She felt him stiffen.

'Ah now, there I think you are mistaken. She understands the importance of maintaining discipline and order.'

'Did she come and see you off when you enrolled and set off on your first shift?' Jemima inquired, knowing full well that Bertha had been waving to the Acton Labour Club marchers at about that time.

'It's hardly a woman's place,' he answered stiffly.

'I would have come and waved you off,' said Jemima softly.

There was a silence.

'Do you think they will take on women bus conductors?' she mused. 'And drivers? After all, women drove buses and ambulances in the War.'

'I don't think it will come to that.'

'I'd volunteer if they did. Perhaps they would put me on your bus? Wouldn't that be funny? I could navigate you to Putney and I wouldn't be scared of any stone-throwing gangs either.'

'I'm sure it won't come to that,' repeated Matthew doggedly.

'Would you like to have me on your bus?'

It was easy, it was so, so easy in the dark, walking side by side, hand on arm, feet marching in unison, staring straight ahead, not a soul around. No one to hear you, no one to see your expression. Just words uttered in the darkness. Words you would never dare to utter in daylight, with other people around.

'I—Of course I would not doubt your capabilities— or your courage!—but I would be concerned for your safety...'

'Would you? How sweet.' She moved a little closer to him, for protection.

They had turned into High Street and Jemima glanced up at the flat. It was dark, no lights on. Ronnie not back then? Maybe he'd been arrested. Maybe Dad had arrested him.

'Looks like no one's home. You will come up, won't you, to see me safely in?'

'Yes, of course. Mr Booth...?'

'Oh, he's off playing strikers somewhere.'

'But the baby?'

'Oh, Baby's alright. Mrs Avery next door's minding.' At least she hoped Baby was alright, realising she had left Baby with Mrs Avery for five minutes five hours ago.

They reached the butcher's and Jemima led the way down the dingy side passage to her porch, then up the unlit stairs to the landing, where she unlocked the door and let them in.

Matthew remained determinedly silent as he stood politely to one side to allow her to pass and she realised he had never been to the flat before. She experienced a moment of shame at this, her home, a poky flat above a foul-smelling butcher's shop. Ronnie's work clothes lay in piles, Baby's nappies hung all over the place and yesterday's tea and today's breakfast things were still piled up in the kitchen sink. But what did it matter? At least she wasn't still living with Mum and Dad.

'Come on,' she said, leading the way into the small lounge. She brushed Ronnie's papers and journals off the armchair and pushed Baby's clothes out of the way with her foot. Matthew stood in the centre of the room looking too big, his hands hanging awkwardly at his side.

'Ronnie's out. Those union demonstrations go on all night sometimes. Often it's just Baby and me here on our own.'

'Really?' said Matthew, clearing his throat. 'That's not, well… Can't be very pleasant for you.'

'Oh, it's not. Not at all. It's not what a woman expects from a marriage.' Jemima sighed.

'No, I'm sure. It can't be.' He frowned.

'Still, I expect I'll be alright here on my own. It seems mostly quiet now.'

'Yes, yes it does. Erm…' He hesitated. 'Perhaps I ought to stay until Mr Booth returns?'

'But sometimes he doesn't return until morning.' And then before he could reply, 'Why don't you sit down? Take your coat off. We have some brandy in the cupboard— that'll warm us,' and she went to the cupboard and poured a nip each into two short glasses, one of which she held out to Matthew.

'I suppose I ought to return soon, they'll be—Bertha will be waiting,' he said.

'Yes, of course,' said Jemima, and she watched as he took the glass and drank from it.

❀ ❀ ❀

It was day two of the strike and Things, Bertha had announced importantly, Were Escalating. The newspapers pinned up on the church noticeboard reported that yesterday two million workers had gone on strike, a figure that was set to double over the next few days. Only a handful of tube trains were running, less than a tenth of the buses and a dozen or so trams. Congestion on the main roads had doubled. People were rising at five to ride bicycles or go on foot to work. Delivery vans and carts ran the gauntlet of the strikers to bring food supplies in from the country, and fights were breaking out as workers attempted to secure a seat in any vehicles that might get them to the office.

Bertha and Janie turned up at the flat a little after eight. Janie was pushing the dribbling Herbert in his perambulator, and was full of excitement because a van-load of cabbages had been spilled all over High Street and a horse had slipped on them and broken its leg and had had to be destroyed.

Jemima listened impatiently. Ronnie, it was clear, had not gone in to work yesterday, though he had said nothing when he had come home some time after midnight, flushed and excited but uncommunicative. And what would happen if he lost his job?

She dismissed the thought irritably. There were, after all, more pressing things to think about. She reached for her hat, glancing at Bertha, but her sister was impassively dabbing a handkerchief at Herbert's chin as though babies' dribble was all that mattered. Then, 'When did Ronnie get back last night?' Bertha asked, cool as you please. 'Is he involved in the strike?' As though it was any of her business what her sister's husband got up to!

'Oh, he was back quite early,' Jemima replied tartly, pulling on her coat and doing up the buttons despite it being a warm spring day outside. 'Though the Lord only knows what he'd been up to. I couldn't be bothered asking.' That, at least, had been the truth.

'Oh,' was all Bertha said, but she continued to stand there and stare.

'Well? Are we going out, or are we going to stand about here all day and miss all the fun?' Jemima replied briskly. Quite apart from changing the subject she was anxious to get the loathsome Herbert and his incessant dribble out of her home.

'Up we go little man!' Janie announced, swinging the baby ceilingward so that an arc of dribble sprayed across the floor. 'Who's a funny little man, then?' she added and Jemima handed her own baby to Bertha and silently held the front door open.

Outside the street had calmed after the morning rush but there was still plenty to see so they strolled along High Street with linked arms, pushing the two perambulators between them.

They came across Dad almost at once.

'Look! There he is! Over there!'

Bertha pointed and on the far side of the road over by the railway bridge they could see Dad, proudly sporting his scarlet armband, standing amid a group of other special constables. She and Janie stood and waved and Jemima took the opportunity to park Baby's perambulator and flop down on a low wall.

'What's he guarding then?' said Janie, waving enthusiastically.

'The Lord only knows.'

'Perhaps they've had a tip-off!'

'About what? A horse?'

'No! A police tip-off. Extremists. You know! Planning on blowing up the bridge.'

But they could see a large tea urn beneath the archway bubbling away on a smoky brazier and it seemed more likely the special constables were there for their morning cuppa.

'Oh,' said Janie, disappointed. 'Where shall we go now then?'

'We could go to the bus garage?' suggested Bertha. 'Matthew drove the early shift so they ought to be getting back to the garage soon. We could watch them come in.'

It was on the tip of Jemima's tongue to point out that if the number 17C had followed a similar route to yesterday it could be some considerable time before it arrived back at the garage. But instead she said, 'Yes alright,' in a bored voice and off they set.

They had got as far as the Red Lion when the number 184 London Bridge bus, barbed wire fastened to both flanks, came careering out of the garage surrounded by a loud and angry mob of strikers. As the bus turned into High Street it swerved, mounting the pavement ahead of them.

All three jumped back in alarm, Janie swinging her perambulator in such an arc it reared up on two wheels and all but tipped over. Janie shrieked and tried to regain control of the wayward perambulator, Bertha made a lunge at the screaming Herbert and Jemima leapt out of the way of the oncoming bus.

She had a confused view of the horrified face of the young man who was gripping its steering wheel, of the bus regaining the road and the word *General*, written in large letters on the side of the bus, flashing before her. The conductor was crouched on the step inside the bus, a passenger on the top deck clutched a bloodied handkerchief to his face, and a running, placard-waving, shouting crowd of young men banged on the bus's side as it swept onwards.

The last thing she saw was Ronnie—her husband— emerging from the throng running alongside the bus to hurl a brick that dented the red paintwork and spun off to land on the pavement about a yard from Baby's perambulator.

In another moment the bus had gone and the crowd had fizzled out. A trail of bricks, broken placards and a single shoe was all that remained of the affray.

There was no sign of Ronnie.

'Alright, Herbie, alright little man, it's all over now. The horrible men have gone,' crooned Janie, soothing the hysterical Herbert. Her own baby, Jemima noted, had slept through the whole thing.

'I think he's alright, no harm done,' said Bertha. She turned her attention to Janie's perambulator, straightening its wheels and making sure all was in working order. 'No damage done. Looks good as new,' she said, experimentally pushing it back and forth a few times. Then she turned to Jemima as though she had just that moment noticed her sister had said nothing.

'Did you see, Jem? That man on the bus was injured. Those men must have caught him with a stone or something. Did you see?'

Jemima *had* seen and she had seen a great deal more than that too, but perhaps, she decided, looking from Bertha to Janie, they had not seen as much as she.

Ronnie. Her own *husband.* In a mob of screaming, stone-throwing men. This was his precious league? This was his glorious revolution? All that talk of solidarity, of the workers' rights, of human endeavour! What it really came down to was one man throwing a brick at a bus in High Street and another man holding a bloodied handkerchief to his face. Pathetic. It was pathetic. *He* was pathetic.

'Let's go in. Let's wait inside the bus garage,' she said suddenly and, not waiting for the other two, set off towards the gates of the garage pushing Baby before her.

There were two special constables on duty outside the garage who wouldn't let them pass so they stood outside and waited. Janie walked Herbert up and down, singing to him in a low murmur.

Bertha asked the special constables whether the 17C had come in yet but they didn't seem to know what had come in or what had gone out. But at that moment the number 17C itself swung around the corner and shot through the garage gates almost before the special constables could open them.

'Hurrah!' someone inside the bus called and a flag waved triumphantly from an upstairs window. Cheers from inside the garage accompanied the 17C's return and, as the bus ground to a gear-crunching halt, the door opened and a rather green-looking conductor reeled out, followed a moment later by Matthew.

'Matthew!' called Bertha, pushing past the constables and in through the gates, waving madly at him.

'The hero returns,' muttered Jemima, but she found herself following closely at Bertha's heels and it was clear, as they approached the bus, that it had weathered a skirmish or two. Most of the windows were broken, a large part of the paintwork was damaged, the windscreen was entirely gone and the streaked remains of a half-dozen eggs were hardening on the upper deck.

'Matthew! Are you alright?' gasped Bertha, taking his arm and looking up into his face.

He nodded and smiled and there was almost a glint in his eye. 'Of course! I'm perfectly fine, my dear. The rabble did their best but we were equal to the task, eh, Bridges?'

The young, green-faced conductor in Oxford bags gave a weak thumbs-up then sat down rather heavily on the step.

'You are brave, Mr Lake—both of you, you really are! Aren't they brave, Herbie?' gushed Janie, forcing the poor child to wave a triumphant fist.

Herbert dribbled in protest.

The garage superintendent, a portly man sporting an important-looking peaked cap and a bushy moustache, emerged from the office and pushed his way towards the returned crew. He shook Matthew's hand then patted Bridges gingerly on the shoulder.

'Alright, lads, well done. Well done all round. Any particular black spots we need to be aware of? What route did you take exactly?'

'Followed the route pretty much exactly,' said Matthew, busying himself with the cash box.

'Think we were in Cricklewood at one point,' said Bridges, looking up at Matthew for confirmation.

'*Near* Cricklewood,' corrected Matthew. 'There was a sign for it certainly, though I don't believe we were actually *at* Cricklewood...'

'Good, excellent. Very good. Now, get yourselves a strong cuppa.'

'And Neasden,' added Bridges thoughtfully. 'Definitely went through Neasden.'

'Doesn't the 17C go to Oxford Circus?' said Jemima to no one in particular.

Bridges was led away by the superintendent and Matthew stepped nimbly down from his bus and almost landed on Jemima's foot.

'Sorry, so sorry,' he muttered, flushing darkly and busying himself with the cash and the door and his armband.

Jemima moved away suddenly, wishing she hadn't suggested coming here, that she had stayed at Mum's house with Baby and watched Mum do the washing. Instead here she was in a bus garage with Matthew, who had just run the gauntlet of the mob halfway across west London (and well beyond, if Bridges was to be believed), and now he was blushing like a schoolgirl because he had almost stepped on her toe. Or perhaps it wasn't that he had almost stepped on her toe, perhaps it was simply because she was here?

And where was Ronnie now, and his little gang of hoodlums? Snatching the purse of some elderly lady in Horn Lane? Pushing over a perambulator? Robbing a charity box?

'Dearest, why are you here? This really isn't a place for women and children,' Matthew was saying to Bertha, having recovered himself after the toe-stepping incident. 'I would much rather you waited for me at home.'

'Oh, but I was worried, my dear—' began Bertha, but she was interrupted by Janie's excited shout.

'Look, look over there! They're enrolling women as bus conductors. There's a sign—look! We could all join!'

The sign, handwritten and stuck on the door of the office, announced:

WOMEN OF ACTION
Are you a Woman of <u>ACTION</u>?
SPECIAL CONDUCTORS NEEDED!
Sign up NOW to help
Your Country in this
TIME OF THE DIRE NEED!
Training and Armbands provided!

Before Jemima could open her mouth to point out the absurdness of such a thing, two young girls in very ugly hats, clutching each other in excitement, appeared in the doorway of the office holding their forms and admiring their new red armbands.

'Fancy!' said Janie. 'Look, Herbie! Do you think Mumsy could be a bus conductor? Do you?'

Herbert replied with a dribble.

As the two young women stood there enjoying the spectacle they were creating Bertha gave a disdainful sniff. 'It's all very well if you're a single young lady but that sort of thing is hardly dignified for the married woman,' she declared, then looked up at Matthew as if she had said this for his benefit.

'What rubbish!' Jemima scoffed. 'You might be too afraid but I shall join up. I expect it will be quite fun.'

'Jemima!' gasped Janie.

'Jem, you can't!' said Bertha. 'What about Baby?'

Baby had so far slept through all the excitement and appeared unconcerned by this latest development.

'Mum will look after Baby.'

'But what about Ronnie?'

'What about Ronnie? He isn't around to object, is he?'

Bertha looked shocked. 'But I mean, he wouldn't like it. What about the league? The workers...?' and here she glanced again at Matthew, but this time tentatively, as though she feared some dark hidden inner sympathy for the strike might suddenly become apparent. 'I mean, you know, all that he's worked for...'

'Pah! A woman can have her own principles, can't she?' Jemima retorted. 'I happen to believe very strongly that the country needs me. At this time of dire need.'

'Bravo!' said Janie.

Bertha just looked at her.

'I think it's marvellous, Jemima—Mrs Booth,' said Matthew suddenly, and they all looked at him. Even Herbert seemed dumbstruck. 'I mean, why shouldn't young ladies be given the chance to do their bit? And it's brave, too, if I may say so.'

Here Bertha appeared to fairly burst with indignation but she said nothing. Jemima smiled.

'I don't know why you don't sign up yourself, Bert, unless you're afraid of a few daft schoolboys calling you names? I'm going to do it right now!' she announced. 'Bert, you and Mum'll have to look after Baby when I'm working.' She turned to Matthew. 'Perhaps I shall be your conductor tomorrow?'

❊ ❊ ❊

But Ronnie *was* there to object. He was sitting at the kitchen table with a scowl on his face when Jemima got home. When she saw him she felt a flicker of something unpleasant in the pit of her stomach.

Was it fear?

She brushed it aside and told herself it was the strike that made him glare at her. She left Baby in the hallway and went straight into the bedroom without so much as saying hello.

'Where have you been?' he demanded, following her and standing in the doorway.

She sighed irritably and took off her hat. God forbid I should be out by myself for a change and not clearing up after you and Baby, she thought, but she concentrated on putting her hat on the hatstand so it would keep its shape.

'I got home and there was no one here,' he continued in an annoying, whining way. 'So I went over to Wells Lane and your mum said you'd all been out since eight o'clock this morning.'

Jemima squeezed her eyes shut so tightly that little lights exploded before her eyes. Then she opened her eyes and turned to face him.

'And what of it? I'm stuck in here with Baby all day every day, but you never think of that, do you? While you're out playing with the other silly little boys, throwing bricks...' She saw him open his mouth then close it again, his eyes dropping from hers, and her anger turned to triumph. 'Throwing *bricks*. Yes, don't think I didn't see you and I was ashamed. *Ashamed*. What kind of a man does that? I was glad no one else saw it. How do you think that made me feel?'

Ronnie was silent but she could see the fury, the shame, the dismay there on his face, and from the perambulator in the hallway Baby stared at him silently, condemning him, it seemed.

'And anyway, Mum will be looking after Baby a bit more from now on. I have signed up as a special bus conductor. I start tomorrow,' and she swept past into the kitchen.

'You've done *what*?'

He stumbled after her.

In the kitchen the remains of a loaf of bread stood on the table and Jemima's hands clenched tightly around its stale exterior, squeezing it between her fingers.

'But...but this is a *betrayal*!'

Jemima picked up the bread knife and calmly began to slice the loaf. She said nothing. She found she had nothing to say.

'This is…' His voice trailed off as though he hadn't the energy to say the word a second time. 'You are my *wife!*' he shouted suddenly. *'MY WIFE!* How *dare* you do this without…without… I *forbid* it, do you hear? I *absolutely forbid* it.'

Aside from an urge to laugh, Jemima found that not only was there nothing to say, there was, rather conveniently, nothing to feel either. There was only a curious throbbing, pulsing beat at her temple making her feel quite light-headed. She hardly noticed Ronnie leave, the front door banging shut. She sliced the now oddly shaped loaf and hummed quietly to herself.

'Here you are, Baby. Let's have some lovely bread and jam. Daddy's gone out for a while but we'll have tea without him and it will be lovely, won't it?'

But there was no jam, there was only dripping and milk, so they had that instead.

❄ ❄ ❄

'Are you really going to go through with it, Jemima?' asked Aunt Nora the following morning as they sat around the table at Wells Lane after breakfast.

Mum was clearing away the breakfast things silently, Janie, round-eyed with envy, was dabbing absent-mindedly at Herbert's chin and Aunt Nora, replete after her third cup of tea, was looking at her niece as though Jemima had just announced she was going to marry a negro.

And Dad was there too, standing silently at the mirror attaching his collar and fussily tying the red special constable's armband around his arm.

'Well, the girl's got spirit, I'll give her that,' was his only comment, earning him a look of horror from his wife. Bertha, watching from the doorway, remained expressionless, her attention focused on Baby, who was obligingly batting at a piece of hat ribbon and seemed oblivious to the adults all around.

'Of course I'm going through with it,' replied Jemima, sitting up straighter. She almost gave Dad a grateful look, but no, she no longer needed Dad's approval. It was no one's business but her own.

'What did Ronnie have to say?' said Mum, glancing at Dad a little fearfully.

'I don't see what business it is of his,' retorted Jemima as she studied Bertha's face carefully. Yes, it was turning red. With fury? Envy? Oh, Bertha, always so predictable!

'I thought your Ronnie was a socialist chap,' said Aunt Nora, looking from Mum to Dad for confirmation. 'Won't he mind you joining the other side?'

'I do have my own opinions and thoughts, thank you, Aunt Nora,' Jemima replied tartly and Aunt Nora bridled, shifted huffily in her seat, and looked at Dad to put his youngest daughter in her place.

'Ha!' was all Dad said, aiming this remark at his reflection in the mirror.

'But won't it be risky, dear?' said Mum anxiously. 'You hear awful things about gangs of delinquents and folk being attacked...'

'I'm going to be a conductor on a bus that might go to Chiswick or perhaps Wandsworth. I'm not leading an expedition down the blooming Zambesi!'

'Language,' warned Dad.

Jemima stood up. 'Well, I must be off.' She smoothed down her skirt. 'Wish me luck!'

At that moment Bertha dropped the ribbon she was holding for Baby and suddenly her face was flushed and angry.

'Anyway I think you're just showing off, Jemima! You don't care two hoots for the strike or the country or anything. You're just doing it to—to show off!'

Mum, Janie, Aunt Nora, even the two babies stared at her.

'Now then,' began Dad, turning around with a frown on his face, but Jemima didn't need anyone to defend her. She tossed her head and reached for her smart black bus corporation hat.

'Think what you like. I shall know in my heart that I'm doing the right thing and that no amount of danger shall put me off.' She turned to the others. 'Well, goodbye.' She went down the passage to the front door, pausing at the last minute to call back, 'And perhaps I shall be on Matthew's bus, Bertha. Won't that be nice?'

Outside, the sun reflected brilliantly off the shop windows and the windscreens of the line of vehicles that had already begun the slow crawl towards the city.

Jemima set off briskly, stepping nimbly over the mounds of steaming horse dung, her head high, the peaked cap cutting a dash in the early morning sunlight, her right arm at an angle that showed off her new armband so that many a passer-by stopped and stared. One elderly gentleman actually patted her arm and said, 'Bravo!'

As she passed the end of Acton Lane a delivery van squeezed beneath the iron railway bridge, loaded so high with wooden crates it had to drive through the central arch, barely scraping through so that the top-most box wobbled and then fell with a crash, splitting open and sending potatoes rolling across the street. Jemima laughed to see it.

At the bus garage on the corner of Steyne Road a small crowd had already formed and the buses stood lined up ready to go. The two young women who had also signed up the day before were being shown to their vehicles and behind them two more women were just signing up. And now, Jemima saw, the sign was asking not just for conductors, but for women drivers too.

'Jemima—Mrs Booth! Hullo there!' And there was Matthew seated in the cab of the number 17C, waving eagerly, and his next words, when he said them, were so exactly the words she had known he would say that it was no surprise at all: 'It seems my conductor, young Bridges, is unwell, so I shall need a new volunteer. Are you game?'

And Jemima laughed and jumped up onto the platform and into his bus.

Caroline and Deirdre

CHAPTER SEVENTEEN

THE PAINT THEY'D USED to decorate the hospital corridor wall was surely the exact same shade of duck-egg blue that had covered the brick walls of the outhouse at 15 Oakton Way.

Caroline attempted to raise her head off the pillow in order to study the colour more closely but it was too much effort, her head being at least three times its normal weight, or else the rest of her was three times weaker. Instead she squinted at the wall through narrowed eyes, but that didn't help either.

She considered asking Mr Milthorpe for his opinion but abandoned the idea almost immediately; speaking was even less of an option than raising one's head from the pillow. Besides, asking Mr Milthorpe whether he considered the corridor wall to be the same colour as the outhouse at 15 Oakton Way might be considered a rather odd question in the present circumstances—quite apart from the fact that Mr Milthorpe had never been to Oakton Way. Indeed no one had been to Oakton Way for the best part of twenty years, the whole street having been demolished to make way for a supermarket. Or was it a new municipal car park? At any rate, Oakton Way was gone, and so too the outhouse and the duck-egg walls.

During the War a number of houses in Oakton Way had been demolished, some in the Blitz, but most later when the V-2 rockets came. Some time in the fifties the council had finally got around to bulldozing what was left and putting up ugly blocks of flats and later those dreadful sixties maisonettes. Not too long after that the entire street—the ugly concrete flats and the hideous maisonettes, even the gasworks—had been pulled down to make way for the supermarket. Or was it a municipal car park?

'You awake, Mrs Kettley? Just tek your temperature, love, and 'ave a luke at your vitals.'

Caroline frowned in an effort to see who was talking and who was being spoken to and into her vision came a very young face, two spectacled eyes and the pale blue of a nurse's tunic. The nurse looked to be about eleven years old and Caroline wondered why the local primary school had seen fit to send its pupils to work in the hospital.

Mrs Kettley. I am Mrs Kettley, she thought with mild surprise. And then she felt surprised that she had forgotten she was Mrs Kettley and that forgetting such a thing didn't really seem so very important. After all, so long as someone knew who you were, so long as the doctor knew and this little nurse and presumably Mr Milthorpe too, that was the important thing.

Mr Milthorpe, it appeared, had discreetly got up and withdrawn to the window so that—what was it?—her temperature and her vitals could be ascertained? Discreet, that was Jack Milthorpe; thoughtful and discreet.

'Just turning your head to one side, dearie. That's grand!' stated the girl-nurse as she placed a digital thermometer in Caroline's ear and glanced at the upside-down watch pinned to her chest.

Dearie! Cheek of the girl, thought Caroline. I am old enough to be... To be what? Her mother? Her grandmother?

But she wasn't anyone's grandmother. Old enough to be her great-aunt then.

'There now. How're you feeling, pet?'

Not waiting for a reply, the girl-nurse had gone and in her place Mr Milthorpe now sat, leaning over with a jovial smile as though a spell in a hospital ward was even better than Scarborough seafront on August bank holiday.

Dear Mr Milthorpe. How long had he been here? she wondered. But to know that, she would need to know how long she herself had been here. Some days? She was sure it was days. But not weeks. She would know, surely, if she had been here for weeks.

Dear Mr Milthorpe, sitting there at her side, patting her hand and wonderfully unconcerned as though she were merely here to have her wisdom teeth out. She'd never got round to calling him by his Christian name, which was Jack, of course. But in the twenty-odd years they had been neighbours, they had somehow never got on to first-name terms.

Jack. It was a good name, a solid, dependable, English name. No pretensions, no nonsense. Jack. She wanted to say it out loud but there you were, just when you really needed to speak you found you couldn't. Ah well, Mr Milthorpe it would have to remain.

How kind, how sweet, how neighbourly of him to sit here with her like this when he wasn't family, when they had only ever exchanged good mornings and discussed twenty years' worth of weather over the garden fence— first with Ted and then, after Ted died, with herself. He had come to the funeral, she recalled, he and Mrs Milthorpe, dropping by afterwards with a bunch of lilies. White they had been, and he'd left them in the doorway. In recent years he'd taken to sweeping the leaves from her pathway in autumn, clearing the snow from her driveway in winter and mowing her lawn in summer, and Mrs Milthorpe had offered cuttings from her fuchsia bush and her delphiniums over the fence. But they had never set foot in each other's house, not once.

'Warm enough?' asked Mr Milthorpe suddenly, and then he smiled and settled back in his chair as if not expecting a reply. 'Mind, it can get that stuffy in these hospitals,' he added as an afterthought, and Caroline remembered with a shock that his wife had died. In this very hospital, not six months ago.

The nurse looked in again, perhaps she had more vitals to take, but she merely glanced at a chart and left without a word.

Jean, that was his wife's name. Jean and Jack Milthorpe. The sort of couple you would meet in the bar of your hotel in Marbella and get to know over a glass of sangria and then swap addresses with at the end of a fortnight and never see again. Not that Caroline had ever set foot in Marbella, nor wanted to, but she could imagine it.

'I telephoned Mrs Denzel for you,' remarked Mr Milthorpe. 'They'll be along shortly. Mind, it's a fair ways to travel in this snow and the days are that short. The Pennines are blocked, I shouldn't wonder. Not that they'll be coming that way; it'll be the M1 to Leeds for them.'

Caroline considered this information carefully. Who was this Mrs Denzel and why had Mr Milthorpe taken it upon himself to telephone her? He certainly seemed very sure that Mrs Denzel would be coming here—and via the M1. So she wasn't local. Caroline felt she ought to know. He obviously assumed she would know.

Mum. Why hadn't he telephoned Mum? They had got the telephone reconnected after the V-2 in Nelson Terrace had taken out the telephone lines, so why hadn't he called her? Perhaps he didn't know her number. Caroline tried to remember. Acton 2867. The numbers popped into her head in a most satisfying way but there was still the problem of speaking them out loud. Perhaps she could write them down? No, little point in trying really.

Acton 2867. Maybe she could think the numbers to him. She concentrated very hard and Mr Milthorpe leaned a little closer and appeared to be listening.

'I meant to say, they did a right good piece on't Radio 4 last evening about dahlias and rhododendrons. You'd have enjoyed that, Mrs Kettley. Fella from 'Orticultural Society, it were, and right interesting, he were, after that daft bugger from Poland last week.'

Caroline gave up thinking *Acton 2867* and found her mind wandering. What daft bugger from Poland? All she could think about Poland was Hitler invading in 1939.

Deirdre, she thought suddenly. Why doesn't someone telephone Deirdre?

CHAPTER EIGHTEEN

DEIRDRE DENZEL PAUSED in her vacuuming of the landing carpet. If she had been alone in the house she would have turned the vacuum cleaner off rather than stand here not vacuuming and therefore wasting electricity. But Eric was downstairs listening to Radio 2 and he might notice she had stopped vacuuming and come and ask her what was going on.

No, he wouldn't. That was exactly the point—he wouldn't notice.

Deirdre took a firmer grip of the handle of the vacuum cleaner. It was a FireFlash™ 3000 with a 1500-watt auxiliary suction vacuum cleaner with a built-in filtration system, 4.5-litre capacity dual dustbags and, according to the salesman at John Lewis's, a little red light that flashed when its bags needed changing. She had had to change the bags twice so far, and to date the little red light had failed to illuminate.

She attacked a particularly resistant dirty spot on the carpet, running the vacuum in a frenzy over the pinkish stain until she remembered this was where one of the girls had spilled a pot of nail varnish in a previous decade and it had left a pale pink stain that no amount of sugar soap or salt or chemically questionable stain-removers had been able to eradicate.

How long had it been like this?

Eric had retired eight years ago amid a blaze of executive farewell drinks and tastefully boxed gifts, of *Enjoy Your Retirement!* cards and demands to Keep In Touch. In the first few weeks there had been a flurry of golf club membership forms, community college enrolment forms and overseas travel brochures. Six months later the *Enjoy Your Retirement!* cards had been recycled, the gifts had been stored in a drawer still in their tasteful boxes, and no one had Kept In Touch. The golf club had proved to be too far away to make it easily accessible and the community college, far from offering the anticipated courses in Advanced Car Mechanics, Basic Italian and An Appreciation of Mahler offered instead courses in Accessing Your Inner Self, Basic Body Piercing and An Appreciation of the Sitar and Indian Music, and was full of dreadlocked youths, expectant mothers and blue-rinsed elderly ladies. The travel brochures had sat in a pile on the telephone table in the hallway offering passers-by enticing glimpses of suntanned flesh, golden beaches and lush green palms. Eric had seemed unable to come to any decision about their first holiday destination.

And that, Deirdre realised with the hindsight of eight years, was the crux of the matter. Forty years of decision-making had used up all Eric's decisions. He had none left.

Deirdre, by contrast, had suddenly found that she had an abundance of decisions. They had been welling up inside her for—well—forty years. Possibly more. And now she had a surplus of them. She couldn't stop making decisions. She had booked them two weeks in Florida. One week in Orlando including Disney World and the Epcot Centre, one week in Miami. And they had gone. It had been relatively successful, though they had exhausted Disney World after one morning and in Miami they had mostly been too terrified to leave the hotel complex. Deirdre had arranged everything: travel insurance, luggage labelling, clothing, medical supplies, maps and schedules, currency and traveller's cheques. It had been terrifying and exhilarating and the holiday itself had proved less significant than the fact that she had organised the entire thing herself.

She led the vacuum cleaner round into the computer room which used to be the study then, for a brief time, Mum's room. Then it had reverted to being the study. Now, as the computer seemed to take up a lot of space and people rarely stayed overnight, it had become the computer room where Deirdre typed up extensive lists of Things That Needed To Be Done and surfed the net comparing brands of venetian blinds and resort prices in Tenerife.

This was a room she enjoyed having under control. The two years in which Mum and a lifetime of Mum's bric-a-brac had squeezed themselves into this room had been traumatic. The system had, in fact, completely broken down. The cleaning and dusting and washing and tidying and vacuuming that went on routinely in other parts of the house had simply ground to a halt here. It had proved too difficult to instigate any sort of routine in this room, and only sporadic incursions could be made when the main opposing force (Mum herself) had been occupied elsewhere (the television). Those two years had seemed like a lifetime of smash-and-grab cleaning and dawn-raid vacuuming. Then suddenly it had ended. So very quickly. And a week later Caroline, who hadn't done much to help during those two years, had swooped in and cleared all Mum's things away and the room had been reclaimed.

There were, Deirdre realised, more people who no longer lived in this house than there were who still did. She led the vacuum cleaner out of the computer room across the landing to the girls' bedroom.

The room looked exactly as it had a week ago when

Deirdre had last vacuumed it. A light layering of dust, yes, but otherwise exactly the same.

She paused in the door, vacuum cleaner in hand, and caught a whiff of the teenage chaos of tangled unwashed clothes, used tissues, open make-up tubes and hairspray cans. It was a whiff, no more. A lingering memory of disorder long reined in. Of people who had moved on. Now if the girls visited they tended to stay an afternoon. Jennifer would start to get fidgety around four o'clock and drive off back to Clapham before the afternoon rush hour began. Charlotte, who visited once or twice a year during the university holidays, did at least stay overnight.

Deirdre sat down heavily on one of the beds. What *had* Jennifer been thinking? What had possessed her? Why had she said those things? And on that awful television program?

Perhaps Charlotte knew something? You could never tell with Charlotte, with either of them. How could you know if anyone was telling the truth?

Could it be true? *Could* it?

She tried, tried, tried to remember the evening Jennifer had talked about but it was so hard. There were so many evenings like that, so many illnesses. There was always one of them wrapped in a blanket on the sofa.

And school uniforms. They were forever tearing and getting holes in and losing bits of it—except Graham, oddly, who never seemed to ruin or destroy any of his uniform.

Suppose something *had* happened and she, their mother, had missed it?

She smoothed down the duvet cover impatiently. Nothing had happened. They were a normal family. They didn't have those kinds of dramas. Boyfriends, of course. Jennifer had gone through a few. She had always seemed very keen on that Darryl boy. No, it was

Darren. Darren McKenzie, and his mother had worked at Lloyds Bank in the high street. Then it had ended— very suddenly, it had seemed at the time. But that was teenagers. There was no accounting for them. Hopeless to even try.

Charlotte had never had any boyfriends as far as she knew—but did mothers ever know? Charlotte had seemed happy enough. Well, no, not happy; moody. She'd always been one for moods, spending all her time with that Zoe from school. But Zoe had moved away, up north some- where with her mother who was that presenter from the telly. And that summer Charlotte had insisted—quite out of the blue—that she be allowed to do her A-levels at the sixth-form college in the town and not at the school, even though it meant two buses and none of her friends being there.

Deirdre fingered the creamy frill of the duvet. The black and red and white duvet that Charlotte had picked out of a catalogue twenty-five years earlier was long gone, replaced by a creamy-white carnation design from John Lewis's.

It didn't make sense. The bed, the empty bedroom, this creamy-white duvet. None of it made sense. It had made sense before. Now, suddenly, it didn't.

Why would Jennifer say that? And on television?

For a few days she had actually considered tele- phoning Caroline.

And now this Mr Milthorpe had telephoned late last night from a hospital ward and she and Eric were about to drive up to Yorkshire. And here she was vacuuming.

From downstairs she could hear Brian Matthew's *Sounds of the Sixties* on the radio followed by a burst of Roy Orbison then abruptly Roy Orbison was cut off and, from the hallway, Eric called up the stairs.

'We should be off, love. Traffic'll be murder. Contraflows round Newport Pagnell.'

'Be right there,' called Deirdre, not moving. She looked at the layer of dust that had accumulated in just one week, pulled herself to her feet and turned the FireFlash™ 3000 to maximum suction. The little red light on the body of the cleaner began to flash urgently.

CHAPTER NINETEEN

IT WAS IMPORTANT SHE speak to Jennifer, there was something that needed saying. And Charlotte, Charlotte too. What was it? And why hadn't they come when she'd called them?

Caroline closed her eyes, opened them again. All she could see were the lopsided venetian blinds at the window, the harsh fluorescent light above her head, the green curtains on metal rails that framed her bed and, on the wall opposite, a large, wistful watercolour of three kittens at play that someone, inexplicably, had gone to the trouble of framing and placing in the ward.

But Jennifer *had* come, she remembered now, only a few days ago. And it had snowed. Mr Milthorpe had cleared the snow off his driveway then done her own, waving to her from the path, and she had just decided to go off and make him a nice strong cup of tea when Jennifer had turned up in her Peugeot, all the way from London. She must have had a day off. People nowadays had all sorts of days off, it was a wonder they got any work done at all. And at the same time all you heard about was people working eighty-hour weeks. How could that be? How could both those things be true? But that was the way of the world now; everything was true and nothing was.

What had they talked of, she and Jennifer?

'Alright, Mrs Kettley?'

The girl-nurse was back. She materialised out of nowhere and picked up Caroline's hand, studying the back of it thoughtfully like some amateur palm-reader who hadn't got the technique quite right.

'Eh, you've had some cuts there, haven't you, love,' she remarked, observing the network of fine white scars that showed faintly on both of Caroline's hands. The girl-nurse adjusted the tube that attached Caroline to a drip, then she tapped the back of her hand. 'Just move that drip,' she murmured, not looking up, and she fiddled with the needle that was sticking half in, half out of the vein.

Caroline watched and wondered if she herself needed to be here, or if the girl could do all this on her own without help.

'There now,' said the girl-nurse, standing up. 'Doctor'll be along presently.' And she left.

Presently. You didn't hear people say that often; it was a word that had gone out of fashion.

Jennifer had driven up and they had talked of Charlotte. Jennifer had been worried about Charlotte. No, not worried, annoyed. There had been a television program. There was always a television program nowadays. You did what you could to escape them but it was a battle you could never win.

High up in the corner of the room was a small television set on a long metal arm suspended on a sort of platform. Mercifully the screen was blank, the set switched off, but as if on cue, from the room across the corridor, came a sudden burst of studio audience laughter. It didn't sound like real laughter, it sounded like people trying too hard to enjoy themselves.

What had Jennifer done? Or was it something Charlotte had done? She had needed to speak to them, it was important, and Jennifer had come but all they had spoken of was the television program then Jennifer had said it was getting late though it wasn't even three o'clock and she had only been there an hour and a half, perhaps two hours. But it was a long drive back to London and in that snow. So Jennifer had left and Caroline hadn't said what she had meant to say.

And Charlotte hadn't come at all.

It had seemed important. But perhaps it wasn't. Perhaps to anyone else, it wasn't important at all. Most things that seemed important weren't important to anyone else.

Dad had said, *Look at that sparrow trying to build her nest before her eggs are laid—do you think she cares if there's a war going on?* He must have said it more than once, for her to remember it all these years later. Funny, it sounded peaceful, almost wistful, when she said it to herself, like a homily you might see beneath a watercolour of a dove stuck on the wall of a church office. But when Dad said it, it was said angrily, resentfully, it was aimed at someone— probably Mum, as though she were the sparrow and she had no business building nests when there was a war to be won.

Yet it was Dad who had died and the war had ended and it was Mum who had lived to build her nest for another thirty-five years, so there you were.

A second burst of studio laughter erupted from the room across the corridor, accompanied, this time, by a titter of laughter from whoever was visiting the old lady in that room. Sad to think of someone coming to visit you and then sitting there and watching the television.

Where was Mr Milthorpe? She realised she hadn't seen him for a while. Perhaps he'd gone home. The snow would be banked up on the path again by now. Little point in clearing it when she wasn't going to be walking up the path for a while. Still, people liked to keep busy, especially at a time like this. People liked to feel they were doing something useful. She'd done it herself when Mrs

Milthorpe was ill in the hospital, baking a casserole or a lasagne and leaving them on his doorstep. He'd especially liked the lasagne, she remembered.

A time like this. What sort of a time was this? There was no other time in her life when she had had a stroke and found herself helpless and uncertain in a hospital bed. It was not an experience she could draw on from her past. There was no 'time like this' to fall back on, it was all new.

She didn't need new experiences at this time of life. She wanted to sit back and enjoy routine, mull over the past—well, parts of it—and know with some certainty what each day would bring. The past, somehow, had become comforting. Which was odd, when the past meant growing up in the war, and people dying.

She thought about William.

CHAPTER TWENTY

FEBRUARY 1945

THE RUSSIANS HAD CAPTURED Warsaw, Dresden was being bombarded, fighting had ceased altogether in Athens and the nightshift at the aircraft factory was finally coming off duty.

It was the last of these circumstances that had any meaning at all as Caroline stepped out of the sandbagged doorway and into the frozen dawn to begin the long trudge home.

It was Tuesday morning—just.

She waved a vague farewell to the other girls of Orange shift, not caring to whom she was waving or in what direction they were trudging, concerned only with pulling the collar of her coat up and the brim of her woollen hat down.

The factory was housed in a vast underground bunker in a disused goods yard, the remains of an aborted underground railway tunnel extension to the District Line that had been abandoned thirty years previously. The bunker now contained machinery, sandbags, workbenches and generators for forty women, a handful of engineers, two inspectors and enough propellers, undercarriages and gun emplacements to maintain a hundred Lancaster and Wellington bombers.

Caroline had worked at the aircraft factory ever since she had left school four years ago: first with Silver shift, stamping, pressing and drilling holes in small sections of aluminium, then with Red shift, riveting, wiring and sheet-metal working. Last year she had volunteered for Orange, which was the nightshift. If you were good—and she was good—you spent most of your time oxyacetylene welding and operating the lathes. It was the lathes and the welding that did the most damage to your hands. After the first week the scabs from white-hot filings and embers covered both hands, despite the gloves. After six months, the scabs had become scars and now she hardly noticed them. She had stopped wondering if she'd ever have beautiful hands again. Or if there'd be anyone left to notice them.

There was always pressure on the Mobiles to do Orange shift. Mobiles were the girls who didn't have a family to look after, meaning they could be moved to anywhere in the country at a moment's notice. Caroline didn't mind Orange shift. The girls tended to talk less and the money was better too—sixty-eight shillings a week, compared to only sixty-three shillings on days. The men, of course—the few that were left—got double that.

She walked head bent, eyes narrowed against the sting of the icy cold air, and thought about lighting a cigarette, but she didn't want to take her hands out of her pockets so instead she walked more quickly. It was three miles each way and, since her bicycle had been stolen, it was an hour's walk home.

Who'd steal another worker's bicycle? It was unthinkable that someone from Orange shift had taken it. Yet there seemed no other explanation given the bicycle was chained up inside the perimeter fence and all that security you had to go through just to get inside the place. Not that it mattered, she realised wearily, at the same time conceding that she really did need that cigarette.

She waited till she had reached the shelter of the old iron railway bridge, fumbling in her pocket for matches and cupping her hands to stop the flame blowing out. The cigarette lit eventually but she stayed where she was, sheltered beneath the bridge for a moment or two, before starting once more on her journey.

How quickly you stopped noticing. She could recall nothing, absolutely nothing, about her walk to the factory last night, about her walk home yesterday morning, about any of her walks last week. They were gone. You just stopped remembering, or you stopped noticing in the first place. You switched off.

She quickened her step.

The dawn was a muddy yellow glow on the horizon. It provided little light and no warmth. Yesterday the daylight had barely scraped above the rooftops before sliding back into evening.

Reaching High Street she noticed through the gloom that the vast crater outside the post office still hadn't been cordoned off. It had been there for over a fortnight, ever since an unexploded bomb that had probably fallen sometime in 1940 had suddenly gone off. If the ARPs didn't cordon it off soon some poor sod would fall into it. Already a foot of frozen water had filled the bottom of the crater.

Hope the sod who took my bicycle is the one who falls into it, she thought, fleetingly enjoying this gratifying image.

As she turned into Oakton Way and approached the house her pace slowed and finally she stopped a few houses short of her own, and stood for a moment in the feeble dawn light opposite number twenty-eight.

Number twenty-eight was now vacant.

Usually she walked straight past, head down, eyes focused, her mind empty. But this morning she looked across at the house, studying its boarded-up windows, the weeds that already, in a few short weeks and despite the winter frosts, had begun to reclaim the path that led up to the front door. On that front door was a single forgotten sprig of dead holly, left over from a Christmas already six weeks past.

Number twenty-eight was a terrace in the centre of Oakton Way, not far from the corner of Nelson Avenue. The Davenports had lived there. They were a large family, the Davenports. The sort of family that seemed always to have someone coming or going and an endless supply of small children tumbling in and out of the front door, the remains of tea smeared over their faces. The Davenports seemed to have been in Oakton Way forever. Mr Davenport had been injured in the First War—you could see his limp sometimes, particularly in cold weather—and after the War he'd worked for years at the railyard round the back of Gunnersbury Lane. Mrs Davenport had been a tiny woman, all untidy hair and apron strings, a baby on her hip. She had raised that family, and kept on raising it, on railyard wages. There had been six, or perhaps even seven of them. It was difficult to recall the younger ones.

The Davenports. They had been such a fixture of Oakton Way that it seemed impossible to imagine the street without them. But the war changed that, as it changed most things, so that one moment there was Kitty Davenport in a smock, ice-cream dribbling down her chin, and little William Davenport chasing a ball across the street and almost going under the hooves of the milkman's horse, then the next minute Kitty was engaged to a corporal from Vermont, William lay dead in an airman's uniform, and number twenty-eight stood empty and deserted.

And then quite suddenly, just before Christmas, they had gone. Of course, William Davenport had been dead two years by then.

Had Kitty gone ahead and married the corporal from

Vermont? They had been such friends once, she and Kitty. All through school, and afterwards. It seemed incredible not to know. Had it been Vermont, or had it been Virginia? She couldn't even recall the man's name.

And two weeks after the Davenports had gone, a V-2 had landed on Nelson Avenue destroying six houses in one go. The explosion had damaged every other house in the avenue and sent debris into every street that bordered it, shattering glass as far away as High Street and the railway station. After that no one thought about the Davenports. And no one stopped to think of little William Davenport who had been born in the upstairs front room of number twenty-eight and who had once fallen from the wall of the gasworks and spent a night in the hospital with concussion and who had stood under a streetlamp—this very streetlamp—and asked a girl to marry him. William, who had been dead these two years past.

The V-2s were falling heavily again now after it had seemed in December they were over. The first one had fallen in Chiswick last September. They'd been sitting down to dinner and just as Mum had been serving out a rabbit stew all the windows had rattled. They'd all stopped and looked at each other but no one had spoken.

The rockets tended to come at night now. This was better as there seemed to be fewer casualties at night and the bombs fell mostly south of the river or in Kent and Essex and Surrey, which made you glad but then made you feel guilty for wishing it on someone else. Croydon in particular was getting it bad, she had heard from a girl in Red shift whose family lived out that way. The V-1s seemed to have petered out altogether, or at least very few were getting through. That was a relief. That horrid droning sound and the sickening, breathless wait to see if it would cut out right over your head or continue on its way was enough to snap your nerves.

The V-2s made no sound, which ought to have been more terrifying but somehow wasn't. The first you knew about it, they said, was when your house collapsed around you.

And William was dead and had been for over two years, long before the first V-1 had fallen, before the Germans had retreated from Russia or Mussolini had been overthrown or Rome liberated. Before D-day. He'd missed so much, there was so much to tell him. And now she couldn't remember what he looked like.

Ahead, number fifteen was in blackout still, as was most of the street. She ought not to have lit her cigarette. It was all but gone now anyway and she paused at the garden gate to light a second from the embers of the first, tossing away the finished butt and drawing on the second one.

Once, a very long time ago it seemed now, she would stand on the corner of Oakton Way hastily taking a few last drags on her cigarette then stuffing a mint in her mouth before going into the house, hiding her cigarettes beneath her bed and her matches at the bottom of her bag. This elaborate charade was for Dad's benefit as Dad did not approve of women smoking. It was 'common'. But now they had all survived five years of war. Now Caroline was nineteen, she worked nightshift in an aircraft factory operating a lathe and, somehow, whether you smoked or not didn't seem to matter. Somehow a lot of things no longer seemed to matter.

She opened the little gate and let it bang shut behind her, walked up the path to the house and pushed open the front door. She could smell coffee, or some hideous wartime version of it, brewing in the kitchen, fat frying in the pan and carbolic soap where Mum had been washing down the walls in the hallway to remove some of the dust from the Nelson Avenue rocket. But mostly she could smell iron filings and hot metal and cigarettes and that didn't come from the house, it came from her.

'Poo, you stink!' announced Deirdre, as she did every morning when Caroline walked into the kitchen.

'Deirdre! Don't be so rude,' replied Mum, her stock response and Caroline ignored them both and went out the back to wash.

'Mornin', love,' said Dad, not looking up from his paper.

'Good shift, dear?' called Mum over the sound of running water, the hiss of fat from the frying pan and the voice of the BBC newsreader who kept up a low but perfectly enunciated commentary in the background.

'How many aeroplanes did you build last night?' demanded Deirdre.

Through the doorway Caroline could see Mum in her floral apron, her grey hair in a net, one hand on the handle of the frying pan, one swirling the coffee dregs in the pot to make it go further, and Deirdre in her school uniform, grey socks pulled up high at her knees, kneeling on the kitchen chair, spreading margarine on her bread, the tip of her tongue poking out, all her concentration focused on making the meagre scrape reach each corner equally. And Dad, sitting with his usual silent frown, listening to the radio announcer, half reading the morning paper, half observing his family as though he was not sure how they—or perhaps he—had come to be here.

'Croydon got it bad again last night,' he announced. 'Hear that, Clive?'

And, as Caroline emerged from her wash, Uncle Clive appeared in the doorway in his slippers and a faded silk burgundy dressing-gown, a matching silk scarf tucked inside the gown. He smiled broadly as though he were on holiday.

'Just as well we don't live in Croydon, then, in't it, Matthew, old boy?' he said brightly, looking at each face in turn so as not to miss the little laugh or the admiring look this comment obviously warranted. No one laughed or looked admiringly at him. Unperturbed he pulled up a chair, sat down and reached for Dad's paper. Dad bristled visibly but Uncle Clive seemed not to notice and settled back in his chair to await his breakfast.

On the first of November last year, a V-2 had landed in Camberwell, killing and seriously injuring over forty people, causing widespread damage and destroying a number of buildings, including the Boar's Head public house in the high street. Uncle Clive, who had been the landlord of the Boar's Head at Camberwell, now lived with the Lakes in Oakton Way.

'There was an egg, love,' said Mum, turning to Caroline, 'but I gave it to your dad.' Mum stood at the sink and looked at Dad to confirm that there had indeed been an egg and that he had been the lucky recipient of it. But Dad was concentrating on the BBC news and offered neither confirmation nor denial.

'Quite right, Berty, old gal. The workers 'ave gotta be fed!' observed Uncle Clive. 'Ain't that right, girls?' And he looked from Deirdre to Caroline. Deirdre wrinkled her nose as though to avoid an unpleasant smell. Caroline looked at his little military moustache and remembered with a slight shudder how it tickled when he kissed you.

Uncle Clive wasn't really an uncle. He was one of those vague uncles-by-marriage of whom no one had even heard, or at least, Caroline and Deirdre and Dad had never heard, until he had inexplicably turned up on the doorstep on a frozen, foggy morning in the second week of November, wearing a grimy trenchcoat and carrying two paper bags of clothes he'd received at the emergency rest centre, waving his replacement ration book triumphantly. He had given a hearty, 'Here I am then!' as though they all knew who he was and had been eagerly awaiting his arrival.

Mum had known who he was: some relative-by-marriage of her dead sister.

So Uncle Clive had moved in and, though it was intended to be a Temporary Arrangement and Dad had made it very clear that giving up the parlour so Clive could have a temporary bedroom was not a long-term solution to anything, it was now the first week in February and Uncle Clive, as he sat at the kitchen table humming to himself and putting down his coffee cup in order to turn the page of the paper, looked in no hurry to depart.

'Delightful drop, Bertha,' he remarked in a pleased voice, nodding towards his cup then looking up and smiling approval.

Mum frowned darkly and attacked the frying pan with a scrubbing brush.

'Ahem,' said Dad sternly, reaching over the table and reclaiming the morning paper, which Clive had momentarily put down on the table.

'Why don't *you* ever make the tea, Uncle Clive?' said Deirdre, looking up from her plate.

'Deirdre, don't be rude,' said Mum, not raising her head. She had spoken mildly enough but the scrubbing increased in ferocity to almost manic speed.

'Ha!' said Dad, shaking out the paper. 'I expect Uncle Clive is far too occupied finding work and a place to live,' but rather than appear abashed, Uncle Clive looked up in surprise and the light from the weak electric light bulb overhead bounced off his Brylcreemed hair.

'Not me. I'm consolidatin',' he declared, and then he looked up at Caroline, who was standing in the kitchen doorway, and he winked at her.

Caroline pulled out a cigarette and ignored him.

The frying pan banged against the enamel of the kitchen sink with a loud and jarring clang.

'For God's *sake*!' snapped Dad.

The scouring abruptly ceased and Mum stood perfectly still at the sink, her arms up to the elbows in soapy water, a sheen of moisture on her upper lip.

What was the matter with her?

'Surrey and parts of Kent again came under heavy enemy fire last night,' reported the man on the BBC news, *'causing damage to a number of residential and commercial buildings, though casualties are reported to be light. Mr Churchill announced that heavy bombing raids by the RAF over Dresden continued to cause substantial—'*

Dad scraped back his chair and turned off the radio, as he always did when he was leaving, as if no one else would be interested in listening to the news.

And perhaps he was right, thought Caroline, sitting down in the vacated chair and pouring herself a cup of grey-looking coffee. Deirdre was only interested in what was playing at the pictures and that morning's hastily completed homework which she was invariably finishing off at the breakfast table. And Mum seemed unaware there was a War on at all—the absence of eggs, meat, clothes, sugar appeared to come as a complete surprise to her every time she attempted to purchase something. And Clive, who, of them all, had the most reason to be wary of the war, seemed the least interested in its progress. His daily perusal of the morning paper was purely concerned with rationing and coupons and what the shops in Bond Street had on sale. How he filled his day, one could only wonder—he certainly hadn't found a job and the only time you saw him out and about was when he was coming out of one pub and going into another. Perhaps he was doing research—after all, he had been a publican for more than twenty years. But somehow you knew that what he was doing was having a drink and playing a game of darts.

'Right, duty calls,' Dad announced, standing in the centre of the room, placing his hat on his head and waiting for everyone to wish him a good day at work.

'Well, I can't hear it,' replied Deirdre facetiously. She tucked her thin, schoolgirl legs beneath her on the chair.

Mum carefully laid the frying pan on the draining

board and dutifully went over and stood before Dad, wiping her hands on her apron and looking as though she would have liked to kiss him goodbye, or at least as if she felt she *ought* to kiss him goodbye. Instead, Dad, as he did every morning—and especially so since being made postmaster—frowned and stiffened and said, 'Mind that doesn't boil over, Bertha,' and Caroline assumed he was referring to the hot water in the kettle rather than Mum's affection for him.

'You enjoy yourself with all them parcels and tele-grams, Matthew,' said Uncle Clive, reaching for the paper. He pushed his cup into the middle of the table. 'Fill 'er up, Deirdre,' he said.

Deirdre pulled a face behind her homework and grudgingly pushed the teapot in his direction with the tip of her pencil.

Dad, having fulfilled his role as head of the house-hold, stood already forgotten in the doorway, a frown on his face as though he was trying to remember something.

As she watched him, Caroline caught his eye, or thought she did. Then she realised it was Mum he was watching as she picked up the frying pan and began furi-ously scrubbing it once more. Dad seemed on the verge of saying something and Caroline waited for her stomach muscles to tense the way they always did when Dad was about to get angry. But they didn't. In fact, she realised, they hadn't for a while now, and not because Dad had stopped getting angry—he hadn't—but just because it didn't seem to matter anymore.

Instead Dad turned on his heel and stomped loudly down the hallway and after a moment the front door closed with a bang.

Deirdre looked up from her homework, chewed her pencil thoughtfully, then looked at Caroline and wrinkled her nose.

'You still stink,' she said.

William was laughing. Balancing on one hand, his legs straight up in the air, feet rigid, his toes pointing to the sky. His old corduroy cap had fallen onto the pavement and his shirt tails fell forward over his head. He held the pose for one second, two, three, then he collapsed and fell with a crash, half onto the roadside, half into Mrs Fielding's privet hedge at number twenty-six. He lay like that, still laughing, but as Caroline held out a hand to help him he jumped nimbly to his feet, scooped his cap off the ground and stuck it on his head—only now, Caroline saw, the cap had become his grey RAF forage cap.

'Invincible, me!' he declared and, grabbing both of Caroline's hands he pulled her towards him to kiss her, but as he did so a huge bomber appeared over the horizon behind him, its engines throbbing, and Caroline realised the sound had always been there, in the background, steadily growing louder and louder. It was a Wellington, you could tell by the sound of the engine, by the silhouette of its fuselage against the sun. A British aircraft, not the enemy's, one of our own, and as William's lips almost brushed hers his hands slid away, *he* slid away, so that no matter how much she reached, she couldn't quite touch him. At the same time the Wellington roared overhead so that it filled the sky, filled the whole world—only it wasn't flying overhead, it was flying directly at them. Caroline screamed though no sound came and she ducked but even as she crouched there on the ground, hugging her knees, she knew, with a dull, sickening awareness, that it wasn't her who should duck, it was William. She opened her mouth to warn him.

'William!'

The word hung heavily in the air, almost visible, and

Caroline found herself sitting up in bed in the half-light of a late afternoon in winter and William was dead.

She looked at the clock by her bedside: five o'clock. Another three hours till the nightshift started. Two hours until she needed to leave the house.

William. She had dreamed of William and his face... his face had been...

She tried to remember what his face had looked like, his nose, his eyes. His mouth. But she had already forgotten in the time it took to wake from a dream. Or perhaps, in the dream, his face had been a blank. She had had the dream before, many times, not quite the same each time, but the main elements were there—William talking, laughing, about to kiss her, about to say something very important. The bomber, the roar of its engine deafening. Herself screaming silently, reaching out, trying to say something, to do something. Then nothing.

Sometimes it was herself building the aircraft, sending it on its way. The bomber she herself had meticulously—lovingly—welded.

It was just a dream, a subconscious visualisation of a scene she had not witnessed. The only witnesses, so Mr Davenport had reported to Dad a few weeks afterwards, had been an AA gunner and the pilot and the navigator of the Wellington. They had returned to the airbase— William's airbase—at dawn from a night bombing mission over Germany. One wing and the undercarriage of the Wellington were damaged and they had flown, out of control, onto the airstrip, slamming into a pillbox, clipping two stationary Mosquitoes and finally coming to rest against a retaining wall. Both pilot and navigator had been badly bruised; the navigator had sustained a wrist fracture and a dislocated thumb, the pilot a nasty cut above the eye that had required several stiches. The AA gunner in the pillbox had leapt to safety. The only casualty, then, had been a member of the ground crew, Airman William

Davenport, a rigger, who had been working on the fuse-lage of one of the downed Mosquitoes and who had been killed instantly.

Killed by the RAF and a Wellington bomber.

At the time Caroline had been working in the machine shop at the aircraft factory, fitting glass covers to instrument panels. Now, two years later, she was part of Orange shift, an all-woman crew who churned out a Wellington every week. It was ironic, if she thought about it. Mostly, she didn't think about it.

She lay in bed and contemplated the ceiling in the half-light. She could hear Mum in the kitchen down-stairs requesting assistance with vegetable peeling and Deirdre's petulant reply. A door slammed followed by Mum's anxious insistence not to be so noisy as they'd wake Caroline. Someone was whistling at the kitchen sink, a vibrant man's whistle, off-key but strong. Not Dad, Dad didn't whistle—and besides, it was too early for him to be home from work. Uncle Clive then, and he was whis-tling 'I've Got a Lovely Bunch of Coconuts', switching to a hum as though he had closed his mouth to shave. Uncle Clive was preparing to go out and soon the odour of cheap eau-de-cologne would snake its way up the stairs and into the small back room she shared with Deirdre.

She should get up. Tea would be ready soon and it was cold lying here in bed despite being almost fully dressed. But she lay where she was. Eventually—after the smell of boiling spinach and carrot and potato and eau-de-cologne had reached her, after Mum had called upstairs that tea was ready, after she had heard the front door open and close and Dad announce his arrival in the hallway, after Uncle Clive had whistled his way down the hall and out the front door—she got up.

It was quarter to six.

Downstairs, Mum was looking distinctly on edge. She stood frozen in the middle of the kitchen with a ladle in her hand. She started when Caroline appeared in the doorway, turning abruptly away.

'Mum, I'm popping out with Anne and Doris,' called Deirdre from the hallway and immediately Dad, who was hanging up his coat and hat, looked over and stood up straight.

'You'll do no such thing. Tonight's a school night. You'll stay in and do your homework.'

'But—'

'And if you've finished your homework you'll help your mum in the kitchen. I'll not have any daughter of mine out after dark.'

Deirdre appeared in the kitchen doorway, changed from her school uniform into a blouse and slacks, a faint red smudge around her mouth as though she had recently put on then removed lipstick. Her face was red.

'But that's not fair! Caroline—'

'I'll not enter into a discussion on this. Go to your room, Deirdre.'

Deirdre clenched her fists and her face became redder and she glared at Dad and then at Caroline, then she pushed roughly past and thudded noisily up the stairs.

Caroline wondered briefly if it really was Anne and Doris waiting for Deirdre outside. Don't be daft, she chided herself, the kid was only twelve for God's sake. It was tempting to go after her with some of the older-sister put-downs she'd used to such good effect over the years. It even crossed her mind to go upstairs and see if Deirdre was alright. But in the end, she said nothing. She went nowhere. None of it seemed remotely important.

'Evening, love. Good kip?' said Dad, standing at the kitchen sink washing his face.

'Don't you want your tea, dear?' said Mum, hovering in an unsettling manner. 'I called up half an hour ago.'

'Not hungry, I'll just take my sandwiches with me.'

'But I saved you some brown soup.'

Mum really did look as if the fate of the brown soup

was uppermost in her mind and Caroline sat down, saying nothing. Mum took this as assent, grabbed a clean bowl and poured a quantity of watery grey liquid into it.

'Here you are,' she said with satisfaction. 'And there's bread in the bread bin. And the potatoes are still warm in the oven. Don't forget to have a nice warming cuppa, too.'

'Don't mollycoddle the girl, Bertha,' said Dad sharply. Normally Mum would have flushed at this and scurried away, but this evening she barely seemed aware of Dad. Instead she looked at her watch and, when she looked up, she looked straight at Caroline.

'I'll just pop out, then,' she said unexpectedly, and Dad looked up from the evening paper.

'Mrs Larkin at number twenty-one,' said Mum by way of explanation. 'Said I'd feed her cat while she's at her daughter's.'

Caroline picked up her soup spoon and dipped it in the uninviting liquid, fully absorbed for a moment by the swirling patterns her spoon made on the greasy surface of the soup. Mrs Larkin had gone to her daughter's a week ago and this was the first time Mum had mentioned anything about feeding her cat.

'*This is the BBC Home Service with the six o'clock news,*' said the announcer on the radio, followed by six crisp pips.

Caroline glanced at the kitchen clock. Still an hour before she needed to leave.

The front door closed quietly behind Mum and Caroline looked up from her soup. Dad reached over and flicked off the radio, listening in the sudden silence, his head on one side like a spotter in a watchtower. Upstairs Deirdre thumped angrily about, making some sort of aggrieved-twelve-year-old's point. Then the thumps ceased and the house fell silent.

Caroline stood up and went into the hallway, snatching up her coat and opening the front door.

'I'm off, Dad,' she called over her shoulder.

Outside night had come quickly and a blast of freezing air hit her like a piece of bad news. The blackout usually plunged the street into total darkness but tonight the full moon and a clear sky meant that, for once, she could see where she was going.

She pulled the front door shut behind her to prevent the light from the kitchen breaking the blackout but she stayed in the doorway, her eyes drawn across the road to where number twenty-eight stood empty. The downstairs windows had long ago been boarded up to keep out looters and other undesirables. But there was a window at the back of the house that was unboarded and had been forced open. You could get in easily enough if you knew where to look.

This evening someone was inside the house.

The blackout curtains had been removed by the Davenports when they'd left and now a figure in the front upstairs bedroom was clearly visible, a figure standing perfectly still so that she almost didn't notice him. Until the figure turned and, stupidly, struck a match to light a cigarette.

William was tall, fair-haired, his shoulders not broad, but strong. He smoked his cigarettes expansively, with big gestures and great gusts of smoke.

But William was dead and the Davenports were gone.

As the match flared and the figure's face was momentarily lit up she saw a thin moustache, a silk scarf, the gleam of hair oil. Uncle Clive.

Caroline remained where she was, watching from the doorway. It was cold and she was late. And as she watched, another figure appeared in the front bedroom. Uncle Clive turned sharply, his cigarette casting a pale glow over the face of the newcomer.

Mum.

A quarter of a mile away the bells of St Mary's struck distantly, carried on the breeze in the clear night air. It was six o'clock.

At six o'clock on Tuesday evening Caroline was standing in the doorway of number fifteen staring up at the window of number twenty-eight opposite. At one minute past she was lying on her front beneath the rosebushes, covered in broken glass, a roaring in her ears that blotted out all else.

As the roaring did not subside, Caroline remained where she was, her hands over her head, and at the same time tried to dig herself into the earth.

A rocket had landed, that much was obvious. A V-2, it would have to be, because she had heard nothing, no buzzing of engines, no drone suddenly cutting out overhead. Just a silent, moonlit night. And then—nothing.

The roaring changed in timbre and Caroline lifted her head. At first, all she could see were millions of tiny, flickering lights in her eyes because she had squeezed them shut so tightly. After a dizzying moment the flickering lights sorted themselves out into a single mass of orange and yellow and the roaring in her ears gradually became a roaring associated with the orange and yellow.

She pulled herself up to her knees unsteadily, a shower of glass and dirt cascading around her. She tried to brush it away but her hand wouldn't do what she wanted. It was shaking too much.

There was smoke, too, great pillars of it, and she put a hand to her face, already choking. The orange and yellow light, roaring and crackling, lit up the whole street. She had to raise her arm to shield her eyes from the light and the heat where a moment ago it had been frozen darkness. The sky was lit up like a brilliant sunset and now she saw the flames and the houses on fire. And the houses were oddly misshapen, stunted. Roofs, whole walls had gone as though a giant had walked right through and crushed them.

Already, people—neighbours, air-raid wardens, fire

crews, the police, you couldn't say for sure who—were there, in the street, running, shouting, doing things. An ambulance crew, a fire tender. People were helping.

Getting to her feet, she stumbled along the front path and paused at the gate. Ahead of her the street glistened with broken glass. Bricks, timbers, roof tiles lay strewn all about. Three houses near the corner with Nelson Avenue had gone. There was nothing there but smoke and a gaping black hole. The houses on either side of the hole were on fire, the flames by now leaping thirty, forty feet into the night sky. Both had lost their roofs. The walls supporting what remained of the timber joists and tiles were warped and buckled from the blast and in imminent danger of toppling right over.

Now, only now, did she think to look behind, at the house. At *their* house. Dad was standing, leaning against the doorway, his face frozen, ashen, bathed in the flickering orange glow of the flames.

Someone screamed, a high-pitched, girlish scream. Looking up, Caroline saw the window of Mum and Dad's room. The glass had gone, only jagged shards sticking out of the frame, and in the window Deirdre's ghost-like figure peering out and pointing. She pointed across the street and Caroline turned to see what Deirdre was pointing at.

Caroline's eyes went straight to the upstairs window of the front bedroom at number twenty-eight where, only a minute before, two people had stood. Now the glass was gone, the window frame buckled, the roof above had come crashing onto the first floor and there was no sign of anyone.

The Davenports' house. Thank God William wasn't in there. William was safe.

But Mum. Mum was in there.

She pointed in the same direction that Deirdre had pointed because the heat and the smoke and the dust in the air made it impossible to talk. Dad was there, she found, standing just behind her. He stared silently at her then, without a word, they set off together across the road, walking quickly. Not running, just a calm, purposeful stride, dodging the rubble and the craters and other debris that had transformed Oakton Way into an alien landscape.

'*Stop, don't go in!*' cried a voice some way off. A man's voice, perhaps one of the fire crew or a warden. '*Don't go in—it's not safe!*'

Was he addressing them or someone else? They ignored him.

'*Here, Dad, at the back,*' she gasped, struggling over a pile of rubble and feeling her way down the side passage between number twenty-eight and number thirty. She led the way, negotiating tiles and bricks, all the time thinking, What will we find? Will it be blocked? She paused at the Davenports' kitchen window to ease it open but there was no kitchen window. Really, there was no kitchen, just an outline of bricks.

Dad pushed past. '*I'll go on! You stay here!*' he shouted, pulling out a handkerchief and holding it to his nose to block out some of the smoke and dust.

'*Upstairs! The front room!*' called Caroline, following him, climbing over the rubble that had once been the kitchen and into the main part of the house. This, at least, was still intact. Something caught her eye: a black shape, on the kitchen floor. A human shape that slowly moved, sitting up and gasping for breath then breaking out in a fit of coughing.

Clive.

She went to him, stumbling and almost falling, and it seemed that, beneath the black coating of smoke and dust, he appeared to be all in one piece.

'*Where's Mum? Is Mum with you? Dad's gone upstairs to find her. Where is she?*'

At her words, he opened his eyes and they were

starkly white against the black of his face. He reached out to hold her arm, nodding, coughing.

'Don't know, don't know, love. Must have been—*cough*—in the doorway when it... Blew me clean down the stairs—*choke*—Your mum...' He jerked his head ceiling-ward. 'Don't know, love.'

Caroline thrust his hand away and stumbled through the hallway and up the stairs, her scarf over her mouth, feeling her way, her head low to avoid the smoke. She was halfway up before it occurred to her the staircase must be damaged, that perhaps it would collapse at even the slightest vibration. She slowed her pace and found she couldn't breathe.

For a moment panic overtook her and she gripped the banister, clawing at the wall. Steady, keep calm, she told herself. It's the smoke. It's panic. Keep going.

She took a step forward, treading carefully, but here the front of the house appeared remarkably intact, so that you could believe, apart from the smoke and choking dust, that there was no damage. Then she turned the corner in the stairs and stopped.

The upstairs was gone. Or rather, it had vanished in a pile of debris where the roof had fallen in. There was moonlight above. But at eye level it was so dark and dusty it was difficult to be certain what she was looking at and for a moment she lost her bearings. But the front bedroom—it must be directly ahead of her. William's house was a mirror image of their own. She continued upwards, following the stair-rail to the landing, her foot slipping, clambering over rubble and bricks, cutting her knees and hands, grabbing where she could find a steady hold. The doorframe to the bedroom was ahead remarkably still intact and she stepped through it. Beyond, she could make out the interior of the bedroom; two of the walls seemed to be still standing but the rest of the room had vanished in a great pile of timber and plaster and bricks.

Before she could call out, she saw movement and there was Dad. He was standing just beyond the doorway, quite still, calmly, his hands loose by his sides like he was on a Sunday stroll in the park.

Then Dad moved. He turned and looked at her.

So Mum was dead. Dad had found her and she was dead.

Caroline stared at him, her heart lurching sickeningly. She pushed herself onwards till she was standing level with him. The debris filled the whole room so that she couldn't make out the start or end of it. It shifted every so often, with a creak and a trickle of rubble and dust. Otherwise it was strangely quiet up here. Her own ragged breathing seemed shatteringly loud. She could hear shouts from the street outside, the crackle of flames from the other houses. Her eyes adjusted to the scene and she saw that not far away, just a few feet really, almost touching distance, was a wooden roof joist, wedged where it had fallen and forming a sort of archway, and in the corner of the arch lay Mum.

And she was alive.

Mum moved her head and groaned. Her body, though, was trapped. A smear of blood across her face glistened darkly in the moonlight. She groaned again but her eyes remained closed.

Instantly Caroline felt all the muscles in her body twitch in her urgency to reach out and grab Mum, to pull her to safety. *But how?* Which part was it safe to pull? What piece of rubble could she lift without bringing the whole lot crashing down on them?

'*Dad!*' she cried. Why didn't he rescue Mum? Why didn't he try to grab her?

But Dad gazed at his wife as she lay trapped and something flickered across his face, something unnatural, something quiet and dead.

Something like hatred.

And Caroline thought, You don't want to rescue her, you want her to die. It was because of Clive, because Dad thought Mum and Clive... No. This predated Clive. It predated everything.

And she realised that it had always been like this. Always.

Around her the house creaked and shifted but in the bedroom no one moved.

CHAPTER TWENTY-ONE

WATFORD GAP OR Leicester Forest?

Deirdre studied the AA road map that lay on her lap, open at the East Midlands. Northampton, Leicester and Nottingham showed as sprawling pink areas one above the other. The M1 was indicated by a thick blue line that bisected the page from north to south. Or in this case, from south to north, as that was the direction in which she and Eric were now travelling.

Eric was driving, not because he was the better driver or because he had necessarily volunteered for this role, but because Deirdre needed her hands and mind free to plan the journey. They had filled up at the BP garage at Elstree just before joining the motorway at Junction 4 and if they kept a good speed the tank should do them there and back. So far, however, it had to be said, they had not kept a good speed. Indeed in some instances they had kept no sort of speed at all, a combination of Saturday morning drivers and contra-flows around Newport Pagnell which meant that, an hour into their journey, they were barely past Northampton. And on the rare occasions when there had been a clear stretch of motorway, Eric, who had been driving for forty years and who had never had an accident, was reluctant to risk all by moving into the fast lane to overtake someone.

Now they were approaching the M6 turn-off and it was time to decide whether to stop at the motorway services to spend a penny and get a quick cup of coffee or press on. And if they stopped, which services to stop at? Watford Gap, which was this side of the M6, or Leicester Forest, which was the other?

She had not, Deirdre realised, been able to prepare for this journey as she would have liked. The phone call from this Mr Milthorpe had come late last night, long after you expected anyone—least of all a stranger—to ring. They'd been getting ready for bed and almost hadn't answered.

Thank God they had.

But to drive straight up to Skipton first thing in the morning, well, it left no time at all for planning, other than a quick call to Charlotte first thing and a note popped through the door of Lorraine and Brian's next door. And now here they were, hurtling north. Well, not hurtling exactly, but making their way at any rate, and it must be five years or more since she'd last driven to Skipton. There had been no time to study the map or plan their stops. All she had was Mr Milthorpe's confused directions and Lord knew what sort of a mess they'd get into trying to find a hospital in a town they had only been to a handful of times.

Watford Gap Services 1 mile, announced the blue and white motorway sign helpfully, followed by a dire warning: *Next services 22 miles.*

It was now or never. *Stop! No, stay on to the next one!* Deirdre gripped the map as the slip lane came into view.

'*Keep going!*' she gasped and Eric started and swerved the car so that they veered left then right as he corrected himself. 'Keep going,' she repeated. 'We'll go on to Leicester Forest, then we'll be nearer our destination.'

'Right-ho,' said Eric, taking a deep breath. 'We could've packed sandwiches and a thermos of tea, then we wouldn't have to stop at all,' he added.

'But there wasn't time!' Deirdre explained. 'There wasn't time. Anyway, it's better to stop.'

She didn't explain why this was so.

Deirdre turned to look out of the window at the empty fields and the bare, leafless trees still covered in early morning frost. Signs for the M6 turn-off appeared, became more insistent, split into different signs, then abruptly ceased. She drew a deep breath.

It was best not to think about Leeds city centre which, on a busy Saturday morning, would be full of shoppers. There were ring roads and bypasses and such like but experience told her that they were heading for the centre of Leeds, no matter what.

'Leicester Forest fifteen,' she noted as another sign came into view.

It was mid-morning as they turned off the motorway at the services, and despite it being late January with the air temperature hovering just above freezing and snow forecast for later and drifts already a foot deep north of York, the place was heaving. What kind of people travelled north on a Saturday morning in January? wondered Deirdre.

They located a parking spot eventually, not far from the farthest boundary of the car park and near to a rather bleak children's playground. They left the car and trekked across the car park to the automatic glass doors of the cafeteria. Deirdre led the way inside.

'You sit down, love, I'll queue,' offered Eric.

Ordinarily Deirdre queued and she looked at him now, surprised. Then she remembered why they were here, and the thought of queuing for what would undoubtedly be disappointing fare seemed unutterably depressing.

'Yes, alright. I'll find us a table,' she said. 'I'll just have a pot of coffee and maybe a biscuit. And if the milk comes in those little cartons, make sure you get two. One's never enough. Don't forget napkins.'

She found a table that wasn't littered with other people's remains and wasn't right next to any families with very young children and sat down. The table was near the window and provided a fine view of the car park, the slip road that rejoined the motorway and the three lanes of northbound traffic. It gave you a sense of movement, made you want to get on with your journey. Or maybe it was just the cafeteria that made you want to move on quickly.

Eric was taking a long time. She could see him deep in conversation with the girl at the tea and coffee counter and she could tell from the nods and the hand gestures and the pointing that this was a discussion about teabags and tea leaves. It wasn't the first such discussion Eric had had with a girl behind a counter. Tea leaves and teabags were something he felt strongly about—Eric, who had once had fifteen staff under him and, for a while, a company car. Now it had come down to teabags and tea leaves.

Deirdre turned back to the window and watched a football coach wheel around in a tight circle beneath the window then head onto the slip road heading north. She looked down at the table which was smeared where a cloth had wiped its plastic surface.

A stroke.

Caroline was past eighty, yes, but she was as strong as an ox, never been sick in her life. She wasn't the sort of person you expected to have a stroke.

What sort of person did you expect to have a stroke?

She raised her head to watch the cars on the motorway. An ambulance went by, blue lights flashing, weaving in and out of the traffic, but no one moved out of its way.

If Caroline died... If Caroline were no longer there...

She blinked and couldn't, *wouldn't* believe it. Not again, not a second time. She had been through it once already.

CHAPTER TWENTY-TWO

FEBRUARY 1945

CAROLINE ALWAYS LEFT TOO early for work and no one ever noticed.

'Cheerio, Mum' she called from the hallway as she left for the nightshift one bitterly cold Monday evening in February—a clear two hours before her shift was meant to start.

Mum didn't notice. She was too busy with yet another horrid recipe from her women's magazine for some inedible stew made from dandelions and nettles and other bomb-crater refuse. And Dad was bunkered down in the lounge engaged in important post office work—as if what happened in a dreary suburban post office could ever be in the least bit important.

So no one noticed that Caroline had left at six when the nightshift didn't start till eight.

And no one noticed Deirdre either, crouching on the stairs then creeping down the hallway and slipping silently out the front door after her.

Once outside, Deirdre felt the frozen February night close in around her, biting at her face and throat and placing icy tentacles along her neck and spine. She pulled her coat tightly around herself and spied Caroline already on the other side of the street.

Where was she going? Who she was meeting? Because she had to be meeting someone. It had been ages since William was killed, after all.

But to her surprise Caroline paused outside number twenty-eight, the Davenports' old house. She opened the gate and walked up the path and down the side of the house.

That was odd. That was *very* odd!

The Davenports' house had been empty for ages— why would Caroline go there? Unless Kitty Davenport had come back and was staying there? But no, that was daft, Kitty was engaged to that Yank, probably even married by now. And if Kitty was back, she would have come round to visit. And that went for any of the Davenports. You would have heard, the whole street would have known if the Davenports were back.

Unless…

It came to Deirdre in a flash so that she stopped dead in the middle of the street, slapping her hand to her head and feeling dazed, breathless.

It was William! William was alive! He had returned, only to find all his family gone! He hadn't been killed by that Wellington bomber, he had survived!

But why keep it a secret? It didn't make sense. Why had Caroline said nothing?

She tried to think. Caroline and William had been stepping out…oh, forever. Everyone knew that. And come to think of it, Caroline hadn't seemed that bothered at all when William had been killed. When they *thought* he'd been killed. She'd just got on with it really. She was sort of quiet, distant. But that was just Caroline… But if William was alive—had been alive all this time…!

A second thought hit her, with at least the same force as the first, though this one made her feel a little sick.

William was a deserter. That was it, it had to be, it fitted so exactly, explained why he was hiding out here, why Caroline had said nothing.

Oh, William! Oh, Caroline! Assisting a deserter, perhaps engaged—or even *married*, God forbid!—to a *deserter!* He would go to prison. Or be on the run, for life. Forever. And Caroline, too, for aiding him.

And what about herself, standing there, knowing there was a deserter in that house? She was an accomplice. She would be arrested. They would all be arrested!

It was better not to know, then there was no question of being involved. She must leave at once and say nothing. Do nothing. Act surprised. Lie, if necessary!

But she had to know...

She approached the house, a feeling of dread dragging her stomach down into her bowels but somehow also forcing her on. She pushed open the gate of number twenty-eight and crept silently up the path.

Deidre wasn't a snitch. She would keep their secret, of course she would, if they asked her to, if they made her.

She paused at the Davenports' front door, listening. Inside there was silence. Outside, a dozen noises suddenly came into focus: men's voices calling, a dog barking, a door slamming and, further off, the splutter of a motor engine, the klaxon of a distant ambulance. There had been no rockets for a while. Mum said it was almost like peacetime.

She slipped silently down the side passage until she came to the kitchen window, which was ajar. She knew the Davenports' house, it was the same as her own house, although in reverse. She had been friends for a time with Jeanie and Dotty, Kitty's younger sisters, though the friendship hadn't lasted. But she remembered the house, its smells, the colour of the walls and carpets.

There was an old wooden crate beneath the kitchen window and after only a slight hesitation she stepped onto it, reached up to the window ledge and pulled herself up. She paused there on the ledge, waiting, reassuring herself all was quiet. Then she ducked inside, and clambered awkwardly down, landing with a thud on the floor and waiting for her eyes to adjust to the darkness.

The kitchen was empty, she could tell instantly because, even though she had made almost no sound, still her breathing, her muffled footstep on the linoleum, echoed in a way they never would in a room full of furniture.

She shivered violently. It was a vacant house in the blackout and God alone knew who might be hiding out here, what tramps and vagrants and looters and spies and murderers might be in this house, in this very room, right now. Watching her.

Sweat burst through the pores on the palms of her hands and her upper lip and under her arms and she became aware of the beating of her heart and the pulse of blood in her head. What if Caroline wasn't here? What if she had been attacked or kidnapped and tied up?

She shouldn't have come. It was stupid! Stupid being in this horrible empty house!

Deirdre scrabbled for the window ledge in the darkness and was about to pull herself up and climb back outside when she heard it.

A groan. Or a grunt. Made by a man.

Oh God.

She froze again. William? Could that have been William?

There it was again, louder, followed by a scuffle or a scraping sound, muffled. And upstairs, definitely upstairs. Were they struggling? But who was it? She couldn't even say for sure that Caroline was up there. It could be anyone.

She left the kitchen and went along the hallway, reached the stairs and began to climb. Each stair creaked loudly, shrieking her presence, and the blood rushed in her ears. As she reached the top stair she heard another grunt followed by a thud. She froze, every muscle taut. If she moved now he would hear her, for sure.

I'm not brave, she realised with a sudden, ghastly clarity. I don't want to be brave. And I don't want to be murdered! Why am I even here?

She felt light-headed.

Ahead, just a couple of feet away, was the doorway of what had been Mr and Mrs Davenport's bedroom. The bedroom door was wide open. The Davenports had taken the blackout curtains with them so that a shaft of yellow moonlight pierced the room, striking the wall, the bedroom floor, and an old mattress that lay in the centre of the empty room. And it struck Caroline, who was on the mattress and…

And Uncle Clive who was on there with her.

Deirdre gasped. She must have gasped because they heard her and as she hurled herself back down the stairs their voices floated after her.

'Bloody 'ell! There's someone there!'

'What? Oh, I doubt it…'

'I tell you, there *was* someone there, in the doorway.'

'Ghosts. Must be a ghost. In this house.'

And it was only moments later, as she was running across the road and stumbling back through the front door at number fifteen, after the initial shock and revulsion had gone, that Deirdre realised that Caroline had seen her, that their eyes had met in the yellow moonlight, that it was Caroline who had said, her voice so quiet, so detached: 'Ghosts. Must be a ghost. In this house.'

She had told Mum, of course.

It wasn't fair of Caroline to expect people to lie for her, especially when what she was doing was so…horrid! Besides, it was for Caroline's own good. Imagine if people found out she had done something like that. With her own uncle! With a man *that old*, a widower! And they not even married or engaged or ever likely to be and Clive's wife—not to mention poor, dear William—barely dead and in their graves. Really, Deirdre had had no choice. Anyone could see that. Caroline was allowed to get away with murder and Mum and Dad never said a thing, never stopped her. It had always been that way, right from when they were children. And it was worse now, with her working at the factory and smoking and coming and going whenever she pleased. Well, this was where it had led, and they would all have to stew in their own juices!

Mum was standing in the hallway as Deirdre stumbled back inside the house.

'Deirdre! What do you think you're doing?' Mum demanded, in that half-tentative, half-authoritative tone she had, and in that moment Deirdre despised her.

'*Out!* I can go out if I want to. Caroline does!'

Mum looked shocked.

'You know you are not allowed out after blackout, it's not safe. You know Dad particularly forbid it.'

But Deirdre stood her ground. She had half a mind to say, *See if I care, after what I've just seen! If you only knew, that would wipe the smile off your face!* Instead she raised her chin defiantly and sniffed.

This seemed to annoy Mum, who countered with: 'You'd better have a jolly good reason for going out, my girl, or I'll be forced to tell Dad.'

'*Tell* him then! And I'll tell him I was following Caroline. She left an hour early for work—again!—and she went into the Davenports' house. And I was the only one who noticed. So I followed.'

She hadn't meant to say that but Mum had made her. Well, it was too bad. But nothing was going to make her divulge the rest of her dreadful secret.

'Caroline?' Mum replied, confused, suspicious, as if the idea of her eldest daughter doing anything untoward had simply never occurred to her. As if she suspected her errant younger daughter was making the whole thing up.

Deirdre felt a rush of fury.

'Yes, Caroline! *And she wasn't alone!*'

Oh that's torn it.

The blood rushed to her face. She hadn't meant to say that. She wasn't sure what she had intended to say, but it wasn't that.

Mum advanced on her, reaching for her arm angrily.

'What do you mean? You ought not to say such horrid things about your sister.'

'You mean, you don't want to hear them!' Deirdre retorted hotly, suddenly glad she'd said what she had. 'Anyway it's *true* and I don't care if you believe me or not! They go there every night at six o'clock. Go and see for yourself if you don't believe me. They're in there right now! In the Davenports' bedroom. There's a way in round the back...through the kitchen window...'

Mum's fingers grasped her arm, squeezing painfully, pulling Deirdre to her, and she suddenly seemed to have become something else entirely, some other person, not Mum at all, and Deirdre felt a flicker of panic.

'*What do you mean* they? Who? Who is it?'

Deirdre's eyes dropped from Mum's face and she wished she could escape. She imagined herself pulling free and making a mad dash for her room. Instead she shrugged and muttered, 'I didn't see...'

'*You said you saw them, who was it?*'

'*I didn't see!* Just two people. Caroline and...a man.'

Mum let go of her arm with a little shake and stepped back, and when Deirdre looked up, Mum had a closed, almost disappointed look on her face.

'I don't believe you saw anything at all,' she said quietly.

'You'd believe it if it was about *me*, wouldn't you?' Deirdre countered furiously. 'Anyway, I *did* see and it *was*

Caroline, whether you believe me or not! And she was with Uncle Clive!'

That was it. There was no going back. Mum had to believe her now, because who could make something like that up?

'Go to your room, Deirdre.'

She had expected anger. She had expected a slap on the cheek. But Mum's voice was flat, quiet.

'Go to your room and stay there and say nothing of this to anyone, do you understand?'

Deirdre had nodded quickly. The only thing that mattered was escaping to her room and staying there.

The following morning Caroline had come waltzing in from the nightshift as bold as brass. And Mum had said nothing, done nothing, only banged the frying pan around a lot. And now it was six o'clock and Caroline was over there doing it *again* in the Davenports' bedroom.

Ugh! Horrible, odious, insidious, disgusting Uncle Clive who always got ready to go out, so promptly, so punctually, at six o'clock. That awful eau-de-cologne, his shiny hair, that moustache, leaving the house just before Caroline did.

And no one ever noticed!

That slimy smile, the slow wink... She'd always assumed that horrid wink was for her! Ugh! And it had never occurred to her—never in a million years—*that Caroline was going to meet him. That Caroline was doing it—*

Poor William! And Mum had done *nothing*!

And at one minute past six the rocket had landed.

One moment Deirdre was in her room staring at a blank school exercise book. The next she was lying on her back staring at the ceiling with all the wind knocked out of her, fighting to catch her breath.

And somehow, seconds or minutes or hours later, she was in her parents' room—how had she got here?—where, until a minute ago, a window had been. Now the window was a thousand shattered pieces all over the carpet and bedspread and crunching beneath her slippers.

'*There! There! In the house! She's in the house!*' Deirdre screamed, pointing through the window frame though there was no one to see her point.

As she pointed, her voice seemed to have dried up, to have evaporated, and she was aware of a great ball of fire at the far end of the street, on the corner of Nelson Avenue.

It had to be a rocket.

But she hadn't heard it! She hadn't heard a thing. It had just dropped, it had just exploded—there was no warning! No warning at all! How were you supposed to know? How could you prepare when there was no *warning*?

And Caroline was there. Caroline was in number twenty-eight. She was there with Uncle Clive and now there *was* no number twenty-eight.

Deirdre gripped the window frame to stop the room spinning off and herself crashing to the floor. Then she let go and stared at the palms of her hands which were laced with little flecks of blood from the broken glass.

Already she could see people running, someone was screaming, men's voices shouted, '*Stop, don't go in! Don't go in—it's not safe!*' The Davies lived at that end of Oakton Way, Mrs Forster and Jack Forster and—

She stopped herself. *But no one knew Caroline was in number twenty-eight. No one but her.* And Clive, of course. Clive, who was in there. Meeting her.

And if Clive had been here in this very room with her now, she would have launched herself at him and punched his face and gouged out his eyes for making Caroline meet him in that house.

She turned and ran out of the room, stumbling in the dark, tripping and flinging out both hands to steady herself, then launching herself down the stairs.

She fell in a heap at the bottom of the stairs with a thud, twisting her ankle painfully, gasping, then, with a sob, she hauled herself up and hobbled towards the open front door. As she reached out for it, the wildly flickering lights from the fires outside danced and bounced off the hall walls like a giant Guy Fawkes bonfire.

The activity at the end of the street had intensified and Deirdre stood in the doorway, her hand shielding her eyes from the heat and the light and the smoke. She had to watch; her eyes were drawn to the roaring, crackling, leaping flames, to the misshapen black forms of the destroyed houses and the tiny running silhouettes of the fire crews as they struggled with hoses.

But that wasn't her concern. There were no flames from number twenty-eight, she could see that. But the bizarrely altered shape of the roof and the first floor made her heart lurch. Where was Dad? And Mum? Why weren't they here? No one knew!

'Help! Help me! Over here!' she cried, calling to the fire crew as she hobbled out into the street, waving wildly. But no one heard her, no one could hear a thing over the roar of the flames, the klaxon of the fire tenders.

She was alone in a world that had burst into flames.

She reached the Davenports' house and stumbled over piles of rubble. It was dark now, away from the flames, too dark to make out clearly what lay in front of her. She tripped and flung out both hands as she fell again then lay, stunned and grazed.

A figure appeared, looming over her, a dark shape, gasping and stumbling. Emerging from the side passage!

Deirdre gasped.

'Caroline?' she cried out as the figure stumbled straight into her then fell backwards against a wall.

'Move!' It was a man's voice. 'Gawd's sake, move out the way! It's all gonna come down!'

Clive!

'But where is she? Where's Caroline?'

Clive simply pushed past her and Deirdre stood frozen in horror, because this was all *wrong*, you were supposed to *help*! And he had *left*. *He had left Caroline in there!*

Was the house going to collapse? What should she do?

She became aware of shouting. It was coming from behind, from the street, and, turning, she could make out Clive calling and waving to the fire crew and in a moment men were running, pushing past her and, at last, no matter what happened, someone was helping.

'*Here, here!*' she pointed, waving frantically. 'The side passage, there's a window, the kitchen window. My sister, Caroline...'

But by then the men—anonymous men with smoke-blackened faces—had disappeared down the passage and there was nothing she could do.

The house was going to collapse. She dragged herself to her feet and backed away down the path, wondering where Clive had gone, whether he had been one of the men who had gone back inside.

She was distracted then by shouts from the front bedroom and as she looked up she saw light from a torch bouncing around the room, lighting up first the wall, then the collapsed roof, then the faces of the men. The shouts were momentarily drowned out by a great crunch then a rush of rubble followed by a silence.

God, please let it be alright, please let it all be alright.

She repeated it over and over again, unable to stop because if she stopped then something bad would happen. As long as she continued saying the words, there was a chance.

She was still saying them under her breath when the men reappeared at the side passage, a stretcher carried awkwardly between them. Deirdre held her breath and waited till the stretcher was level with her and she could see that the occupant was alive and breathing and had a makeshift bandage across her forehead and was...Mum.

Mum?

And behind her was Dad, his face serious, and behind him was...Caroline. Pale, a streak of dirt across one cheek, but otherwise perfectly unharmed.

Deirdre stood and gaped, shaking her head, trying to make sense of it. Mum had been there when the rocket fell? Mum had gone to meet Clive instead of Caroline?

Her stomach plummeted through the floor. Of course she had. That was exactly what Mum would do—the only way, in fact, that Mum could deal with a situation like this. She would meet Clive, warn him off. Tell him she knew, give him a chance to explain—or to deny it. Tell him to go. Anything that meant not telling Dad. And Deirdre had supplied her with the information: *every night at six o'clock. In the Davenports' bedroom. There's a way in round the back. Through the kitchen window.*

So Mum was here—had come here this evening— because she, Deirdre, had told her about Caroline and Clive. And if Mum had died...

She felt her knees give way and she was violently sick. By the time she had got to her feet the stretcher had been carried down to a waiting ambulance and loaded on board. She could see Dad standing silently, watching, before climbing on board himself.

It was her fault.

No. No, that wasn't true. She turned to face her sister, who until a moment ago had been all but dead.

'What if she dies? What if Mum dies now?' she screamed, launching herself at Caroline, when what she meant to say was, *I thought you were dead.*

'It's a knock on the head, just a knock,' said Caroline, holding her off and staring after the ambulance. Or perhaps she was watching the flames.

Deirdre felt sick again. She wanted to scream out, *You killed her, you almost killed Mum!* but instead she said, with a sob, 'Where's Clive? Is he here? He nearly died too!' because she wanted Caroline to realise what might have happened, that this was all her fault.

But Clive was nowhere to be seen and Caroline said nothing.

The sob came again, shaking her whole body, and she couldn't stop it, she couldn't push it down.

'Did Dad rescue her?' she gasped, after a moment, after it became clear that Caroline wasn't going to say anything. 'Did he dig Mum out?'

She needed to know what had happened.

She couldn't stop the sobs.

'Yes, of course he did,' said Caroline, turning to face her. 'He wouldn't just stand there and let her die, would he? What kind of man would do that?'

Deirdre didn't know what kind of man. Apart from Uncle Clive, who seemed to epitomise that kind of man. She began shivering again, suddenly realising how bitterly cold it was and that she wasn't wearing a coat or anything.

'Come on,' said Caroline calmly, putting an arm around her shoulders and guiding her towards the house.

The door stood wide open as they had left it. Deirdre reached the front step and stumbled through the doorway, breathing into her cut hands to get the circulation back, to try to stop the shivering.

It was bitterly cold and she turned back to hurry Caroline inside so they could shut the front door.

But Caroline had stopped and was standing there in the middle of Oakton Way just as though she couldn't feel the cold, just as though nothing had happened at all.

CHAPTER TWENTY-THREE

'DID YOU CAME UP M1 and past Leeds, or A56 from Preston?' asked Mr Milthorpe from the position he'd taken up just inside the doorway of Caroline's hospital room.

Deirdre ignored him—those were the sort of questions you had a husband for.

'Leeds,' said Eric, who was sitting beside her nursing a plastic coffee cup on his lap, turning eagerly to take up Mr Milthorpe's line of questioning. 'And Wetherby,' he added.

'Wetherby!' said Mr Milthorpe, surprised.

'M1 seemed the best route. Once you get past Leeds you're okay. A56 might be less congested but it takes you too far west.'

'Aye. Aye, that's as may be. But it's a gamble, either way,' agreed Mr. Milthorpe thoughtfully, as though they were discussing some vital military strategy.

Meanwhile, Caroline lay unconscious on the bed before them, hooked up to half a dozen bleeping, flickering, buzzing machines. It was a strange social occasion, where the person on whose behalf you were all gathered, family and strangers alike, wouldn't—couldn't—speak to you. Left you all to your own devices to make the best of it, to find some topic of conversation, some part of your lives in common.

Why didn't the irritating man just leave?

Deirdre turned to her husband. 'Eric, why don't you see if that doctor's around?'

'Oh, right-ho.' Eric stood up and sauntered off in search of the doctor.

Mr Milthorpe sat down in the vacated chair and fell silent.

The doctor, Dr Ormerod, was a very young Asian woman who spoke with a strong Birmingham accent. She'd greeted them with a cheery 'Alright?' soon after they'd arrived and ushered them into a horrid little office 'for a little chat, like'. The office had been so cluttered with metal filing cabinets and a desk piled high with manila folders stuffed to overflowing with papers that the three of them had barely been able to stand comfortably without touching some part of each other. As Eric was her husband and the doctor a stranger, albeit another woman, Deirdre had stood very close to Eric and had listened to the doctor's solemn report on Caroline's condition as the corner of a filing cabinet had dug into her lower back.

Caroline had had an ischaemic stroke, which was, the doctor had explained pleasantly, a clot in an artery in the brain. They'd put her on thrombolytic drugs which would, they hoped, break up the blockage and reopen the artery.

Eric had nodded and said, 'Ah,' and Deirdre had listened and felt a sort of rising panic because she didn't know what it actually meant.

Caroline's condition, said the doctor, summing it all up for them, was critical but stable. Critical meant her life was in danger. Stable meant she hadn't died yet. She had a fifty-fifty chance of survival, but an eighty-twenty chance of sustaining some permanent paralysis or other disability. There was a fifty-fifty probability that she would remain in a coma and not regain consciousness.

The odds and percentages were hard to take in. Eric had said it was like going to Walthamstow dogs and trying to decide which greyhound to back. At least in a greyhound race there were usually only six to eight runners and you felt like the odds must be in your favour. They weren't of course, because a one in eight chance is no chance at all, really.

Dr Ormerod had walked them back to Caroline's room and silently touched Deirdre's arm in a way that was oddly comforting—you somehow didn't expect someone with a Birmingham accent to have a good bedside manner. Then she had drifted away, murmuring that she would return soon to 'see how they were all doing'.

That was three hours ago. It was late afternoon and the weak January sun had already slunk beneath the cooling towers of the hospital laundry.

Deirdre shifted in the small orange plastic chair that the hospital provided for the use of visitors. She had sent Eric from the room in search of Dr Ormerod and now she was left with Mr Milthorpe.

She glanced discreetly at her watch. It was a little after four thirty in the afternoon. Outside (what you could see of outside through the venetian blinds and the grime on the window) was dark. There was a canal nearby, the Leeds and Liverpool Canal, they had passed it on the way in, and the castle up on the hill, though you couldn't see it from this window.

It was evident that she and Eric weren't going anywhere tonight. Or perhaps they should spend the night at Caroline's house? They would need to get her keys from the nurse—unless Mr Milthorpe had them? When Mum had died she and Eric had waited in a corridor. She couldn't recall being there for more than a few hours, certainly not overnight. Mum had collapsed on Sunday evening, an ambulance had arrived, they had waited outside, then sometime around midnight Mum had gone.

Caroline hadn't arrived until midday the next day.

And now it's your turn, she thought, watching her sister's still face. But such thoughts made it seem as though the end, Caroline's end, was inevitable.

It was best not to think.

'Looks like snow,' observed Mr Milthorpe, peering through the blinds.

After a while the nurse returned and Deirdre got stiffly to her feet then hesitated. She wanted to ask, Do you think she can hear us, do you think she's awake? But she said nothing.

The nurse was monitoring the intravenous drip. She smiled vaguely but didn't even glance down at Caroline to see if there was any change. The nurse's manner, her expression, made it clear she believed in instruments and electrical monitors. The change in a patient's pallor, a shift of their head, an opening of their lips, meant nothing to her.

When she had gone Deirdre sat down again and watched Caroline's eyelids as her eyes flickered back and forth. It looked like she was dreaming.

CHAPTER TWENTY-FOUR

D EIRDRE HAD BEEN HERE, sitting by the bed, talking to Mr Milthorpe, which seemed to Caroline rather like Alice talking to the White Rabbit. Well, not really like that, but it was as unlikely a scenario.

What had they talked about? Alice and the White Rabbit had talked about time. An appointment, being late. What would Deirdre and Mr Milthorpe find to talk about? Gardening. Yes, they both loved gardening. She hoped they would find that they had that in common. But the talking seemed to have stopped and she was no longer sure who was sitting by her bed or if anyone was.

I really ought to speak, Caroline realised. At the very least, she should acknowledge Deirdre's presence. After all, her sister had travelled some distance, all the way up from London presumably. It must be a long way, as they rarely seemed to undertake the journey north. But then, if you were being fair, she had rarely undertaken the journey south herself. There was so little need. Especially since Ted had died.

In the years immediately following Mum's death, when Ted had had the Sierra and had liked to drive and the traffic hadn't been quite so bad, they had gone down two or three times a year. The children had suddenly become interesting, had developed distinct personalities. And she and Ted had had no children of their own, of course. She had been past that age long before Ted came on the scene. But since Ted's death she'd gone south less. It was an unpleasant journey by car, worse by rail. She had all she needed right here.

You were meant to get nostalgic for the past once you reached a certain age but it hadn't happened. And why would it? The past wasn't somewhere any right-thinking person would wish to dwell. It contained far too much that you were sad had gone forever, and so much more that was just plain unpleasant. And it got no less unpleasant just because the years had passed. You just felt the pain of it less, that was all. You could look at a death—Dad's during the war and then Mum's years later. William. Ted. You could see them from a distance, as an observer rather than as a participant, which was a relief. But it certainly didn't make you want to go back there; it didn't make you want to relive a single God-awful minute of it.

Besides, she found that most of the memories that popped into her head at odd times were insignificant and inconsequential, quite meaningless to anyone but herself: the prickliness of sunburn on her legs after a daytrip to Scarborough just after the war; the smell of a biology classroom in summertime over sixty years ago; the feel of a school tunic against her skin; the sound of the old Ford reversing up the street. And others—the rubber of a gasmask pressed against her face, the smell of bodies burnt to a crisp, the sound of a buzz bomb cutting out overhead. The shock of losing someone.

Not that you remembered shock or loss. You just remembered that it had happened and that you had done this or that at the time.

The sound of an ambulance siren floated up from below, muffled and then louder as the wind changed direction.

There was something she needed to do. The electricity bill was due today or tomorrow. No, it wasn't the electricity bill. An iron left on? Well, if the house had burned down they would probably have told her it about by now. She had been doing the ironing, moving a load of clothes from the ironing board in the kitchen to the cupboard under the stairs, when the room had started spinning, had gone red then black, the floor had rushed up and hit her... and here she was.

Doing the ironing. Not very glorious. Not at all heroic. Most accidents happened in the home. And sometimes they happened in the street in the middle of the afternoon: Dad falling into the bomb crater right outside the post office in March '45. Lying in a foot of water at the bottom of the crater all night until a returning nightshift worker had spotted him early the next morning. Dead, his neck broken.

Nowadays you'd get compensation—you got compensation for anything if the newspapers were to be believed, even tripping over your own feet. All Dad had got was a minor obituary in the *Gazette* and Mum had got a small pension from the post office and a brief letter of condolence in recognition of services rendered. And that was that, really. A hurried wartime funeral, quickly forgotten. Dying accidentally in the blackout, falling into a bomb crater outside the very post office where you'd worked for thirty-odd years, did not get you a state funeral or your name inscribed on the town war memorial. Or even on a bench in Acton Park.

Dad would have hated to go that way. So undignified. He would have loved to have his name on the war memorial. William was there, or so Deirdre had once said. She'd never gone there herself to see it.

So many people gone and soon no one left to remember them. Whole families with nothing to show for their time on Earth. There was Grandma and Grandpa Flaxheed, whose house in Wells Lane she could recall— just—visiting as a child of four or five. Walking through the silent, sunny Sunday afternoon streets, holding hands. Whose hand? She couldn't remember. A man's hand. Going round for Sunday afternoon tea.

How shrunken and dour they had always seemed. Grandma fussing over a dropped stitch or a draught at the window, Grandpa in his big old armchair, pointing at some story in the newspaper or trying to engage her in some child-like conversation. And always on the mantel-piece the wedding photograph of Jemima, the daughter who had died young, and her husband, who had died a short while later of diphtheria or scarlet fever or some such old-fashioned disease. She could remember sitting on Dad's knee, had a vivid impression of rolled-up white shirt sleeves, a lap to perch on, scratchy tweed trousers. The smell of sawdust and raw meat.

Was it Dad?

Deirdre would know. She would ask Deirdre.

She remembered then what it was she had meant to tell Jennifer. It was about Charlotte. Charlotte had come up to stay that December of Mum's funeral. Had told them—herself and Ted, after some persuasion—what had happened, why she was looking so peaky. They had been sworn to secrecy. And they had kept that secret for twenty-five years—well, Ted wasn't going to be telling anyone anything was he? Not now. But herself... She had prom-ised. And now she had decided to break that promise. But Jennifer had come and gone and she had said nothing.

Well, it wasn't too late.

Jennifer and Charlotte

CHAPTER TWENTY-FIVE

'HOW DO I LOOK?' SAID Charlotte, inspecting herself doubtfully in the car's wing mirror.

'Like someone going to a funeral,' replied Dr Ashley Lempriere, glancing over from the driver's seat. Then she swerved left off Princes Street and into North Bridge without indicating, causing the Volvo behind to blast its horn angrily and Charlotte to grip the handle above the passenger-side door.

'Jeez, people get so hung up about which lane they gotta be in in this city,' Ashley observed, turning indignantly into the forecourt of Edinburgh's Waverley Station.

'Yes. If we could just loosen up and do away with road rules altogether, I'm sure we'd all be a lot happier,' agreed Charlotte dryly.

'Funny,' said Ashley, narrowing her eyes and tail-gating a slow-moving Subaru.

Charlotte didn't feel funny. She felt like someone who was going to a funeral. She closed her eyes and tried not to think about the day ahead. And she was pretty keen not to think about the previous evening either. She opened her eyes and concentrated on the rear of the white Subaru instead.

'Where are you meant to drop people? There's, like, not even a turning circle!' said Ashley, swinging her car in a tight circle and almost collecting a courier on a bicycle.

Last night the Cultural Studies department, following a particularly depressing staff meeting that had seen Tom Pitney bemoaning the usual things (budget cuts, teaching loads, tutorial double-ups, student numbers), had somewhat surprisingly, and at Dave Glengorran's suggestion, adjourned to the Union Bar. There, having consumed a number of 99p pints of Auld Augie, Charlotte had found herself in the pub car park around midnight being propositioned by the eminent Dr Lempriere, a proposition that had involved a taxicab ride to Ashley's Canonmills flat and a warm, electric-blanketed double bed.

This was baffling because she hadn't been looking for anything; had, in fact, finally reached a stage in life where she was happy being celibate and single. And, more to the point, she had most definitely had her mind on other things last night. Perhaps she looked more attractive when she was grieving and in shock? This was unfortunate.

It was also complicated.

And the complications had started this morning, the morning of the funeral. She had awoken in a strange bed with a colleague whom, until twelve hours ago, she had barely trusted and whom she had spent a fair part of the last term avoiding. Her only choice of clothes had been the ones she had been wearing the night before and her train left in less than an hour. She now found herself in a silver Audi in a borrowed black suit, about to be dropped off in the early morning gloom at Waverley Station, and no, she did not feel in the least bit funny.

'You want me to drop you here?' said Ashley, looking around for a spot to pull over near the brightly lit station entrance. *No Waiting* and *No Parking* signs flashed in the car headlights, crowding both sides of the kerb.

'Thanks. You're going to be late for work,' she said.

That wasn't funny, it sounded like someone's mum. But she was going to a funeral—what did she care if Ashley was late for work?

'First lecture's not till eleven. I got plenty of time. Here you go.' And Ashley swung into a spot that had suddenly been vacated by a taxi and pulled up with a jolt.

Charlotte focused her attention on unfastening her seatbelt, opening the car door and going round to the boot. The air was freezing and she pulled up the collar of her borrowed jacket. Ashley was already there and as the boot swung up they both reached for Charlotte's purple backpack, which still contained yesterday's unmarked semiotics essays. It was Charlotte's bag, so she made a grab for it and Ashley stood back and shut the boot.

She called it a trunk.

Charlotte hesitated, standing in the icy road, holding her backpack and awaiting the moment of parting. She was going to a funeral, it was okay to be emotional, highly strung, taciturn even. She smiled, a smile that was intended to convey a casual farewell, tinged with sadness because, after all, her aunt had died, and yet with a certain restrained tenderness in acknowledgment of last night. It came out like a grimace.

'Should I come with you?' said Ashley, touching her arm, and looking searchingly into her face.

Charlotte blinked in astonishment. 'To Skipton?'

'No, to the ticket office. See you off, that kinda thing.'

'No need,' said Charlotte, brusquely, to cover her embarrassment. To Skipton, indeed! How absurd. 'Thanks for the lift.'

'No biggie. My fault you needed one.'

This reference to last night seemed to hang in the air, demanding some kind of response. What? Another smile? Charlotte hitched the backpack over her shoulder, giving herself time. Should they kiss?

'Were you close? Will it be a horrible ordeal?' said Ashley, reaching out and touching both arms now, and this reminder of the funeral was a welcome distraction.

'All funerals are an ordeal, I suppose,' Charlotte replied, choosing to ignore the first question, and then realising she had only ever been to one other funeral, Grandma Lake's, over twenty years ago. That had been an ordeal, she realised, though not because Grandma Lake had died.

'Well, you got my cell phone number,' said Ashley, and then she settled the problem of the farewell by offering a quick hug.

Charlotte released herself from the hug as soon as was decently possible and, with a vague wave, dived through the darkness to the station entrance.

Once inside the vast station concourse, she paused and took a deep breath, relaxing—until she saw the queue at the ticket hall. She hurried over to join it, dodging around a stationary group of backpackers and a pigeon that swooped her from its nest in the glass-domed ceiling high above. The snow meant that most of the northbound services had been cancelled but the train for Bristol Temple Meads was still scheduled to leave in fifteen minutes. Three hours to Leeds then the local train to Skipton and a minicab to Aunt Caroline's house. She would arrive at about midday.

''Scuse me? Are ye in this queue?' said a young woman in a suit and Charlotte mumbled a reply and shuffled forward in the line.

An uneasy thought was nagging her. Aunt Caroline had rung a few days before her stroke and invited her down for tea. And she hadn't gone. Well, you didn't go all the way down to Yorkshire for afternoon tea, did you? She'd said, Yes, of course, though it would have to be during half-term. And a few days later Aunt Caroline had had the stroke.

She wished she had gone.

She wouldn't mention it, she decided, as the queue inched forward. Not that she had done anything to be ashamed of, it was just that no one needed to know. There was nothing to be gained by it. And there would be plenty of other things to talk about, or to avoid talking about, beside that.

Jennifer's spectacular television debut, for one. Christ. Would they talk about that? How could they avoid it? Graham would mention it, surely.

And me? she wondered. Will I mention it?

A scruffy young man carrying a large musical instrument case was ahead of her in the queue and he knocked the case against her shins as he manoeuvred it then stared blankly at Charlotte when she protested.

Ten minutes till departure. There were five ticket windows open and as one became free a hand from inside the window shot out and flipped over the *Open* sign to read *Closed* and pulled down the shutter. Four windows open. Above the ticket windows was a huge advertising hoarding promoting *Focus on Scotland*, a weekly current affairs program on Scottish Television. Most of the poster was taken up by a vast head-and-shoulders close-up of a heavily made-up woman in her late fifties with smooth, flawless skin and a most unScottish tan, sporting a newsreader's coiffured hairstyle. She was Naomi Findlay, long-time presenter of the program.

'Ha!' Charlotte said out loud, and what ought to have been an ironic laugh merely sounded bitter, as it did each time she saw this particular poster. That would be right, she thought, that would be too bloody right.

CHAPTER TWENTY-SIX

JULY 1981

A̲N UNACCOUNTABLY HOT and cloudless after-noon meant that everyone at Henry Morton Secondary was suddenly in shirt sleeves with their socks rolled down. The upper-school boys had removed their grey-and-red-striped school ties. The fifth-form girls lounged in groups on the grass of the school field, their skirts hitched up high to tan their legs, listening to radios and swatting lazily at wasps. No one looked like they had a maths O-level to sit in less than an hour.

A noisy game of football was going on in the school playground, two discarded jumpers on the ground acting as goalposts and, crossing the playground, Charlotte ducked to avoid the ball as it flew past her head.

'Oi! Throw us it back then!' called one of the boys, but she ignored him. She barely heard him.

She was heading towards the girls' toilet block, the one behind the science labs. She didn't often go there. Smokers congregated there and you learned early on to avoid the place unless you wanted to be ambushed. But if there was any smoking and ambushing to be done today she hoped it would be done outside in the sunshine. She hoped there was no one in the toilet block at all.

Someone's written stuff about us on the wall of the girls' toilets.

Zoe Findlay had said this. Had come up to her in the library, pulled up a chair, leaned over, looked left and right, then made her dramatic announcement. Then she had added, mysteriously, 'You didn't write it, did you?'

Charlotte had stared at her.

Zoe, who at sixteen still had the small frame and fresh unmade-up face of a thirteen-year-old, had looked as though the idea of someone writing anything about her on the wall of the girls' toilet was the most exciting thing that had ever happened to her. Charlotte had pushed back her chair and left the library. 'Don't follow me,' she muttered furiously through clenched teeth. *Do not follow me.*

The toilet block loomed ahead on the far side of the playground. The bike rack that ran the length of the wall was crowded with badly parked bicycles and bike chains with elaborate padlocks but was otherwise deserted.

What would someone write about us? she wondered, and a prickle of fear crawled up her spine. Something bad? Of course it was something bad; people didn't write good stuff about you on a toilet wall, did they? Had Zoe herself written it?

'Hey, Charlotte, there's something written about you in the girls' toilets!'

Charlotte spun around to see a friend of Jennifer's— Julie Fanshawe , it was—standing in the doorway of the sixth-form common room, her face a mask of fake schoolgirl concern. 'You better go look,' Julie added, and then she smothered a laugh and disappeared inside. A moment later Jennifer herself suddenly burst out of the common room, running—yes, actually running!—across the path, looking up and seeing her and then, with a kind of wild-eyed glance, diving into the toilets, looking like she was being chased. Or about to throw up.

Charlotte stared.

According to Jennifer—who liked to exaggerate—the sixth-form common room was awash with bottles of Woodpecker cider and Liebfraumilch that someone's older brother who worked in an off-licence provided at discount prices. No doubt this accounted for Jennifer's white-faced dash for the toilets.

No doubt. It could not be that Jennifer knew anything about what was allegedly written on the walls of the toilets.

And who else was in there? Who else knew?

The playground had gone silent. All games had stopped. Every pair of eyes was trained on her, she could feel them crawling over her shoulderblades, down her back.

She turned slowly around to face them and what she saw was—

Was Zoe's mum climbing out of her red BMW, and all thoughts of Jennifer and what might or might not be written on the wall of the toilets vanished.

Naomi Findlay, in a dark trouser suit and high black boots that clicked on the tarmac, strode from the visitors' car park towards the school office. A red leather bag was slung over one shoulder and she clasped her car keys tightly before her like a weapon.

Charlotte stared in surprise.

Naomi? Here?

She began to walk quickly over to her, almost breaking into a run. 'Hello!' she called, wanting to add, 'Naomi!', but suddenly, here in the school grounds, it seemed wrong. Inappropriate.

Naomi stopped and looked around. She saw Charlotte and seemed to hesitate, head turned towards her, body turned towards the steps of the school office as though she wished to keep on walking. Her eyes were hidden behind large dark glasses but her head moved slightly from left to right and back again, taking in the car park, the bike racks, the playground, the noisy game of football and, last of all, returning to Charlotte.

Charlotte reached her and smiled breathlessly. Then she realised she didn't know what to say. She realised that Naomi wasn't returning her smile.

'Hi,' Charlotte gasped, wishing she wasn't so out of breath. 'What are you doing here?'

Naomi didn't take off her glasses and all Charlotte could see was the bright midday sun reflecting off the lenses. She felt a flicker of something cold run down her arms.

'Just came to see the Head,' said Naomi casually, as though she often popped by for a chat with the headmaster.

'Oh, Zoe in trouble?' said Charlotte with a grin, because the idea of Zoe doing anything as interesting as getting into trouble was absurd.

'No,' Naomi replied, taking the question at face value. 'It's—' she paused for a fraction of a second, 'the move. I'm moving her. To a different school. Well, we're both moving really. It's work.'

Naomi raised her chin, her gaze directed over the roof of the school building towards some distant horizon. The sunlight seemed to melt her lip gloss, turning her lips into pools of liquid silver.

Charlotte said nothing for a moment, feeling her breath coming in and going out.

'Moving?' she repeated, and everything seemed to slow down.

'Yes. Didn't Zoe mention it?'

Mention it? No, Zoe had not mentioned it. And neither had Naomi. The coldness had reached Charlotte's fingertips. She couldn't feel her hands. Around the playground had faded away. The game of football continued but no sounds reached her ears.

'Yes, I've got a job at Granada. Newsreader.' And Naomi hitched up her bag and glanced ever so casually at her wristwatch.

Granada? Charlotte swallowed. Surely that was in...?

'So naturally we're moving to Manchester. During the school hols. End of August.'

Charlotte found her heart was pumping so fast she couldn't quite draw breath. She couldn't speak.

Naomi glanced a second time at her watch. 'I'm afraid I have to go. I've got...there's a lot to do. I need to...' And only now did she finally, seem...what? Embarrassed? Awkward?

And Charlotte thought, I bet she wishes I hadn't come over. Hadn't seen her. That she could just pack up and leave and not have to say anything. That she could pretend nothing ever happened.

But something *had* happened.

A football sailed over their heads and from far away a cheer went up.

Would Naomi have done that? Just packed up and gone?

'But I—' Charlotte began.

Naomi interrupted with a tight smile. 'Well, I expect you and Zoe will remain friends.'

Charlotte fell silent, appalled. Why is she pretending? she wondered. Why is she making it sound as though I came round every night to visit *Zoe*?

Something had happened.

'I thought you—I thought *we*—'

She found that she couldn't locate the words. That she was no longer sure what the words were, or what she thought about anything.

'Please, Charlotte. Don't let's make a fuss.' Naomi reached over and touched her arm lightly, the way you might touch someone at a funeral whom you knew only slightly. Then she smiled gently. 'Let's be sensible, shall we?' She half turned her head as a teacher walked close by, her eyes following until the teacher was out of earshot.

'Sensible?' Charlotte repeated, not knowing what such a word meant in this context but knowing it wasn't good.

'I'm sure we'll stay in touch.'

But that was what you said to people when you had no intention of ever seeing them again.

'I do have to go,' said Naomi again. 'But look, your exams. You have one today, don't you?'

Did she? Charlotte couldn't remember.

'Well, best of luck. I'm sure you'll do well. I really do have to go,' and she reached out and squeezed Charlotte's arm. Then she turned and walked with a click of her boots up the steps.

Charlotte watched until she had disappeared inside the office.

Something *had* happened.

Three weeks ago she had gone round to Zoe's house but Zoe had been away at her dad's and Naomi had said, Stay Charlotte, stay for a drink!

Naomi had been in high spirits, something had happened at work. She had been talkative, excited.

And Charlotte, who had never once gone around to Zoe's house because she wanted to see Zoe, had stayed. Had drunk a glass of champagne from an expensive bottle with a French label, had drunk a second glass, had followed eagerly as the party had moved upstairs to Naomi's bedroom. Here she had found that she was really quite drunk and that her first sexual encounter was therefore both blurred around the edges and startlingly lucid in the middle.

At around midnight Naomi had silently driven her home and, dropping her a block away, had said, Best not mention it. Not to anyone, not to her parents, least of all Zoe.

As if she would mention it to her parents.

Then for three weeks Naomi had worked late at the television studio, sometimes not returning till eleven o'clock or midnight, and Charlotte knew this because she had sat in the park opposite the house, waiting. And it turned out that what Naomi had meant was: Don't mention it to anyone—including to me.

And the reason for Naomi's excitement that day—her high spirits, the expensive champagne with the French label, the silent drive home at midnight—was now clear. She was moving to Manchester.

Now it was the last week of the summer term and the final exam was maths in the gymnasium in half an hour.

Take me with you.

But Naomi had gone and the words hung in the air as heavy as a death sentence. Then they were gone and no one had heard them except Charlotte.

There was still time. She could run after her. She could wait until Naomi came out. She could go round tonight, tomorrow night. They wouldn't be leaving immediately, would they? Naomi had said the end of August. It took ages to plan something like this. Perhaps Naomi *had* been planning it for ages? Perhaps this was the final phase? Perhaps she was just waiting till Zoe's final exam and then they were off?

She found herself walking across the playground but it was as though she wasn't really there. There were people moving all around her, their voices muffled as though heard from another room. She reached the gym and stood in the doorway staring at the rows of desks, each with a chair behind it. She must ask Zoe, find out the exact date they were leaving. Why had Zoe said nothing? Had she not known?

It was because Naomi had told her to say nothing. Best not mention it.

The gym filled up and Charlotte sat down at a desk. Someone put an answer booklet in front of her, then after a while another person placed an exam paper on her desk. Someone at the front of the room spoke, everyone turned over their papers and the room fell silent.

'A man walks five miles on a bearing of 092 degrees and then three miles from M to N on a bearing of 345 degrees—'

Naturally, we're moving to Manchester.

'...calculate the distance NQ...'

Let's not make a fuss.

'...and the bearing of Q from M. Show your working out in the space provided.'

I'm sure we'll stay in touch.

Charlotte pushed back her chair so that it fell with a thud on the parquet floor. She stood there for a second, two seconds, aware that every head had turned to stare at her, and as she stumbled out three invigilators started up after her, but no one tried to stop her.

She fled the hall, escaping across the quadrangle and through the teacher's car park to the side gate and away. Then she turned left, in the opposite direction to home, and only stopped when she had reached Beechtree Crescent. There was no For Sale sign outside the Findlays' house. It looked exactly as it always did.

Perhaps it had all been a mistake, a joke?

But you could sell a house after you'd moved out. You could do anything you liked, once you were an adult with a job and a car and an income. You could make decisions, do things, play with other people's lives if you wanted to.

Let's not make a fuss.

And Charlotte thought, If I hadn't run into her just now. If I hadn't seen her crossing the playground. Would she have told me? When? Would I have gone round there one evening and found them gone? The house deserted, empty. Boarded up.

She went home. Went upstairs and shut herself in the room she shared with Jennifer. If Mum had been in the house she might have wanted to know why Charlotte was home at three forty-five when the maths O-level wasn't scheduled to finish till four o'clock. But Mum was out so when Charlotte arrived home with her school jumper tied around her waist and her face pale and carrying only a pencil there was no one to notice.

Let's be sensible, shall we?

And soon after dinner Darren McKenzie had come round and Charlotte had stood on the landing staring down at his silhouette through the frosted glass. The door to the lounge was ajar and on the television Naomi Findlay said, *'…a sheep dip in Tower Hamlets.'*

Darren McKenzie had come round in search of Jennifer and then he had left, never to return.

❀ ❀ ❀

'Can I help ye?' said the man at the ticket office at Edinburgh's Waverley Station, speaking through a microphone and a glass partition.

Charlotte stared at him blankly. 'Oh, yes. Day return to Skipton, please.'

'That'll be via Leeds. Ye'll have to hurry now. Leeds train is just now boarding,' the man replied helpfully. 'Platform six.'

Thanks for nothing, thought Charlotte. Make me queue for half an hour then tell me to hurry.

She grabbed her bag and walked quickly out of the ticket hall, glancing, despite herself, at the station forecourt where Ashley had parked. The silver Audi had gone. But it hardly seemed to matter. She set off across the concourse for platform six.

CHAPTER TWENTY-SEVEN

'I'M SORRY, MR GASPARI'S phone is unattended at present. May I take a message?'

'No, thanks.'

Jennifer jabbed at the disconnect button and threw her mobile down on the passenger seat beside her.

Still unattended! No one could be in the office but away from their desk *all week*. She was being screened, that was the only explanation. The board had clearly read her letter about that stupid television appearance and was still deliberating about what action to take. She was going to receive a pathetic letter of reprimand, she was certain of it. Why else would Gaspari and the rest of his geriatric cronies be avoiding her? It would probably be waiting in her in-tray Monday morning. Gloria, no doubt, would have opened it and read it and gleefully passed it around the department, never mind it would be marked confidential.

Well, there was no time to worry about it now, she had a funeral to attend.

Jennifer studied her face in the car's rear-view mirror, reapplied her lipstick, adjusted a strand of hair and took a deep breath. Here goes nothing, she thought, opening the car door and getting out.

She was parked in the street outside Aunt Caroline's bungalow beneath a bare and leafless yew tree. She would have parked in the driveway where she'd parked—was it really only last Thursday?—but Mum and Dad's Vauxhall was already there.

It was eleven forty-five. The funeral was at twelve fifteen at St Luke's parish church. Presumably Mum and Dad knew where St Luke's was as she had no idea herself and she owned no map that extended further north than Watford.

It was bitterly cold though a clear, brilliant blue sky made her reach for her sunglasses and blow the dust off them. It had snowed up here again in the last few days and small drifts and unmelted patches glistened in the sunlight on people's lawns and in the gutter. On the neighbour's lawn stood the melting remains of a dwarf snowman lopsidedly sporting a woolly blue, white and yellow Leeds United hat and a broken clay pipe. The snowman stared sightlessly at her through eyes made from two small stones.

Lucky I came up to visit last week, thought Jennifer, approaching the house. She nearly hadn't but something—probably guilt—had made her, and she must have been the last one of them to see Aunt Caroline alive. It was important to make the family aware of this point.

Aunt Caroline's front door opened before she had gone two steps down the garden path and Dad emerged, followed closely by Mum.

'Hello, love,' he said, meeting her halfway up the path and touching her elbow, which was about as tactile as anyone was likely to get today. Dad was in his old dark-grey work suit that still fitted him perfectly eight years after retirement and, despite his slight stoop, seemed to give him an air of authority that his usual cardigans and BHS permanent-press trousers didn't. 'Good trip up?' he said, because it was expected.

Jennifer shrugged, 'Contraflows round Newport Pagnell but otherwise okay. Hi, Mum.'

'Oh, hello, dear,' said Mum vaguely, scrabbling in her handbag for something.

Mum was wearing her 1980s black skirt suit that had done many a funeral in its day, the skirt horribly pleated and shoulder pads that would have looked more at home on a Denver Broncos' quarterback.

'Did you end up in the centre of Leeds?' said Mum. 'We always do. Where *are* they? Eric, have you seen the car keys?'

'I've got them,' said Dad, holding them up as proof.

'Oh,' said Mum, looking a bit peeved. Then she pulled herself together and held up a map. 'I'll navigate. We'll all go in the one car, saves petrol.'

'Is this all of us?' said Jennifer, looking back into the house and imagining a funeral with only three people— four if Charlotte bothered to turn up—sitting in a vast, empty church. And where was Graham?

'No, no, no. Ted's sister Iris and her husband are here.' Mum jerked her head back towards the house. 'And the neighbour, Mr Milthorpe. He's gone on ahead. Graham and Su are meeting us there.'

Iris and her husband, Arthur, emerged from the house. Iris, an elderly lady with a pink tinge to her hair who walked with the aid of a stick, and Arthur, who followed one step behind, carrying her bag and sporting an ancient trilby hat, allowed themselves to be shepherded by Mum into the back of the Vauxhall. Jennifer fled to her own car, calling out, 'I'll follow you.'

'Oh, all right, dear,' said Mum, clearly not pleased by this deviation from her plan.

They set off in convoy, Dad driving, Mum navigating with wild gesticulations, Iris and Arthur wedged patiently in the back and Jennifer behind, keeping a safe distance in case of sudden and unexpected turns.

Where's Charlotte? she wondered irritably, as the Vauxhall indicated right and Mum pointed vigorously out of the window as though she didn't think Jennifer could work out where they were going. Perhaps Charlotte was going direct to the church?

Perhaps she wasn't coming?

The convoy successfully negotiated a mini round-about and a set of traffic lights.

Would Charlotte miss Aunt Caroline's funeral? She'd missed Christmas, spinning some tale about end-of-term papers and departmental meetings that no one had believed for one minute. Well, Jennifer hadn't believed it. Mum had spent Christmas Day banging on about how Charlotte was about to be tenured or made emeritus professor or vice-chancellor of the whole bloody university or something. Charlotte hadn't even rung up till halfway through the Queen's speech.

The church, a small stone and slate affair with an ivy-covered lichgate, was on the left and Mum leaned out and pointed to a suitable parking spot. Jennifer ignored her and pulled up on the other side of the road. She sat for a while, watching in her rearview mirror as her family plus extras climbed out of the Vauxhall, retrieved hats and gloves and bags and walking sticks, and generally sorted themselves out. Only when it was safe did she venture to get out of her own car and join them.

One or two elderly people dressed similarly to Iris and Arthur were standing about outside the church and in the vestibule. In the middle of this group stood Graham and his girlfriend, Su. Graham, despite the fact he must have driven up from Bristol this morning, was in a suit that looked as though it had come straight from the dry cleaners, it was so precisely pressed. His shoes had a shine to make a drill sergeant drool.

Beside him, Su was dressed in a woven cotton longyi in different hues of red and brown that wrapped around her slender waist and reached almost to the ground, and over this a short white tunic buttoned to her throat.

Despite the fact that her outfit was clearly more suited to a rubber plantation than a Skipton churchyard in very early February, she still managed to look serene. She was busy explaining to the group of elderly listeners why Burma was now called Myanmar. There was a lot of smiling and nodding and arm touching and they all appeared to be getting along famously.

Typical, thought Jennifer. If Graham and Su didn't score invites to tea from most of Skipton's over-seventies it wouldn't be for want of trying. Had they played their trump card yet, she wondered, looking around for Su's two little boys, but there was no sign of them. This didn't mean the boys weren't here—it wouldn't occur to Graham or Su that kids might not be appropriate at a funeral— it simply meant they were sitting somewhere looking impossibly cute.

Graham looked up and gave a wave of welcome, indicating their arrival to Su with a nudge, and Su gave a big smile as though she had been waiting all morning for Jennifer to arrive. Jennifer raised her hand in a half-wave but didn't go over.

Hovering in the church vestibule with two elderly mourners was a very young vicar. When he spotted them, he excused himself and came over with both hands outstretched, producing a warmly sympathetic smile as though it was something they taught you at theological college.

'Mr and Mrs Denzel! Welcome to St Luke's.'

The very young vicar ('Oh, please call me Justin') took both her parents' hands and clasped them for a moment longer than was necessary before guiding them all into the church.

Not a bad turnout, thought Jennifer, turning discreetly around from her seat in the front pew to survey the congregation. She counted fifteen who had now entered the church and were sitting in twos and threes just behind the family. There were still a few minutes before the service was set to begin and she slipped her mobile out of her bag and glanced at it. No messages. *Damn* Gaspari!

She was distracted by someone appearing at the end of their pew and, looking up, she saw Charlotte slide in next to Dad.

Well, *finally*! What she had done, *cycled* here?

Charlotte was wearing a surprisingly smart black jacket (surely not D&G?) and noisy black boots, and had a scarf wrapped tightly around her neck. She was carrying a purple backpack (a backpack, for God's sake!) which she slid under the pew, then she slumped down in her seat the way she had done since she'd been a teenager.

For a second Jennifer remembered another funeral and another church and Charlotte sitting just like that, slumped in a corner, silent.

The vicar appeared magician-like from behind a curtain, robed up, and a hush fell over the congregation.

'Hello and a very warm welcome to you all on this cold, cold morning,' he said with a big smile.

Charlotte looked up then and for a brief moment their eyes met. And Jennifer thought, I never said sorry. I never told her it was all my fault and I'm sorry about what happened.

CHAPTER TWENTY-EIGHT

DECEMBER 1981

'DEARLY BELOVED, WE ARE gathered here today in the sight of God our Father to mark the life and the sad passing of one of our flock.

'Bertha Mavis Lake, née Flaxheed, lived but a short time in this parish, where she came in the twilight of her years to be cared for by her loving family.'

Jennifer fidgeted irritably in her seat. It was *freezing* in here! Why didn't they put on the central heating? How could anyone be expected to sit through a church service in this cold? No wonder people didn't go to church anymore. It wasn't exactly welcoming.

A fierce glare from Mum brought her attention back to the service.

'Though Bertha Lake lived less than two years in this parish and I did not have the pleasure of being acquainted with her personally...'

Lucky you, thought Jennifer automatically, then she felt guilty and made herself pay attention.

'...I know from my conversations with her family that she was a caring and loving daughter, mother and grand-mother, and a much-loved and much-*valued* member of our community.'

The elderly vicar, Mr Gilchrist, paused for effect

or perhaps to check his notes. He was knocking on a bit, Jennifer observed; his shoulders were stooped and a tremor passed over his hands as he held tightly onto the pulpit. His voice rasped the words with difficulty but then, she had to concede, it would be a challenge for anyone, giving a funeral service for someone they'd never even met. Although nowadays vicars probably did more funerals for people they'd never met than for those they had.

Sitting beside her, Graham was flipping through his hymnbook in preparation for the first hymn. He held the hymnbook up between them as though he fully intended to sing. As though he expected Jennifer to sing too. Jennifer glared at him and he withdrew the book. On the other side of Graham, Charlotte was slumped in her usual bad mood, not paying attention to anyone, and probably wishing it was her own funeral.

Jennifer winced.

And then she felt a rush of irritation. It was getting so she couldn't even think her own thoughts anymore without someone to make her feel guilty for it.

Suppose it *had* been Charlotte's funeral?

'Let us stand for hymn number one hundred and four on page ninety-eight of your red hymnbooks.'

The vicar had to say that, 'your red hymnbooks', otherwise most of the congregation wouldn't have a clue what book he was talking about.

Everyone got to their feet with a rustle of clothes and a rustle of hymnbook pages. Jennifer glanced sideways at the line of mourners. It was odd to see people—well, basically her own family as that was all that was here—dressed in black suits and looking very sombre. And inside a church.

Aside from Graham, who looked as though he was enjoying the whole affair immensely, everyone looked very ill at ease. Mum was trying very hard to give out a dignified 'I come here every Sunday' sort of air that was fooling no one. Dad perched on the edge of the pew gripping his hymnbook, glancing from side to side to see when to stand and when to sit and when to kneel, and clearly hadn't set foot inside a church since his own wedding day.

Uncle Ted, who was a valuer and auctioneer from North Yorkshire and presumably spent the majority of his time tramping about in James Herriot boots in muddy farmyards, had scrubbed up surprisingly well, though his suit was more *Incredible Hulk* than *Dynasty* in terms of its vintage and fit. His large round face and large round ears were bright pink from the cold though you'd think he'd be used to it, being from Up North.

Beside him, Aunt Caroline looked very elegant, and whereas Mum had spent the morning orchestrating everyone and getting quite hot under the collar doing so, Aunt Caroline had spoken very little. Whatever she thought of the proceedings, she wasn't letting on.

Charlotte, who had so many black clothes she must have been spoilt for choice this morning and whom you'd think would therefore be right at home in a funeral, had fidgeted and scowled and glared at everyone all morning so that even Mum hadn't approached her.

'Charlotte's just sad that Grandma's gone,' Mum had explained, as they all waited silently in the car for her to come downstairs and join them. This had seemed so patently unlikely that Jennifer had almost laughed out loud.

'She's probably in the second stage of grief,' Graham had explained helpfully. 'Shock is the first, then denial. The last is acceptance.'

'And the fourth is a belt round the head with a cricket bat,' Jennifer had observed, and Mum had said, 'Jennifer!'

The thing was, no one appeared to be grieving for

Grandma Lake. Or at least no one had been shocked by her death. She had died at the hospital at midnight on Sunday following an angina attack the previous evening. Her rapid deterioration during the night and the final, sudden end had seemed the most anticipated thing on Earth. As for denial, well no, there didn't seem to be much of that either.

Acceptance, yes. They had all, as far as Jennifer could tell, accepted Grandma Lake's parting with surprising ease, and already her room had reverted back to being the study. Dad had reclaimed his favourite chair, moved his stuff out of the garage and driven the car back in. Mum had cooked a really spicy chicken curry then a bolognese, they had had takeaway from the Bamboo Palace and Dad was openly watching *Match of the Day.*

All in all, they seemed to be coping very well. And any acting up from Charlotte had nothing whatsoever to do with Grandma Lake's death. That Mum would have no idea of this, or of anything really, was entirely natural. Anything else would be shocking.

The hymn ended in a straggle of voices and a loud chord from the organist, who obviously thought he was Elton John. Everyone sat down with more rustling of coats and bags. Someone dropped their hymnbook with a sharp thud. Mr Gilchrist gripped the pulpit once more and everyone settled back, content to let him run the show.

'Bertha Lake lived a long life. A life that spanned a large part of this century. And, we must suppose, she would have experienced first hand much of the good and the evil that man has produced during this time.'

That Grandma Lake could experience good and evil was hard to imagine, she having spent her final years waddling from her room to the television set to the bathroom in a sort of eternal triangle of torpidity. But no doubt this was the customary sort of twaddle that vicars were meant to come out with at a funeral for someone about whom they knew nothing. Or knew only what the relatives chose to tell them.

Had Mum or Aunt Caroline provided him with the relevant biographical details or was he flying solo? Aunt Caroline had only come down south this morning so it seemed unlikely she had spoken to the vicar. Mum then. Mum must have given him some brief outline. Very brief, by the sound of it.

'She was born at the start of the century...'

There! He didn't even know what year Grandma Lake had been born.

'...in Acton, a suburb where she grew up and married and where she lived as a wife and, for many years, as a widow, until just two years ago.'

When she was forcibly wrenched from her home and dumped here.

'She married Matthew and they enjoyed a happy and successful marriage that spanned twenty years until Matthew's untimely death in 1945.'

Mr Gilchrist paused to allow the impact of this tragedy to sink in.

'As a widow in post-war London, Bertha raised her two daughters, Caroline and Deirdre, on her own and she was fortunate enough to live to see both her children marry and make homes of their own and present her with three grandchildren, Jennifer, Charlotte and Graham.'

Jennifer frowned to cover her embarrassment. Graham beamed and looked around at everyone as though seeking congratulations from the congregation for a job well done. Charlotte continued to sulk in the corner and probably wasn't even listening.

So, Grandma Lake's life was to be judged by how long her marriage had lasted, how many offspring she had produced and how many grandchildren she had had. What about Aunt Caroline? Never mind that she'd existed for fifty-odd years on her own, all that mattered was that she was now married and settled down with Ted.

Jennifer tried to imagine what Mr Gilchrist might say about her if she should happen to die tomorrow: poor, sweet Jennifer, struck down in her prime, denied the joy of motherhood, of holy union with another—well, that's what the vicar would say and Darren, sitting in the congregation gripping Roberta Peabody's hand and fighting back tears of self-recrimination, would know it wasn't true, would know they had shared holy union on a number of occasions, thank you very much, in Darren's bed no less, while his mum and dad were downstairs entertaining their city friends over dinner. Oh yes! Darren would be remembering all that and he'd regret dumping her then, wouldn't he!

The vicar peered short-sightedly at a piece of paper he was holding in his hand, his eyes scanning the contents to make sure he had missed nothing. Then he looked up at the congregation brightly. 'Let us pray.'

Is that it? thought Jennifer, outraged. Eighty-odd years and all Grandma Lake got was three paltry sentences? It was *nothing*. Couldn't Mum have come up with more than that?

She turned to look at her mother but Mum was already rearranging herself on the kneeler before her and didn't seem the least bit outraged. Further along the row Aunt Caroline wasn't kneeling. She was sitting up in her seat and didn't even bow her head when Mr Gilchrist began the prayer.

At least it meant they could all go home soon to the mushroom vol-au-vents.

Mum had explained that after the service, the family were expected to stand at the church door and shake hands with everyone who had attended. In reality, this meant shaking hands with the vicar and that was it. Apart from the family no one else had come.

They piled into two cars, Dad's red Cortina and

Uncle Ted's large and mud-splattered dark green estate ('I do think he could at least have given it a wash before coming down,' Mum had observed in an aside to Dad), and drove off after the hearse to the crematorium. Here a nervous, shuffling wait was followed by a ten-minute service, a moment of horror as the coffin slid soundlessly and eternally behind a curtain and vanished, then a half-hour journey home again, by which time Jennifer was starving.

'I set the oven to come on at twelve,' Mum explained as they filed into the house. The dining room table was already groaning under the weight of a ton of cheese, ham and tomato sandwiches, a vast bowl of French onion dip, pineapple chunks and little cubes of Red Leicester held together with cocktail sticks, plates of Ritz biscuits and rolls and rolls of neatly folded table napkins.

'Tuck in,' said Dad, nodding towards the feast he had been heroically slicing and buttering that morning before anyone else was even awake. 'Tea or coffee, Ted?'

Ted, who was removing his boots in the doorway, met Dad's suggestion with a barely concealed look of dismay.

'I could sink a nice glass of bitter, if you've got one, Eric-lad.'

'Aren't you driving, Ted?' said Mum, shocked, standing forlornly in front of the oven with a tray of frozen vol-au-vents in her hands.

'We both drive, Deirdre,' said Caroline coming in from the hallway and removing her coat thoughtfully as though she hadn't quite made up her mind to stay.

'I'll have a beer, too,' Jennifer called out as Dad went to the fridge.

'Tea or coffee?' said Mum firmly. She glanced up at the clock on the kitchen wall. 'Now I've put the vol-au-vents in but they'll take about 35 minutes so don't fill yourselves up.'

'Grand,' said Ted obligingly, helping himself to a plate

and a napkin and a huge spoonful of coleslaw. 'Mek em yourself, did you Deirdre?'

'Fat chance,' muttered Charlotte, who had come slinking into the room last and was now sitting in her usual spot in the furthest corner of the sofa.

'Caroline? What can I get you?' said Dad, hovering halfway between the fridge and the dining-room table.

'Well, what have you got in that drinks cabinet of yours, Eric?' she replied, earning her the instant respect of Jennifer. Graham looked up from his inspection of the potato salad to gauge Mum's reaction. Mum straightened up, having placed a quiche in the oven alongside the vol-au-vents, and made a great show of regarding the kitchen clock. Then she surprised them all.

'Oh, why not? Eric, I'll have a tiny sherry,' she said, throwing caution to the wind.

Dad blinked. 'Right-ho,' he said. 'Caroline? Sherry? Or we've got Dubonnet, vermouth, advocaat or Cinzano.'

Ted spluttered and a mouthful of lager dribbled down his chin. 'By 'eck,' he muttered, for no obvious reason except that this choice of drinks was not, perhaps, what he had been expecting.

'Sherry's fine, thanks, Eric,' said Aunt Caroline and she sat down beside Charlotte on the sofa. 'After all, it's not every day you bury your mother, is it?'

'We didn't bury her,' Graham corrected, and before he could add, 'We burned her,' Mum leapt in.

'You girls? Tea or coffee?'

It's not every day you bury your mother.

Jennifer regarded Aunt Caroline and noticed that Charlotte was watching her too. She'd always been different, Aunt Caroline. Different from themselves, at any rate, and that was the only difference that mattered. It was hard to picture Mum and Aunt Caroline as sisters, let alone Aunt Caroline being Grandma Lake's daughter. They had hardly been in the same room as each other twice in the last two years.

'You're looking peaky,' said Aunt Caroline, taking the tiny sherry glass that Dad offered and studying Charlotte's face.

Charlotte turned away furiously.

Aunt Caroline reached out and touched her knee. 'You know, you can always come and stay with us. If you need a break.'

What about me? thought Jennifer indignantly. I'm the eldest! Why can't I come up? What if *I* need a break?

'There you are, dear,' said Mum, handing her two cups of coffee. 'Pass one to Charlotte.'

So now they all had drinks in their hands and Dad and Mum and Ted were standing in the middle of the lounge, Mum with her tiny sherry, Dad and Ted nursing lagers, and all looking at each other.

'Not a bad drop this, Eric-lad,' said Uncle Ted, holding up his can of lager to the light appreciatively. 'I mean for Southern-poofter beer,' he added with a wink at Graham.

'Don't have more than one if you're driving, Ted,' said Mum.

'The missus is driving us 'ome, an't ya, love?'

'Actually, many of the stronger ales and bitters are brewed by breweries in the south and southwest,' Graham pointed out, earning him a withering look from both his sisters.

'You're lucky you both drive,' observed Mum, as though being able to drive was something you were either born with or you weren't. 'Dad never drove, nor did Mum.' It seemed that now Grandma Lake was gone it was okay to get nostalgic about her. 'Do you remember that old Ford Dad had for years, Caroline? But he never would drive it.' She looked over at Caroline to confirm this but Caroline took a sip from her drink and seemed in no mood to confirm or deny anything.

'Well, he must 'ave driven at some point, Deirdre,'

said Uncle Ted. He turned towards Caroline. 'You've got a photo of him sitting in the cab of a bus, an't ya, love?'

Caroline stood up abruptly and sniffed. 'I think your vol-au-vents are burning, Deird.'

Mum spun around, flustered, and rushed into the kitchen.

And as far as Jennifer could remember, no one had mentioned Grandma Lake again that day.

CHAPTER TWENTY-NINE

'WILL YOU COME BACK to the house for a bite to eat, Vicar—Justin?' said Mum, putting on her Margot Leadbetter voice, as they left Aunt Caroline's cremation.

'I won't, thanks.' The vicar extended his hand and beamed at her. 'I've got another funeral at one.'

'Goin't down like flies, Vicar?' wheezed the elderly Arthur, who had been Ted Kettley's brother-in-law.

Charlotte stood impatiently in the driveway to the crematorium and turned up the collar of her jacket—Ashley's jacket. Public displays of affection, no matter how mild, made her nervous. However, they'd got through the funeral and the cremation, so that just left the wake.

Was it called a wake if you weren't Catholic? Mum had called it 'a bite to eat', which sounded much more secular, if middle class and much less emotional. All very Protestant, in fact.

Everyone was outside now, milling around, slapping gloved hands together in the frozen air and talking loudly. There was a distinct sense of release and perhaps relief that the formal part of the proceedings was over. The elderly folk, perhaps hardened to such occasions, congregated outside the church, glad of an excuse to gossip.

'Ron Briscoe had Ardley Colliery Brass Band play at his funeral,' observed a frail old man in a long raincoat who was leaning heavily on a walking stick.

'I remember that dog at Marge Compton's funeral,' said his wife, a large woman with a vast flowery hat.

'Ron Briscoe played second trombone,' said Arthur.

'It were a dalmatian. Do you remember, Iris?'

'Aye, but he played trombone with the Taddlethwaite lot, not with Ardley.'

Finally, when the pleasantries with the vicar had been completed and instructions given to everyone, Mum gave the word that it was time to depart.

Charlotte saw Jennifer standing impatiently in the crematorium doorway, holding her mobile phone to her ear and trying to escape Aunt Caroline's neighbour, which gave Charlotte time to seek out Graham and Su and make her way over to their shiny new Golf.

'Can I beg a lift to Aunt Caroline's? I don't have my car.'

''Course you can,' said Graham, then he fixed her with a speculative look. 'You made it by the skin of your teeth,' he observed, unlocking the car with an electronic beep. 'Did you have second thoughts and nearly not come?'

'Have *you* ever tried getting from Edinburgh to Skipton on public transport?' she countered. 'Hi, Su.' She kissed her almost-sister-in-law on the cheek.

'Charlotte. How are you? I once travelled from Margate to Paisley on public transport,' remarked Su in her precise English. 'Of course I was a student then,' she added, which explained why she'd been on public transport though not why she'd been in either Margate or Paisley.

'Direct train to Leeds then change for Skipton— simple,' said Graham. 'And you could go via Carlisle, too—though that would mean two changes. Oh, watch out for the child restraints,' he warned, as Charlotte slid into the back seat and immediately got tangled up in various child-sized seats and safety belts.

'How are the boys, Su?' she asked, because she felt she ought to.

'Fine. Spending February with their father.'

'Oh. Is he still in Rangoon?'

'No. Paisley.'

Well, that explained it.

'And how is the university, Charlotte?' asked Su, turning around in her seat and fixing Charlotte with such a direct gaze that she was forced to concentrate on the suburban delights of Skipton through the window in order to avoid it.

'Fine. Well, I'm still there, that's the main thing. They haven't replaced me with a twenty-two-year-old PhD student—yet. And you? How are things in Bristol?'

Su worked for a merchant bank as some kind of investment analyst, which meant she worked a million hours a week and earned an absolute fortune. The Golf they were now sitting in was Graham's. Su owned a late-model gold Mercedes, though she claimed this was only for tax purposes. Graham worked for Social Services in Bristol and worked nearly as many hours for substantially less. They lived in a three-storey terrace house near the city centre which Su owned and Graham liked to renovate.

'As well as can be expected,' said Su, which from anyone else would have been enigmatic and perhaps a little sombre, but Su said it with a gleam in her eye so that you had an uncomfortable feeling she was laughing at you. 'Graham has reversed our feature walls. The feature walls are now white and the white walls are now a feature colour. Avocado.'

'Aubergine,' corrected Graham, as they turned into Aunt Caroline's street. 'The home section of the *Bristol Evening Post* is doing a feature on us next week.'

Aunt Caroline's street had a silent, suburban weekday feel to it. Mum and Dad were already getting out of the Vauxhall and Arthur and Iris emerged from the back seat.

Aunt Caroline's front door stood open and for a second you expected to see her appear in the doorway, wiping her hands on her apron and making some announcement about scones. Instead, the neighbour who had been at the church appeared in the doorway then stood aside, smiling a welcome. Mum, who was coming up the pathway armed with the front door key, paused.

'Mr Milthorpe. I thought you were behind us?' It sounded like an accusation.

'Thought I'd go on ahead and open up. Kettle's on.'

There was going to be a turf war, that much was obvious, and Charlotte waited beside Graham's Golf until everyone else had gone inside and terms had been agreed on before venturing inside.

In the hallway Mum was in full swing.

'This is Iris and Arthur Pearson, dear,' she said to Graham, indicating the elderly couple she had given a lift to. 'Iris was Ted's sister. My youngest, Graham, and his... Su.'

Su smiled serenely and Charlotte sighed. Mum couldn't say 'girlfriend' because Su was forty-two and had two children.

'Hello, love. And where are you from?' Mr Pearson asked Su, picking up on her dark complexion and Oriental eyes, to say nothing of her unusual attire.

'Bristol,' Su replied charmingly. 'And you?'

'We live in Ilkley, love,' said Iris. 'Though I were brought up 'ere in Skipton and Arthur in Blackburn.'

'Aye, we've come a long way,' agreed Arthur, and it was difficult to tell whether he was being ironic or not.

'And this is...' Mum hesitated as the man with the long raincoat and the large woman with the vast flowery hat stepped into the hallway.

'Bill and Mavis Rudley,' announced the man, stomping his feet on Aunt Caroline's doormat and unbuttoning his coat.

'We live in Firth Street,' said his wife, as though this explained their presence, then she busied herself untying her hat, removing it and looking around for a hook large enough to hang it on.

''Scuse me,' murmured Charlotte, squeezing past the log-jam of mourners that had stuck fast in the hallway.

'Oh. Dearest, this is—'

Charlotte smiled wanly. 'Hello. Shall I serve the drinks?' and she escaped into the kitchen.

The neighbour, Mr Milthorpe, was already there, pulling milk out of the fridge, the kettle steaming behind him, a tray of biscuits and sliced cakes on the bench top. He looked as though he knew his way around.

''Ello, love,' he said, looking up. 'Jack Milthorpe. I live next door. Me and your aunt were old pals.' He stuck out his hand.

'Hello. I'm Charlotte,' and she shook his hand, wondering how he knew she was Aunt Caroline's niece. Perhaps it wasn't too hard to work out, if he knew as much about Aunt Caroline's family as he appeared to know about her kitchen.

'I've seen the photos on't mantelpiece,' he explained, as if she had asked. 'Shall I do you a nice cuppa?'

'Thanks, yes. Oh, let me help,' but she didn't move. He seemed to know what he was doing. Perhaps he was one of those people who liked to be doing something rather than just standing around. She watched him go unerringly to a cupboard and pull out a tin and spoon tea leaves into a large green teapot. Or perhaps he didn't like to think of strangers in Caroline's kitchen. That's what we are, I suppose, she thought; strangers.

'Hello? No, look I'm after—yes, can you hear me? I'm after Mr Gaspari. Is he—'

Jennifer.

And on her mobile. She must have got here soon after Mr Milthorpe as Charlotte had seen her standing on her own in the lounge when everyone else was still removing their coats and scarves in the hallway. And she was talking to her office on her mobile.

'No. No, I'm not on the bus. I'm at a funeral,' said Jennifer testily, as if that explained something vital. Perhaps it explained poor reception. Perhaps she earned extra brownie points if she called the office from a funeral? Charlotte could imagine Tom Pitney's reaction if she rang him from a funeral. Tom didn't really like you to ring him at any time.

'I have left about four messages already... Yes, it is important. Do you think I'd be phoning from a funeral if it wasn't?'

Yes, thought Charlotte, entering the lounge and going past Jennifer to get to Aunt Caroline's drinks cabinet, I think you probably would.

The drinks cabinet held a surprisingly good supply of sherry—old ladies' tipple, thought Charlotte—plus a bottle of port, one of brandy and something that looked suspiciously like cherry liqueur. The sherry seemed the safest bet and she pulled out the bottle and decided there were some advantages to taking the train after all—she could get quietly drunk in a corner and not have to worry about driving home.

'Thank you, that would be most helpful,' said Jennifer sarcastically and the snap of plastic on plastic, followed by a petulant sigh, seemed to indicate that the phone call had ended.

'I'll have one of those,' said Jennifer in a different voice—long-suffering now, rather than angry. Charlotte studied the labels on the various bottles and did not turn around. She reached for two glasses and poured a generous quantity into each. She turned and held out one of the glasses.

'Thanks.' Jennifer took a sip from the glass and looked away, not meeting Charlotte's gaze. 'Ugh,' she commented. 'How old is this? Pre-war?'

Charlotte said nothing but took a hefty swig of her own glass. She winced. It really was hideous.

There was a moment's silence.

'So. And how's things in the wonderful world of academia?' said Jennifer, as though they were strangers meeting after a year apart. Which wasn't far from the truth.

'A lot better than things at your workplace, by the sound of it,' Charlotte replied.

Jennifer frowned. 'That? Oh, just some useless secretary on a power trip. They know where I am, they can contact me if anything urgent crops up.'

'Get many urgent things cropping up, do you, in the toy department?' said Charlotte with a wide-eyed look. 'Teddy bear revolt? Rogue Action Man sexually assaulting promiscuous Barbie doll?'

Jennifer produced her most withering look, which was very withering indeed. 'For your information, we don't do Action Man and Barbie dolls nowadays. It's all computer toys.' Then she seemed to remember something, perhaps that they were at Aunt Caroline's funeral, perhaps that she was supposed to have been talking about computer games on Kim's television program. Either way, she fell silent and gingerly took a second sip of the sherry.

'How's Nick?' Charlotte asked, knowing this would annoy Jennifer. Mum always asked about Nick and her questions were always a thinly veiled criticism of Jennifer's divorce.

'Fine. He's fine,' replied Jennifer, not rising to the bait, or perhaps saving herself for Mum. 'And you? Are you seeing anyone?'

Charlotte suddenly remembered that she was wearing Ashley's jacket, had spent last night at Ashley's flat, that she had had sex and that Jennifer, from the sound of it, had not. Then she realised that Ashley's contract ended in July, that she allegedly had some fiancé or other awaiting her in Canada, that last night had all the hallmarks of a classic one-night stand, and—what was more surprising—that it didn't really matter. All these thoughts skimmed across her mind in an instant. She shrugged.

'No. No one really.'

'Hey, that reminds me,' said Jennifer, suddenly becoming animated. 'Guess who I ran into? You'll never guess!' And before Charlotte could make a guess, she triumphantly provided the answer. 'Zoe Findlay! On the Bakerloo line. Southbound. She was going to Elephant and Castle.'

Charlotte sighed. Not the Zoe Findlay thing again.

'So?' she replied.

'So! You and her were...well,' Jennifer shrugged, 'best friends,' and perhaps she meant it euphemistically. However she meant it, Charlotte was not about to enter into this discussion now. Perhaps not ever.

'She asked about you.'

'Look, I really don't care about Zoe Findlay. I never did. Why are you so obsessed with the past?'

Jennifer looked surprised. 'I'm not. I—'

'Oh?' She regarded Jennifer over the top of her sherry glass. 'Kim's TV program?' she prompted. 'You went on there and said...*that. Why?* Why would you *do* that?'

She hadn't meant to say that. Hadn't meant to speak so angrily. Didn't want to be having this conversation at all. The glass shook slightly in her hand. She steadied it with her other hand.

Jennifer looked away. She swallowed a mouthful of sherry. 'Yeah, sorry 'bout that.' She paused. 'I mean, mostly it was just a silly mistake. I went on as a favour to Kim and they told me it would be about violence in kids' computer games. But some specialist dropped out at the last minute so they switched to next week's topic, which was "I Saved My Sister's Life!". Kim said it was karma.'

Karma, was it? A silly mistake?

Charlotte experienced a disturbing rush of ground and sky all at once, not unlike what you felt when you stood on the edge of a very steep drop and felt yourself falling. She spoke slowly. 'But... But why didn't you say Sorry, I'm on the wrong show, and just *leave*?'

'Kim was desperate. This psychologist bloke had dropped out at the last minute. I couldn't let her down.'

'Why not? Someone else obviously didn't think twice about letting her down!'

She'd raised her voice and from the hallway Iris Pearson stared at her. Charlotte lowered her voice. 'I mean, it's television, it's not emergency surgery. It's not some military operation. *It's just television.* A poxy television program.'

'Oh really? And you've made your career out of analysing them. How's the book going by the way?'

There was a silence. Charlotte took another swig of the dreadful sherry and found her glass was empty. She wasn't going to let Jennifer change the subject on her.

'*Look.* No one believed it was true, anyway,' hissed Jennifer with a sideways glance at Mr Milthorpe, who was passing by with a tray of what looked like Madeira cake.

A silence fell.

'What are you two drinking?' asked Mum suspiciously, coming over.

Sometime during this exchange the other mourners had entered the lounge and everyone was now munching on scones and Madeira cake and sipping percolated coffee.

'It's sherry,' said Jennifer. 'Charlotte broke into Aunt Caroline's stock and dug out this pre-war vintage.'

'I thought we could all go out to dinner tonight,' said Mum, undeterred by talk of sherry. 'Mr Milthorpe suggested a nice trattoria in town. I wonder if we ought to invite him? He's been very sweet helping out—'

'Can't,' interrupted Jennifer. 'I've got paperwork I need to do in the office tonight for a board meeting tomorrow.'

'Oh.' Mum looked a little surprised. Then she turned to Charlotte.

'I'm catching the four fifty-six train back. I've got a tute first thing tomorrow,' Charlotte said with an apologetic shrug. It was true, and she wasn't about to jeopardise her position in the department by failing to turn up or, worse, asking another member of staff to fill in for her.

'Oh. Well. I'm sure Graham and Su will be able to come.'

No one answered her.

'And if not, your father and I will go on our own. It's been ages since we've eaten out. Or I could heat up a shepherd's pie in the microwave.'

She turned away to supervise Mr Milthorpe in the kitchen.

Charlotte's glass was empty and she picked up the bottle to refill it.

'Anyway, I told Mum I invented the whole thing,' said Jennifer after a moment. 'That's what she wanted me to say.' She held out her glass for a refill. 'And why would anyone believe it anyway? I mean, if something like that had happened, surely everyone would have known. It's not something you can keep secret for twenty-odd years, is it?'

They looked at each other for a moment and there seemed nothing further to say.

I never thanked her, Charlotte realised. I never thanked her for saving my life.

Bertha

CHAPTER THIRTY

MAY 1926

O N THE THIRD DAY of the strike an amazing thing
had happened. A sign had appeared on the front gate of
the bus garage calling for volunteer bus drivers—and they
were taking women!

Jemima had announced it that evening.

She had returned, triumphant, from her first shift as
a volunteer conductor, sweeping into the kitchen in Wells
Lane, sporting her red armband and her conductor's cap,
full to bursting with her own self-importance, and Bertha,
feeding Baby at the kitchen table, wanted to slap her.

Naturally Mum and Cousin Janie and Aunt Nora had
been agog and never mind they had all been dead against
it the night before, and that Ronnie had forbidden it and
as far as anyone knew wasn't even talking to her, or that
Bertha and Mum had had to look after Baby all day. And
never mind that Jemima didn't care two hoots for the
Good of the Nation or the Rights of the Decent-Minded
Citizen or any of that other claptrap the government was
spouting. You'd think she was the first woman to volunteer in the whole of Acton, in the whole of London. You'd
think a woman had never driven an ambulance in France
or nursed soldiers at the front or marched on parliament
with a placard demanding the vote. You'd think a woman

had never even set foot on a bus before yesterday morning. You'd think Jemima had kept the very life-blood of the capital's transport system flowing and had single-handedly prevented a bloody revolution to boot.

And Matthew had arrived at Wells Lane with her, as breathless and as flushed as she, so that Bertha stared at them both and realised that she had never actually seen him breathless or flushed before, not even on their wedding night.

Jemima, he had explained, had been conductor on his bus—imagine!

She did imagine.

'We ran the gauntlet!' Matthew announced, standing in the middle of the kitchen with his chest puffed out and everyone congratulating him.

And Mum said, 'Aren't you *brave*!'

And Dad said, all gruff like, 'Aye well, we all have to do our bit in a time of crisis.'

And Janie said, 'Was it frightening, Mr Lake? Were you set upon by gangs of strikers?'

And even though he was her husband and she was proud of him—she really was—and she was pleased that everyone was so thrilled, still... Bertha found she was unable to say anything. Anything at all.

Jemima flung her cap down on the kitchen table and herself in an empty chair and launched straight into a particularly hilarious incident that had occurred somewhere near Chiswick involving a rowdy band of strikers and an angry passenger with a carton of eggs.

'Oh, it was too funny!' she exclaimed. 'Go on, Matthew, tell them!'

Matthew, was it now? Yesterday she had called him Mr Lake, if she had spoken to him at all.

On her lap, Baby made a sort of gurgling noise and Bertha stood up abruptly and pushed her way out to the hallway where she busied herself settling Baby in the large black perambulator.

'Fellow must have been a sniper in the War,' she could hear Matthew saying, just as though he had been in the trenches and had personal experience of such things. 'He stood outside on the top deck and hurled eggs—with marksmanship accuracy, mind—at any of the ruffians who came within so much as five yards of the bus! You should have seen the mess!'

And then Jemima said, 'And what do you think, Mum? Now they are calling for women drivers too! I think I might try out for it.'

Women drivers? In the hallway Bertha stopped settling Baby and listened. They wanted women drivers? And Jemima wanted to sign up for it! But it was she who had driven Uncle Alan's old traction engine all those years ago, not Jem. It was she who should be a driver!

She stood in the kitchen doorway, her heart pounding, looking from Dad to Aunt Nora to Janie, at Mum standing at the sink swirling the tea leaves around in the pot, at Jemima who sat in the centre of the room.

It's me, thought Bertha, *this is my time. I must say something.*

But she knew if she did that they would say no. They would come up with a dozen reasons why she should not.

She would say nothing.

Then Matthew announced it was time to leave— Mother and Aunt Daisy would be awaiting their tea. And in the hallway Baby started up such a wailing and Jem marched out to the hallway and shook the perambulator but that only made Baby wail all the louder so she announced she would take the wretched thing home.

Matthew said, It's dark outside, and Lord knew what sort of persons might be roaming High Street and he would see to it that she and Baby got safely home.

When they had gone, Dad said darkly, Her husband ought to be the one seeing her safely home, it wasn't right. And Aunt Nora sighed and looked at Janie who was bouncing little Herbert on her knee and said, Ah well, things don't always turn out like you expect, and Mum said, Who wants another cuppa, then?

Bertha went into the lounge and stood at the window watching until Matthew and Jemima and the perambulator had turned the corner of Wells Lane and disappeared from sight. Did Matthew expect her to go home? Or would he come back for her? Mrs Lake and Aunt Daisy would be awaiting their tea. She grabbed her hat and gloves, called out her goodbyes and hurried from the house, but rather than head towards Oakton Way she turned instead in the direction of Uxbridge Road.

If she didn't go now, she might never go.

It wasn't really dark outside. The sun had barely sunk below the row of houses opposite and there was an orange glow over the rooftops and the chimneys of South Acton and Gunnersbury Park. There were lots of folk out on this balmy May evening and Bertha joined them, knowing that she had a role to play, that her part, finally, had been revealed to her.

The bus company wanted volunteer drivers and they were taking women. A week ago it would have seemed absurd, laughable. Now it seemed…obvious. A gift from heaven.

She crossed Horn Lane and passed the King's Head then waited impatiently at the corner of Steyne Road for a horse-drawn coal cart and a slow-moving meat delivery van to pass. Ahead were the gates of the garage.

Don't pause, just walk in and sign up.

The special constables guarding the gates tipped their hats at her and waved her through as though they had been expecting her, as though they knew she had important business within. She crossed the yard and made for a small superintendent's office at the rear where the portly man with a creased uniform and a huge moustache appeared to be awaiting her arrival. Instead of scowling or laughing at her or inquiring what her business was, the superintendent merely nodded, touched his cap, called her 'Miss' and handed her a clipboard with a printed form on it.

'Thank you,' she replied calmly, taking the form as though she signed up as a volunteer bus driver every day of her life, and produced, with a flourish, a good fountain pen that she had placed in her bag for just this purpose.

After asking the usual questions—her name and address and her husband's name and occupation—the form asked, Had she ever operated machinery or driven a vehicle before? She proudly wrote, *Yes, farm traction engine on uncle's farm in Shropshire.* Writing 'Shropshire' made it seem more plausible somehow—there weren't many traction engines in Acton. Then she wondered if she was right to have mentioned it was her uncle's farm. Did that perhaps imply she had been childishly playing and hadn't really driven it on her own? And then she had wondered if she ought to have mentioned Shropshire after all. Did the bus company really care where she had driven the vehicle? But in the end she left it there, as it seemed to add an air of authenticity. After all, anyone could claim to have driven a vehicle, couldn't they? Then the form asked about her general health and she wrote *Excellent* in bold, healthy letters. And finally it asked if her husband had given his permission for her to sign up and Bertha chewed her lip and looked around but the superintendent had retired to his office and was engrossed in reigniting the large tea urn in the corner.

It was true that Matthew had not exactly given his permission in so many words but he had applauded Jemima's decision to sign up as a conductress—and her a mother!—and he had applauded the idea of women drivers, so it stood to reason he would have given his approval, had he been specifically asked. She wrote *Yes* in firm letters. Then she signed the form and handed it back and in return received a smart black cap, a red armband, a stack of route maps and an instruction to turn up promptly at six o'clock the following morning.

And it was done, all in a matter of minutes. She was a bus driver.

She must tell someone! Now, right this minute! She thought about the house in Oakton Way and Mrs Lake and Aunt Daisy sitting patiently awaiting their tea and her standing in the middle of the lounge telling them. No, she could as easily tell them she was leaving Matthew to live with a tribe of nomads in the desert for all they would understand. She set off back to Wells Lane, hoping everyone was still there.

What if Ronnie was there? She experienced a qualm of unease suddenly, imagining Ronnie's dismay, his disbelief. But Ronnie wasn't her husband, what did it matter what he thought? Was it a betrayal? No; it would have been, once.

❋ ❋ ❋

At Wells Lane, there was—predictably—uproar.

Mum and Dad were there and so too were Aunt Nora and Janie, Herbert lying asleep on Janie's lap with his wet mouth open, a line of drool stretching from his chin to Janie's knee. They were sipping tea in the lounge, eating a plate of Mum's fish paste sandwiches. Bertha paused in the doorway and wondered if they had even noticed she had gone out? Apparently not.

But it hardly mattered. She had signed up.

'Pour yourself a cup, dear, there's enough in the pot,' said Mum, not looking up.

But Bertha didn't pour herself a cup. Instead she stood in the doorway and announced that she had gone down to the bus garage and signed up as a driver and she started tomorrow. At six o'clock sharp. And that Mum would have to look after Baby on her own as she would no longer be able to.

There was a moment's silence. It ought to have been thrilling, but somehow it wasn't. Then uproar.

Mum gasped in dismay and cried, 'Bertha!'

Janie gasped in awe and cried, 'How exciting!'

Aunt Nora put her hand on her heart and said, 'Well I never did!'

And Dad got slowly to his feet, took a deep breath and said, 'So that's how it is,' with a deep frown as though he had been expecting something along these lines and, now that it had happened, his worst fears had been realised.

'What does Matthew say?' asked Mum, and Bertha sat down, busying herself with the teapot, putting down her new cap and armband.

'Matthew's in complete support of the government and all the people who are trying to keep the country running,' she replied truthfully.

'You're never going to drive one of them big old Generals?' Aunt Nora exclaimed.

'How exciting, Bertha!' Janie gasped a second time, her eyes wide with the thrill of it all. 'Wish I could sign up...' A glance at her mother quickly put paid to that idea.

'It is a General, yes,' Bertha confirmed. 'I explained to the superintendent that I had driven before and they were very impressed. They signed me up on the spot. I receive my training at six o'clock and then I do my first shift at seven.'

'Well, I never did!' said Aunt Nora again.

It was dark and quite late by the time she arrived home. Mrs Lake and Aunt Daisy had finished tea, washed up and put everything away, and were sitting in the lounge expectantly.

'But where's Matthew?' Mrs Lake inquired, looking past Bertha as though she suspected her of leaving him out in the street at the mercy of itinerant robbers and bandits.

'Escorting my sister home,' Bertha replied tartly. 'It was dark and she had the baby and there are so many people out on the streets...'

'Goodness!' said Mrs Lake, alarmed, and Aunt Daisy looked quite faint and asked did she think they were quite safe alone here in the house, especially during the day when Matthew was out?

Bertha smiled wordlessly at Mrs Lake and fetched Aunt Daisy's rug from upstairs and made them both another cup of tea, washed up the empty milk bottles and placed them outside on the doorstep.

'Where *can* Matthew be?' said Mrs Lake for the fifth time, peering at the clock on the mantelpiece as if it would provide some clue. The clock said it was half past nine.

'Do you think something has happened?' replied Aunt Daisy, but no one could answer her.

At ten o'clock Aunt Daisy put away her knitting and Mrs Lake set out the breakfast things on the table for morning, then they said their goodnights. Where was Matthew? *Could* something have happened?

Bertha waited till the quarter hour struck then she too climbed the narrow staircase to the bedroom at the front of the house that she and Matthew had shared for the last six months. She undressed and lay awake beneath the cold sheets.

Footsteps in the street outside, the squeak of the gate and a key in the lock downstairs heralded Matthew's return. The floorboards in the hallway creaked then a moment later she heard heavy footsteps on the stairs, the bedroom door open and close. A smell of damp outside air, tweed and smoke filled the room. He undressed in the darkness, slowly, folding his clothes as he always did:

trousers and braces over the back of the chair, shoes side by side beneath the bed, jacket on a hanger in the wardrobe, shirt carefully folded and placed on the chair…

No. Shirt not folded. Bertha peered at him in the moonlight. Shirt screwed up and pushed hastily beneath the bed.

Then he pulled on his nightshirt and climbed into bed. All in the dark, all in silence. He turned over, pulled the bedclothes over himself, and Bertha couldn't tell whether he slept or not.

She imagined him running the gauntlet through Chiswick, driving his bus through a throng of angry pickets. Fearless. A volunteer. She ought to be proud. Any decent wife would be. Was she proud? She didn't know. She had said nothing. And she had intended to tell him she had signed up but had said nothing about that either. Now it was too late.

Now his shirt lay screwed up beneath the bed. Out of the way. Out of sight.

The old grandfather clock in the hallway struck eleven times and in six hours she would rise.

She was up at five o'clock, indeed had hardly slept more than a few hours. It was light outside and she dressed silently and crept down the stairs. No one else was awake and she cut herself a slice of bread and butter and drank a mug of milk rather than risk the sound of the kettle waking them.

Matthew hadn't stirred though he would be up soon. The huge number of telegrams created by the strike was swamping the post office and he had been told to begin his shift early this morning. His shift on the bus would have to be allocated to another driver.

To me? she wondered. Did you choose which route you did? No, of course not, it wasn't a schoolyard game; this was Real Life.

She let herself out of the front door, wincing as the door latch slid noisily back into place.

Ought she to have told him?

He would have stopped her. She knew it as surely as she knew anything. She would tell him, of course, but afterwards. When it was too late.

Outside the sun was shining brightly and the dawn chorus was loud in the sycamores. The blossom on the cherry trees glowed in the morning light and she was going off to drive a bus in the strike. Everything was perfect.

She was early so she walked along Acton Lane and beneath the red-painted iron bridge over which the trains to Kew and Brentford rattled. She crossed Winchester Street, walked briskly along High Street and turned into Steyne Road. The early workers were already beginning their steady trek eastward on foot and the first delivery carts rattled in from the provinces heading towards the city and Bertha smiled and waved at every driver that caught her eye. Ahead was the bus garage and she was relieved to see there were no strikers outside yet.

Turning in through the gates she saw five big red Generals lined up and waiting to go. Beside them, two young men in Oxford bags and college scarves and a stout middle-aged lady with her sleeves rolled up and a determined look on her face turned to stare at her.

'Miss Flaxheed?' called the lady.

Bertha nodded. 'Yes, I'm here to—'

'I'm Miss Gordon. This is Mr Parks,' she said, indicating the first young man, 'and Mr...?'

'Sutton,' supplied the other young man, reaching out to shake Bertha's hand.

'Hello, I—'

'Good, good. Now, you'll soon pick it up. Step this way and we'll do a bit of theory to get things rolling.'

Bertha and the two young men, Parks and Sutton, followed at a respectful distance as Miss Gordon led them over to the first bus, flung open the engine cover and proceeded to give them a brief lecture on the mysteries of the internal combustion engine.

Bertha listened and nodded and began to be alarmed. Would they be tested on this? She watched the two young men who leaned eagerly over the engine and nodded vigorously and made 'Oh, right' and 'Yes, of course' noises every so often. Bertha felt fairly certain neither one of them had ever looked inside an engine before in their lives.

'Now, this is your standard S-Type omnibus,' Miss Gordon was saying, closing the engine cover and standing back to indicate the massive vehicle with a flourish.

All three of them nodded wisely.

'The S is gradually replacing the older K-Types which were only twenty-eight horsepowers. This is a Daimler engine, thirty-five horsepower.'

She paused to let this sink in and they all looked impressed.

'She's got a twenty-four foot, eight-inch body and weighs four tons unloaded. Carries fifty-four passengers: twenty-six downstairs, twenty-eight outside. You've got your forward control, of course.'

'Forward control?' prompted Parks—or was it Sutton?

'Driver sits beside the engine rather than behind it.'

'Ah...'

'You've got your basic bell-and-cord arrangement inside, means your conductor or your passengers can tell you when to stop.' She reached inside the bus and pulled the cord to demonstrate.

'Right then, who's first?' and Bertha gulped and realised this was it.

'Well done, Miss Flaxheed. Now, there's your steering column, your gearstick, your accelerator, and—most important of all—your brake. Now, who can tell me the speed limit?'

'Twelve miles an hour?' hazarded Sutton.

'Excellent! Now then, Miss Flaxheed, once around the block then you're on your way!'

With Miss Gordon sitting behind her and Parks and Sutton cheering encouragement from behind, Bertha lurched and ground her way out of the yard and into Steyne Road then left into High Street. Really, once you got the hang of the gears, it was just like driving the traction engine! She turned left twice more and sailed—with some aplomb—back through the gates of the garage just as Jem appeared in her conductor's cap and armband, ready to start her shift, Mum waiting with Baby and the perambulator just beyond the gate.

Jemima jumped out of the way and stared openmouthed and wide-eyed as Bertha swung the General round the corner and turned a neat circle in the yard, bringing the bus to a halt facing the gates. Then she missed the gear and the bus lurched then the engine cut out with a bump.

'Bravo! Well done, Miss Flaxheed,' said Miss Gordon beaming, and Bertha sat in the driver's seat glowing and not a little flushed.

The superintendent lumbered out of his office, a cigar in the side of his mouth, carrying a sheaf of papers.

'This one ready?' he inquired of Miss Gordon with a nod towards Bertha.

'Ready for action, Mr Royale!' confirmed Miss Gordon, climbing down.

Mr Royale turned to Bertha and regarded her through a puff of cigar smoke. 'Right you are. Here's your route map. Don't worry about the schedule. Just get her there and back. In one piece. Got it?'

Bertha took the map and nodded grimly.

Jem, who had been sitting on a wall watching with a raised eyebrow, now stood up.

'Extraordinary,' she observed dryly. 'Are they really going to let you out with this?'

'Of course,' replied Bertha annoyed.

Jemima looked up and down the yard and her frown deepened. 'Where's Matthew?'

Bertha restarted the engine and gripped the steering wheel so that her knuckles turned white. In front of her was the high brick wall of the garage and beneath her hands the engine of the four-ton General throbbed disarmingly. What would happen, how much damage would there be, if the bus shot forward and smashed into the wall? Would it smash, a jumble of shattered glass and twisted metal? Or would the bricks crumble and disintegrate?

'Matthew's working', she replied. 'Early, at the post office. He won't be here till later. Much later. You can ride with me. Is that all right, Mr Royale? If I take Mrs Booth as my conductor? She's my sister, you see.'

'Is she?' Mr Royale looked at Jemima through another cloud of cigar smoke as if such a thing was hardly to be contemplated. 'Well. That should be fine. Hurry up then, no time to be dallying here.'

Jemima stood very still and said nothing and for a moment it seemed she would refuse to get on board. Then she hitched up her ticket machine and climbed up on the platform, pausing as she passed the driver's cab.

'You think, don't you, that by being here you can keep an eye on him?' And she laughed.

There was already a line of people waiting to board and Bertha sat quite still, her foot poised over the accelerator, as an elderly gentleman and a nanny in a black uniform and a cloak, clutching a small child, climbed on board and went up top, Jemima close on their heels. The engine chugged erratically as she idled, waiting for the gates to be opened once more.

It was seven twenty.

'Are we ever going to get a move on?' called Jemima impatiently from her position halfway up the stairs.

'Remember your route!' called Mr Royale as he swung back the gates and stood to one side to let her pass.

Bertha eased down on the accelerator and the bus lurched forward. She waved goodbye to Mr Royale and to Miss Gordon and to Parks and Sutton and to the other volunteers who were arriving to start their shifts. Beyond the gates Mum stood beside the big old perambulator, Caroline perched on her hip, Mum holding the baby's hand up in a wave of farewell.

The S-Type General, all four tons of it, roared into life and thundered out through the gates and onto Uxbridge Road, swinging out between a private motor car that swerved to avoid it and a charabanc loaded with shopgirls who cheered as the bus shot across the Gunnersbury Lane junction and disappeared from view.

AUTHOR'S NOTE

While I have taken every care to produce a work that is historically correct, some inaccuracies will inevitably have occurred, and for these I beg the reader's indulgence and trust that they do not detract from the reading experience. The discerning enthusiast will spot at once that the tram route number 36 taken by Bertha and Jemima from Acton to Park Lane does not, in fact, exist. And, sadly, Acton Bus Garage closed its doors in March 1925, some ten months prior to many of the events described in this novel. Acton is, of course, very much a real place, though the reader will not find Wells Lane nor Oakton Way on any map of the area. The reader will also face certain disappointment if they attempt to apply to study at Edinburgh's Waverley University or to purchase goods from Messrs Gossup and Batch.

SOURCES

The following organisations, publications and articles proved invaluable to me during the writing of this book:

Staff and volunteer researchers at the Information Desk and Library, London Transport Museum, Wellington Street, London.

Staff at the Local History Centre, Ealing Library, Ealing, London.

Are Department Stores Dead? by Amy Merrick, Jeffrey A. Trachtenberg and Ann Zimmerman.

A Social History of the English Working Classes, 1815–1945 by Eric Hopkins (Edward Arnold: London, 1979).

A Traveller's History of London, Second edition, by Richard Tames (The Windrush Press: Gloucestershire, 1992).

Blitz on Britain: The bomber attacks on the United Kingdom 1939–1945 by Alfred Price (Ian Allen Limited: London, 1977).

Britain 1926 General Strike: On the verge of revolution by Phil Mitchinson (In Defence of Marxism, http://www.marxist.com/britain-1926-general-strike-revolution.htm.

Daughters of Britain: An account of the work of British women during the Second World War by Vera Douie (George Ronald: Oxford, 1950).

Early Years in Acton by C. W. Herbert from *London Bus Magazine*, No. 31 (Winter 1980), pp. 7–23.

Express and Star, Bulletin No. 2, 5 May 1926.

Foundations of the Film Industry: 1920s (http://www.
filmsite.org/20sintro.html).

Going Green: The story of the District Line by Piers Connor
(Capital Transport Publishing: London, 1993).

Images of London: Acton by Jonathan Oates (Tempus
Publishing: London, 2002).

Life Between the Wars 1920-1940 by Pauline Weston
Thomas (www.fashion-era.com).

Life in Britain Between the Wars by L.C.B. Seaman (B.T.
Batsford: London, 1970).

London Buses: A brief history by John Reed (Capital
Transport Publishing: London, 2000).

London: A history by Francis Sheppard (Oxford University
Press: Oxford, 1998).

Royal Mail: The post office since 1840 by M.J. Daunton (The
Athlone Press: London and Dover, 1985).

The Acton Gazette and West London Post, 14 May and 21
May 1926 editions.

The Cuss-less, Girl-less Telephone and *First Exchanges in
Britain* (http://strowger-net.telefoonmuseum.com/
tel_hist_cussless.html).

The Defence of the United Kingdom by Basil Collier (HMSO:
London, 1957).

*The Glory Game: The rise and rise of Saturday night telly.
Part Three: The Golden Goose* by Jack Kibble-White
and Steve Williams (http://web.archive.org/
web/20041119072044/http://offthetelly.co.uk/
lightentertainment/glorygame/part3.htm).

The Historical Development of BT and *Events in
Telecommunications History* (http://www.btplc.com/
Thegroup/BTsHistory/BTgrouparchives/index.htm).

The Victorian Post Office: The growth of a bureaucracy by
C.R. Perry (The Boydell Press: Woodbridge, Suffolk,
1992).

Trolley bus history: Current collector design
(www.trolleybus.co.uk).

Women Workers in the Second World War: Production and patriarchy in conflict by Penny Summerfield (Croom Helm: London and Dover, 1984).